# HONOUR AND VENGEANCE

DREDA SAY MITCHELL

Love and Hate Series Book 2

The right of Louise Emma Joseph and Anthony Philip Mason writing as Dreda Say Mitchell to be identified as the Authors of the Work has been asserted by them in accordance Copyright, Designs and Patents Act 1988.



All characters and events in this publication other than those clearly in the public domain are fictitious and any resemblance to any real person, living or dead is purely coincidental and not intend by the author.

The moral right of the author has been asserted.

Print ISBN 978-1-0685091-2-4

Editing and formatting: https://studioenp.com
Additional Editing: Lily and Christine Dunlop
Cover design: Mitchell and Joseph Ltd/ Book Brush
Cover Photographers: Iniraswork, Eyecan and Feedough

# Praise for Dreda Say Mitchell & Ryan Carter

'As good as it gets.' **Lee Child**

'Great book by a great girl.' **Martina Cole**

'A truly original voice.' **Peter James**

'A fast-paced thriller that will keep you guessing until the very last page.' **Paula Hawkins**

'Sharply observed and a moving story of conflicting loyalties and unfinished business.' ***Guardian***

'Zippy, twisty plot…and a bevy of memorable supporting goodies and baddies.' ***Sunday Times***

'Thrilling.' **Sunday Express Books of the Year**

'Awesome tale from a talented writer.' **Sun**

'Fast paced and full of twists and turns.' ***Crime Scene Magazine***

# Free Novella

Join Our Exclusive Book Club

If you haven't already, plunge into the gangland world where the Steele and Watson Crime Family Drama started.

**DANGEROUS**

A LOVE & HATE SERIES PREQUEL

**Fate throws them together. The streets try to tear them apart.**

Bertram Watson, aka Brother Bertie, newly arrived from Jamaica, finds himself on the run in London's gritty streets. Jimmy Steele, son of a feared gangster, is bleeding out in a warehouse after a botched heist. Their paths cross in a twist of fate that will change their lives forever.

As Bertie's Jamaican street smarts clash with Jimmy's East End savvy, they form an unlikely alliance. But with rival gangs closing in and dangerous secrets coming to light, their newfound friendship is put to the ultimate test.

In this thrilling novella, loyalties are tested, blood is spilled, and love is pushed to its limits in the unforgiving world of London's underworld.

Visit www.dredamitchell.com

# Prologue

'You two-faced fucking traitor!' Jimmy bellowed, his silver-grey eyes blazing with murderous intent that sent a chill through even the hardest men present. 'You're dead to me!'

Brother Bertie spat a mouthful of blood onto Jimmy's shoes. 'Big man, aren't ya?' he snarled, all pretence of friendship gone. 'Look at yourself. You ain't nothing but poison!'

Their black suits were torn and splattered with each other's blood. They stood toe-to-toe on the edge of the river, fury and rage boiling between them. Blood trickled from Jimmy's split lip as he lunged forward at Brother Bertie, fists raised high to do serious damage.

The crowd of mourners gathered at Sugar Cane Wharf's waterfront, gasped and recoiled in horror, watching in utter disbelief while both men slogged it out. No one could understand what the hell was going on. These men were closer than brothers. Now look at them, at a bloody funeral, for crying out loud. Tearing each other apart like animals.

Brother Bertie ducked the blow, his eyes savage with venom that shocked the onlookers.

This wasn't just a punch-up between mates. This was brutal, naked hatred. Whatever had gone on, the love these two men had once shared had turned into something twisted and ugly.

Jimmy charged again. This time Brother Bertie met him head-on, his right hook connecting with Jimmy's temple with a sickening crack. Jimmy staggered but didn't fall.

'You know what you did!' Jimmy roared, saliva spraying from his lips.

His one-time best friend's laugh was cruel and sharp. 'And you know what you did!'

The mourners formed a loose semi-circle around the two former friends, their faces twisted with ghoulish fascination. Black-veiled women whispered feverishly while men in dark suits nudged each other, eyes gleaming with unholy excitement. Violence at a funeral - prime East End entertainment. They'd be talking about this in the pubs for months.

Brother Bertie's chest heaved, veins bulging in his neck. 'Some things a man can't forgive!'

'LIAR!' Jimmy howled, launching himself at Brother Bertie with such force they both crashed onto the sandy, stone-strewn shore. Their grunts punctuated the air.

They rolled together, each blow delivered with savage intensity, each curse dripping with loathing. Years of brotherhood dissolved into primal, animal hatred. They grappled at the water's edge, the icy river water soaking through their funeral attire, turning expensive cloth into sodden rags.

'Someone get Danny!' a voice shouted from above.

'Get Gertie!' another cried.

The Thames surged hungrily, ready to claim whichever man lost.

With a roar that barely sounded human, Jimmy gained the upper hand, straddling Brother Bertie's chest, pinning him down where the river lapped at his shoulders. His hands found Bertie's throat, thumbs digging into his windpipe.

This was it. The moment when everything changed forever.

When brotherhood became murder.

'I'll fucking end you today!' Jimmy's face contorted beyond recognition, a mask of pure malice. Blood from his wounds dripped onto Brother Bertie's face. 'You were the man I trusted most in the world!'

His once best friend thrashed beneath him, still fighting despite his air being cut off. His hands tried to claw at Jimmy's face, but the filthy river water weighed him down.

'I'm going to kill you!' Jimmy screamed, pressing harder, eyes bulging with rage. 'KILL YOU!'

# Chapter One

1969
Months Earlier

'She's coming in,' hissed the voice through the murky darkness of Sugar Cane Wharf.

Danny Steele's scarred knuckles whitened as he dragged them through his silver-streaked hair. 'About bloody time.'

The jagged scar on his cheek pulled tight in the bitter night air, a permanent reminder of old battles won and lost.

Twenty-eight minutes. That's all the time they had left before the gates slammed shut forever.

Danny peered through the thick fog rolling off the Thames, his cold eyes calculating every angle, every risk. Any normal geezer would be pissing himself right about now, heart banging like the clappers, but Danny wasn't wired that way. He'd built his reputation staying three moves ahead of the Old Bill and five ahead of rival firms. The King of the Docks – that's what they called him from Wapping to Whitechapel.

But what use was a crown when your kingdom was about to disappear?

The rotting wooden planks groaned beneath his feet, ancient timbers that had seen more blood and betrayal than a Pentonville exercise yard.

Jimmy stood shoulder to shoulder with his old man, every muscle coiled tight. His silver-grey eyes, so like his mother's, hardened with resolve as he scanned the darkness. His championship boxing dreams were buried six feet under, but this – this was where he belonged. In the thick of it with Danny, where blood meant everything and loyalty was the only currency that mattered.

Twenty yards away, Brother Bertie crouched behind a stack of rope, his trademark pork pie hat tilted at that cocky angle. Watching the river, a reckless gleam deepened the darkness of his eyes. The bastard could spot trouble from a mile off, which made him worth his weight in stolen gold.

Checking her watch, Rita Lawless announced, 'Twenty-five minutes until they padlock this shithole for good.' She'd crammed her dangerous curves into docker's gear, tucked her hair under a flat cap, but nothing could disguise those killer hips or the way she moved – pure sex wrapped in working-class brass.

Danny's granite jaw worked, and he snapped back, 'We'll be long gone by then.'

Ten of his hardest men dotted the wharf, brutal bastards who'd busted skulls and spilled claret in Danny's name for years. Now they waited in deadly silence, each one knowing this was the funeral of an era.

Jimmy's voice came tight with tension, whispering, 'You certain about this, Dad?'

Danny's features hardened into something carved from East End stone. 'That posh wanker gave me his word.' His voice carried the bitter edge of a man who'd learned too late not to trust the upper classes. 'One final shipment before the suited cunts move in – that was the bloody deal.'

Jimmy had no clue which toff his father meant, but the rage burning in Danny's eyes told him everything he needed to know. Questions in their world got you a permanent dirt nap.

Brother Bertie's smooth voice called softly through the fog, 'There she is.' He pointed through the swirling mist, his body coiled with anticipation.

The ship materialised out of the Thames darkness – a black metal beast sliding through the water without lights except for a single yellow beam cutting through the gloom. Deep in her steel belly lay enough treasure to make Croesus weep with envy.

Brand-new Japanese electronics. Colour tellies when most punters still watched fuzzy black-and white pictures. Stereos that could blow your eardrums to kingdom come. Transistor radios smaller than a packet of Embassy that rich tossers would pay stupid money for in Harrods.

All of it smuggled past the customs boys without a penny to the taxman. Worth enough folding money to set Danny up proper until he figured out his next move. He had buyers across London waiting with vans and cash, ready to make the goods disappear before dawn broke over the rooftops.

His mind already racing with possibilities, Danny ordered, 'Get ready, you bastards. Quick and quiet gets the job done.'

The ship bumped against the wharf with a grinding screech of metal on wood. Jimmy caught the thrown rope with practiced ease. Biceps bulging, he secured it to the bollard. Relief softened his tense features; the initial part of the operation went smooth.

The first container swung over the ship's side, spinning slowly on its steel cables. Danny's crew moved with the precision of a well-oiled killing machine, twenty years of graft burned into their muscle memory.

The crane operator – one of Danny's bought-and-paid-for men – guided the load down steady and smooth. Jimmy and three dockers positioned themselves underneath, ready to receive their prize. Brother Bertie directed with sharp hand signals, no words needed, a tentative smile playing at the corners of his mouth.

The crate hit the planks with a bone-deep thud that vibrated through the ancient wharf. Danny's men swarmed it immediately, crowbars and bolt cutters appearing from nowhere. They attacked the steel bands.

Inside, rows of boxed electronics gleamed under the dock lights, each one wrapped in protective plastic that crinkled under their eager fingers.

Stroking a television box with the reverence other men reserved for their wives, Danny whispered, 'Fucking beautiful.' His heart clenched with hope – this could be the score that set them all up for life. 'Bloody gorgeous.'

Rita checked her watch again, her face pinched with worry, tightening around her eyes. 'We need to shift our arses, Danny.'

The crew doubled their efforts, forming a human chain to the lorry hidden in the shadows nearby. The second container was already swinging over, rocking dangerously, a Thames breeze catching it.

His face draining of colour, Jimmy hissed, 'Watch that fucker!' The crate lurched sideways.

The crane operator steadied his load, the men tensed—

Then the night exploded with police whistles, the sound slicing through the fog.

'POLICE! NOBODY FUCKING MOVE!'

Brother Bertie leaped down from his lookout, his eyes wide with panic, the reckless gleam replaced by cold fear. 'Filth everywhere! They're swarming from both ends!'

Danny spun to see torch beams stabbing through the murk, his face turning an alarming shade of purple with rage. Veins standing out on his forehead, he roared, 'Jesus fucking Christ! Some grass bastard's sold us out!'

*That lying posh cunt gave me his word. Should've known better than to trust a toff.*

Jimmy grabbed his father's arm, fingers digging in hard enough to leave bruises. His voice came fast and desperate, face white under the sodium lights. 'We're fucked! We need to leg it now!'

Danny wrenched free, nostrils flaring, resembling an enraged bull. 'Fuck that!' Rolling up his sleeves to show forearms scarred from decades of dock fights, he snarled with quiet, deadly certainty, 'Nobody takes my gear! If we're going down, we're taking some of these cunts with us.'

The coppers closed in, truncheons raised, their faces twisted with bloodlust. But East End dockers didn't roll over for anyone.

Throwing his head back, Danny bellowed, 'COME ON THEN, YOU BASTARDS!'

The wharf erupted into chaos.

Jimmy's fist exploded into a copper's face, the sickening crunch of breaking nose echoing across the water. Blood sprayed in a wide arc, and the officer dropped, like a sack of cement. Brother Bertie moved, his body coiled with violent grace. He ducked under a truncheon to crack his opponent across the skull with a length of iron pipe.

Grabbing a copper by his uniform, Danny commanded through gritted teeth, 'Secure those crates!' He smashed the man's face against a wooden post, the wet sound of splintering bone music to Danny's ears.

More Old Bill poured onto the wharf, their numbers overwhelming. For every copper they dropped, three more emerged from the fog, truncheons swinging, ready to do damage.

A portly sergeant bellowed, his bloated face glowing with triumph, 'You're nicked, Steele!'

Voice deep and threatening, Danny growled back, 'Fuck your mother!' He charged with his head down, cold fury driving every movement. The sergeant's eyes bulged with terror before Danny's shoulder caught him in the gut, sending him crashing into his mates. They went down in a tangle of limbs and screaming curses.

A truncheon smashed down with brute force across Danny's shoulders, white-hot pain shooting down his spine. He stumbled but rolled away at the last second, lashing out with a vicious kick that connected with a kneecap. The snap echoed across the wharf.

The copper shrieked, 'My fucking leg!', collapsing in agony.

Through the mayhem, Danny spotted Jimmy cornered by two burly sergeants wielding their truncheons. His son's face was a mask of determination and fear, silver-grey eyes blazing with defiance. Brother Bertie was pinned against the crates, blood streaming from a gash above his eye, turning his face into a crimson mask. But his eyes still held that reckless gleam – the bastard was enjoying the fight.

Danny's loyal dockers were falling one by one, outmanned by the swarming coppers. The night air shattered with curses, grunts of pain, and the wet sound of wood on bone.

Three officers finally brought Danny down, driving his scarred face into the rough planks. The taste of blood and defeat filled his mouth with bitterness. Realising it was over, an emotional lump formed in his throat,.

*Fuck, fuck, FUCK!*

Feeling robbed of breath at the catastrophic turn of events, Danny's crew dropped their fists. Jimmy spat red beside a copper's boot but stopped struggling, his chest heaving with exhaustion and rage. Brother Bertie stood motionless, locking eyes with Jimmy in silent understanding – they'd gone down fighting, and that counted for something.

The Bill hauled Danny upright, wrenching his arms back until his shoulders screamed. The sergeant in charge, a lanky, scarred prick with pockmarks covering half his face, leaned in close, breath reeking of cheap booze and victory.

Crowing with sadistic pleasure, he said, 'Daniel fucking Steele. Caught red-handed with your cock out. Smuggling charges carry serious bird time, sunshine.'

Danny's features twisted into a snarl of pure hatred. 'Shove it up your arse sideways.'

The sergeant's cruel eyes narrowed. He raised his truncheon. 'Let's see if we can't rearrange that ugly mug of yours.'

'That won't be necessary, Sergeant,' a smooth voice interrupted, cutting through the chaos.

The crowd parted. A gleaming Rolls-Royce Silver Shadow purred onto the wharf. A uniformed chauffeur jumped out to open the rear door with practiced servility.

Lord Alexander Blacklock, 9th Viscount, known as Xander to many, stepped out looking fresh from a Mayfair dinner party, camel hair coat spotless, silver hair perfectly groomed. His silver-topped cane tapped against the weathered planks with deliberate precision. At sixty-eight, he still carried himself with the insufferable arrogance of inherited wealth.

Danny's guts twisted at the sight of him, his heart thrashing against his ribs.

*You treacherous snake. Your own flesh and blood, and you grass me up without blinking.* Not that anyone here – including Jimmy – knew that this posh bastard was Danny's real father. That he was his wrong-side-of-the-blanket son.

*After everything, I believed your word.*

*Stupid, stupid, STUPID!*

Addressing the sergeant with bored indifference, Lord Xander continued, 'I've spoken with the Chief Constable. As legal owner of Sugar Cane Wharf, I won't be pressing trespass charges.' He cast a cold glance at Danny, his eyes calculating every weakness. 'These men are… desperate. With the dock closures and all.'

The condescension made Danny's stomach churn with rage, his face turning a deeper shade of purple.

*One day, old man. One day you'll push me too far.*

Examining his manicured nails with theatrical precision, Xander continued, 'The contraband, however, will naturally be confiscated.'

Danny bit back his fury, knowing he had to swallow this crippling turn of events. His resistance was crumbling, but his pride kept his back straight.

Xander cleared his throat, his voice echoing in the sudden stillness. 'The world is changing, gentlemen. The docks, this way of life – it's finished. Perhaps it's time you changed, too.'

Danny's harsh laugh made several coppers step backwards, the sound bitter as wormwood. 'Our world might be changing, but some things never do. Like backstabbing toffs who'd sell their own mothers for a shilling.'

For a heartbeat, Xander's mask slipped, revealing genuine hatred beneath the aristocratic facade. Then it vanished, buried under generations of breeding faster than a bookie welching on odds.

Then he spoke the words Danny and his men had been dreading, his voice slowed with meaning.

'Sugar Cane Wharf is officially closed.'

After the coppers released them, Danny, Jimmy, Brother Bertie, Rita, and the bloodied crew didn't slink away. Instead they gathered across the street to witness the execution. These were men whose families had worked these docks since Queen Victoria's time.

The massive iron gates of Sugar Cane Wharf groaned shut with a final, terrible clang that echoed across the entire East End. The pockmarked sergeant turned the oversized key in the padlock with deliberate slowness, the metallic click sounding the same as nails being hammered into a coffin lid.

One by one, the dock lights went dark, swallowing Sugar Cane Wharf in absolute blackness. Danny's men stood in silence, watching their world die. Some of the older dockers removed their caps in respect, mourning the death of everything they'd ever known.

From somewhere down the Thames came the lonely wail of a ship's horn, a funeral dirge for the dying docks.

His voice carrying to every man, rough with emotion he refused to show, Danny said finally, 'The bastards can padlock our gates. But they can't chain what we are. What we've always been.'

He stared at the locked gates, feeling the crushing weight of history pressing down on them. Sugar Cane Wharf had pumped lifeblood through this community since his grandfather's time. Now it was just another gravestone in the East End's cemetery of progress.

Jimmy's silver-grey eyes burned with determination rather than defeat as he said quietly, 'The docks are finished. But that don't mean we are.'

Danny nodded slowly, his scarred cheek carved from granite resolve. The world might be changing, but Danny Steele wasn't ready for the scrapyard yet.

Not by a long fucking shot.

But what was a king without a kingdom?

# Chapter Two

The slick black figure slithered over the stone balcony of the Grosvenor Square mansion, a shadow come to life. Rain drummed against the leaded windows, nature's perfect cover for a break-in. Cold fingers worked the antique window latch with practiced precision, barely making a sound as it gave way. The intruder's breath fogged in the night air – the only visible sign of humanity beneath the black mask.

Inside, the opulence was suffocating. Thick Persian carpets muffled footsteps down the darkened corridor. Original paintings worth more than most people's houses lined the walls. Aristocratic ancestors with pinched faces staring down their painted noses, generations of blue-blooded bastards with the same cruel eyes.

A sliver of light spilled from beneath a doorway. The intruder froze at the sounds floating through the heavy oak. A woman's whimpered protests punctuated by a man's guttural grunts. Animalistic, selfish pleasure with no thought for his partner.

'Please, Xander… it hurts…' whimpered the woman, posh accent broken.

The only response was a disgusting wheeze followed by a final, guttural groan. The springs creaked with his body shifting on the bed.

'For God's sake, Prudence, must you always lie there like a corpse?' The intruder imagined the man's lip curling with contempt. 'If I'd wanted to fuck a dead fish, I'd have visited the bloody docks.'

The intruder's jaw clenched behind the mask. Something about that tone – entitled, cruel, familiar – made bile rise in their throat.

The bedroom door swung open. Lord Xander emerged, viciously knotting his silk dressing gown, his face twisted with disgust. At sixty-eight, the pompous old git still strutted about like he owned the world – spine straight, chin up, every move designed to remind everyone else they were shit on his shoe. Raking his hand through thinning silver hair, the low light caught the signet ring glinting on his bony finger. Beneath all that posh charm and wit lurked a greedy parasite who'd married young Lady Prudence for her money after pissing away his own family fortune at the gaming tables. The refined mask was perfect – fooled half of London society – but strip away the expensive education and what was left? Just another vicious bastard who took what he wanted and fuck everyone else.

'Useless frigid cow,' he spat, stalking down the corridor. 'Can't even wrap her cunt around me, let alone breed a fucking heir.'

The figure melted into the shadows of an alcove, closely watching the old man's retreat. Rage and something else, something deeper, more complicated, twisted in his gut.

Xander disappeared into his own suite at the end of the hall. Inside, a four-poster monstrosity dominated the space, embroidered with the Blacklock family crest that had intimidated commoners for centuries. Xander shrugged off his dressing gown, letting it puddle on the priceless carpet. He slipped between Egyptian cotton sheets with a satisfied groan. Within minutes, his breathing settled into the heavy rhythm of sleep.

The masked figure waited, counting each breath, watching the rise and fall of the other man's chest. Ten minutes passed before approaching the bed, steps silent as death itself. The blade appeared. Wickedly curved steel that caught moonlight filtering through the curtains. With precise, delicate control, the cold metal pressed against Lord Xander's throat, just hard enough to dimple the loose skin.

Xander's eyes snapped open, momentary panic flooding his face red before recognition dawned. His pulse beat against the wicked edge of the knife, but his aristocratic features quickly rearranged themselves into an expression of bored calm.

'Ah,' he drawled, 'I've been expecting you, Daniel.'

Beneath the mask, Danny's lips contorted into a savage smile. The knife pressed a fraction deeper, drawing a single drop of blue blood. He could end it right here. One quick slice and decades of humiliation would be over. But even now, even with a blade at the bastard's throat, Danny couldn't quite bring himself to sever the connection from his blood father.

*Christ, what kind of twisted son am I?*

***

'I should cut out your tongue for that stunt you pulled.' Danny's voice was barely more than a whisper, but in the quiet room, it carried the weight of a death sentence. The silk mask clung to his sweating face, revealing only the cold glint of his eyes. 'Double-crossing me is a dangerous fucking game.'

Lord Xander managed a smirk despite the steel at his throat. 'Come now, Daniel. You're being overly dramatic.'

Danny eased back reluctantly, stepping away from the bed. His fingers twitched with the urge to finish what he'd started, but he sheathed the blade instead. The old bastard would live. For now. Because somewhere deep in his fucked up psyche, Danny still craved something from this man. Respect, acknowledgment, maybe just the simple admission that his bastard son had made something of himself.

*King of the Docks, my arse. You're nothing but a trained dog begging for scraps.*

Xander rose with practiced elegance, knotting his dressing gown tighter. He moved to a crystal decanter set on a mahogany sideboard, pouring amber liquid into two heavy tumblers. The casual way he turned his back on a man who'd just held a knife to his throat spoke volumes – either supreme confidence or complete madness.

'Drink?' he offered, extending one glass towards Danny.

'Not thirsty,' Danny bit out. He tore off his mask.

He watched Xander knock back the expensive whisky, studying the lines of his face. The high cheekbones, the aristocratic nose, the same cold calculation in the eyes that Danny saw every morning in his own mirror. It made his blood boil and sing all at once. Two vicious predators circling, each waiting for the other to show weakness. The only difference was the accent and the postcode.

'My boys barely escaped before customs swarmed the fucking place,' Danny finally let his secret father have it with both barrels, his scarred face convulsing with fury. 'You set me up, you silver-spoon tosser.'

Xander refilled his glass, unmoved by the accusation. His calm was more infuriating than any insult. 'Business complications arise, Daniel. Hardly catastrophic for a man of your… resourcefulness.'

'Business?' Danny's laugh was harsh and hard. 'That shipment was my last chance at Sugar Cane

Wharf. My reputation's in bleedin' tatters. Half the East End thinks I've lost my bottle.'

And wasn't that the bitter fucking truth? Years building his empire, clawing his way up from the gutter, and one botched job and the closing of the docks had the sharks circling. Scumbags who'd crossed the street to avoid him last month were now meeting his eyes in pubs, testing his resolve, vultures sensing weakness. Respect was a fragile thing in his world. One sign of weakness and the wolves came running.

The old man's thin lips curled with disdain. 'And you blame me for your failures? How very… common of you.'

Danny forced himself to breathe through clenched teeth, fighting the familiar red mist that was part of his relationship with this man. How many times had he stood in a room with Xander, being made to feel small? How many times had he walked away promising himself it was the last?

'You could've warned me with one fucking phone call,' Danny hissed, his face inches from Xander's. 'But you wanted to see me scramble, like a rat in a flooding sewer, didn't you?'

A flash of triumph crossed Xander's aristocratic features, there and gone in an instant. But Danny caught it – that moment of satisfaction, the pleasure the old man took in his bastard son's humiliation.

'King of the Docks,' Xander mocked, each word dripping with disdain. 'Tell me, Daniel, how does one rule what no longer exists?'

Cold understanding crystallised in Danny's mind as he stared at the bastard who shared his blood but never his suffering. The docks were closing, had been closing for years. Everyone knew it, but Danny had convinced himself he could adapt, evolve, find new territories to conquer. But Xander saw the truth, saw that the kingdom Danny had built was crumbling beneath his feet.

'So that's your game,' Danny's voice dropped to a deadly whisper. 'You want me broken? On my knees begging for scraps like some manky old mutt?'

For the first time, genuine emotion flickered across Xander's face – not quite satisfaction, but something close. 'I require your services, Daniel. Nothing more, nothing less.'

'You've got some brass neck, old man.' Danny scoffed. 'Why would I do anything for you after this betrayal?'

'Because,' Xander's eyes gleamed with cold calculation, 'I can give you something far more valuable than that pitiful dock operation. A chance to become King of London's Underworld.'

Despite every instinct screaming at him to walk away, Danny felt the familiar pull. The promise of power, of proving himself worthy in the eyes of the man who'd never acknowledged him. Every cell in his body wanted to spit in Xander's face and storm out, but his feet remained rooted to the expensive carpet. When this man beckoned, Danny responded, a trained animal. The realisation burned through him, more painful than any knife wound.

*What gutless piece of shit have you become, Danny Steele? Fifty years old and still desperate for Daddy's love.*

'What needs doing?' The question tore from his throat unbidden, and Danny despised himself for asking it.

Xander smiled, wolfish and slow like he had Danny by the nuts. 'I want you to rob the Anglo-Merchant Bank in the City.'

Danny lost some of his colour, staring at Xander as if he'd lost his marbles. 'No fucking way. The last crew who tried that place ended up splattered across the pavement. Three blokes turned into street art.' He leaned closer, studying Xander's face. 'Why the hell would you want me to rob a bank? What's in it for you?'

'I can only tell you if you agree to do it.' Xander's eyes remained cold and frigid, giving nothing away. A canny glint suddenly gleamed in his gaze. 'Whoever pulls off that job will be hailed as the King of London's Underworld. Not just the docks but the whole of this city.'

Danny felt his pulse popping beneath his ribs.

*King of London's Underworld.*

The words bit into him, burning through his veins with dangerous heat. He could see it – his name whispered in every boozer, every manor boss from South London to the West End paying tribute. The ultimate crown. The top of the pyramid. Every villain in London looking up at the high and mighty Danny Steele, knowing he was the geezer who'd pulled off the impossible.

The bastard who'd robbed the unrobbable bank and lived to tell the tale. A criminal empire that would make running the docks sound like child's play.

But even as the vision seduced him, a warning voice clawed at the back of his skull. This was Xander's game, and the old man never offered anything without extracting a price that left you bleeding. Still, the temptation gnawed at Danny's guts – that chance to prove he was more than just another East End thug with delusions of grandeur.

For a moment, Danny saw himself clearly – a grown man begging for scraps from a father who would never love him. The image was so pathetic it made his stomach churn. Maybe it was time to break the cycle, to prove he didn't need Lord Xander Blacklock's approval to be somebody.

'That's your price?' Danny scoffed, his face twisting with disgust. 'The only way back into your good books is suicide? Bollocks to that. I've got other ways to climb back up. Don't need your poxy bank job to make my mark.'

Something flickered in Xander's eyes – surprise, maybe even a hint of respect. 'You're making a mistake, Daniel.'

'Wouldn't be my first.' Danny straightened his shoulders. 'But it might be my last mistake with you.'

He moved towards the balcony, then paused, turning back with a twisted grin. The old Danny – the one desperate for approval – would have left quietly. But tonight was different. Tonight, he had nothing left to lose.

'By the way,' Danny's voice carried a cruel edge, 'sounds like you married a defective model. All that money and breeding, and you still can't get your shrivelled old todger to plant an heir? Poor Lady Pru. Must be like trying to stuff spaghetti through a keyhole.'

Fury flashed across Xander's face, a rare crack in his aristocratic mask, the first genuine emotion Danny had seen all night. 'Get out.'

'Touched a nerve, did I?' Danny savoured the momentary victory with triumphant relish 'Don't worry, I'm going. But remember this – I'll find my way back to the top without you. And when I do, it'll be me calling the shots.'

Slipping back onto the balcony, rain hitting his face with cold slaps of reality, Xander's final words followed him into the darkness:

'Hailed as the King of London's Underworld.'

# Chapter Three

'Daddy! Mummy won't wake up.'

The words sliced through Jimmy, although he didn't quite catch them, but they stopped him mid-swing at the punching bag that hung from the iron beam on their roof terrace of his home on Molasses Quay that overlooked the river.

Jimmy Steele commanded respect across the East End, six feet of muscle and menace with piercing silver-grey eyes that held the kind of cold intelligence that made hard men reconsider their life choices. Two years it had been since he'd lost his boxing championship, two years deeper into his father's criminal empire, and Jimmy had everything he'd thought he wanted. A gorgeous wife who'd followed him from enemy territory, three healthy kids, this bloody great house. Respect on the streets and fear in his enemies' eyes.

But the guilt he'd buried kept clawing its way back to the surface. The belt he'd used on his sister, Sin, still haunted his nightmares, and something had shifted in his relationship with the man who was his blood brother, Bertram Watson, a distance that gnawed at his gut. In the gangland world, family was supposed to be everything.

Jimmy was learning it could also be the very thing that destroyed you.

Something was wrong because seven-year-old Violet stood in the doorway with her nightdress buttoned all crooked, wild hair framing her small face. Six-year-old Robbie hovered behind her, thumb stuck firmly in his mouth, a habit Mini had been trying to break for bloody ages.

Flexing his scarred knuckles unconsciously, Jimmy muttered, 'What'd you say, princess?' Sweat trickled down his bare chest despite the Thames' chill cutting through the morning air.

'Mummy's still sleeping.' Violet's bottom lip trembled. 'And Harry's been crying forever and ever.'

Now he heard it, their ten-month-old's desperate wails cutting through the house. Ice water replaced the blood in Jimmy's veins. Mini never left the baby crying, not for a bleedin' second. She'd be up with first light, tending to their youngest, getting the older ones washed and dressed for school with military precision.

Forcing a grin bright enough to reassure his two children, though his heart raced with worry, he told them, 'Mum's just having a lie-in, that's all. Right, you two, get yourselves down to the kitchen. Rustle up some bread and jam while Daddy sorts things out.'

After they'd scampered off, Jimmy snatched his vest from the bench and yanked it over his head, the fabric straining against his immense chest and rock hard abs. He took the stairs three at a time, his heavy footsteps echoing through their home.

In Harry's nursery, he found the ten-month-old, standing and gripping his cot bars, face blotchy and red, tears streaming down chubby cheeks. His nappy sagged, heavy and soaked through, the poor little mite.

'Come here, son.' Jimmy lifted the baby with hands that could snap necks but cradled his youngest with impossible tenderness.

Harry hiccupped, his sobs subsiding as he buried his face in his father's neck. Jimmy kissed the top of his head, breathing in that sweet baby smell that always made his chest tighten with fierce love.

In the master bedroom, Jimmy's heart nearly stopped. His wife lay buried beneath covers, only a tumble of dark-brown hair visible against the white pillowcase. When he'd left for his morning routine, she'd been sleeping peacefully, soft breaths easing through the dawn quiet. This wasn't right.

Jimmy approached the bed cautiously, shifting Harry to his other arm. Mini didn't stir, so Jimmy perched on the mattress edge and gently pulled back the covers, and the sight he found stole his breath.

His wife's face was ghostly pale, dark shadows carved deep beneath her eyes. Mini's chest rose and fell with shallow breaths, her nightdress clinging damply to her small frame. Choking anguish gripped his throat as he reached out to brush damp strands from her forehead. Her skin burned beneath his touch. She was on fire from the inside out.

'Mini, wake up, love.' His voice echoed in the emptiness, raw with desperation.

Her eyelids fluttered, revealing bloodshot eyes that struggled to focus. 'Jimmy?' The word emerged, dry and rasping, barely audible.

Pausing only to press a desperate kiss to Mini's forehead, Jimmy said, keeping his tone gentle despite panic building inside him, 'It's gone eight o'clock, darlin'. The little ones are still in their nightclothes.'

Confusion clouded her features before horror dawned. Her face turned an alarming shade of red. 'Eight? But… the children… school…' She struggled to push herself upright, arms shaking with effort.

'Easy now.' Jimmy eased her back into the pillows with gentle pressure, his massive frame casting a shadow over her. 'Kids are downstairs having breakfast. They're sorted.'

'Harry—'

'Got him right here.' Jimmy adjusted the baby on his knee, forcing a nervous smile. 'Bit wet, but nothing I can't handle.'

An emotional lump formed in her throat. She whispered, 'I've never slept this late. Never. Not once since the children were born. What kind of mother doesn't hear her baby crying?'

'The kind who's bloody ill, that's what.' Heart clenched with hope that he was wrong, Jimmy cupped her cheek, his thumb brushing away tears that scalded his palm. 'You're burning up, Mini.'

That familiar stubborn glint returned to her eyes, the one that had made him fall head over heels for her all those years ago. She lifted her chin defiantly and shot back, temper flaring, 'Don't be daft. Just been up late with those sewing orders. Got Mrs Carpenter's daughter's Holy Communion dress to finish by Friday.'

She pushed herself upright with trembling hands, flinging back the covers. Jimmy watched her stand, his body coiled to catch her if needed. Mini took two steps and swayed, her knees buckling beneath her. His free arm shot out, wrapping around her waist and pulling her against him.

'For fuck's sake, woman.' Fear made his voice low and dangerous. 'Get back in that bed before you collapse.'

'The children need breakfast. Harry needs changing.' Mini leaned into him, her tiny frame practically disappearing against his bulk. She planted her small hand on his chest, fingers splayed over his galloping heart, and continued between ragged breaths, 'I'm fine, Jimmy. Really. Just need a cuppa to get me going.'

'You need a doctor, is what you need.'

She stepped back, her lips curled into a dismissive smile. 'We don't waste money on doctors for a bit of tiredness.' Mini reached for her youngest child, who gurgled and eagerly extended his chubby arms towards his mother. 'Our Harry's soaked through. Give him here.'

Jimmy reluctantly surrendered their son, watching as Mini cradled him close, pressing kisses to his damp hair. Maternal instinct overrode everything else – that was his Mini.

'I'll change him, then get the children sorted. Violet's got that spelling test today.'

When she turned away, Jimmy gently caught her arm, his fingers circling her delicate wrist. 'You can barely stand. Let me take care of things today.'

She mustered a small, sarky smile. 'The great Jimmy Southpaw, changing nappies and packing school lunches? That'll be the day.'

Confidence bolstered, he managed a sheepish grin, relieved to see a bit of her old fire back. 'I'm not completely useless, you know. Been watching you do it for years, haven't I?'

'And taking notes, were ya?' Her dazzling smile widened, bringing some colour to her pale cheeks.

He took Harry from her arms, setting the baby on the bed to kick his legs, then drew Mini against him.

'I love you,' he whispered into her hair, the words torn from somewhere deep in his chest where fear and devotion warred. 'You know that, don't you? More than anything in this bloody world.'

'I know,' she breathed, leaning up on tiptoes to brush her lips to his. 'I love you, too, you great big softie.'

Holding his wife close, his gut clenched with sudden unease, squeezing until he could barely breathe. He'd never seen Mini laid low like this, not once in all of their years together.

If anything happened to her, if he lost the woman who was his anchor, his reason for everything, how would he survive? Mini was the light that kept him from drowning in the darkness of his father's world. Without her…

No.

He shook his head violently, banishing the poisonous thoughts.

*Don't be daft, Jimmy. She's just got a case of that nasty sniffles doing the rounds. Nothing more than that. She'll be right as rain in a day or two.*

# Chapter Four

'Daddy!' Six-year-old Precious squealed, launching herself into her father's arms, yellow ribbons flying from her neatly plaited hair.

Bertram Watson, known to one and all as Brother Bertie, scooped her up outside St Mary's Primary School. It was his turn to collect her and take her home for the night before bringing her back the following morning. He was never going to see eye to eye with Claudette, Precious' mother, or the man who was now her stepfather, but at least he'd used the law's clout to ensure he had visitation rights.

He still wore that trademark pork pie hat and flashed his wicked grin, and the ladies still melted when he turned on the charm. But heartbreak had carved something vicious into Brother Bertie's soul.

The carefree rogue who'd talked his way out of any trouble now carried a bitter darkness beneath that easy smile. Simply put, falling in love with Sin Steele had ripped his heart out.

He hadn't given a toss that she was his best mate's sister or that society said a black man shouldn't touch a white woman.

Fuck 'em!

Love didn't give a toss about rules, and he'd loved her with everything he had. But Sin had walked away to protect him, leaving him gutted and hollow.

Two years of living with that agony had turned him reckless. Gambling and screwing around like a man with nothing left to lose. Because without Sin, that's exactly what he was – a man with fuck all to care about except the next thrill that might make him forget her face for five bloody minutes. The darkness ate at him daily, turning his charm brittle and his laughter false.

But Brother Bertie had learned to wear his mask well, even when it was killing him from the inside out.

'I can't wait to see Auntie Gertie,' Precious chattered. 'She says she's going to teach me how to make bread.'

Her brown eyes widened with delight at the sight of the multicoloured sweetie necklace he pulled, magician-style, from his pocket. 'For my baby-gal,' he declared, looping the string of brightly coloured sweets around her neck.

'Before we see Auntie Gertie, we just got to make a quick stop first,' he informed her, taking her small hand in his.

He took her to the Tube station which she adored. Precious was mad for trains and tunnels.

'Is it the red line or the black line?' She stared up at him with those trusting eyes, lifting her sugary necklace to bite off another sweet.

'The black one, baby-gal. Northern Line.' Brother Bertie squeezed her tiny hand, guilt stabbing his chest. His smile never reached his eyes. 'Taking you on a little adventure.'

If his sister got wind of where he was taking her niece she would kill him on the spot. But he couldn't help it – the itch was back, and he had to scratch it.

They reached Dean Street in Soho and an unmarked painted red door. It didn't have a number or a name, those looking for it knew where to go.

Brother Bertie tapped a specific rhythm on the back door. A peephole slid open, then the door.

'Well, well, well, Brother Bertie,' Rita Lawless drawled, arching a pencilled eyebrow. 'Ain't you a sight for fucking sore eyes.'

Rita had kissed goodbye to the East End dives ready to strut her muff Up West, hunting for bigger prey with the patience of a shark. The closure of Sugar Cane Wharf had been her cue to reinvent herself as something classier. Well, that was the plan anyway.

Standing nearly six feet in her stocking feet, Rita commanded attention whether she wanted it or not. Her willowy frame and sharp-featured face told the story of a woman who'd clawed her way up from the gutter using nothing but raw cunning, her body, and a switchblade she kept with her twenty-four hours a day. She was a mistress of reinvention, all right – had to be in her line of work. You either adapted or ended up back selling your arse for a fiver behind Woolworths in Whitechapel.

The Red Door Club was the start of her new hunting ground, and the flat above it her base for her operations. This afternoon found her in a silk kimono hanging open, blonde hair wrapped in curlers, mascara smudged under tired eyes. Half past four and she gave the impression she'd just crawled out of some punter's bed, which wasn't far from the truth.

Same old Rita, just with a posher postcode.

But Rita had a weakness when it came to kids, which was why she levelled Brother Bertie with a killer glare when she spotted Precious. 'You better tell me you never brought your little girl here.'

He shifted uncomfortably, knowing she had every right to tear a strip off him. 'Need to see Miles. Won't be long.'

Rita's flashing gaze hardened to flint, and she lowered her voice so that Precious couldn't hear. 'You brought a fucking child to the Red Door? What kind of numpty father are you?'

'Just a quick game. Half hour, tops.' He pasted on that one-hundred-watt smile of his that usually did the trick with Rita.

This time it didn't work, she appeared about ready to clock him one.

'Half hour, my sweet fanny,' Rita scoffed, eyes flashing with disgust. She knelt to Precious' level, her voice softening. 'Hello, little queen. I'm Rita. Your daddy's got some boring grown-up business. Want to come upstairs with me? Got some comics and lemonade.'

Precious shyly checked with her father first, who nodded. 'Be good for Miss Rita, yeah? Daddy won't be long.'

He stroked her cheek, the gesture tender though his eyes darted towards the club's depths like a junkie spotting his dealer.

Rita led them up a narrow staircase to her flat above the club. The place screamed delusions of grandeur – cheap leopard-print throws over knackered furniture, tacky porcelain angels next to posh perfume bottles. But surprisingly tidy.

Drawing Precious close to her, she point-blank warned him, 'I've got to head out in an hour for a fitting. Don't make me regret this, Brother Bertie.'

'I'll be quick. In and out,' Brother Bertie promised, already edging towards the side door that led to club

Rita grabbed his arm, her talon-long nails digging in hard enough to draw blood. 'I fucking mean it. If you're not back within the hour, I'll go knocking on your sister's boarding house and give Gertie chapter and verse about what you've been up to.'

The thought of his devout sister finding out he'd brought Precious here made him shudder. He'd rather face Danny Steele in a dark alley than disappoint Gertie.

He gave Precious a quick kiss. Rita took her upstairs, and he entered the door to the club. The club floor lay empty, waiting for the night's punters to fill it with blokes sniffing around for entertainment and dirty old codgers getting their rocks off watching tarts gyrate for tips.

Green velvet booths hugged the walls, their fabric stained with God knows what from years of spilled drinks and seedier activities. The gilt-framed mirrors were cracked and tarnished, reflecting nothing but lies and broken dreams. Every surface felt sticky to the touch, coated in a film of cigarette smoke, cheap perfume, and the desperation that clung to places where hope went to die.

At the far end, a stage dominated with a single spotlight hung overhead, casting harsh shadows down on the striptease performers. Empty beer bottles and overflowing ashtrays still littered the tables.

Brother Bertie passed through and stopped at a reinforced door with a metal grille. The doorman, a mountain with a busted nose and cauliflower ears, nodded him through to the basement.

Stepping from daylight into permanent midnight, smoke hung thick as fog on the Thames, lighting amber from shaded lamps over green baize tables. Three card games operated in full swing despite the early hour. The air crackled with tension, desire, and desperation. London's underground never slept, not even for a bloody wink.

Gambling.

That was the itch Brother Bertie needed to scratch.

Gambling was the only thing that numbed the constant ache in his chest since Sin had left him. The rush when he placed a bet – heart banging, palms slick with sweat, blood pounding in his head – it hit him just like Sin used to. That same gut-punch feeling. That same buzz that made everything else fade to bollocks. Made him feel like a proper man again, not some pathetic mug crying into his pillow.

When he won big, his body rippled with the same electricity he'd felt when Sin whispered, 'I love you.' The mindless hours at the table, where nothing existed but the next card, the next bet were the only times his brain wasn't torturing him with could've beens and should've dones.

At the tables, he wasn't the sorry bastard who'd lost the love of his life.

Miles Harker presided over the main table, a spider in an expensive suit. Everything about him screamed class, from his movie star good looks to his Savile Row tailoring to his posh school accent. But beneath all that Mister Sheen polish lurked something rotten. His smile never reached those dead eyes, and when it came to money owed, Miles took things very fucking seriously indeed.

He kept a ledger in his head for every debt, every slight, every punter who thought they could take liberties. And when collection time came, Miles always got his pound of flesh. With interest.

'Mr Watson,' he smoothly greeted. 'I'm glad you came back.'

Brother Bertie made a point of using his real name here so Miles Harker hadn't put two and two together and connected Bertram Watson to the Brother Bertie who was an associate of the feared Steele family.

'Haven't seen you in days.' Miles smiled, long and oily. 'I was beginning to think you'd found Jesus.'

Brother Bertie silently acknowledged the other players before dropping into an empty chair.

'Jesus and me ain't exactly on speaking terms,' he replied with a brittle laugh. Back in the day his laugh had been filled with cheek and warmed with cheekier charm. 'Besides, the only praying I do these days is for a good hand.'

'Five-card stud,' Miles announced, shuffling the deck with machine-like hands. Then he announced what the minimum stake was.

Brother Bertie slapped his cash on the table. Two weeks' honest work plus a bit extra from helping Jimmy shift some questionable merchandise.

He was on a winning streak from the off. Blood rushed through his ears as he raised, and raised again.

Brother Bertie flipped his cards, a manic grin splitting his face. 'Read 'em and weep, gentlemen! The Lord provides!' he crowed, arms spread wide. 'And today he's providing for me!'

Raking in the pot, an electric high flooded his whole body. This was what he craved. This searing sensation of triumph that reminded him of being in Sin's soft, tender arms.

Thoughts of Precious flickered at the edges of his mind. He should go upstairs. Collect her. Take her home…

Just one more hand.

One more time.

One more…

Two hours later, Brother Bertie was flying high, his pile of chips had quadrupled, and a brunette called Maggie had draped herself over his shoulder.

A newcomer entered the room who Miles greeted: 'Norman! Didn't expect you till tomorrow.'

'Just passing through,' he explained. 'Thought I'd drop by for a quick game before I head to the tailor's to get a new whistle made.'

Miles asked, 'And what would you need a new suit for?'

'Danny Steele. That daughter of his is getting married. I've got an invite to her upcoming engagement party, so I'd best get myself suited and booted.'

Brother Bertie felt like a lorry had crashed into him at full speed. The room seemed to implode around him, air evaporating, sound warping into meaningless noise. He couldn't find any oxygen to fill his lungs

'Sin?' The name tore from his throat, jagged and raw, barely audible above the pounding in his skull.

His heart wasn't just breaking, it was being ripped from his chest, still beating, exposing every nerve ending to unfiltered agony.

Sin.

His Sin.

Getting married.

Terrible images flooded his mind unbidden. Sin in another man's arms. Sin in another man's bed.

'You all right, mate?' someone asked. The voice seemed to come from miles away, distorted and meaningless.

Brother Bertie couldn't respond. Couldn't do anything but grip the edge of the table as his world collapsed inwards. Gone. All of it gone.

Recklessly, to ease the agony inside, he ploughed on with the gambling. But his luck vanished. Losing one hand after another, chasing losses with bigger bets, until his beautiful pile of chips dwindled, then disappeared like smoke.

Maggie slipped from his lap without a word, drifting to stand behind a player on a winning streak. Brother Bertie barely noticed her leaving, focused only on the cards, on the next hand that had to, HAD TO be a winner.

'I'll stake you,' Miles offered when Brother Bertie had nothing left.

Brother Bertie nodded, missing the predatory gleam in Miles' eye.

Another fifty quid. Gone.

Fifty more. Gone.

Another hundred. Gone.

'That's two hundred you're in the hole, Mr Watson,' Miles informed him with narrow-eyed relish. 'Think it's time to call it a day.'

Reality crashed back into Bertie. Two hundred quid. Might as well be two thousand for all he could pay it.

'I'm good for it.' Brother Bertie fronted it out, knowing full well he was skint.

'Course you are,' Miles agreed too easily. 'But I'll need it soon. You've got forty-eight hours.'

No fucking way! 'Need more time—'

'Forty-eight hours,' Miles repeated, the nasty dirt beneath his carefully cultivated polish on full display.

That's when Brother Bertie remembered…

*Precious.*

He'd forgotten his own bloody, young daughter.

Fuck's sake, what time was it? Panic seized him. He checked the clock. Half past fucking six.

Flying out of his chair, towards the exit, Miles Harker's threat followed him. 'Don't make me have to get creative about collecting, which usually involves me sending the boys around.'

'Your girl's with Charlie,' the bouncer said, lifting his chin in the direction of the bar.

Precious lay curled up asleep in one of the booths, her small, innocent form so horribly out of place in surroundings that screamed sex and sin. The remains of her sweetie necklace hung limply around her neck, just a lonely strand with a few sweets left. Brother Bertie's steps faltered, shame washing over him in a sickening wave.

'What kind of fuckery father…' he choked, shame eating him alive.

Blood fire! His own daughter sleeping in a strip club. Some father he turned out to be. Raasclaat! Gertie had raised him better than this bollocks.

Gently, he scooped Precious into his arms and kissed her forehead. Her eyes fluttered open, drowsy and confused.

'Daddy!' Her sleepy voice was full of undeserved trust. 'Charlie let me help put cherries on sticks! Can we get an ice cream now?'

The innocent question stabbed deeper than any blade. His arms tightened around her protectively as emotion throttled his throat.

'Tomorrow, baby-gal,' he promised, voice thick. 'First thing.'

Sleep pulled her under before he could say more.

Sin was getting married.

Sin was getting married.

Brother Bertie wanted to howl his rage at the Heavens.

To burn the whole fucking world to ashes.

And he needed to get Miles Harker his money in two days.

# Chapter Five

Sin Steele plastered herself against Adrian, her fiancé, grabbing at his hair like some desperate slag in a back alley. She forced her mouth hard onto his, trying to convince herself this meant something, anything. But even as she ground into him, all she could think was if she kissed Ade hard enough, long enough, she might actually feel something beyond lukewarm affection.

Twenty-six meant a woman was well and truly on the shelf according to most, but Sin had geezers doing double-takes whenever she walked into a room. Her striking beauty, those sharp cheekbones, full lips, and the dangerous glint in her eyes, had blokes practically breaking their necks for a second butchers at her. Her chestnut hair now fell to her shoulders in a sexy Jane

Fonda, 'Barbarella' style, all volume and tousled. Combined with her willowy frame, clad in a deep-purple minidress that showcased her shapely legs, she could have been a model rather than a hairdresser. That had been the dream once, before everything went to shit at the hands of an evil manipulative photographer. Still, her unmistakable East End edge was exactly what her wealthy Soho clients were gagging for – authentic grit they could enjoy without getting their own manicured hands dirty.

The back office of the hair salon smelled of expensive products and ambition. Glossy magazine cutouts of the latest hairstyles plastered the walls. Twiggy's iconic pixie cut, Jean Shrimpton's flowing locks on the cover of *Harper's Bazaar*, Jimi Hendrix's fuck-you afro from his *Electric Ladyland* album cover, Marsha Hunt's magnificent natural hair from her *Hair* musical promo, and a treasured vintage copy of Donyale Luna's groundbreaking 1966 *Vogue* cover that Ade had framed as a statement piece.

This place, where she'd worked for years before Ade bought it last year, was her escape route from the East End, her ticket to respectability, even if it meant ignoring the hollow ache in her chest.

At thirty, Adrian 'Ade' Mack was one of Soho's golden boys. Sharp-suited, Chelsea-booted, with dark hair sculpted into perfection and a grin that could melt steel. The trendy sod had clawed his way from nowhere to owning a number of London's hippest hair salons, where rock stars clinked glasses with gangsters and everybody paid through the nose for the privilege.

He name-dropped famous clients with practiced ease, and Sin Steele was his prize exhibit. The East End beauty draped on his arm at every fashionable party. He treated her right, showed her off proper and claimed he was saving himself for their wedding night. *Old-fashioned respect,* he called it.

But something had shifted lately. Something that made him feel like a right fraud every time Sin kissed him. She thought he was perfect. Always bloody perfect.

If only she knew.

'Easy there, gorgeous,' he murmured to Sin, his voice carrying that polished accent that had initially attracted her. 'There'll be all the time in the world for that after we're married.'

Sin fought the urge to roll her eyes. 'That's months away.' Her fingers played with the collar of his shirt while she batted her lashes at him. 'Don't you want me?'

Ade kissed her forehead with infuriating tenderness. 'More than anything.'

*I'm not your effing sister,* Sin thought, irritation flaring hot, flushing her skin. *Kiss me properly, for crying out loud.* Was it too much to ask for a bit of proper passion?

She knew what it was to be with a man who couldn't keep his hands off her, who'd have her knickers off before she could catch her breath, who made her body sing like a blooming opera star. Now look at her, engaged to a fella who treated her like she was made of bloody glass, ready to shatter if he so much as copped a proper feel.

*Be truthful. His hands will never drive you wild. Not like…*

She shut that thought down in an instant.

The past was dead and buried, along with her dreams of becoming London's next 'it girl' model. This was her future now, and she'd make it work if it killed her.

'I just think it'll be special if we wait.' His eyes, a clear, untroubled blue, held none of the fire she craved.

'You're a good man, Ade Mack,' she forced the words past the lump in her throat. 'Better than I deserve.'

His smile brightened the room. 'You deserve the world, Cynthia. We'll be happy. I promise you that.'

She knew Ade could deliver on that promise, too. His salon was the talk of Soho, frequented by musicians, models, and the occasional film star. He moved in circles where creativity and money flowed freely, where the old rules about class and background meant nothing. At his parties, she'd schmoozed with people who couldn't point to the East End on a map, much less know the unwritten laws that governed life there. Just last week, he'd taken her to a private club where some up-and-coming band had played until dawn, and nobody had blinked twice at her accent or asked about her family. That freedom was intoxicating, almost enough to make up for the spark that wasn't there between them.

The door burst open, banging against the wall with enough force to make them both jump.

'Bloody hell!' Kathleen Doherty stood framed in the doorway, her round face flushed with embarrassment. 'Sorry! Didn't know you two were...' Her eyes darted between them, taking in Sin's slightly smudged lipstick and Ade's tousled hair.

Kath had stood by Sin's side since they were schoolgirls, barring those years when Sin got shipped off to that school run by the holy sisters in Kent. Her copper hair and warm smile made her the sort of person strangers confided in within minutes. Everything about Kath was generous - her laugh, her figure, her enormous heart that left her vulnerable to every sob story in East London. People mistook her bubbly chatter for empty-headedness, dismissing her as another brainless Barbie. The twats couldn't have been more wrong. Beneath all that sunny disposition lurked an instinctive understanding of human nature.

Kath could spot a liar faster than a pickpocket in Petticoat Lane.

Ade's entire body language shifted, becoming oddly rigid. He stepped away from Sin, creating distance between them. 'Kathleen.' He cleared his throat, shoving his hands behind his back, like he had no business touching Sin in the first place. 'We were just—'

Sin watched his discomfort with mild curiosity. Odd reaction for a man caught snogging his fiancée.

That was the third time this week he'd jerked away from her when someone walked in. What man didn't want to be seen with his hands all over his gorgeous wife-to-be?

The awkward moment dissolved when Dilly appeared behind Kath, her sweet face breaking into a hesitant smile at the sight of Ade. At twenty, Kath's sister moved through the world with careful, hesitant steps, her soft brown eyes holding a distant gaze that had been her constant companion since some bastard had run her over when she was a kid, then done a runner.

Though Dilly never spoke, her silence wasn't empty. Tiny little gestures, like the lift of her hand, the small shake of her head, or the change in the expression in her gaze, that's how she communicated to the world. Any man interested in putting a ring on Kath's finger, she made it clear from the off that there would be three of them in the marriage – Dilly came, too. Most men waved goodbye after that. Good riddance! 'There's my favourite girl!' Ade's demeanour transformed completely as he crossed to Dilly, crouching to her eye level. 'Those are brilliant new shoes, Dilly! Did you pick them yourself?'

Dilly nodded, her eyes bright with pleasure at being noticed, at being treated like a person rather than a problem.

'She chose them special for your engagement party coming up soon.' Watching her best friend's intended with her sister softened Kath's gaze.

Sin's chest tightened. This was why she needed to marry Ade. Any man who treated Dilly with such genuine kindness couldn't be all bad, even if kissing him felt like pressing her lips against warm cardboard.

Ade straightened, giving Dilly's shoulder a gentle squeeze. 'Ladies, you'll all look beautiful, I'm sure of it.' He glanced at his expensive watch. 'I've got clients all afternoon. We'll catch up later, yes?'

He pressed a chaste kiss to Sin's cheek and headed for the door. 'Wonderful seeing you both,' he added to Kath and Dilly before disappearing into the bustle of the salon.

The moment he left, Kath raised an eyebrow. 'He couldn't get out of here fast enough.'

'He's busy,' Sin defended automatically. 'He's a man everyone wants to see.'

Sin nodded, busying herself with tidying Ade's desk, needing something to do with her hands. 'Getting closer every day. Hardly seems real.'

'And you're sure?' Kath's voice dropped low, concern etched into every word. 'About tying the knot with him?'

Sin's eyes snapped with indignation. 'Course I'm bloody sure. Why wouldn't I be?'

Kath wouldn't let it go. 'Because when you look at him, your eyes don't go all swoony-woony like they did with—'

'Don't you dare go there.' Sin stabbed a warning finger at her. Hearing his name would break something inside her that she'd spent two years carefully patching together. 'I've told you, Kath. That's over. I'm looking to the future now, and that's all that matters.'

The truth was, she couldn't allow herself to think about what she'd given up. If she did, she might not have the strength to go through with saying, 'I do', to another man. And then what? Living under her despised father's roof and thumb for eternity?

Kath sighed, crossing the room to take Sin's hands in hers. The gesture – so simple, so full of genuine affection – nearly broke Sin's carefully constructed composure.

'I want you happy, is all,' Kath said, her teeth worrying her bottom lip the way they always did when she was concerned. 'You're like a sister to me. And Dilly. If Ade makes you happy, then I'm over the bleedin' moon for you both.'

Sin forced a smile, squeezing Kath's hands. Ade would give her children, respectability, a life free from her father's shadow. That was enough. It had to be.

As for love?

She'd been burned by that particular fire once before, left with scars that still ached in the quiet moments. She wouldn't make that mistake again. Love was a luxury she couldn't afford.

# Chapter Six

'How come you never told me that Sin was getting married?'

The question made Jimmy frown, confusion flickering across his sharp features. He glanced sideways at Brother Bertie, who stood with his hands jammed deep in his pockets, his pork pie hat tilted at that familiar rakish angle. But there was nothing familiar about the tension radiating from his blood brother's frame.

*You beat her, you bastard. You took a belt to the woman I love.* That's what Brother Bertie wanted to bellow at him. But he'd perfected the bloody art of pretence. Two years of laughing at Jimmy's jokes while rage burned through his veins. Two years of slapping the back of the best friend he'd ever had while imagining his hands squeezing around his neck.

They were standing on the golden stretch of sandy beach that the Thames revealed when she pulled back from Sugar Cane Wharf. Quiet these days. Too bloody quiet. No sound of dockers shouting, no cranes groaning under massive cargo loads, no ships blasting their horns. The docks had died, taking with them the heartbeat of the East End.

'Didn't think you'd be interested.' Jimmy shrugged, trying to keep his voice casual. 'She's found herself a good un. Adrian owns a number of businesses in Soho. And I'm not talking the shady-shit kind. He's aboveboard which is what my sister deserves.'

Brother Bertie kicked at the wet sand, his jaw clenched. Every shared drink with Jimmy tasted bitter as piss. Every moment of their old easy friendship felt like Jimmy was slowly knifing him in the back.

'Yeah, but why didn't you tell me?' Brother Bertie pressed.

Jimmy turned fully now, studying his friend's face with those sharp grey eyes that missed nothing. Something in Bertie's tone snagged his attention. The bloke was trying to act normal, but Jimmy caught the jagged edge underneath, sharp enough to cut.

*What's eating at him?*

'What's going on with you, Bertie?'

Brother Bertie managed a sudden, wide grin. The smile was all show, no substance. He'd been living this twisted charade, pretending everything was tickety-boo between them when all he wanted was to smash Jimmy's face into the Thames' mud.

'Nothing, Southpaw. Just asking, that's all.'

The laugh never reached his eyes. Jimmy had known his blood brother long enough to spot when something wasn't right. The man had been scarce these past months, showing up less at Jimmy's gaff, disappearing for days on end, coming back looking like he'd been dragged through hell backwards.

Truth was, Jimmy missed his mate. Missed the easy rhythm they'd always shared. Since moving into Molasses Quay two years back, there was a difference in their relationship. Jimmy could feel it. A distance he couldn't put his finger on, slipping away every time he tried to grasp it.

'Anyroads,' Jimmy emphasised, 'look at all this.' He swept his arm across the vista of abandoned wharves and empty warehouses, their broken windows staring out. 'A couple of years back, Dad said one day this will be worth a goldmine. I thought he was talking out of his rear end.'

He scowled hard. 'But lately I got to thinking, what if he's right? So I've been buying up properties, which are going dead cheap because no one wants to live here no more with the docks shutting—'

A woman's scream tore through the air, raw and terrified, cutting through Jimmy's words.

They spun towards the sound, exchanging a lightning-quick glance before breaking into a run. Their feet pounded across the wet sand, each step splashing through shallow pools left by the retreating tide. A small crowd had gathered near the old jetty, mostly women with pinched, worried faces trying to push between a hulking brute and the cowering figure pressed against the rotting wooden pilings.

'Fucking hell,' Brother Bertie breathed, his voice tight with controlled fury. 'That's Hughie.'

Brian Hughes, known to everyone as Hughie, had worked the docks for thirty hard years. His meaty fist was raised above his sobbing wife, Nancy, whose face already bloomed angry red where he'd struck her. The stench of cheap booze rolled off him in sickening waves, his bloodshot eyes wild and unfocused, and he swayed on his feet.

'You worthless bitch!' Hughie roared, spittle flying from his twisted mouth. 'Can't even put decent food on the table!'

'Leave her alone!' One of the women grabbed his arm and got shoved hard for her trouble, stumbling backwards into the crowd.

Jimmy and Brother Bertie closed the distance in seconds. Bertie's shoulder drove into Hughie's side, knocking the bigger man off balance, while Jimmy caught his raised arm and twisted it behind his back with practiced efficiency.

'What the bloody hell d'you think you're playing at?' Jimmy hissed into Hughie's ear, cranking the pressure on the joint until the man howled. 'Nancy's never done nothing to deserve this kind of treatment.'

Brother Bertie knelt beside the trembling woman, his normally animated features hardened into a mask of barely controlled rage. The sight of Nancy's battered face sent something dark and violent coursing through his veins.

Sin's back. Purple stripes where Jimmy had assaulted her.

'Easy, sweetness,' he murmured to Nancy, his voice gentle despite the fury burning in his chest. 'You're safe now.'

Nancy's left eye was already swelling shut, blood trickling from a nasty split in her bottom lip. 'It's all right,' she mumbled through damaged tissue, though it clearly wasn't. 'Just a misunderstanding, that's all.'

'Misunderstanding, my arse.' Jimmy tightened his grip and studied Hughie's face contorting with pain. 'Since when do you go around knocking seven bells out of your missus? Everyone knows you worship the ground Nancy walks on.'

The fight drained from Hughie suddenly, his massive shoulders slumping forward. When Jimmy cautiously released him, the man didn't lash out, he crumpled, dropping to his knees on the wet sand. Great heaving sobs tore from his chest, his face buried in his hands.

'I've never, never, raised a hand to my Nancy,' he choked out between ragged breaths. 'Not in twenty-five years of marriage. Not once.'

'Yet here we bloody are,' Jimmy chucked back at him in disgust.

*You fucking hypocrite,* Bertie viciously cursed in his head. *You raised your hand against your own sister. Against the woman I love. And here you are playing the righteous raasclaat hero.*

Hughie's words spilled out. 'Since Sugar Cane Wharf closed I can't find no work. No one wants to hire an old-timer like me. Forty-eight years old and on the bleedin' scrapheap.'

One of the older women stepped forward, her weathered face grim with understanding. 'It's the truth, Jimmy. Never known Hughie to so much as raise his voice to Nancy before this. They've always been solid as rock, them two. But since the docks shut down… well, he's been hitting the bottle something chronic. And he ain't the only one around here.'

Jimmy stepped back, the hot anger in his chest colliding with unwelcome understanding. The heart was being ripped clean out of Sugar Cane Wharf's community. Family businesses boarded up overnight, their owners fleeing to the suburbs. Pubs that had conducted business for decades now stood empty, windows smashed and covered with corrugated metal. Families that had lived in the same streets for generations packed up their lives and disappeared to Essex or Kent, chasing work that might not even exist.

Men who'd known nothing but honest dock work their entire adult lives suddenly found themselves useless, their hard-earned skills worthless in a rapidly changing world.

'Listen to me very carefully, Hughie,' Jimmy cautioned and crouched down, his gaze boring into the man's bloodshot ones. 'If I ever hear you've put your hands on Nancy again – even once – I'll do you so badly your own mother won't recognise what's left. That crystal clear?'

Brother Bertie watched Jimmy play the protector, the righteous husband defending the innocent woman. The hypocrisy burned in his throat. Where had this righteous fury been when Danny ordered Jimmy to beat Sin? Where was this protection when his own sister needed it?

*You hypocritical bastard. Standing there like some knight in shining armour when your hands are just as dirty.*

Hughie nodded miserably, tears cutting tracks through the grime on his cheeks.

'But you come see me tomorrow morning at the River Rat. I know someone who's looking for experienced men on building sites. Won't be what you're used to, but it's honest graft with decent pay.'

Hughie stared at him, hope flickering across his battered features. 'You'd do that for me? After what I've done here?'

'Not for you.' Jimmy straightened up, his voice harder than Thames ice. 'For Nancy and your kids and those grandbabies of yours. Now get yourself home and don't show your face again till you're stone-cold sober.'

As the small crowd dispersed, Jimmy and Brother Bertie watched Nancy being led away by the group of kindly women.

Brother Bertie suddenly checked his watch, his entire body tensing. The pretence was wearing thin. But he'd almost forgotten, he only had two days to pay Miles Harker. He had a plan to get the money. One that made him sick to the core.

'Shit, I've got to scarper.'

'What?' Jimmy's voice carried genuine disappointment. 'Thought we were hitting the River Rat for a pint?'

'Can't. Got somewhere important to be.'

Before Jimmy could press him further, Bertie was striding away across the sand, moving faster with each step until he was almost jogging. Jimmy watched him go, that familiar feeling of something being seriously off settling in his chest.

*What aren't you telling me, Bertie? What's got you so twisted up inside?*

The worst part was the suspicion growing in his gut, that whatever was eating at Bertie, whatever had put that haunted look in his eyes and that rage beneath his smile, it had something to do with family.

And in Jimmy's world, family secrets were the most dangerous kind of all.

# Chapter Seven

Twenty-four hours. That's all the poxy time Brother Bertie had left before Miles Harker's goons came hunting.

One more day to scrape together two hundred quid, or he'd be decorating all four corners of London with his body parts. The thought sent arctic dread crawling up his spine. He stood in the narrow hallway of Gertie's boarding house, cold sweat breaking across his skin.

'Gertie?' His call tore through the silent stillness. 'You home, girl?'

Nothing but the tick of the grandfather clock and his pulse thrashing in his ears.

Here he was, praying his beloved sister wasn't home so he could rob her blind. What kind of manky bastard did that make him? The worst kind. How could he steal from the one person who'd never turned her back on him?

But Miles Harker didn't give a toss about family loyalty. The sadistic knobhead would carve Brother Bertie up for sport, debt or no debt. Two hundred pounds stood between breathing and feeding the rats in some Whitechapel gutter.

He climbed the stairs; each step echoed his shame, each footfall a countdown to betrayal. The thin metal pick slid from his jacket lining, shaking in his fingers. Gertie's door lock surrendered without a fight, ironic, considering the war tearing his chest apart.

The door swung open.

The room was pure Gertie. Vibrant Caribbean colours blazing warmth and faith from every corner. The hand-stitched bedspread in brilliant greens and golds made him think of home, of better times when his biggest worry was dodging Mama's wooden spoon. Gertie's dressing table sat opposite, covered with pristine white crochet, every corner perfectly straight, not a thread out of place.

No makeup cluttered the surface – Gertie called it vanity, pure and simple. But pride of place went to that pale-blue Avon powder compact, its lid decorated with two white doves. Above the bed, a massive two-tone image of Christ watched over everything. Hands clasped in prayer, eyes that seemed to track Brother Bertie's every movement. Judging every rotten thought in his head.

Those painted eyes seemed to darken, boring straight through him. Brother Bertie could almost hear Gertie's voice echoing off the walls: 'The Lord sees everything, Bertram. Every wicked thing.'

The dressing table drawer slid open without a sound. Inside, nestled between a prayer and hymn book and rosary, sat Gertie's bank book. The sight of it twisted his insides into barbed wire. This wasn't just paper and ink, this was his sister's life savings, her security, her future in this country she had battled to make her own.

Inside were handwritten records of how much his sister had deposited into her account.

Nearly five hundred poxy pounds.

Every penny represented sacrifice, represented hope. And here he was, about to piss all over it.

Slipping the bank book into his jacket, Brother Bertie felt his conscience shrivel and die inside his chest. The crucifix watched. Christ's eyes followed. And somewhere in the distance, he could swear he heard the sound of his own soul shatter.

***

The Anglo-Merchant Bank in the financial section of the City of London rose before him like a cathedral to money. All marble columns and gleaming brass, designed to make a man like Brother Bertie feel small. A temple where the likes of him didn't belong.

He hesitated on the threshold, pork pie hat clutched in his trembling hands, Gertie's bank book burning a hole in his pocket. Inside, men in expensive tailored suits moved with the confidence of those born to privilege, women in neat skirts tapped at typewriters. A world apart from the grime of the docklands and Whitechapel where he hustled to survive.

Stepping across the polished marble threshold, he felt a faint rumble vibrate beneath his feet – the Underground running beneath the bank. The same tremor he knew from Sugar Cane Wharf when the East London line rattled below the docks.

Suddenly he felt suffocating. Couldn't breathe.

Fearful he was going to chuck up, he veered sharply left, following brass signs to the gents'. Inside the spotless lavatory, he locked himself in a stall and sat heavily on the closed toilet lid. He buried his face in his hands, breathing hard through his fingers.

'What kind of monster steals from his own flesh and blood?' he growled to himself, low and thick with self-hatred.

He finally emerged from the stall, approached the sink nearest the window, twisted on the tap, and splashed water on his face. Then he leaned his palm on a maintenance access panel in the wall that he suspected connected to the building's service areas or even the Tube below. And stared into the mirror.

Instead of his reflection, all he could see was Gertie. The way she'd worked her fingers to the bone to give him opportunities. Her unwavering faith in him, even when he repeatedly proved he didn't deserve it. Gertie at the kitchen table, counting pennies, working out if they could afford both heat and food that week. Never complaining, just figuring it out. Always figuring it out.

'Rob my own sister.' With contempt, he kissed his teeth hard, shaking his head. 'I'd rather take a blade to my neck than stick one in the back of the only person who's never turned theirs on me.'

A saying from his Jamaican childhood hit him full force: *The serpent that bites the hand that feeds it is cursed for all eternity.*

Miles Harker and his thugs could break every bone in his body. They could send him to an early grave. But betray Gertie?

He would rather cut himself into a million pieces.

# Chapter Eight

'You're a teef and I want you out of my yard!'

The sound of his sister's furious voice hit Brother Bertie hard, slamming into him before he'd even opened the front door. Full-throttle Jamaican, using 'teef' instead of 'thief' and 'yard' meaning her home. Gertie was in a proper uproar. Her bank book, pressed on his chest, burned through his skin, branding him with his betrayal.

Brother Bertie pushed through the door and followed the commotion to the dining room, his stomach twisting hard, churning with dread. The scene that greeted him froze his blood cold.

Gertie stood in the centre of the room, her distinctive red, gold, and green paisley bandana wrapped tightly around her head, face contorted with righteous fury. She brandished a large steel pot spoon, jabbing it at Dr Finch, one of her long-term lodgers, pinning him to the floral wallpaper. The former physician cowered, his bloodshot eyes wide with terror, gin fumes radiating from his pores, the stench filling the room.

'And after all Gertie has done for you.' This admonishing voice belonged to Ruddy, Brother Bertie's close friend and fellow lodger in his sister's boarding house who leaned on the doorframe, arms adamantly crossed over her chest, her signature beehive hairdo adding inches to her average height.

'I see you take my kindness for weakness?' Gertie jabbed the spoon towards the doctor's chest, steel glinting under the electric light, her voice trembling with a lifetime of disappointments. 'After all these years, you come in my bedroom? My sanctuary? Rifling through my drawers like some common criminal?'

'I never—' Dr Finch attempted, his voice quavering as though he were standing on a gallows, fingers clutching at his threadbare collar.

'My bank book is gone!' Gertie thundered, her voice carrying enough power that Brother Bertie was certain they could hear her all the way back to Whitechapel station. 'And you the only one with sticky fingers round here!'

The doctor's seasoned face crumpled. 'Gertrude, please, I wouldn't—' he stammered, backing away until the wallpaper pattern pressed into his sweat-soaked shirt.

'Don't you Gertrude me!' She hissed and whacked the spoon on the dining table, her eyes blazing with flames hot enough to scorch. 'You had your last chance, and the one before that, and the one before that, too! My patience has run dry like the Jordan River in drought!'

Brother Bertie couldn't bear it another second. 'It was me, Gertie,' he confessed, his face firing up with shame.

The words dropped into the room, like a match into petrol.

All eyes turned to him. The silence that followed was deafening.

His hectic gaze snapping between brother and sister, Finch seized his opportunity, and bolted from the room, footsteps fading rapidly down the hallway.

Gertie stood frozen, her eyes widening with disbelief. Her usually glowing brown skin took on an ashen tinge, the life draining from her face. The steel spoon slipped from her fingers, clattering onto the worn wooden table with a finality that stabbed at Brother Bertie's heart.

She sank heavily into a chair, her entire body suddenly looking smaller, frailer, like she'd aged a decade in seconds.

Ruddy remained near the wall, remaining quiet.

'What you saying, little brother?' Her voice emerged with disbelief tinged with devastation, her hands gripping the edge of the table as though it might anchor her to a world suddenly spinning out of control.

Brother Bertie pulled the bank book from his inside pocket and placed it gently on the table before her. The blue cover gleamed in the light, mocking him with its innocence. His heart thrashed against his ribs, about ready to flee before all hell broke loose.

Gertie stared at the bank book, then up at her brother, her dark eyes swimming with hurt that cut him deeper than any blade ever could. 'But why?' she whispered, her voice cracking on the question, fingers hovering above the bank book but not touching it, as though it had become something alien. 'Why would you do this thing to me?'

'I'm in trouble, sis. Deep trouble.'

It spilled out of him – the gambling, the debt, the forty-eight-hour deadline which was now one day. He couldn't look her in the eye. Couldn't deal with the wounded expression crippling her face. His shoulders hunched forward as though trying to make himself smaller, to disappear entirely from her heartbroken gaze.

He left out Sin. Couldn't bring himself to admit that part of his spiral began the day Jimmy's sister walked away, leaving an emptiness he'd tried to fill with cards and booze and other women.

Gertie's face had hardened by the time he'd finished. She appeared older than her forty years, the lines around her mouth deepened by sorrow, marked there by his betrayal.

'Since you come to England, I give you everything.' She spoke quietly now but sharp enough to draw blood. 'Everything I have, I share. My home. My food.

My love.' She picked up the bank book with trembling fingers, cradling it against her chest,. 'And this is how you repay me? Stealing from your own blood?'

'I didn't go through with it,' Brother Bertie pleaded, raising his eyes now, desperately, feeling like he was drowning, his hands outstretched in supplication. 'I couldn't. I went to the bank but I couldn't do it.'

'But you thought about it. You went.' Gertie's eyes burned through his flesh and bone, right down to the rotten core beneath.

She stood, rearing up, drawing herself to her full height. She stabbed an accusing finger at him, close enough that he could see the calluses earned from years of hard work keeping them both afloat.

'You haven't been right since that damn girl,' she growled, each syllable vibrating with a mixture of anger and maternal worry, her finger trembling with the force of her emotion. 'She twist and wring you up inside until you have no sense left. That girl is pure wickedness dressed up in pretty clothes.'

Brother Bertie felt like his sister had struck him across the face. The mention of Sin was a physical blow that left him breathless. He tried to open his mouth to deny it, but his lips refused to move, throat working uselessly around words that wouldn't come. And he knew why – there was no way he was going to lie to his sister again.

'I need to pray on this,' Gertie muttered, her bank book clutched tight to her chest, her troubled expression turning inward, seeking guidance beyond the human realm. 'I need guidance from the Lord, because right now, I don't recognise my own brother.'

The silence she left behind pressed in on Brother Bertie from all sides. He'd faced down armed men without blinking, but his sister's disappointment crushed him, breaking him down, threatening to shatter him completely.

Ruddy pushed herself off the wall, her eyes assessing him from her vantage point. He'd forgotten she was there, witnessing his disgrace.

'Never thought I'd see the day when you did the dirty on your own sister.' Her mouth drooped with disdain. 'I like a flutter with the cards as much as you, but there's rules, ain't there? Never bet more than you can pay without ending up six feet under.'

Brother Bertie couldn't argue. He slumped into a chair, his hat still clutched in his hands, crushed beyond recognition like his own self-respect.

Ruddy shook her head. 'Since Sin dumped you—'

Brother Bertie's eyes flashed with indignant fire. 'She never dumped—'

''Course she bloody did.' His close friend rounded on him. 'I don't care what excuses she gave you, if she loved you, she would've fought for you. Not gone waltzing out the door at the first opportunity. Now she's wearing the ring of some other fella?'

Brother Bertie cocked his head and watched his friend intently, a flicker of defiance sparking in his eyes. 'You never liked her, did you?' he challenged, a hint of his old swagger surfacing momentarily through the shame.

Considering her words carefully, Ruddy's mouth twisted, 'What I don't get is why didn't she stick two fingers up to her old man and Jimmy? Tell them to fuck right off? That this is her life and no man gets to lay down the law about who she loves?'

'You're wrong—' The words felt hollow even to his own ears, the fight draining from him as quickly as it had come, leaving him deflated and small in its wake.

'Maybe. Maybe not.' Ruddy's tone softened, only ever so slightly, mind you. 'But I tell you what I'm not wrong about. You owing that big bastard Miles Harker money, which he'll want back with interest and perhaps a few of your fingers for good measure.'

Brother Bertie dragged in a rough breath. 'What am I going to do?'

Ruddy's hand landed on his shoulder, warm and solid, offering silent support even as her eyes remained hard with reality. 'First off, you need to pull your head outta your lovesick arse and start living again. We'll figure it out, we always do.'

But for the first time in his life, Brother Bertie wasn't sure they could fix this mess. Some betrayals slashed too deep, left scars that never faded. He stared at the doorway where his sister had disappeared, feeling the distance between them stretch into an unbridgeable chasm of his own making.

# Chapter Nine

'Lord, give me strength.'

Gertie prayed with all her heart as she walked down the dark narrow steps to the gambling room in the basement of the Red Door Club in Soho. Each step took her deeper into a world that would be at ease in Sodom and Gomorrah.

The basement opened into a den of vice that made her stomach clench. Clearly a gambling den with men hunched over cards and dice, their faces twisted with greed and concentration. Scantily clad women moved between the tables, painted angels of temptation, refilling glasses and whispering encouragement into sweaty ears.

Gertie clutched her handbag tighter, feeling the thick envelope of notes pressing against her palm through the leather.

'Well, well.' A smooth voice cut through the cigarette smoke. Miles Harker emerged from behind a poker table, his big frame casting shadows across the green felt. He caught her in the trap of his predatory eyes, taking in her modest coat, her red, gold, and green head wrap, the way she held herself apart from the corruption surrounding her.

*Despite his smooth tongue, the Devil comes in all guises,* Gertie fiercely thought, meeting his stare without flinching,

'Odds on you being a church lady,' he summed up with a cruel smile. 'What's a good Christian woman doing in my den of iniquity?'

Gertie's chin lifted slightly. 'I come about my brother's debt.'

Miles' laughter boomed across the gambling den, causing several players to look up from their games. 'Your brother owes me two hundred quid, plus interest. That's two-fifty now, love. Time is not free.'

'I have the money.' She patted her handbag, the gesture nervous and uncertain.

'Of course you do.' Miles circled her, a shark scenting blood. 'But where's the fun in that?'

He faced her square on. 'Tell you what, church lady, takes guts coming down here. So let's make this interesting.'

He gestured towards an empty poker table, its green surface scarred with cigarette burns and ring stains. 'Five-card stud. You win, your brother's debt disappears completely. You lose...' His grin revealed tombstone-like teeth. 'You double the debt. Four hundred pounds.'

Gertie's eyes widened, her hand flying to her throat. She worried her bottom lip between her teeth, searching the room as if seeking divine intervention among the gamblers and painted women.

'I... I don't know nothing about cards,' she stammered.

Miles' smile turned wolfish and widened. 'Even better. Sit down, dear lady.'

***

Miles Harker had been taking money from fools since he was old enough to hold cards. This church biddy would be easier than stealing sweets from a baby. Clutching her handbag tighter than a virgin's knickers, her trembling hands betrayed her fear when she sat. Inside his head, Miles rubbed his palms with relish – she'd fold faster than a house of cards in a hurricane.

He dealt with practiced ease, explaining the basics as if she were a child. 'Pair beats high card, two pair beats one pair, and so on. Simple as Sunday service.'

Gertie nodded earnestly, studying her cards with the concentration of someone trying to decipher ancient scripture. When she had to bet, her shaking hands counted out notes, placing them on the felt with the reverence of a church offering.

'Fifty pounds to start,' Miles announced, sliding forward his own stake.

'Fifty pounds?' Gertie's voice pitched higher with alarm. 'That's… that's so much money.'

'Scared, love?' He grinned at her, his gaze gleaming with greed. 'You can always just pay me the two-fifty and walk away.'

She shook her head, jaw setting with determination. 'No. I won't let my brother down.'

The first hand went to Miles – pair of jacks against her nothing. She stared at his cards as if they'd personally betrayed her, then slowly slid forward more cash.

'Don't worry, darling,' Miles said with saccharine sympathy. 'Beginner's luck comes to everyone eventually.'

The second hand was his, too. And the third. Each time, Gertie's face grew a more unnatural brown, her breathing more hectic. She fumbled with her cards, dropped cash and asked question after question about the rules. By the fourth hand, she was down nearly a hundred pounds of her precious savings.

Miles was enjoying himself immensely. Watching her suffer was almost as satisfying as taking her money.

Then something shifted.

The fifth hand he dealt her he was sure was pure rubbish because her shoulders sagged. But when he bluffed with his pair of tens, betting another fifty pounds, she surprised him.

'I… I think I'll try raising,' she told him uncertainly, adding her own fifty to the pot.

Miles called, confident in his hand. When she laid down three queens, his jaw nearly hit the felt.

'Oh my,' Gertie breathed, eyes glued to the cards as if she couldn't believe what she was seeing. 'Did I win?'

'Lucky hand,' Miles growled, but something cold was creeping up his spine.

Gertie won the next hand, too. She bet timidly at first, then with growing confidence.

'I don't rightly know what I'm doing,' she exclaimed, raking in the winnings, 'but the Lord seems to be smiling on me today.'

Miles' smarmy smirk was long gone. This wasn't how it was supposed to go. Church ladies didn't catch cards like this. They didn't sit there calmly while the pots grew larger, their initial nervousness replaced by something resembling… composure.

Hand after hand, she gutted him at the table. Not through skill – at least, not that he could see. She still asked questions, still seemed uncertain about her bets. But the cards kept falling her way, and somehow she always seemed to know exactly how much to bet, when to fold, when to go all in.

By the time the smoke cleared, Miles Harker was down three hundred pounds – more than her brother had ever owed him. He stared at the mountain of chips in front of the church woman, his throat dry.

'Seems the Lord was watching over you,' he relayed with hoarse disbelief.

Gertie's smile was innocent as a child's. 'He works in mysterious ways.' She began sliding the entire stash of cash back across the table towards him. 'But I didn't come here to take your money, Mr Harker. I came here to save my brother.'

Miles shifted his gaze from the money to her face, searching for the trick, the angle. There had to be one. 'What do you want?'

'My brother's debt marked as paid. In full. No interest.'

He glanced at her, long and hard for a moment, then slowly nodded. What choice did he have? By now everyone in the room was watching. The woman had just cleaned him out, then handed back his money like she was returning a lost wallet.

'Yeah,' he said through gritted teeth. 'We got an understanding.'

Gertie stood, smoothing down her coat with hands that had never once trembled during the final rounds. 'Thank you, Mr Harker. The Lord bless you.'

She walked towards the stairs with the same measured dignity she'd descended with, leaving Miles Harker staring at his money and wondering what the hell had just happened.

***

On the narrow staircase leading up from the basement, Gertie allowed herself one small smile. The familiar thrill still coursed through her veins – the sweet rush of reading an opponent, of knowing exactly when to push and when to fold, of letting them think they had you beat right up until the moment you took everything.

Before she'd found the Lord, her lover back in Kingston had taught her every trick in the book. Cards, dice, reading men's souls through their tells. She hadn't just been good at it – she'd been a master.

Some skills, once learned, never left you. Even when you buried them beneath years of prayer and righteousness.

Gertie breathed a huge sigh of relief and hoped that this would be the end of the matter.

# Chapter Ten

'You accusing me of rolling over for some bloody ponce in a suit and selling you down the fucking river?'

Danny's harsh accusation sliced through the bitter morning air, confronting the crowd of dockers whose faces were wreathed in a toxic combination of anger and fear. He stood alone, outside the closed gates of Sugar Cane Wharf, the enormous rusty chains wrapped around them.

'You promised us, Danny!' A burly docker with shovel-sized hands jabbed a condemning finger in his direction, the digit trembling with barely suppressed rage. 'Said Sugar Cane was different. That it wouldn't go the same way as Wapping.'

Desperation hung in the air thicker than the fog that came off the river. The dockers were fathers, husbands, and sons, each carrying the weight of families depending on their wages. Unemployment wasn't just about losing a job, it was the gut-wrenching fear of watching your kids go without. Generations of families had been dockers, and now – nothing. What were they going to do? They didn't know any other type of work. The community was built on the docks. Without it, the community would wither and die.

*They're looking at me,* Danny thought, *like I'm the one who shut the bloody gates. Like I'm the villain here.*

*I ain't fucking having that!*

'I fought tooth and bloody nail for you lot!' he bellowed back, fighting to maintain his composure, the scar on his cheek throbbing visibly. 'You think I wanted this? Think I wanted to watch everything we built turn to rat shit?'

*My word. My reputation.*

Danny felt something twist inside him with the viciousness of a knife between his ribs. A man was nothing without his word, especially in the East End. He'd built his whole empire on fear and respect. If they stopped respecting him, what was left?

'Don't matter what you wanted, does it?' A docker's face mottled with fury as he spat the words out, spittle flying from his lips. 'You gave us your word, and now look at us, standing "on the cobbles" again!'

A visible shudder of horror rushed through the crowd at those words. Being 'on the cobbles' wasn't just a phrase to these men, it was a nightmare of desperation from their fathers' and grandfathers' days. For generations, desperate dockers without steady work would stand on these very cobblestones outside the wharf gates before dawn, hoping to be one of the lucky few picked for a day's labour. The ghost of that humiliation – men fighting like dogs for scraps, foremen picking favourites, families going hungry when you weren't chosen – was etched into the collective memory of every docker family in the East End.

'Christ almighty,' an older docker muttered, staring down at the stones beneath his feet with sudden awareness. 'My old man swore I'd never have to stand on the cobbles like he did. Said that's why we fought for the unions. Said that's why he got his bloody head stoved in by peelers during the strike in forty-six.'

From the rear of the crowd, a gruff voice pierced the gloom, desperation dripping from every word. 'Heard tell that they're gonna concrete the whole bleedin' lot! Just like they're planning to do with the docks in Wapping. Pour a concrete fucking gravestone right over our lives.'

Danny's eyes narrowed to dangerous slits. 'Concrete over the Thames? What next, flying bloody pigs?' he mocked, his teeth bared in what was more snarl than smile. Features hardening to stone, his hand dramatically traced the jagged scar on his right cheek, the puckered flesh white against his flushed skin. 'I hope no one's doubting my conviction because I've spilled blood for this place just like the rest of you sorry bastards.'

A docker stepped forward, his cap clutched in calloused hands, his voice tinged with hope and fear in equal measure. 'Danny's the only one who's prepared to help us. Always has been.'

'Yeah,' another chimed in, nodding vigorously. 'He's had our backs since Old Salt – God rest his soul – back in 'sixty-two.'

The memory of Lou 'Old Salt' Higgins' death under a rusty crane hung over the docks like toxic smoke. The docks were always hungry for their next victim, and the bosses couldn't give two fucks about a docker's life. Old Salt's blood staining the planks, Danny's fury had reached boiling point. He'd had enough of this shit. It was time to step up and take on management for the sake of the men.

While that bastard, rat foreman, Rawlings, had tried to sweep the mess down the river, Danny set his plan in motion. He'd thrown open The River Rat pub's doors, got the booze flowing, and had every docker from Wapping to Tilbury digging deep for Old Salt's family. The strike Danny organised became the stuff of dockland legend. Two weeks of chaos that had the bigwigs pissing themselves in their wood-panelled offices. He'd played it like a pro, firing up the dockers with rousing speeches while working every connection to keep their families fed.

But it was when he faced down Rawlings in front of everyone that Danny stamped his reputation in blood. He had that piss-poor excuse of a foreman spilling his guts about unsafe conditions concerning Old Salt's death. Rawlings was out on his arse faster than a tart's knickers on payday. Old Salt's family were taken care of, and Danny secured safer conditions on the docks.

They'd proclaimed him the 'King of the Docks', and the title became his tailor-made suit of power.

What most hadn't sussed was that Danny had cleverly eliminated a rival, taking over the former foreman's criminal operation in the process and using it as the springboard for the massive illegal empire he'd once run through the docks.

'Don't listen to this lying scrote!' a belligerent voice suddenly interrupted Danny in mid-flow.

The crowd parted like the Red Sea as Eric 'Batters' Rogers put in an appearance. A shock went through the dockers, men instinctively stepping back. His ever-present shadow, Lucas, his son and right hand trailed behind, pulling himself up to his full six feet five, ensuring that all-comers understood not to take the piss. The giant's knuckles were scarred and his eyes cold as January water.

Hatred was Eric 'Batters' Rogers' daily bread, and Danny Steele the poison he couldn't stop swallowing. Standing a few inches shorter than his son with shoulders that could block out the sun, Batters commanded his corner of Sugar Cane Wharf through brute force and settling disputes the old-fashioned way – with bone-crushing finality. Those canny enough to look beneath the brutality would recognise that the lines deep around those eyes told the story of sleepless nights spent missing his precious daughter, Mini, the girl he'd sworn to his dying wife, Fleur, he'd always protect.

But Mini had chosen Danny Steele's boy over her own blood, and that betrayal cut deeper than an enemy's blade which meant he'd turned his back on her. He'd never been one for fancy words or clever schemes, when trouble came calling, he answered with his fists. The docker nickname 'Batters' wasn't just about his love of violence; it was a warning that you crossed his path at your own bloody peril.

'If it ain't the rat from the other end of the wharf.' Danny slathered on a mocking, sarky tone, but his eyes turned to chips of ice, his body tensing with a street dog's menace scenting a rival.

The two men were archenemies. Two sides of the same grimy criminal coin on the docks, but their methods couldn't have been more different. Danny played the game with a veneer of respectability. Batters, on the other hand, was a creature of the shadows. He made no pretence of being anything other than what he was, a hard-nosed gangster who'd sooner crack skulls than negotiate. His power came purely from fear and brute force. The Dockside Devil, a boozer at the opposite end of Sugar Cane Wharf, served as his headquarters. It was a place where only the brave or the foolish dared to tread without an invitation.

Batters swaggered forward, jabbing a thick finger at Danny. 'He knew! He knew Sugar Cane was going to turn into a dead ringer for the Marie Celeste.' The veins in his neck bulged with each accusation, his face flushing crimson. 'Your guardian angel knew full well it was marked for the knacker's yard and said fuck all!'

'Piss off back to whatever hole you crawled out from,' Danny growled. His jaw muscles twitched with the effort of restraining himself, tendons standing thick as ropes on his neck.

Batters sidled closer, breathing in Danny's humiliation, a cruel smirk playing across his lips. 'Told these boys you were pulling the wool over their eyes, didn't I? That Sugar Cane was marked for death just like the rest.' He turned to address the crowd, arms spread wide like a preacher. 'While Danny here was feeding you fairy stories and lining his pockets, I was preparing.'

'Preparing for what?' a burly docker demanded, his massive chest heaving.

'For the future, lads! The docks are dying, but there's plenty of other work for men who know which horse to back.' Batters patted his coat pocket, the implication of ready cash clear as day.

Danny spat on the ground, the glob landing inches from Batters' polished shoes. 'He's talking bollocks. This slag wouldn't piss on you if you were on fire and had twenty quid in your pocket.'

'Who are you gonna believe, eh?' Danny fought to keep his tone even despite the fury threatening to boil over inside him, his fingernails digging half-moons into his palms. 'Me, who's been working to keep this place running to the bitter end? Or this piece of dockside scum who sits on his fat slag rear-end every day while you're out making an honest day's crust?'

Batters threw his head back, roaring with nasty laughter that bounced off the empty warehouses. 'Honest? That word must taste like shit in your gob. A two-faced tosser like you wouldn't know honest if it kicked him square in his cunty-nuts.' He quickly turned his attention back to the men.

"I've got three warehouses running in Hackney and Bow, all fully staffed with former dockers taking home a plump wage.' He paused for effect, savouring the moment. 'Men who had the sense to know when a ship was sinking.'

The looks on the dockers' faces changed from anger to consideration. Hungry children at home had a way of clarifying priorities. Money was money, and principles didn't feed hungry kids.

'You'll work for him?' Danny exploded, unable to contain his rage. 'After everything? After what he did to Tommy Wilson's family? After he tried to flood the docks with that cut-rate gin that blinded three men?'

A weathered old docker stepped forward, shoulders hunched with defeat. 'What choice have we got, Danny? You promised us the docks would stay open. You said we had nothing to worry about.'

'He knew, as surely as I'm standing on this here ground.' Batters pointed dramatically to the floor at his feet.

'Come a bit closer and say that, you fucking wank job!' Danny lunged closer. He could feel the respect from the men dwindling away. That had always been his fear when the docks shut, that they would no longer call him king.

Lucas stepped forward, his massive fists clenched, forearms thick as dock pilings, but Batters held him back with a raised hand. 'No need for that, son. Danny's done himself in better than I ever could.' His eyes glittered with malicious triumph.

Turning back to the crowd, Batters raised his voice again. 'Any man who wants honest work, come down to the Dockside Devil tonight. I'll be sorting jobs then.' He locked eyes with Danny one last time. 'Unlike some, I keep my promises.'

As Batters and Lucas strutted away, the dockers began to drift away, too, their boots scraping on the ancient cobbles like a funeral procession. Some couldn't meet Danny's eyes; others shot him looks of pure betrayal. A few nodded curtly, acknowledging the end of an era.

One by one, they walked away until Danny stood alone at the gates of his fallen empire.

The King of Nothing. Danny fucking Nobody.

He knew he no longer had a choice. He had to turn to Lord Xander. Which was no bad thing. Danny straightened his shoulders.

What better way to forge a new kingdom than to carry out the biggest bank robbery London had ever seen?

Become the Underworld King of this city.

# Chapter Eleven

Danny Steele bulldozed his way through the Voodoo Lounge entrance. His black mood from his encounter with Batters circled him, a vulture trying to pick him clean and hanging heavy around him.

The club buzzed with Friday night debauchery. Topless women dancing for rough-faced men in sharp suits leering through whisky fumes. Sequined hostesses with practiced smiles steered punters towards private booths for 'special entertainment'. Blue-tinged cigarette smoke drifted through amber lighting, casting everybody in a hellish glow.

'All right, guv'nor?' the barman called over, already reaching for Danny's usual Ron del Barrilito Puerto Rican rum.

Danny Steele owned this place, lock, stock, and secrets, though only his inner circle knew that particular fact. At least he still had this place, a reliable money stream now that the docks were going under. He intended to extend his reach further, but for that he needed serious capital, and fast.

He nodded curtly at several regulars, maintaining appearances while raw fury boiled through his veins. The whispers had already started – East End gossip burned through every boozer and betting shop and brothel. People watching, waiting to see if the great Danny Steele would fall on his arse.

''Ere he is,' a voice rang out, loud enough for all to hear above the music. 'The King of the Dock-less! How's it feel having your crown jewels lopped off, Danny boy?'

The club fell deathly silent, the music suddenly seeming distant and hollow. Customers froze, drinks suspended midway to lips. Even the dancers stopped mid-writhe, eyes wide with horrified anticipation.

*You fucking what!*

Danny turned nice 'n' slow towards the source of the disrespect. A ratty-faced, two-bit tosser, years younger than Danny, stood against the bar surrounded by his grinning cocksure cronies. The dumbnuts bastard wore an expensive suit that screamed more money than taste, his greased-back hair gleaming under the lights, chunky gold sovereign rings flashing on most fingers. Danny recognised him now – one of Batters Rogers' up-and-coming boys, barely out of nappies but already shooting his mouth off. Trying to make a name for himself by thinking he could drag Danny's nuts over his face and take him down in public.

Danny's voice dropped to a dangerous whisper that nonetheless carried through the silent club. 'What did you just say to me, you manky scrote?'

The younger man straightened, too thick or too drunk to recognise the danger signals crackling through the air.

His grin widened. 'I said, I'd call you King of the Docks, but you ain't king of dog shit no more, are ya?' He glanced around, playing to the crowd. 'Word on the cobbles is old Danny boy's washed up. Batters says it's time for fresh blood.'

*This nobody cunt thinks he can take my place. Thinks the old lion's teeth have fallen out. And using Batters' name, bold as brass.*

Inside, Danny's guts twisted with fury and something else. An ice-cold flicker of fear. This was exactly what he'd dreaded. That someone would challenge him in public. His reputation hung in the balance. One moment of weakness now, and the whispers would become roars. His reputation would be in the gutter, and Batters Rogers and all-comers would be measuring up Danny's territory for new carpets by Monday morning.

In one fluid motion, he reached for a pint glass and smashed it into the younger man's face. The sound was unforgettable, a wet crunch of glass meeting bone, followed by an animalistic high-pitched squeal.

Blood sprayed in a claret arc across the bar top as shards embedded themselves in flesh.

The loud-mouthed ponce staggered backwards, hands flying to his ruined face, blood spurting between his fingers. Danny went in for the kill. He grabbed a fistful of hair and yanked downwards with savage force, feeling strands rip from the scalp. Danny forced the shrieking man to his knees.

'You fucking what?' Danny roared. 'You stand in MY club and tell EVERYONE I'm washed up? That some jumped-up, has-been, wank-shite like Batters Rogers is taking over?'

He smashed the man's face into his knee with a sickening crunch. Teeth and blood sprayed across the floor. The distinct crack of a breaking nose echoed through the club.

'You worthless piece of shit!' Each word thundered through the club while Danny dragged the bleeding man across the floor by his hair, leaving a glistening scarlet trail. 'Who the fuck do you think you are? Some worthless, tarnished flash thinks he can waltz in and drop Batters' name in my gaff?'

Danny kicked him viciously in the stomach, feeling the nauseating give of cracking ribs beneath his handmade Italian loafer.

'You tell Batters I wiped better things than you off my bloody khazi this morning.' Danny delivered another savage kick that lifted the man's body several inches off the floor.

'Please…' the man burbled through blooded lips, a flap of torn cheek moving grotesquely as he spoke, 'I didn't… Batters just said…'

'Shut your fucking north and south before I cut your tongue out!' Danny bellowed. He grabbed the man's splayed fingers and deliberately stomping on them, the crack of breaking bones punctuating his fury. 'You disrespect me in front of my people? You mention that dogshit Batters' name in my club? I'll fucking bury both of you.'

Danny seized the bleeding man by his collar and half dragged, half carried him towards the exit, blood spattering the floor with each step. The metallic tang of fresh blood filled his nostrils, coating the back of his throat. The crowd parted like frightened sheep, faces pale with shock.

'This,' Danny announced to the silent room, his voice dropping to a deadly calm, 'is what happens when any fucker dares his boys into my territory.'

Two bouncers appeared instantly at Danny's shoulder.

'Make sure that dogshit understands who's boss,' Danny growled, his chest rising and falling with his rough breathing. His shirt clung to his sweat-drenched back, adrenaline still pumping through his system.

He turned back to the club, where silence still reigned supreme. Every eye in the place was fixed on him, faces displaying a mixture of terror, respect, and morbid fascination. Danny casually pulled out a handkerchief and wiped his hands, the white cloth quickly turning crimson.

Then, as if a switch had been flipped, his face transformed into a charming grin. The bloodied handkerchief disappeared into his pocket with a flourish.

'Now I've taken out the rubbish,' he announced, voice warm and inviting, 'how about a drink on the house for everyone? Can't have one mouthy, insignificant tosspot ruining our Friday night, can we?'

The tension broke. Nervous laughter rippled through the crowd.

*Fifty percent of this job is front,* Danny thought behind his jovial mask. *Give 'em the impression you're always in control, even when the world's going to shit around you.*

He turned his attention to what he'd really come to the Voodoo Lounge for.

***

The stairs leading to the lower level stretched before him, taking him into the members-only section of the club. The boisterous noise upstairs faded behind him, replaced by the hushed murmurs of serious men conducting serious business. The basement casino glowed with golden light from crystal sconces, flattering even the most haggard faces. The air was heavy with expensive cigar smoke and the subtle notes of rare whiskies and eau de cologne. A circle of expensively dressed men huddled around a green baize table, hanging on every syllable from the distinguished figure commanding their attention.

Lord Xander dominated the room without apparent effort. Though pushing seventy, he radiated unnatural vitality, the kind only obscene wealth and privilege could preserve. His thick silver-streaked hair swept back from sharp features that had grown more refined rather than decrepit with age. The tailoring of his suit was subtle perfection, the fabric alone probably worth more than what most working men earned in a month.

Reciting one of his far-fetched tales with perfect aristocratic timing, his plummy accent filling the room. '…and there I was, starkers as the day I was born, the diplomat's wife hiding in the wardrobe, wearing nothing but my diamond cufflinks, when who should barge in but the archbishop himself!' Lord Xander delivered the fabricated anecdote

The assembled erupted in raucous laughter, except for Danny. He was tired of his father's nudge-nudge-wink-wink stories of his naughty days fucking every woman who looked at him.

Danny straightened his blood-spattered tie and strode forward, cutting through the crowd. 'A word,' Danny growled directly into Xander's ear, his voice vibrating with barely contained aggression. 'We need to talk.'

His father levelled him with a smile that didn't reach his eyes. 'I do hope it's what we discussed before.'

When they were settled in large armchairs in a discreet corner, Xander commented dryly, 'I see you've been entertaining the masses upstairs.' He glanced over Danny's bloodied appearance with clinical detachment, as if examining an insect. 'One hopes the unfortunate recipient will recover. These public displays are so… crude.'

'He'll live,' Danny grunted.

'Indeed.' Xander studied him with cold detachment, his manicured hands resting precisely on his knees. 'I assume this means you've made your decision about my little proposition?'

Danny leaned forward, the leather chair creaking beneath his weight. 'I'll do your bank job,' he said, voice barely above a whisper. 'Now I want the details. Why this bank of all banks?'

Xander's icy gaze stared back at him. 'The money is yours, entirely. Take every penny you find in the bank with my blessing.' His tone suggested he was bestowing some great honour upon Danny, like throwing scraps to a stray dog.

'But?' Danny's jaw tightened, the scar on his cheek whitening with tension.

'There's a safe deposit box. Number 718. It contains documents I require.' Xander's expression remained perfectly composed, giving away nothing.

Danny fixed his father with a hard stare. 'What documents?'

'That,' Xander replied, 'is none of your concern.' The words were clipped, final.

Danny's temper went on the rise again. 'If I'm risking my neck and my men, I want to know what for.'

'You're risking your neck for a lot of money,' Xander countered smoothly, crossing one immaculately trousered leg over the other. 'The contents of that box are my affair. Simply bring what you find to me.'

Nostrils flared, Danny fought hard for control. Upstairs, he would have already smashed the smug bastard's face in. Down here, in this basement, with this man, different rules applied. Rules he'd never been able to break.

*Still treating me like some errand boy even when I've got blood on my hands.*

'You got yourself a deal,' Danny finally agreed.

He gazed intently into the distance. 'Time to show London what a real firm can do.'

# Chapter Twelve

Danny thumped his empty glass onto the mahogany desk in his private office above the River Rat pub. The sticky Bacardi residue glistened in the bottom, caught by the lamplight.

'What's this about then, Dad?' Jimmy's fingers drummed against his thigh, nervous energy running through him.

He sat with Brother Bertie on the other side of the desk, facing his old man. The two younger men exchanged wary glances. Word had come through earlier that Danny wanted a late-night sit-down, and those never ended well for someone.

Danny locked his fingers together, savouring the moment. 'We're going to do a job. A proper bleedin' one.'

Brother Bertie straightened his pork pie hat, sharp interest flickering in his eyes. 'What sort of job?'

'We're going on the pavement.'

Bank robbery. Jimmy's stomach plummeted through the floorboards. This was madness, even for his power-hungry father.

'Bleedin' Christ!' Jimmy exploded, kicking back his chair and shooting to his feet. His face flushed puce with shock. 'You've gone proper barmy! Career armed robber now, is it? The Old Bill would have us banged up before we could count the readies!'

'Shut your bone box and park your bum!' Danny snarled. His meaty fist slammed on the desk. The rum glass jumped. 'This isn't some half-arsed smash and grab from some poxy corner shop. One job, Jimmy. That's all it takes for enough readies to set us up proper in new business ventures.'

Jimmy's chest heaved. He assessed the greedy bastard he'd looked up to all his life, then slowly retook his seat.

Brother Bertie rubbed his hands together, undisguised enthusiasm blazing in his dark eyes. When Gertie had told him what she'd done – gone to Miles Harker's lair and paid his debt off – he'd nearly lost his bloody mind. Anything could have happened to her there. And if it had, it would have been his fault. Yet again his devoted sister had saved his worthless hide. He'd promised her that his reckless ways would be behind him.

But the chance to rob a bank…

That spoke to the thrill-seeking fool in him.

Danny carried on, savouring their attention. 'We're going to turn over the Anglo-Merchant—'

'Bloody hell!' Brother Bertie interrupted with shocked excitement. 'Mr Steele, let's do a rewind right there! You can't be talking about the cursed Anglo-Merchant Bank where…'

Jimmy finished, equally stunned. '…six members of the Flanagans walked in, none walked out. Then bits of them were found scattered across half of London.'

His best mate could barely get his words out. 'One gang blew themselves up with dynamite. Another ended up in a shootout with the coppers.'

'Dad, that place is cursed,' Jimmy tried reasoning with the stubborn old git. 'That's why no firm will touch it.'

Danny grinned, savage satisfaction spreading across his scarred face. 'Exactly why it's perfect, you muppet. No one would expect us to try it. They reckon they're untouchable.'

Brother Bertie suddenly straightened, excitement flashing in his eyes. 'There's an escape hatch in the gents'!'

Jimmy and Danny both snapped their heads towards him, surprise etched on their faces.

'What you on about?' Danny demanded, thick eyebrows knitting together.

'There's a maintenance access point in the men's toilets that I'd bet my last quid leads down to the Underground tunnels. Probably connects to the Central Line running underneath.'

Jimmy's eyes narrowed with suspicious interest. 'And how the bloody hell would you know that?'

Brother Bertie shifted in his seat, clearly uncomfortable, tugging at his collar. Burning shame crept up his neck. There was no way on God's green earth he wanted Jimmy to know that he'd tried to steal from his own devoted sister.

*But at least I didn't beat her senseless!*

Brother Bertie crushed his bitter resentment down deep. Enough! He'd tortured himself long enough with this poison eating away at his guts. Sin was gone, lost to him forever. And this festering hatred towards Jimmy was killing him from the inside out. He was drowning in it, and if he didn't find a way to let it go, it would destroy him completely.

Time to bury it deep. Time to dig a grave for this rage and shovel dirt over it. Because the alternative – losing Jimmy completely, watching their blood brotherhood crumble into nothing – that would finish him off for good.

He told them, 'I was at the bank a few weeks back.'

'Doing what exactly?' Jimmy pressed, stubborn curiosity blazing.

Brother Bertie waved a dismissive hand. 'Just business, wasn't it? Nothing worth gassing about.' He arched a knowing brow. 'Point is, I saw it. Always good to have another exit point other than the front door.'

'There's more,' Danny poured another generous finger of rum into his glass. The amber liquid caught the light. 'I'm on commission for this job.'

'Commission? From who?' Jimmy demanded, nostrils flaring.

'Doesn't matter who,' Danny snapped, knocking back the rum in one burning swallow. 'What matters is the prize. We hit the main vault, but we also need to empty safety deposit box 713. Special contents.'

The other two considered his words and nodded.

Relaxing back, Danny added, 'This stays between the four of us. Not a whisper elsewhere.'

Brother Bertie frowned, glancing around the empty room. 'Four? There's only three of us here.'

The door creaked open. 'He means me, darling.'

Rita strutted in as brazen as you like. Now that she'd gone all West End, she was pure class, a very dangerous Miss Hoity-Toity. Her honey-blonde hair fell in a sleek bob that kissed her shoulders, not a strand out of place. The cream wool shift dress hugged her tall frame perfectly, ending a respectable inch below the knee, paired with matching court shoes. But underneath all that expensive polish, Rita was still pure East End steel. She'd climbed the social ladder, all right, but she'd kept her street-fighter claws for the journey.

Rita clip-clopped towards Jimmy, sliding into his personal space with sultry grace. 'Look at you, handsome. Still married to that prized little wife of yours? Shame.' Her expensive perfume engulfed him – musky, heady, dangerous.

'Pack your antics in, Rita,' Danny barked, though reluctant affection tinged his gruff voice. 'We ain't got time for your prick-teasing.'

She flashed a wicked smile but backed off, perching herself on the edge of the desk, crossing her long legs with deliberate slowness. 'Just saying hello to an old friend, Danny-boy. No harm in that.' Her sly stare lingered on Jimmy, making him shift uncomfortably.

'Rita's our wheel-woman,' Danny explained. 'Best getaway driver this side of the river.'

Rita pulled out an Embassy, lighting it with a silver Zippo. 'My considerable talents are wasted behind the wheel, but a girl takes what she can get.' Smoke curled from her glossy lips.

The sexual tension crackled between them. Danny tore his gaze away first.

'You two.' Danny jabbed a thick finger Jimmy and Brother Bertie's way. 'You'll run the show, plan it over the next eight weeks. I'll stay in the background.'

Brother Bertie asked, 'So we'll be calling the shots?'

'Within reason,' Danny cautioned, his voice dropping to a dangerous growl. 'But you better listen good, you cocky little bastards. Whatever happens, whatever goes down, you leave with the contents of box 718. Nothing else matters – not the money, not each other, not your bleedin' mothers. That box is everything.'

'What's in it?' Jimmy asked, angling his body forward with burning curiosity.

Danny didn't answer because it was a question he desperately wanted to know himself.

The Anglo-Merchant Bank job was coming, curse or no curse. And God help any poor bastard who got in their way.

# Chapter Thirteen

I'm as fake as the brass on them new decimal coins they're bringing in, Sin sadly decided, staring at the pristine ivory silk dress hanging from Mini's cluttered fitting room door. The exquisite garment seemed to mock her with its untainted perfection, with all its empty promises of happily ever after that Sin knew in her broken heart were hollow.

The bright converted room with a view of the river in Jimmy and Mini's house on Molasses Quay was a colourful testament to Mini's remarkable talents. Vibrant bolts of luxurious fabric lined one peeling wall in a gaudy rainbow of textures and patterns. A heavy industrial sewing machine dominated a scarred wooden table. Three headless mannequins stood in silent, judgmental formation, their wire frames draped with half-finished garments.

Sin ran her fingers over the cool, slippery silk of her engagement dress. Mini had bloody outdone herself this time. The expensive fabric had cost a small fortune, which Ade had ponied up to pay for, and Mini's skilful hands had transformed it into something that belonged in the glossy pages of posh *Vogue*. Sin had seen similar fashionable designs in trendy Carnaby Street boutiques going for prices that made her eyes water.

Mini bustled into the cramped room carrying a battered box of sharp pins, her keen eyes immediately taking in Sin's hesitation. Tilting her head with a shrewd look, she rattled the pins in their box.

'You getting cold feet or what?' Mini asked, her nimble fingers already busy with a frayed tape measure. The directness in her tone made Sin flinch. 'That fancy dress ain't gonna try itself on, darling.'

Sin's fingers clutched at the edge of the dress, her knuckles whitening with tension before she willed them to relax. 'Just admiring your brilliant handiwork.' Her response came out with a forced brightness that didn't reach her eyes.

She shrugged off her cardy with a dismissive flick of her wrist, as if shedding her doubts along with it.

The luxurious dress slipped over her head in a cool, seductive whisper of delicate fabric. Mini circled her, making tiny, precise adjustments, her pursed mouth full of shiny pins. At five feet nothing, Mini had to stand on a rickety wooden box to reach Sin's slender shoulder.

'Gordon Bennett,' Mini breathed reverently, stepping back to take in the stunning effect. Her tired eyes widened with genuine amazement, a rare, unguarded moment of appreciation softening her usually sharp features. 'You look the dog's bollocks in that.' With a wink she added, 'Or should that be, the bitch's tits.'

They both giggled at that. Mini surveyed her handiwork with pride. 'Bleedin' Buckingham Palace level. Adrian's gonna fall over his feet when he claps eyes on you.'

Sin turned reluctantly to the mottled surface of the full-length mirror. The unexpected reflection startled her. The high-necked, sleeveless column of pristine ivory silk skimmed her reed-thin figure perfectly before flaring slightly at the modest hem. Delicate silver embroidery traced intricate patterns across the fitted bodice, catching the dim light with each shallow breath she took. She barely recognised her wretched self.

Sin caught her sister-in-law's thoughtful eye in the mirror, biting the inside of her cheek until she tasted metallic blood. Her restless fingers twisted the expensive silk at her sides, knuckles whitening against the delicate ivory fabric.

Swallowing hard, Sin asked, 'How did you know?'

'Know what, pet?' Mini stilled her hands momentarily on the silk, sensing the weight behind Sin's question.

Struggling to keep her voice steady, Sin pushed out, 'That Jimmy was the one. That he was worth giving up your entire family for.' Her eyes locked with Mini's in the mirror, desperately seeking something she couldn't name.

Mini's usually busy hands stilled on the shimmering fabric. Her normally brisk movements frozen in mid-air. In the foggy mirror, Sin watched her petite sister-in-law's expressive face transform, the sharp angles of determined concentration melting into something wistful, almost dreamy.

'Some things you just know, deep in your aching bones.' Mini's husky voice dropped to a passionate whisper, her bright eyes taking on a faraway, glassy gleam. 'First time I laid eager eyes on your handsome brother, it was something proper. Would've followed that magnificent man to hell itself if he'd asked.'

Her chin lifted, a sudden flash of raw defiance hardening her delicate features. 'My miserable dad being a right vindictive bastard about it only made me more dead cert, if I'm honest.'

Sin caught the slight, vulnerable tremble in Mini's quivering bottom lip, the way her slender throat worked to swallow down ancient pain. Even after all these troubled years, the festering wound of her father's cruel rejection hadn't fully healed. Sin reached out impulsively, squeezing Mini's bony shoulder, feeling the fierce, unexpected strength in that compact frame.

Her hand falling away, Sin was suddenly unable to maintain the lie of enthusiasm about her own upcoming marriage.

'Ade's a proper doll. Everyone says I'm ridiculously lucky.'

'Lucky, my skinny arse.' Mini fixed her with a penetrating, shrewd look, her suspicious eyes narrowing. She planted her work-worn hands firmly on her narrow hips. 'Real question is, does he light that passionate fire in your cold belly? Or are you just settling for a nice, safe warm glow?'

Sin's eyes darted away, seeking escape. 'He's wonderfully kind to Dilly. You should see how patient he is with her. Never treats her different or damaged.'

'Ain't answering my nosy question, though, are you?' Her penetrating gaze cutting through all pretence, Mini leaned closer, voice dropping to a concerned murmur. 'You can fool everyone else with that plastic smile, but I've known you too long. Something ain't right, and we both bloody know it.'

Sin's restless mind drifted to Bertie. Her secret Bertie. His dazzling smile that lit up dingy rooms. The way his expressive eyes crinkled adorably at the corners when he laughed his deep laugh. The electric-warmth of his strong hands. The husky sound of his velvet voice when he'd whispered her name passionately in the darkness.

The bittersweet memory burned through her traitorous body, eating away at her fragile insides. Two agonising, brutal bloody years since she'd ended their dangerous relationship, and still the searing pain felt fresh.

*Stupid numpty,* she chided savagely. *You had something precious and real and you carelessly threw it away. And for what? To please judgmental people who'd never accept your happiness anyway?*

*Mind you, he's not exactly pining for miserable me, is he? Making his arrogant way through half the women across Soho, from all accounts. Probably laughing his head off at pathetic me with them between the sweaty sheets. Poor little frightened Sin, too bloody scared to follow her treacherous heart.*

Then again, it didn't have a rightful claim on him anymore. She'd made her cowardly choice, hadn't she?

Mini's voice cut through her bitter thoughts. 'Men are thicker than a docker's greasy sandwich, love. Running around with floozies doesn't mean a bloody thing,' she remarked carelessly, misinterpreting Sin's distant, tortured expression as general doubts about Ade's faithfulness.

The words escaped Sin's lips before she could stop them, raw and wounded. 'I ended it,' she whispered hoarsely, horrified at what she'd almost revealed. Her hand flew to her mouth, eyes widening with alarm.

Mini glanced up sharply from her pinning, eyebrows drawing together in confusion. 'Ended what, hun?' she asked, her voice tinged with sudden concern.

Sin's face flushed hot with panic. She forced a bright, artificial laugh that echoed hollow in the small room. 'Nothing. Just thinking out loud.' She turned away, pretending to adjust the dress' sleeve.

Mini stepped back to admire her meticulous work once more, but instead of her usual satisfied, proud nod, a strange, alarming expression crossed her pale face. She pressed a trembling hand to her heaving chest, her slender fingers clutching desperately at the rough fabric of her faded blouse.

'Mini?' Sin's voice rose with alarmed concern, all thoughts of her own troubles instantly forgotten.

The small woman doubled over suddenly, a violent, racking cough tearing from her constricted throat. She gripped the edge of the cluttered sewing table with white-knuckled intensity, her small body convulsing with each brutal spasm.

'Mum!' Sin shouted frantically, genuine panic rising in her constricted chest. 'MUM!'

Heavy footsteps pounded up the creaking stairs, and Iris appeared breathlessly in the doorway, sleepy baby Harry balanced precariously on her bony hip. Her widened eyes took in the distressing sight of Mini's hunched form.

'What happened?' Iris demanded sharply, her voice cutting through the panic. She thrust the squirming baby unceremoniously into Sin's unprepared arms, already moving towards her daughter-in-law with practiced efficiency.

'She just started coughing violently,' Sin explained, her voice shaking with fear. She awkwardly adjusted the baby in her arms. 'One minute she was completely fine, and then—'

Iris guided Mini gently to a rickety chair, kneeling protectively beside her. Her voice softened with maternal concern. 'How long has this worrying cough been going on?'

'No need to make a big song and dance about it,' Mini insisted stubbornly between ragged, painful breaths, waving away Iris' helping hand even while she leaned on it. 'Just a persistent tickle in my dry throat.'

'Don't give me that old codswallop,' Iris snapped decisively, though her capable hands were gentle; they rubbed Mini's trembling back in soothing circles. 'Sin, mind Harry carefully. I'm taking her downstairs for a strong cup of sweet tea.'

'I don't need—' Mini began weakly, attempting to rise from the chair with a show of defiance that collapsed almost immediately.

'I wasn't asking politely,' Iris interrupted, her tone brooking no room for argument. The worry in her eyes betrayed her brusque manner.

***

'What's going on? And don't give me any of your cobblers, young lady,' Iris confronted Mini, her gentle voice belying the directness of her words.

The fierce concern in her eyes made Mini glance away.

Mini wrapped her small fingers around the chipped mug, grateful for the warmth seeping into her trembling hands. The sweetened tea's steam rose in delicate wisps, momentarily obscuring her troubled face. Her insides twisted under a crushing weight. Every breath produced a frightening crackling sensation deep in her fragile chest.

Perched on chairs at the wrought-iron table on the small terrace overlooking the Thames, Mini and Iris sat in uneasy silence.

With a stubborn set to her jaw, Mini responded. 'I'm all good, honest.' Her fingers tightened around the mug to hide their uncontrollable trembling. 'Just been working harder with so many orders coming, including making Sin the most spectacular wedding dress ever.'

Iris reached across the weathered table and placed her warm hand over Mini's cold one. 'Are you sure that's all it is? Because you look dead rough around the edges and properly done in.'

Mini tossed her head with practiced defiance, her small chest aching with the effort. 'You think a little tickle in my throat is going to keep me down?' She managed a dismissive wave, forcing steadiness into her shaking hand. 'I've already made an appointment with the doctor tomorrow, so you can stop your endless nattering.'

Abruptly, her mother-in-law lowered her voice. 'If you need to see a doctor away from here, private-like, I can help you pay for that.'

That took Mini by surprise which showed in the confusion contorting her features. 'Where would you get a few extra bob from? I'm not taking your housekeeping money.'

Iris went a bright red, which Mini didn't understand. 'All I'm saying is if you need me, I'm always here.' Her fingertips patted the back of Mini's hand with care and reassurance.

After Mini left to go back to Sin and Harry, Iris remained on the terrace, watching the rise and fall of the river. The clouds had darkened, threatening imminent rain, perfectly matching the growing unease settling in her knotted stomach.

The disturbing image of Jimmy's wife's pinched, grey face haunted her troubled thoughts.

# Chapter Fourteen

The doctor's words kept ringing in Mini's ears like a cruel bell that wouldn't stop.

*'Mrs Steele, I'm concerned about these results... need to run more tests... your mother's medical history... come back next week...'*

Mini stepped out onto the East London street, her face ghostly white, drained of all colour. The pavement beneath her feet didn't feel real, like she was floating somewhere outside her own body. Her hand clutched her handbag with knuckles bleached bone-white. A wave of nausea crashed over her, and she stopped, leaning against the rough brick wall of the chemist's, the coarse texture grounding her to reality.

For a moment, she thought she might pass out right there in broad daylight. How fucking ridiculous would that be? Mini Rogers, known for being tougher than most men in the East End, sprawled out on the pavement like some delicate flower.

*Get a fucking grip, girl.*

Mini straightened, shoulders thrown back, chin lifting with deliberate defiance. She was Jimmy 'Southpaw' Steele's wife, mother to three beautiful children, a woman who'd faced down Danny Steele himself without flinching. She wasn't about to fall apart on the bleedin' street.

She took a deep breath and started walking again, the click of her heels against the pavement now deliberate and strong. But inside her head, the doctor's office played on endless repeat.

*'Something in these scans… concerning pattern… your mother had similar symptoms… need to be thorough…'*

Something prickled at the back of her neck. The unmistakable feeling of being watched. Mini had grown up in the East End, daughter to Batters Rogers. She knew danger when it breathed down her neck. Without breaking stride, she deliberately took a sharp left down Thorpe Street instead of continuing straight towards home. No one who knew her would expect her to go this way.

Mini slipped her hand into her bag, fingers wrapping around her silver fabric shears. Seven inches of razor-sharp steel that could slice through the toughest materials – or a man's jugular if needed. She'd been carrying them since she was fourteen, back when her dad's rivals thought grabbing the boss' daughter might be good leverage.

She ducked around the corner into a narrow alley, pressing herself to the wall, shears now held ready at her side, the metal cold against her palm. Heavy footsteps approached. Big, male footsteps. She held her breath, muscles coiled tight as piano wire.

As the figure turned the corner, Mini lunged, pressing the gleaming tip of the shears up against the man's kidney. 'One fucking twitch and I'll open you up like a bleedin' Christmas present.' And she meant every last killer word of it.

'Christ almighty, Mini!' The man's body froze in recognition. 'Go easy on a fella!'

Mini stepped back, lowering the shears, her posture relaxing though her eyes remained vigilant. 'Lukey? What the effing hell are you playing at?'

Her brother stood there, big and tall, hands raised in surrender, his face contorted with shock, eyes wide beneath his heavy brow. 'I wasn't playing at nothing,' Lucas protested, his massive frame making the alley feel claustrophobic. 'I was just—'

'Following me?' Mini's eyes flashed dangerously, her jawline clenching hard. 'Spying on me?' Her words sliced the air between them, sharp as her shears.

Lucas lowered his hands slowly, his dark eyes – so like their mother's – filling with unconcealed worry. 'I saw you coming out of the doctor's,' he said, his booming voice deliberately hushed. 'You looked terrible.'

'So what? You thought you'd tail me like I'm some slag who needs watching?' The anger felt good, electric and vital, pushing away the hollow fear that had been gnawing at her insides since she'd sat in that sterile office.

'Don't be like that, Min,' Lucas said, his voice softening to a gentleness that seemed impossible from a man with hands the size of dinner plates. 'I was worried. You're my baby sister.' He reached out, his scarred knuckles brushing against her cheek with unexpected tenderness.

The touch nearly broke her. Mini felt her bottom lip tremble and bit down on it hard enough to taste copper. 'You can't be seen with me.' The last thing she wanted was to bring trouble to her brother's door. 'If Dad caught wind—'

'Fuck Dad.' A rare flash of defiance darkened his usually compliant face. 'You think I give a toss what he says? You're my blood.' His hands balled into fists at his sides.

Mini shook her head, but there was the ghost of a smile on her lips. 'You daft bugger. You never did have the sense God gave a gnat.'

'What happened in there, Min?' Fear twisted his features. 'You've got the same look Mum had when she—'

'Don't!' Her whip-crack tone lashed him off.

The word hung between them, raw and desperate. Mini's hands were shaking now, proper shaking, and she couldn't make them stop. All these weeks she'd been telling herself it was nothing – just a persistent cough, just being run-down, just the damp off the river getting into her chest. But deep in her bones, she'd felt the creeping fear.

She'd been so young when Mum started coughing. Watching her beautiful mother fade away bit by bit, the doctors scratching their heads and muttering about 'something growing' and 'nothing more we can do.' Mini remembered the way Mum's hand had felt in hers at the end – paper-thin skin over bird bones, so fragile she was frightened to squeeze.

Mini finally was brave enough to tell her brother what she hadn't dared breathe to anyone. 'I'm having tests—'

'What?' He sucked in an alarmed punch of air so loud it vibrated around them.

Quickly moving forward, she ran her hands over the front of his donkey jacket to calm him. 'The doctors aren't sure what's going on. But if anything comes up, they have medicines now, techniques that can help.'

What a relief to finally share the terror she'd been carrying alone for weeks with another person, her beloved big bruv. She'd been too scared to voice it, too scared to even think it properly. Because once you said a thing out loud, once you put words to your worst fear, it became real. It became something that could actually happen.

Composing himself, Lucas asked, 'What's that husband of yours got to say? I hope he's treating you like the most precious thing…' Seeing her gaze sharply dart away, his voice dribbled to nothing before it came back with a ferocity. 'You haven't let on to Jimmy?'

All of a sudden, it was too much for Mini. She buried her head in the security and comfort of her brother's chest. He hugged her tight, soothing her with words, strength and fierce protection.

His chin rested on top of her head, his breath warm against her hair. 'Whatever it is, Min, we'll face it. You ain't alone.' His voice rumbled through his chest, vibrating against her cheek.

'You always were a soft touch,' she murmured into his jacket, clutching the worn leather with her fingers. But she tightened her arms around him, betraying her need for his strength.

For just a moment, Mini allowed herself to be held, to be the little sister rather than the strong woman who faced down the world without flinching. But the doctor's words wouldn't stop echoing in the darkest corners of her mind.

*'These symptoms concern me… your mother's history… need to prepare yourself… specialist appointment next Wednesday…'*

Mini pulled back, composing herself with visible effort, blinking rapidly, her jaw setting into that stubborn line Lucas had known since she was a toddler. She reached up and patted Lucas' cheek. 'I need you to promise me something.' Her voice emerged steadier now, a quiet authority in its tone.

'Anything,' he answered without hesitation, his scarred hands settling on her shoulders, squeezing gently.

'If anything ever happens to me—' The words emerged clipped, each one deliberately formed.

'Mini, don't—' Lucas interrupted, his face paling with alarm.

'Shut it and listen.' She dug her fingers into his arm with surprising strength. 'If anything happens, you be there for my kids. Through rain or shine, you be the best uncle those children could have. You hear me?' Her eyes hardened to flint. 'You protect them with your life.'

Lucas stared down at her, his eyes widening like he was staring over the edge of a cliff.

'Promise me, Lucas.' The words emerged as a command, not a request.

'I promise,' he whispered, his voice rough with emotion, a vein pulsing at his temple.

Then she was gone, walking with her head high towards home, shoulders squared against the weight of her burden, while inside her mind the doctor's words continued their terrible echo.

*'Something in these scans… concerning pattern… your mother had similar symptoms…'*

Mini kept walking, her heels striking the pavement with determined precision. Whatever was coming, she'd meet it head-on. She was a Rogers by blood and a Steele by marriage. She gripped her handbag tighter with resolve. And neither family ever went down without a fight.

# Chapter Fifteen

'Standing up to eat? What are we, soddin' animals?' Uncle Don boomed across the posh chatter at Sin's engagement party inside the ballroom in the swanky hotel in the City. Glaring at the buffet spread and the lack of chairs, his wizened face screwed up in disgust. 'In my day, only dogs ate standing up.'

Another chimed in, 'Balancing your grub while trying not to spill your drink down some ponce's shirt.' Their plate wobbled precariously. 'What's this then? A plate for my thumb? I've seen bigger ashtrays in a knocking shop. What do they expect me to eat – air sandwiches?'

Sin cringed but couldn't help smirking. It had never occurred to her when Jimmy booked this upmarket hotel to celebrate her engagement to Ade that some of the older members of her family would have been sniffy about a buffet. But, of course, it was a new thing for them. One of Ade's smooth mates smiled condescendingly.

'It's frightfully modern, actually. Much more sophisticated than those dreadfully formal dinner parties.'

Don snorted. 'Sophisticated? Load of cobblers, mate. You want sophisticated? Try eating a proper meal without being a dead ringer for a twat.'

Adrian appeared at Sin's side, cutting an impressive figure in his tailored suit. He slipped an arm around her waist, the expensive cologne he wore mingling with the scent of his natural warmth.

He kissed her on the cheek. 'You're a knockout.'

And she was. Sin could have stepped straight off the cover of *Vogue*. Her chestnut hair was swept into a sleek bouffant that would've made Brigitte Bardot weep with envy, every strand lacquered into submission. The deep burgundy silk shift dress Mini had created for her skimmed her curves perfectly, hitting daringly mid-thigh with a high neckline that somehow managed to be both modest and seductive. Her cream leather T-bar shoes with chunky heels complemented the tiny silver beaded bag that caught the shimmer of the chandelier light above.

Sin stared down at the sparkling diamond on her finger, the weight of it feeling heavier than it should. This was supposed to be the happiest moment of her life, wasn't it? Every girl in London would kill to be in her shoes. So why did she feel like she was suffocating?

'Having any second thoughts, gorgeous?' Ade's voice cut through her internal turmoil, smooth as aged whisky.

Sin's head snapped up, her practiced smile sliding into place with the ease of a West End performer. 'Not on your life,' she heard herself say, the words tumbling out without hesitation.

'Congratulations to the happy couple.'

Sin went rigid at the sound of her father's deep tone. God, if she could have got away without inviting him she'd have done it in a heartbeat. Plastering a civil smile on her lips, she turned. Her mother's hand was tucked properly in the crook of her father's arm.

Danny Steele was every inch the East End patriarch in his best three-piece charcoal suit. His white shirt was crisp as fresh snow, French cuffs gleaming with gold links, and his burgundy silk tie was knotted to perfection. Danny understood the power of appearance, knew that looking the part was half the battle in commanding respect. His dark hair was slicked back with Brylcreem, not a strand out of place, and his black Oxford shoes shone like mirrors.

'Congratulations, my darling,' Iris said warmly, releasing Danny's arm to embrace her daughter. 'Don't you both scrub up well.'

Sin's gaze flew instinctively to the scar she'd carved into her dad's cheek when she was fifteen, that jagged reminder of the first time she'd learned sometimes you have to fight back.

To onlookers, it appeared that Danny bestowed the sunshine smile, but Sin knew him well – the smile never reached his eyes.

He surveyed Ade before telling him, 'I hope you know what you're getting yourself into, son. My Cynthia is a wilful little madam. Needs a strong male hand to keep her in line.'

Hatred pulsed in the air between father and daughter, a poison that had festered for years.

Danny's eyes gleamed with that familiar malice, his voice dripping false concern. 'Best way to deal with a woman like her is to put a baby in her belly, keep her too busy to cause trouble.' His gaze burned into Sin, every word a deliberate twist of the knife. 'One a year ought to do it, don't you reckon, Ade? The only reliable way to handle a lippy mare like her. You don't want her getting ideas above her station, thinking she's something special just 'cause she cuts hair Up West.'

Sin felt the blood drain from her face, rage and shame battling for dominance in her chest.

Ade caught her trembling hand in his. He held it for a few seconds, then brought it to his lips, pressing a gentle kiss to her knuckles. The tension in his shoulders was the only sign he'd registered Danny's venom.

'Sin will be my queen,' Ade announced, with a dazzling smile but some of its sparkle vanished when his direct gaze rested on Danny. 'Every empress deserves her crown, Mr Steele, and I intend to make sure she wears hers proudly. A woman with her talents should be treasured, not constrained.'

*There*! Sin thought with triumph. *Smoke that in your fecking pipe… and choke*!

Danny's face darkened. Around them, the party continued, completely oblivious to the drama going on.

Iris applied a touch of pressure to her husband's arm. 'Isn't that cousin Mary? She told me she wanted a word with you.'

While her mum manoeuvred her father away, Ade placed a comforting palm on her shoulder. 'You okay?'

Sniffing and fluttering her lashes, Sin grinned. 'He doesn't like me. Never will—'

'Ade,' an excited voice called.

It was Kath. Sin watched as he was whisked away by her best friend, who was struggling to manage Dilly's excitement at the elaborate dessert table. With natural grace, Adrian crouched to speak to Dilly at eye level, the way he always did. Within moments, he had her giggling, her face lighting up with simple joy.

'What'd you think of this drum then?' Jimmy gave her a quick peck on the cheek. 'Cost me an arm and a leg to get this place, but you're worth it, sis.'

Originally, Sin and Ade were going to hire a place in town to celebrate their engagement, but a few weeks back Jimmy had surprised them by getting this swanky hotel in the City. It was his engagement present to them.

'It's beautiful,' Sin admitted, running her fingers over the damask tablecloth. 'Too good for the likes of us, probably.'

A muscle in Jimmy's jaw twitched. 'Did you hear Uncle Reg?' He winked. 'Reckons the toilets here are posher than his sitting room.'

That suffocating silence descended on them like it always did for these past couple of years. His words were for their ears only. 'I wanted everything to be perfect for your engagement. I—'

'You don't have to keep trying to make up for what happened,' Sin butted over him, her annoyance coming to the surface 'This,' she gestured at the opulent room, 'doesn't fix anything.'

Jimmy flinched from the lash of her words. 'Will you ever forgive me?'

The question hung between them, loaded with history and pain. Sin opened her mouth to answer, but the words died in her throat, her attention fixing on the entrance to the ballroom.

Brother Bertie stood framed in the doorway, his skin set off by a sharp navy suit and his pork pie hat held in his hand. The world tilted on its axis, everything blurring except him.

The noise of the party faded to nothing, replaced by the thundering of blood in her ears. *God, he's magnificent.* So bloody tasty it hurt to feast her eyes on him. Sin's throat closed up, an invisible fist squeezing until breathing became a conscious effort.

'What's he doing here?' The rough words tumbled out seemingly of their own accord, sharp with accusation.

Jimmy's face creased in puzzlement. 'Why shouldn't my best mate be at my sister's engagement party?'

Sin caught herself quickly, realising her mistake. 'I just haven't seen him around, is all.'

*God, how many times am I going to have to wear this Tupperware smile?*

Spotting Ade making his way back towards them and, with the desperation of a drowning woman, Sin made a decision. Once he reached her, she possessively threaded her arm through his, clutching so tightly he glanced down, slightly baffled.

'There's someone I want you to meet,' she said with a brittle brightness, steering him directly towards Bertie before her courage failed her.

*Better to face this head-on*, she convinced herself.

Bertie's easy smile slid into place, but Sin alone caught the split-second flash of raw emotion in his eyes before he buried it.

'Adrian, this is Bertram Watson. Brother Bertie to most,' Sin managed, astonished how steady her introduction came over because her tongue felt thick and uncooperative, her mouth bone-dry. 'He and Jimmy go back years.'

'The boxing days,' Brother Bertie added. He extended his hand to Adrian. 'Heard plenty about you.'

'All good, I hope.' Adrian laughed, shaking his hand firmly with that effortless charm he wore like a second skin.

''Course,' Brother Bertie responded, his gaze finally shifting to Sin. The weight of it was almost a physical caress. 'Congratulations on your… engagement.' His hesitation before the word was microscopic, detectable only to her. 'You look…' He paused, desire dark and hungry flickering behind his eyes, his heated gaze dropped briefly to her lips before snapping back up. 'Happy.'

Sin felt a familiar pull low in her belly, a dangerous hotness unfurling like smoke. Her skin prickled with awareness, every nerve ending suddenly, painfully alive in a way she had no business feeling on her engagement night to another man.

Seemingly oblivious to the connection between his fiancée and the man just introduced to him, Ade tightened his arm about her waist. 'Sin's made me the luckiest man in London…' His eye line jerked across the room. 'I think we may have a situation.'

A drama was indeed playing out. Aunt Marge, a formidable woman in her sixties with hennaed hair piled high, was jabbing a finger at a young man in a fashionable wide-lapelled suit, one of Ade's Soho crowd.

'Don't you deny it, you cheeky little git!' she bellowed, face flushing to match her hair. 'I know when someone's had a grope, and I've had more than me fair share!'

The young man was horrified, his public school accent thickening with indignation. 'I beg your pardon? That's utterly preposterous! I would rather embrace a lamppost!'

A muscle in Sin's cheek twitched. The room had gone deathly quiet, expensive glasses frozen mid-clink, the refined hotel staff staring on in horror.

'You calling my mum a liar?' Eddie, Marge's son, stepped forward, all eighteen stone of bristling indignation, meaty hands balling into fists. 'Apologise before I knock your teeth so far down your throat you'll be chewing your own arsehole!'

'Now, Eddie—' Jimmy started, moving towards the scene, but it was too late.

'Enough!' Danny sliced through the proceedings. 'You're embarrassing yourselves at my princess' engagement party.'

Eddie's face drained of colour, remembering whose celebration he was disrupting. 'Danny, I—'

'Shut it,' Danny hissed, then proceeded to make things all hunky-dory again.

Sin turned to speak to Bertie, but the space where he'd been was empty. Her heart sank with something she refused to identify. Then her gaze found him, with Jimmy, both heading towards the ballroom door.

Sin touched her engagement ring with her thumb, rotating it slightly. She wondered if she was making the biggest mistake of her life. Or finally doing something right by trying to move on from the one man she couldn't have.

# Chapter Sixteen

'You keep your trap shut, got it!' After his warning, Jimmy pressed a backhander into the hotel worker's sweaty palm.

Nodding, the bloke pocketed the cash with practiced speed, glancing nervously over his shoulder. Passing Jimmy a brass key in exchange for the money, the man mumbled, 'Third floor. Suite 309. Just be quick about it.'

His eyes darting everywhere but Jimmy's face. He didn't hang around, scurrying off.

'Staff lift's this way,' Jimmy muttered to Brother Bertie, nodding towards a dingy corridor behind the kitchens, a world away from the glittering reception where Sin's engagement party was in full swing.

The service lift was the total opposite of the gold-plated beauty laid on for the guests in the main lobby. This one was all scuffed metal and flickering lights, stinking of bleach and yesterday's rubbish. Jimmy jabbed the button with his thumb, impatient.

'Not exactly The Ritz back here, is it?' Brother Bertie remarked, spinning his pork pie hat on one finger, a performative casualness that didn't reach his eyes. 'Your sister's got the fancy digs while we're skulking about with the fucking bin men.'

The lift jerked upwards, cables creaking overhead. Brother Bertie leaned against the wall, cool as you like, but Jimmy caught the calculation in his eyes. Always thinking, always watching. Made him the best partner for a job like this, even with the tension that'd been brewing between them lately.

Two minutes up, two minutes looking, two minutes down. In and out. No one the wiser.

The service lift jerked to a halt on the third floor. The doors scraped open with a metallic groan that set Jimmy's teeth on edge.

'Come on.' Jimmy stepped into a dim corridor lined with service trolleys and laundry carts. 'Should be down this way.'

They passed numbered doors, their footsteps muffled on the thin carpet – nothing like the plush red stuff in the guest areas. This was the bowels of the hotel, where the shine wore off and reality leaked through. A chambermaid scurried past, eyes down, not wanting to know what two hard fuckers were doing in the staff area.

'309.' Jimmy stopped, slid the brass key into the lock. 'Sin's getting ready in here. It's the honeymoon suite. Best in the house for my little sister,' he added, a flicker of brotherly pride coming through despite the job at hand.

Jimmy turned the key in the lock and pushed open the door. 'Fuck me sideways. Jackpot.'

The honeymoon suite sprawled before them, a palace of excess that stank of old money. Cream silk wallpaper, gold-leaf ceiling patterns, and a four-poster bed big enough for a football team. Sin's belongings had colonised the space – makeup explosion across the marble vanity, designer dress hanging from the wardrobe, killer heels scattered across the plush carpet. Her signature red lipstick stood next to a bottle of French perfume that probably cost more than most dockers made in a month.

The distant sound of laughter and clinking glasses drifted up from the party below – a different world from the one they inhabited. Down there, Sin was playing the blushing bride-to-be. Up here, the real business was about to happen.

'Ten minutes, tops.' Jimmy stalked across the thick carpet, his heavy boots leaving temporary dents with each step. 'Someone catches us up here instead of down at the party, we're in deeper than a docker's hook.'

Brother Bertie moved with practiced quiet, following Jimmy towards the balcony doors. 'Your old man thinks of everything, don't he? Getting Sin engaged at a hotel with a direct eyeline,' he observed, jaw tight, an undercurrent of something hard and bitter in his tone.

'Wasn't the old man's idea. It was mine.' Jimmy grunted, reaching for the heavy curtains, shoulders squaring defensively.

He yanked the balcony doors open. Cold air rushed in, bringing with it the smell of London – exhaust, old stone, and rain-washed pavements.

'Bloody hell,' Brother Bertie breathed, stepping onto the balcony.

There it was. Right across the narrow street. So close you could almost reach out and touch it.

Their target.

The Anglo-Merchant Bank.

Three imposing storeys of Portland stone and old-world power, standing fortress-solid directly opposite them. Security lights cast eerie shadows across decorative columns and heavy brass doors that guarded millions.

Jimmy's chest tightened. He'd genuinely booked this place for Sin because she deserved the best – his baby sister, about to be married, needed something special. But he wasn't stupid. Two birds, one stone. Give Sin her dream engagement bash while getting a perfect vantage point for the biggest score of their lives.

Golden opportunity, that's what it was. Sin happy, Danny impressed, and Jimmy acting like he had his head screwed on right for once.

'Perfect view.' Brother Bertie stepped forward and gripped the railing, knuckles tensed around the metal.

'Christ, you can see right into the security office when they change shift.'

St Paul's loomed behind the bank, its massive dome rising above the City, catching moonlight on its weathered stone. The ancient cathedral had seen centuries of London's criminals come and go, plots hatched and men hanged, and now it was witnessing another scheme unfold in its shadow.

Through an open window of the bank, they could hear a wireless playing – some posh classical rubbish, Mozart or something. The sound of wealth, floating on the night air.

'See there?' Brother Bertie pointed, momentarily forgetting whatever had been eating at him. 'They've added another camera since I was inside. Covering the east corner now.' His finger traced the route. 'But they still change the tapes at three a.m. Night guard takes a slash, leaves the monitors for nearly four minutes,' he added, drumming his fingers against the railing with precise, measured taps.

Jimmy nodded, cataloguing every detail. 'What about the toilets? That maintenance route still good?' he pressed, focus absolute, the outside world falling away.

'Better than good.' Brother Bertie's face lit up with boyish excitement, momentarily transforming him back into the carefree friend Jimmy remembered. 'Found something new when I was scouting. When the Central Line trains pass underneath – every fifteen minutes exactly – the whole building trembles. Not much, just enough to feel it in your feet. Perfect cover for when we're cracking the vault. No one'll notice a thing.'

Jimmy smiled – the first genuine one all evening. This was why they were blood brothers. No one saw opportunities like Bertie.

'Plus, that security guard – the one with the gammy leg – he's predictable as sunrise,' Brother Bertie continued, eyes bright with the thrill of the plan. 'Does his rounds at quarter past and quarter to. Twenty-three minutes exactly, then back to his desk for a cuppa and *Racing Post*.'

Below them, the City streets were empty except for the occasional black cab or late-working suit. The financial district at night was a different beast – all the money locked away behind alarm systems while the gents who shuffled it slept in their Surrey mansions.

'Who's that?' Jimmy tensed suddenly, eyes narrowing to slits, the hunter's instinct taking over.

A lone figure emerged from the service entrance. A woman, moving quick but not rushing, her hand fussing with her skirt. Straightening herself after being thoroughly messed up.

The woman stepped under a streetlight, the harsh glow catching platinum-blonde hair and a figure that could stop traffic at rush hour.

'Fuckery!' Brother Bertie choked, his pork pie hat nearly slipping from his fingers, composure cracking completely. 'You've gotta be having a giggle…'

'Chrissie.' Jimmy couldn't believe what the bloody hell he was seeing. 'Aunt bloody Chrissie.'

No mistake about it. The platinum-blonde hair, all bubbly and wavy, the hourglass figure poured into a skirt tighter than a duck's arse. Chrissie with her blood-red lipstick and Marilyn Monroe swagger, unmistakable even from this distance. She glanced around before strutting off in her stilettos, disappearing around the corner.

'What the actual fuck?' Jimmy's knuckles turned bone-white on the railing. His heart thumped hard and fast. 'What's she doing coming out of the bank?' he demanded, disbelief etched into every line of his face.

Brother Bertie's face had gone deadly serious, the playful spark vanishing. 'Your old man know about this?' he asked quietly, already calculating odds and angles.

Jimmy shook his head, mind racing. 'Not a fucking chance. Dad would've said something,' he insisted with growing alarm.

Pure fucking panic seized Jimmy, a wave of dread wash over him. He strode urgently towards the door.

Behind him, a crash. Jimmy spun to see Brother Bertie fumbling with one of Sin's perfume bottles he'd knocked from the small balcony table. It smashed before he could catch it.

Jimmy frowned because his best friend wasn't usually this clumsy. Something was off with him tonight.

'You go on ahead.' Brother Bertie nodded towards the door, not meeting Jimmy's eyes. 'I'll clean this up, make sure everything's exactly how your sister left it.'

'Right, you do that,' Jimmy said, eyeing his friend. 'Though if I didn't know better, I'd say you've got your mind so twisted up you couldn't find your arse with both hands and a map.'

Yanking open the door, Jimmy turned his mind back to his Aunt Chrissie. What the bloody hell was his aunt doing at Anglo-Merchant Bank?

Jimmy fucking hated complications.

And his Aunt Chrissie was always a cunty bollocks complication. Always an unpredictable spanner in the works.

# Chapter Seventeen

The whole bloody engagement party was suffocating her. Sin needed to get out. The hotel ballroom was doing her head in, all that chatter and laughter. She couldn't breathe properly. Every time she smiled at another guest, it felt wrong.

Sin slipped away from the crowd, mumbling something about powdering her nose. The lift was quiet after all that noise downstairs. She was knackered. Properly done in. Playing happy fiancée was exhausting work, and she'd been at it for months now.

Jimmy had gone all out for the venue and the plush suite upstairs. His way of saying sorry, she supposed. Like throwing money at something could make up for what he'd done. The bastard thought expensive wallpaper could erase the memory of the belt across her back. Some things couldn't be bought off.

The corridor was empty, just thick carpet and silence. She put the key in the lock and pushed the door open, already thinking about kicking off these bloody heels and maybe having a good ole cry before she had to go back down and pretend everything was all sunshine and happiness.

She stopped dead.

Bertie was there, on his knees picking up bits of a broken glass. The sight of him knocked the breath right out of her.

He jumped up, dropping the pieces. 'Sin.'

The way he'd said her name…Christ. It went right through her, stirring up everything she'd been trying to bury for two years.

'You shouldn't be here,' she said, but her feet were already moving towards him.

'I know.' His answer was rough and hoarse. 'Don't care.'

The air sparked between them. Her skin was tingling, every part of her suddenly awake in a way she hadn't felt for two years. Her heart was going mental, battering against her ribs.

She couldn't say who moved first. One second they were apart, the next they were crashing together. His mouth found hers, and everything else disappeared.

Brother Bertie's hands cradled her face, his fingers trembling along her skin. The gentleness in that touch, contrasted with the desperate hunger of his mouth, undid something deep in her chest. All the feelings she'd locked away came flooding back, drowning her in sensation and memory.

She clutched at his shoulders, his back, anything to anchor herself to the tide of desire threatening to sweep her away.

'Fuckery,' he groaned into her mouth, the word torn from somewhere deep. 'Sin—'

Words dissolved. Brother Bertie walked her backwards until her spine met the wall, the solid pressure grounding her even as everything else tilted off its axis. His hands found the backs of her thighs, and Sin wrapped her legs around his waist with instinctive ease, their bodies remembering this dance even after all this time.

His hardness pressed at her core, separated only by silk and wool and cotton. Their eyes locked. For one breath-held moment, they remained perfectly still, suspended in time and possibility.

'I've dreamed of this,' he whispered with feverish need. 'Every bloody night.'

Sin's fumbling fingers worked at his belt. 'Don't talk,' she breathed. 'Don't say anything that'll make me think.'

Her body craved him with greedy hunger.

Brother Bertie pushed her dress up, his hands rough against her thighs. When his fingers found the silk barrier between them, Sin's breath caught. He tore the delicate fabric with one sharp movement, the sound obscene in the quiet room.

'Look at me,' he commanded, and Sin opened her eyes to find his gaze devouring her. Dark and hungry and absolutely focused. 'I need to see your face when I—'

He pushed inside her, and Sin's world contracted to that single point of connection. A half gasp, half sob tore out of her. Completion. That's what it was. Finding a missing piece of herself she hadn't realised was gone until it returned.

Her head fell back to the wall, eyes fluttering close. Her body trembled with barely contained energy. Too much and not enough all at once. The stretch and burn of him filling her, the familiar sensation of his body, the way he fitted inside like she'd come home.

'I've missed you,' he purred along the sensitive skin of her throat. 'Missed this. Missed the way you feel around me.'

They began to move together, finding their rhythm instinctively. No awkwardness, no hesitation, their bodies spoke a language that needed no translation. Sin bit down on his shoulder to keep from crying out his name, tasting the fabric of his suit jacket, feeling the solid muscle beneath.

Brother Bertie buried his face in her neck. 'I've tried to forget you,' he confessed against her ear with honesty. 'Tried to move on. But you're in my blood, Sin. Under my skin. In every breath I take.'

The distant sounds of the party filtered up from downstairs. Laughter and music and voices celebrating her future with another man.

Brother Bertie's rhythm faltered, his movements growing more urgent. One hand slipped between them, finding the place where Sin needed him most.

She gasped, electricity shooting up her spine, pleasure coiling tighter and tighter at her core.

'I've got you,' he whispered, straining with the effort of holding back. 'Let go, Sin. Let me see you come apart for me.'

His words, the way his breath buzzed across her skin, the way he knew exactly how to touch her – it was too much. Sin shattered, pleasure exploding outward from her centre, radiating through every nerve ending. She buried her face deep into his neck to muffle her cries, feeling his pulse racing beneath her lips, tasting salt and desperation on his skin.

Brother Bertie followed moments later, his hips stuttering with hers, her name a broken prayer on his lips. For several heartbeats, they remained locked, breathing hard, sweat cooling on flushed skin. Their foreheads pressed together, sharing the same air, the same space, the same impossible moment.

Then reality came crashing back.

Sin's legs were shaking as Brother Bertie lowered her to the floor. Her dress fell back around her ankles. She could feel the evidence of what they'd done on her thighs, and part of her didn't want to wash it away.

Brother Bertie stepped back, sorting his clothes out. His hair was a mess, his shirt creased, his mouth swollen from her kisses. The space between them felt huge now.

This time when he looked at her, his expression had changed. 'I'm not doing this again,' he said quietly. 'Being your dirty secret. You need to choose, Sin. Him or me. But I won't share you anymore. I won't be the bloke you come to when you need to feel alive, then watch you walk away and marry someone else.'

His harsh declaration hit her hard. She opened her mouth, but he held up his hand.

'Don't answer now,' he said, heading for the door. 'Think about it. Think about what you actually want, not what everyone expects.'

Brother Bertie stopped at the door. 'When you decide what matters more – keeping them happy or being happy yourself – you know where I am.'

***

Sin collapsed against the wall, her heart beating beyond control and her eyes shut tight. Bertie's ultimatum banged in her skull.

You need to choose.

A bloody earthquake threatening to swallow her whole.

She smoothed her wrinkled dress with shaking hands. What was she going to do? Ade represented everything she'd convinced herself she wanted. Stability, respectability, a clean break from the East End and her father's shadow. But Bertie… God, he was a piece of her very soul. Two years of pretending hadn't changed that fundamental truth.

Sin stumbled to the ornate mirror hanging above the dresser, gasping at her reflection. Her carefully applied lipstick was smudged beyond repair. Her hair, which the salon had spent an hour arranging into an elegant updo, now tumbled in wild disarray around her flushed face. Eyes too bright, pupils still dilated with desire. Anyone with half a brain would know exactly what she'd been doing.

The door burst open without warning.

'Sin! There you are! I've been looking all over for you—' Kath stopped dead, her hand still clutching the doorknob.

Dilly hovered behind her, fingers intertwined with her sister's free hand.

Sin whirled around, her heart thundering like crazy. 'Kath!' Her fingers frantically patted at her dishevelled hair, mind already racing with excuses. 'I was just—'

'I saw Brother Bertie getting into the lift.' Her best mate cut over her, stepping into the room, pulling Dilly gently along with her. The warmth that usually radiated from her face had vanished, replaced by something harder as her gaze travelled from Sin's mussed hair to her rumpled dress, lingering on a small tear at the hem. 'Now why would he…?'

The words died on her lips. The confusion that initially showed on her face was soon replaced by something harder, unfamiliar on Kath's usually sunny features.

Dilly shifted from foot to foot, her soft brown eyes darting between the two women. She squeezed Kath's hand tighter, sensing the suffocating tension in the air.

'You haven't.' Her best friend was outraged. All the animation drained from her face, leaving it mask-like and pale. 'Tell me you haven't.'

'It's not what you think.' The lie tumbled from Sin's mouth before she could stop it. She tugged at her dress, smoothing non-existent wrinkles, hating how her tone still shook with the aftereffects of passion.

'Don't.' Kath's hand sliced through the air with surprising ferocity. 'Don't insult me, Cynthia Steele. I might not be the full ticket some of the time, but I've got a pair of eyes all of the time, that work just fine, thank you very much.'

The harshness of Kath's words, slapped Sin square in the face. In all their years of sisterhood, Kath had never spoken so much as a cross word with her, with such cold fury. Kath was sunshine personified, determined to see the best in people, always ready with a smile or a kind word. This rigid, angry woman was a stranger.

'It just happened.' Sin's shoulders sagged, her hands fluttering uselessly at her sides. An emotional lump formed in her throat, nearly choking her.

'It just *happened*?' Kath bit out like she couldn't believe what she was hearing. She took a step forward, then seemed to remember Dilly and stopped herself. 'What, you tripped and fell on his—' Her eyes flicked to her sister, who was watching with anxious eyes. Kath pressed her lips together, inhaling deeply through her nose. 'Things like this don't "just happen", Sin. Not at your own engagement party. Not with two hundred guests downstairs celebrating your future with Adrian.'

Sin flinched at the name, turning back to the mirror. In the reflection, she could see the accusation burning in Kathleen's eyes.

'I know it's wrong.' Sin braced her hands against the dresser, head dropping forward, the severity of her actions pressing down on her shoulders so hard she thought she was going to collapse. 'I know that.'

'Then why?'

Sin turned to face the fury in Kath's eyes. Not just disappointment or hurt, but genuine, blazing anger.

'I still love him.' The confession tumbled out before Sin could catch it. 'I never stopped.'

Pain so raw and personal flashed across Kath's face that Sin drew in a sharp breath. Dilly made a small, distressed sound and tugged at her sister's hand, her brow furrowed with concern.

'How could you?' Kath's fingers curled into a white-knuckled fist at her side. Her chest rose and fell rapidly, as though she'd been running. 'How could you do that to Adrian? He's a good man. A decent man.' Her voice broke slightly, betraying deeper emotions than mere disapproval. 'Any woman would be made up to have him on her arm.' Her eyes glittered like she was on the brink of tears, a reaction far more intense than Sin had expected.

The vehemence in Kathleen's defence of Adrian struck Sin as odd, even through her emotional turmoil. Yes, Kathleen had always spoken highly of him, especially his kindness towards Dilly, but this level of personal outrage seemed excessive, even for loyal Kathleen.

'Kath, please.' Sin reached out, taking a step towards her friend, desperate to bridge the sudden chasm between them.

Roughly shaking her head, Kathleen jerked backwards as if Sin's touch might burn her. She bumped into a small table, sending a vase wobbling. 'Don't.' Unshed tears magnified her anger. 'You've made your choice, Sin. You just couldn't bear to admit it until you'd hurt everyone around you.'

The accusation landed, a hard blow. Sin wrapped her arms around herself, suddenly freezing despite the warmth of the room.

'Kath—'

'No.' Her friend's head snapped side to side in a sharp gesture, the pulse in her jaw visibly throbbing. Her fingers laced more tightly through Dilly's, her grip tense. 'I don't want to hear it. Not tonight.'

She turned to her sister, her whole demeanour transforming in an instant. The hardness melted from her face, replaced by gentleness as she glanced at Dilly. 'Come on, sweetheart. We're off.'

Dilly's gaze darted between the two women, distress evident in her suddenly drawn features. She hesitated, then pulled free from Kathleen's grip. With slow, deliberate steps, she crossed to Sin and touched her arm with featherlight fingers. The simple gesture of comfort nearly broke Sin completely.

'Thank you, Dilly,' Sin whispered, tears spilling down her cheeks and dropping onto the girl's hand.

Dilly's eyes, so much wiser than anyone gave her credit for, held Sin's for a long moment.

Kathleen watched this exchange, her jaw working silently, blinking away what might have been her own tears. She held out her hand, and Dilly returned to her side with one final glance at Sin.

'Don't come back downstairs until you've fixed... this,' Kathleen hissed, gesturing with disdain at Sin's dishevelled appearance. 'I can't even look at you right now.'

She spun on her heel, pulling Dilly along, and left, a raging whirlwind. The door slammed behind them with such force that the crystal chandelier above Sin's head trembled, sending fractured light dancing across the walls.

Sin stared at the closed door, alone once more with the wreckage of her choices. Brother Bertie's ultimatum on one side. Kath's righteous anger on the other. And somewhere downstairs, Adrian waited, blissfully unaware that his world was about to collapse.

Sin's legs finally surrendered. She slid down against the dresser until she hit the floor, her expensive dress spreading out around her in a white puddle. For two years, she'd constructed a careful façade, brick by brick. Now, in the space of thirty minutes, the entire structure had crumbled to dust.

# Chapter Eighteen

Chrissie Steele strutted her muff through the middle aisle of the typing pool on the third floor of the Anglo-Merchant Bank, hips swaying with an unapologetic East End swagger. Danny Steele's baby half-sister was a vision straight out of a gentleman's magazine. Platinum-blonde hair teased to perfection, a voluptuous figure poured into a tight pencil skirt that had more curves than the Thames at low tide. At forty, ten years younger than her brother, she exuded the glamour of Diana Dors with a healthy dose of East End brass thrown in for good measure. Her heart-shaped face, framed by plump, full lips that could tell tales to make a docker blush, drew daggers from the typists who clocked her entrance.

The clickety-clack of her heels announced her arrival with fanfare, and she knew it, too, putting an extra swing in her walk just to watch the old bints' faces sour. She carried herself with more front than Selfridges, cigarette holder between manicured fingers that had seen their share of scrapping. The other secretaries might give her the evil eye, but Chrissie didn't give two fucks. Behind those entrancing eyes sparkling with mischief was a woman who'd been dragged through the hedge backwards by life and come out the other side looking like she'd stepped off a film set. Beneath her bombshell exterior lurked something dangerous – a bird who'd sooner peck your eyes out than let you see the vulnerability she kept locked up tighter than the bank's vault.

Chrissie reached the imposing mahogany door at the end of the typing pool. Not your everyday wood, this, it was polished to within an inch of its life, gleaming under the overhead lights as though it had been burnished by angels with diamond cloths. The brass nameplate read 'Edward Turner, Senior Manager' in elegant script.

'Enter,' barked a clipped male voice from within.

Grabbing the ornate handle, Chrissie pushed the door open, stepped inside, and closed it behind her with a deliberate click that echoed across the room.

Edward 'Teddy' Turner sat behind his expansive desk, and Christ, the poor bastard was the spit of death warmed up and served cold. In his early forties, he was the picture of banking respectability gone wrong – a dull, pasty-faced, unassuming man who wore tortoiseshell round glasses that couldn't hide the sheer terror in his watery eyes. His bland appearance and forgettable demeanour usually made him blend into the wallpaper of the financial institution, just another faceless banker shuffling papers.

But today? Today he appeared like a man facing the gallows.

Sweat beaded on his pale forehead despite the office's cool temperature. His hands trembled as he straightened already-perfect papers, the careful movements betraying a desperation that had nothing to do with order and everything to do with barely contained panic. The man lived with his dear old mum, doted on her like she was the Queen herself, and had probably never so much as stared sideways at another person. Now he sat there about ready to spew his guts all over his pristine blotter.

'Will we get away with it?' The words tumbled from his lips. 'Chrissie, will we actually get away with it?'

She smiled, that too sweet grin that had been getting her out of trouble since she could walk. 'Of course we will, darling,' she purred with East End confidence. 'Trust me.'

Moving with the fluid grace of a woman who knew her power, Chrissie slinked around the desk and settled herself in his lap, a cat claiming its throne. Her fingers ruffled his thinning hair with mock affection, and she felt him shudder beneath her touch.

*Poor Teddy,* she mused, studying his sweating face with amusement. *Such a naughty boy with such a dark secret.*

The memory unfolded in her mind, sharp and clear. Three months ago, she'd been heading to the more private ladies' loo on the vault level, strutting down those marble steps in her new white kitten heel slingbacks. That's when she came across Teddy Turner, Senior Manager, lurking near the safety deposit boxes like a guilty schoolboy caught smoking behind the bike sheds. The way he'd jumped when he saw her – Christ, the man had nearly leaped out of his skin. His face had gone from pasty white to beetroot red in seconds, those watery eyes darting about like a trapped animal.

'Miss Steele!' he'd stammered, fumbling with what looked like a small cloth bag. 'I didn't expect… that is, you shouldn't be down here.'

Chrissie had tilted her head, studying him with the calculating gaze of a predator sizing up prey. Something was off. Teddy Turner was many things – dull, forgettable, the kind of man who faded into the background at parties. But a nervous wreck? That was new.

'Shouldn't I?' she'd drawled, stepping closer. 'Funny thing, that. Because I could've sworn I saw you slip something into your pocket just now.'

The colour had drained from his face faster than water down a sink. 'I… no, you must be mistaken.'

But Chrissie Steele hadn't survived this long by being stupid. She'd cornered him then and there, backing him against the cold metal of the deposit boxes with nothing but her smile and the promise of what she might do if he didn't start talking. It hadn't taken much – a few well-placed threats delivered with her sweetest expression, and poor Teddy had crumbled like a week-old custard cream biscuit.

The whole sordid tale had poured out of him. His mother's mounting medical bills. The private treatments the National Health wouldn't cover. The desperation that had driven him to skim money from unclaimed safety deposit boxes – just small amounts at first, then more when he realised how easy it was. Now there was an audit coming in four months, and he didn't have the funds to replace what he'd stolen.

'They'll send me to prison,' he'd whispered, his face crumpling with shame. 'My mother… she needs me. The treatments, the medications… without them, she'll…'

That's when Chrissie's mind had shifted into overdrive. Here was opportunity wrapped up in a neat little package, tied with a bow of desperation and guilt. Teddy Turner needed saving, and Chrissie Steele never did anything for free.

'You don't need to worry about anything.' Her scarlet nails trailed along his jawline, feeling him quiver at her touch. 'I told you I'd sort it, didn't I? And true to my word, I've got a plan that'll benefit us both.'

She'd become his salvation and his downfall, his mistress and his conspirator. The poor sod thought she was helping him out of kindness, but that sentiment, as a general rule, wasn't Chrissie's thing.

Well, not when it came to most of the men in her life. This arrangement was going to set her up beautifully – money, security, and all the fine things she'd been denied growing up in the shadow of her brother's empire.

'But what if—' Teddy started to protest…

She silenced him with a finger pressed to his lips. 'No more talking,' she breathed, using that husky whisper that made strong men weak. 'Time to show me how grateful you are.'

'I've got your documents right here,' she purred, crimson-tipped fingers working the buttons of her straining blouse until it fell open to reveal her magnificent bosom barely contained by a lacy black bra.

Teddy's watery eyes widened behind his glasses, panic flashing across his otherwise composed features. 'Christ almighty, Chrissie!' he squealed, tight with desperation. 'Not here. Everyone will hear us.'

'Leave the worrying to me, sugar.' Buttering him up, Chrissie reached his chair and pushed it back from the desk with a strength that made him gasp. 'You've been stuck in this prison all day with those numbers and doddering old men. Time for something more… interesting.'

She made quick work of his flies, her expert fingers finding their target with practiced ease. Leaning close to his ear, her hot breath tickling his skin, she growled, 'I'm not wearing any knickers. Not a stitch beneath this skirt.'

Teddy nearly lost control then and there, trembling beneath her touch, his face flushing so dark he looked about ready to pass out.

'Christ, Chrissie,' he groaned.

Straddling him, she slid down onto his eager cock with a satisfied sigh.

'Teddy, you've been a naughty, filthy boy,' she whispered, moving against him in a rhythm as old as time itself. 'Working too hard, neglecting what's important.'

His fingers dug into her luscious hips, face contorted in pleasure and exquisite pain. The expensive chair creaked dangerously beneath them, keeping time with their frantic movements.

'You like that, don't you?' she taunted, taking absolute control of their pace. 'Your little secretary giving you what you need.'

Teddy's breathing grew ragged, pathetic whimpers escaping his throat. 'Chrissie, I can't – I'm going to—'

A sudden sharp knock at the door interrupted them. Teddy's eyes flew open in panic.

'Come back in five minutes!' he bellowed, breathing heavily.

'Talking of coming…' Beaming, with a wicked smile, Chrissie moved hard, increasing her merciless pace until Teddy's eyes rolled back, his rigid body tensing, and he reached his completion with a muffled groan.

She smiled, satisfied. Good. She'd got that business out of the way. She had Teddy wrapped around her little finger so tight, he'd do anything for her.

Straightening her rumpled clothing, Chrissie noticed the troubled expression clouding Teddy's sweaty face again. His glasses sat askew, and he appeared like a man who'd just survived a natural disaster.

*Here we go,* she thought with internal irritation. *Time for all the bloody hand wringing to kick off again.*

'The plan. You're absolutely sure it'll work?'

Hells bells. How many times was she going to have reassure this four-eyed twat, for crying out loud!

Chrissie pulled out her compact and reapplied her very red lipstick with theatrical drama, watching him squirm in the reflection.

'Darling,' she drawled, snapping the compact shut with a decisive click, 'when have I ever let you down? Trust me, by the time I'm finished, you'll be in the clear and we'll both be laughing all the way to the bank.'

She leaned down and pressed a lingering kiss to his damp forehead, leaving another scarlet mark of possession.

'Literally.'

***

Feeling very satisfied with herself, Chrissie strutted away from the bank's imposing stone facade, her hips swaying with triumphant rhythm. She wore the very expensive and very nice Persian lamb jacket that Teddy had gifted her. Last month he'd been given the devastating news that there was nothing more the doctors could do for his mother, which had hit him hard. Now he was using the money to keep Chrissie in a life style she was becoming accustomed to. It beat being banged up in Holloway any day of the week. It had cost that boring sod a pretty penny, but she was worth every bleeding shilling.

Mind you, her heart went out to his poor mum. She might have a reputation as a right piece of work when it came to blokes, but she'd always had a soft spot for women getting a raw deal.

The evening air had a nip to it, but Chrissie barely noticed, warmed by the glow of another successful conquest. That pathetic banker would do anything for her now, eating out of her hand like a starving mutt. Just as she'd planned. Though a tiny part of her had to admit that Teddy wasn't too bad. And, strangely, when he got really going he wasn't half bad between the sheets

The purr of a car engine crept up behind her, but Chrissie paid it no mind. Just another admirer gawking at what she liked to call her 'state-of-the-art bum', most likely. But then the unmistakable prickle of danger crawled up her spine. The sudden heat of a presence behind her, so close she could feel hot breath tickling the back of her neck.

'Do what you're told,' a controlled growl whispered, low and deadly as a grave digger's shovel.

Chrissie's hand instinctively reached for her hatpin, seven inches of steel disguised as a fashionable accessory, tucked into the lining of her jacket. She'd stuck it in more than one grabby bastard over the years.

'I wouldn't do that if I were you,' she was warned, menace dripping from every word. 'Not unless you want those pretty fingers broken one by one.'

A Ford Zodiac screeched to a halt beside them, its navy-blue paint job dented and scratched, the chrome bumper hanging slightly askew. Not a flash motor, but solid and anonymous, perfect for the job at hand. The back door thrust open with a rusty groan.

'Get in.'

Chrissie's mind raced. She could scream, but the street was nearly empty, the few passersby keeping their heads down in typical London fashion. She could fight, but the iron grip on her arm told her that wouldn't end well. Her options had shrunk to minus zero.

Knowing she had no bloody choice unless she fancied getting her brains splattered across the pavement, Chrissie slid into the car's musty interior. The door slammed shut behind her.

The car lurched forward, tyres squealing in protest, taking Chrissie away to God knows where.

# Chapter Nineteen

'You're making a big mistake,' Iris warned her husband between tightly clenched teeth. Her arms were wound around her middle across her convulsing tummy.

While she perched nervously on the edge of the settee in their sitting room, Danny paced, wearing a hole in the carpet. His hands clenching and unclenching, strangling invisible enemies. That sickening feeling in his gut knotted with each step, the same sensation that always came before everything went to rat shit.

'What choice do I have?' He hissed. 'The bank job's on the line here.'

Iris' eyes followed his restless movement. 'You know what I'm telling you is the truth. You're bringing grief to our doorstep.'

The knock at the door cut through the tension. Three sharp raps that made Danny flinch.

'I'll get it,' Iris muttered, tight with resignation.

Danny remained frozen, muscles knitted and twisted, listening to his wife's footsteps in the hall. The murmur of voices reached him, then the decisive click of the front door closing.

Iris appeared in the doorway, her face pale as chalk. She walked back into the room with the careful steps of someone crossing thin ice.

'What's with all the drama, Danny?' came a throaty female drawl. 'If you wanted a family reunion, you could've just sent an invitation.'

Turning slowly, face blanching, Danny watched Chrissie saunter into his home with the confidence of a woman who owned the world.

Danny's stomach dropped to his boots. His baby sister stood there in all her dangerous glory, and Christ, she was a sight to behold. Too much of a sight. The platinum-blonde hair was still perfect, the curves still packed into that dress snug enough to stop traffic. But her eyes, those eyes that had once stared up at him with pure adoration when they were younger, now were hooded, concealing her emotions from him.

'What the hell are you doing in the bank?' he fired at her.

Chrissie never did anything without an angle, and her timing stank worse than low tide at Rotherhithe.

***

Chrissie had taken Iris' place on the settee, but taking over it completely by spreading out her body and placing her Chanel black quilted leather handbag beside her. The air between sister and brother simmered. Never turn your back on his sister, that was Danny's golden rule. He'd never know whether she'd put her arm around his waist or stick a blade in his spine. Their whole relationship balanced on a knife's edge.

Love and hate dancing together in the dark.

Before Chrissie could answer his question, although she was taking her sweet time about it, Iris shuffled in with a tea tray, cups rattling against saucers from her gin-shaky hands. She set it down without a word, lips pressed into a thin line, her features etched with worry. While she poured, her jittery gaze darted between husband and sister-in-law.

When Iris handed Chrissie her cup, his sister leaned close, her lips brushing near Iris' ear. 'You still washing his dirty underpants?'

Iris recoiled, colour draining from her face. Tea sloshed over the rim onto her trembling fingers.

'It's 1969, sweetie,' Chrissie continued, her slow smile revealing perfect white teeth. 'There's a whole other world out there for women nowadays. Women's lib and all that. You don't have to be chained to his laundry basket till death do you part.'

A muscle jumped in Danny's temple, blood rushing hot in his ears. Heat climbed his neck, fury building in his chest. 'Knock it right off!' His tone dropped to a dangerous growl. 'Leave Iris out of your twisted games.'

This is what she does, Danny thought with bitter recognition. *Finds the weak spot and presses until something breaks. She learned it young, learned it hard, and I'm the bastard who should've protected her from it and didn't.*

A sharp rap at the door cut through the tension, and Iris practically sprinted from the room, relief washing across her hunched shoulders.

Heavy footsteps approached. Jimmy appeared in the doorway with Brother Bertie right behind him. Jimmy stood solid as Tower Bridge, filling the frame with his boxer's build. His grey eyes were flint-hard. Brother Bertie positioned himself against the far wall, arms folded across his chest, his usual easy grin replaced by a stony expression.

Chrissie sat bolt upright, both feet hitting the floor with a thud, all playfulness evaporating. 'What's all this then? A firing squad?' Her hectic gaze darted between her nephew and his best friend. 'Someone want to tell me what the fuck is happening here?'

Neither man spoke.

Danny rose slowly, lowering himself next to Chrissie, crowding her deliberately.

'I'll ask you again. What are you doing at the Anglo-Merchant in the City?'

Initially she stubbornly pursed her lips together. Then, 'I'm Edward Turner's secretary. He's one of the senior managers. Everyone calls him Teddy.'

Danny's eyes narrowed to dangerous slits. His sister working at a bank? Might as well tell him the Pope was running a knocking shop off Commercial Street.

'How'd you get the job?' he demanded with rough suspicion. 'Last I checked, your typing skills were limited to forging betting slips.'

Chrissie tossed her bright hair, squaring her shoulders. 'Through a friend of a friend. You know how these things go.'

'The type of friends you've got,' Danny spat, 'are all banged up in Brixton nick. Try again, darlin'.'

Her face crumpled, the glamorous mask slipping to reveal something raw underneath. 'You've always seen me as no good, haven't you?' Moisture gathered in her eyes. 'Just the family fuck-up.' Chrissie couldn't hide her genuine pain. 'I'm doing my best here, Danny. Is it so hard to believe I just got a proper job? That I'm trying to get on the straight and narrow?'

The words hit Danny in the gut harder than any fist. Guilt crashed over him, fierce and unexpected. Christ, his baby sister, the girl who used to climb into his bed during thunderstorms. Now she sat there with tears threatening to spill, convinced he thought she was worthless.

*But you do think that, don't you?* The truth cut deep. *You've written her off as damaged goods. Just another casualty of the life you chose.*

What lay between them was written in scars only they could read. When she needed him most, Danny wasn't there. God, if she ever found out the truth…

'It doesn't matter.' He cut the past dead and slammed shut its fucking door. 'You're gonna be my eyes and ears in that bank.'

Her jaw dropped, genuine shock freezing her features. 'You what?'

'You heard. I need someone on the inside.'

'Are you having a bubble? I can't—'

'You can and you will,' Danny cut her off sharply.

Understanding dawned in Chrissie's eyes, her breathing becoming erratic. 'Oh. My. God. You're planning a blag. You're gonna turn over the bank.'

Her disbelieving gaze darted from Danny to Jimmy, then landed on Brother Bertie, something unreadable flickering across her face, the pieces clicking into place.

Chrissie fell silent, her expression back to being hooded. Slowly, she leaned back into the cushions, reaching for her teacup and taking a deliberate sip that revealed nothing of what was ticking away in that unpredictable mind of hers. Danny watched her carefully.

Finally, she placed her cup down with a delicate clink in the saucer, smoothed her pencil skirt with practiced hands, and stared him dead in the eye.

'All right,' Chrissie agreed, words smooth as expensive whisky. 'I'll help you. But on one condition.'

Danny wasn't surprised. There were always conditions where his baby sister was concerned. She'd learned early that everything came with a price, and she'd never forgotten the lesson.

Chrissie's lips spread into a slow, knowing smile.

'I'll help you, brother dearest, as long as I get a cut.'

# Chapter Twenty

Batters was feeling like the mutt's nuts. Standing on the edge of what remained of the East End docks, the bitter wind snapping at his heavy cashmere overcoat, he surveyed his expanding territory with frigid satisfaction. The dark Thames slapped against rotting wood, hungry and relentless. Abandoned cranes loomed over the night sky, mimicking giant gallows, their shadows stretching across concrete split by weeds where Danny Steele's men had once called the shots.

Batters bit down on his Romeo y Julieta cigar, its glowing tip momentarily illuminating his hard face in the darkness. The expensive Cuban tobacco tasted like victory. Sweet bloody victory.

Times had changed and he'd planned ahead. Always had multiple revenue streams. Protection rackets, gambling dens, smuggling operations that ran smoother than a virgin's thighs. And, of course, that little moneymaker no one knew about. The docks had only ever been one slice of his pie, not the whole bloody bakery like that jumped-up prick Danny Steele.

'Saw Mini yesterday,' Lucas ventured hesitantly behind him. 'From a distance, of course.'

Every muscle in Batters' body tensed. But he didn't turn around.

'That right?' He kept his voice unnaturally level, fingers tightening around his cigar.

'The little girl's the spitting image of Mum,' Lucas quickly added, 'She didn't see me.'

His words hung in the frigid air between them. The lie tasted familiar on Lucas' tongue. He'd been secretly meeting his sister for years now, playing uncle to her children, doing what his mum had asked him with her dying breath – to look out for his sister.

Batters said nothing. A distant part of him suspected the truth, but tonight his mind was elsewhere, drifting to grandchildren he'd never met because his daughter had chosen Danny Steele's boy over blood.

'How many kids she got now?' The question emerged rougher than he'd intended.

'Three. The way I hear it, the oldest boy's starting school and the baby is just learning to walk.'

Batters nodded, something tight and painful shifting under his ribcage. Then he hardened his heart.

'She chose her path. Made her bed with the Steeles.'

He grimaced because lately his justification for not seeing his daughter and her kids left the taste of bitter poison in his mouth.

His good mood suddenly gone, he left his son behind and stalked off through the shadowy passages of Sugar Cane Wharf towards home. Something prickled at the back of his neck. A sixth sense developed over decades of watching his back.

A presence.

Someone was there.

Deliberately, Batters slowed his pace, every nerve ending on major alert. His hand slipped inside his overcoat, fingers closing around the cold grip of his Webley revolver. He continued walking, keeping his movements casual while his ears strained for any telltale sound. His breathing remained steady, and he navigated beneath a broken lamp post, using the deeper shadow as cover.

Another step.

The whisper of fabric behind him.

Closing in.

In one explosive motion, Batters spun, drawing his shooter in a practiced arc. He lunged forward, seizing the shadowy figure by the throat with his free hand and propelled them backwards into a narrow passageway between two warehouses. The brick wall met their back with a satisfying thud. He pressed the gun barrel hard against their temple.

'One wrong move and you're dead where you stand,' he snarled, his finger tightening on the trigger.

'It's only me,' came the familiar throaty announcement, remarkably calm for someone with a shooter to their head.

Batters tensed up again. The grip on his gun didn't waver. 'You want to watch your step in the dark. Good way to get yourself killed.'

'I think you mean you could get killed.' Something cold and sharp pressed against Batters' belly, sliding between the buttons of his shirt to kiss the skin beneath.

Batters felt the knife point dimple his flesh, his breathing controlled. He eased the gun barrel away from the figure's head. Only then did the knife withdraw, disappearing as quickly as it had appeared.

Moonlight caught the blonde curls.

Chrissie Steele revealed herself.

***

Taking a deep drag on her fat joint, Chrissie kicked off her heels and got comfy on Batters' creaky leather chair. The smoke curled in the air, and she watched him pour two generous measures of good Scotch. His terraced house on the edge of Sugar Cane Wharf was obsessively kept, not a speck of dust anywhere. Every surface gleamed with polish, a silent tribute to his dead wife, Fleur, who'd kept their home with the fierce pride of a woman who'd clawed her way up from nothing.

'Make yourself comfortable, why don't you?' Batters' attention was pointedly fixed on her bare feet propped on his immaculate coffee table.

Chrissie wiggled her jet-black-painted toes, deliberately defiant. 'Always do, Eric.'

Batters handed her a glass. 'Get this down you,' he excitedly ordered. 'To the biggest score of our lives.'

Grinning for all he was worth, Batters strutted around his front room. 'Can you believe it? I'm pulling off the big one. Robbing the Anglo-Merchant Bank.'

That's what no one knew he was up to, making preparations for a heist that would keep this country talking for years to come. Suddenly he moved across the room, cupped a startled Chrissie's face in his large hands, and gave her a huge, loud smacker on the lips.

'And it's all down to you,' he beamed at her.

'Eh!' She shoved him off. 'None of that, thank you very much.'

Straightening, Batters laughed out loud, then plonked his large self down. 'And aren't I the lucky one having an inside man?' He chuckled, pride swelling his chest. 'Or should that be an inside woman? You, Chrissie.'

'Best idea I ever had,' Batters continued, boasting, raising his glass in self-congratulation. 'Seeing you at The Flamingo that night was like fate stepping in. Poor Chrissie Steele, down on her luck, needing a helping hand. And old Uncle Batters comes to the rescue, doesn't he? Got you to see how you could enhance that job at the bank.'

'Stroke of genius,' Chrissie agreed, her mind spinning with the delicious complication of it all. She bit the inside of her cheek to keep from smirking, recalling how different their meeting had actually been.

*He thinks he's so clever, but I set him up from the start.*

She'd needed a resolution to the Teddy problem and when she'd seen Batters she'd found it.

Three months ago at The Flamingo Club she'd made sure to be in his line of sight, all dolled up and seemingly vulnerable. By closing time, with whisky loosening his tongue, she'd carefully steered the conversation towards money troubles, then banks, then security. The idea of pulling a blag on the bank had seemed to spring from his mind, but in reality she'd planted every seed.

When he'd suggested her becoming his inside eyes and ears, she'd acted reluctant at first – making him think it was all his brilliant plan.

The bank robbery would explain away the missing contents of those safe deposit boxes by putting the blame on the robbers, and Teddy would be in the clear.

And, as for Chrissie?

A cut of Batters' stolen cash plus a cushy-comfy future as Teddy's mistress.

Perfect.

'Any changes inside worth knowing about?'

Now this was the complication.

What Chrissie could never have foreseen was that her own brother was planning to turn over the bank, too. That unexpected twist had nearly given her heart failure, but after the initial shock, she'd realised it might work even better.

Two robberies at the same time. More chaos, more confusion, and an even better smokescreen for the police to believe that the safety deposit boxes were cleaned out by the villains.

Tell Batters about Danny planning to hit the same bank on the same day?

Not bloody likely.

Chrissie smiled her best smile. 'No changes. Everything is on course for the bank heist of the century.'

Batters glared hotly at her. 'You're lucky I even brought you in on this job after that stunt you pulled two years back.' He bristled, the memory clearly still a raw nerve. 'Fucking stabbed me in the back and made a right twat out of me in front of that cunty brother of yours.'

For the first time, Chrissie let her true colours show, irritation flashing across her face.

'I'm sorry about what happened with that car business,' she snapped. 'But let's be honest here, Eric. You needed someone inside that bank, and I was your only bloody option.' She shook a Rothmans from her packet, lighting up with a sharp flick of her lighter. 'So we're in an "I'll scratch your back, you scratch mine" situation, aren't we? You want that bank job done, you need me. Simple as.'

She blew smoke directly at him, all pretence of the apologetic little girl gone. 'Danny's my brother, yeah, so I had to support him back then. But this ain't about family. It's business. Just don't forget which side your bread's buttered on.'

He sent her a hard stare.

'Funny how things change.' Chrissie blew smoke towards the ceiling. 'Remember when you and Danny were thick as thieves? Running around the docks together, causing mayhem? Never thought I'd see the day you'd be at each other's throats.'

Batters' face darkened like a thundercloud. 'Ancient history. We were just kids then.'

'What happened between you two anyway?' Chrissie pressed, genuinely curious after all these years. 'One day you're best mates, the next you're mortal enemies.'

'Some things don't need digging up,' Batters replied sharply, slamming the door on that conversation.

Chrissie got back on with business. 'Everything's ticking along just as expected.' She lowered her lashes accompanied by a girlish smile. 'Not a dickybird has changed. Everything's exactly as we discussed.'

What Batters would never understand was that Chrissie had figured out early never to pin her hopes on just one horse. Growing up in the role of Danny Steele's baby sister meant watching how quickly fortunes could change in their world. One minute you're untouchable; the next, you're being fished out of the Thames with concrete boots.

Women in their world were always collateral damage, used when convenient, discarded when not. A shudder ran through her at the hard lesson life had taught her as a girl. When things went pear-shaped, she'd been left to fend for herself, just like always.

*Never again,* she silently promised her younger self. *I look after ME now.*

'To your crowning moment,' Chrissie toasted, saluting him with her glass.

'Our moment,' Batters corrected, his face flushed with greedy anticipation and good whisky. 'Our bloody moment of glory.'

Chrissie clinked her glass against his, her smile tight and controlled.

*Poor bollocks. Thinks he's got me eating out of his hand.*

Men never learned. That was their biggest weakness. And her greatest advantage.

# Chapter Twenty-One

Wind cut through the City of London Cemetery, biting at the edges of the tiny woman kneeling before a well-tended marble headstone. Mini Steele removed dead flowers from the brass vase with practiced movements, her wedding ring flashing defiantly in the autumn light. She positioned fresh blooms with the precision of someone who'd performed this ritual many times before.

'I don't know what to do, Mum,' Mini whispered, her teeth worrying her bottom lip, her fingers tracing the engraved letters:

FLEUR ROGERS BELOVED WIFE AND MOTHER.

'The doctor says I need to tell Jimmy soon, but how do I break his heart like that?' The thought of telling him left her quaking inside. 'He's lost so much already.'

Violet placed a small bunch of daisies on the grave while a solemn-faced Robbie clutched a bright-yellow sunflower almost as big as himself. Mini always brought her children here. Her mother might be gone, but that didn't mean they couldn't know her.

Mini pressed the heels of her hands against her eyes, the pressure building behind her temples. 'I'm scared, Mum. Not for me… for them.' She glanced at her children, her stomach twisting. 'For Jimmy. He acts tough, but he's not ready for this. Nobody ever is.'

Violet looked up, her eyebrows slanting upwards in the centre. 'Are you talking to Nanny Fleur in Heaven?'

Mini arranged her features into practiced brightness. The last thing she wanted was for her kids to see her down on her luck. 'Yes, baby. Telling her all about my beautiful children.' The words flowed smoothly, a mother's practiced shield.

'Does she hear us?' Robbie asked, his small face lined with confusion.

''Course she does,' Mini replied, ruffling his dark hair with quick, nervous fingers. 'And she'd be dead proud of you both.'

Violet shifted from foot to foot in the cold. 'Can we leave the flowers now?'

'Soon, sweetheart. Just give Mummy a few more minutes, yeah?' Mini turned back to the grave, her shoulders hunching forward. 'What would you do?

Would you tell him everything straight away, or wait until…' The words died in her throat.

The distinctive crunch of footsteps on gravel jerked Mini's head up. A tall figure approached from the cemetery gates, broad-shouldered and unmistakable even at a distance. His deliberate, bloody threatening walk hadn't changed in all these years.

Eric 'Batters' Rogers halted abruptly, his time-beaten features transforming in stages: surprise, hunger, then hardening to granite. A bouquet of posh roses dangled from one massive hand, the other clenched into a fist at his side.

'Mummy, who's that man?' Violet tugged at Mini's coat, her voice small.

The blood drained from Mini's face, leaving her chalk-white. 'That's your grandad.'

Batters stood rooted, his eyes fixed on Mini with uncomfortable intensity. For a heartbeat, his features softened, the hard mask slipping to reveal naked longing, drinking in the sight of his daughter after years of self-imposed separation.

Mini rose slowly, chin tilting upwards, every muscle in her body coiling tight. Her hands trembled before she forced them steady. 'What, aren't you going to say hello to your grandchildren?' Her in-your-face challenge stabbed through the air, raw with years of rejection and the agony of being cast aside by the one man who should have protected her.

Batters remained silent, his muscles visibly bunching beneath his coat. His breathing had turned shallow, the air catching in his chest. Sweat beaded along his hairline. The roses trembled in his grip, petals beginning to scatter at his feet.

'Look at them, Dad.' Mini's demands escalated, her eyes blazing with sudden fury. Every inch of her small frame vibrated with defiance. 'Really bloody look at them. Your own flesh and blood, and you've never once bothered to know them.'

Her father's gaze reluctantly shifted to the children, his gaze lingering on Violet, who had Fleur's eyes, the same eyes that stared from the wedding portrait still hanging in his hallway.

'This is Violet,' Mini introduced, her hand protectively gripping her precious daughter's shoulder. Her voice caught, then hardened. 'She's seven and brilliant at maths, just like you always were.' The words turned sharp again. 'And this is Robbie. He's six, fearless as anything.'

The children stared upwards at the towering stranger, Robbie edging behind his mother's leg, small fingers clutching her coat.

Batters massaged his tense jaw, the motion jerky, uncontrolled. 'They shouldn't be here.' Each word emerged clipped, betraying the effort it took to maintain composure.

'Where should they be, then?' Mini snapped, colour blazing high on her cheekbones. 'Not with their mother visiting their grandmother's grave? Or just not anywhere near you?'

'You know bloody why.' Years of rage coughed out of his mouth.

'Because I married a Steele?' Mini laughed, tossed her head with pure brass. 'It's been years, Dad. Years! What, are you going to hold on to this hate until you're in the ground next to Mum?'

His massive hands opened and closed at his sides. 'You made your choice.'

The words hit Mini's chest with brutal force, stealing her breath for a moment. 'I made my choice to be with the man I love. Not to lose my father.'

Batters' expression collapsed into raw sorrow before his features reassembled themselves into practiced stone. But his hands couldn't stop trembling.

'Is Mummy crying because of you?' Robbie suddenly demanded, glaring up with all the outrage his small frame could muster.

Mini knelt quickly, her hands trembling as they framed Robbie's face. 'No, darling. Sometimes grown-ups just disagree, that's all.'

'Are you a bad man?' Violet stepped forward, her chin raised in a gesture so reminiscent of Mini at that age that Batters unconsciously took half a step backwards, his face draining of what little colour remained.

He opened his mouth, closed it, swallowed hard with his Adam's apple bobbing frantically. 'Some people think so,' he finally muttered, his tone gruff but oddly vulnerable.

Mini watched him, her gaze boring into his defences, looking for cracks in his armour. A cold fury settled in her stomach. 'I'm not asking you to like

Jimmy. I'm asking you to love your grandchildren. I'm asking you to be my dad again.'

'You should go.' His glassy gaze was fixed determinedly on a point beyond her shoulder.

The light died in Mini's expression.

'Fine.' The word emerged flat, drained of everything she had left to give. 'I tried. For Mum's sake. She'd be heartbroken seeing what a coward you've become.'

She gathered her children with quick, efficient movements, swiping angrily at her eyes, her throat burning with unshed tears.

'Come on, loves. We're going home.'

'But the flowers—' Robbie protested, still clutching his sunflower, his lower lip jutting stubbornly.

'Put it down for Nanna, darling.' Mini's voice gentled when addressing her son, though her hands still shook.

Robbie placed the sunflower beside his sister's daisies with gentle care, then turned his serious gaze upwards. 'My daddy says flowers make ladies happy.'

Batters' face aged ten years in an instant. His features went rigid, then crumpled around the edges. A strangled sound escaped his throat. But he remained rooted to the spot while Mini led the children away, his body rigid with the effort of not following, his chest heaving with suppressed emotion.

Only when they'd almost reached the cemetery gates did he move, approaching the grave with heavy, unsteady steps. He laid his roses beside the children's flowers. His grandchildren.

He crouched by the grave of his cherished dead wife.

'She's the spitting image of you,' he whispered, fingers brushing against the cold marble, all his grief spilling out. 'Both of them are. The girl has your eyes, Fleur.'

# Chapter Twenty-Two

'Miss Gertie!' Charlie called out, raising his bottle of VP wine in an exuberant greeting. His weathered face creased with genuine pleasure. 'You're looking mighty fine today. A vision for these tired old eyes!'

Gertie had just exited Whitechapel station, the weight of her shopping bags pulling at her arms. Despite the discomfort, her face broke into a warm smile at the sight of the three dishevelled men slouched against the grimy wall. They were the resident boozers who'd made their lives outside Whitechapel station, fixtures as permanent as the brickwork itself.

'Charlie.' She nodded at him, then at his scruffy companions. 'Billy. Frank. Enjoying the sunshine, I see.'

Charlie struggled to his feet, his threadbare army jacket hanging loose on his skeletal frame. 'When such a beautiful day presents itself, who are we to waste it indoors?'

'True words,' Gertie agreed, then significantly arched her brow. 'Though some might say you're enjoying the wine more than the sunshine.'

The men chuckled appreciatively. Frank, the smallest of the three with a face like crumpled paper, gave her a yellow-toothed grin. 'We was just speaking of you, Miss Gertie.'

'Oh?' Her eyebrow arched higher. 'And what mischief are you planning?'

'No mischief,' Billy said earnestly. His rheumy eyes brightened. 'Charlie here was saying how long it's been since we had some of your ackee and saltfish.'

'Was he now?' Gertie couldn't help but laugh. These men with nothing to their names except the clothes on their backs and their daily bottle, they reminded her of the village elders back home, sitting under the breadfruit tree, spinning stories.

Charlie appeared sheepish, swaying slightly on his feet. 'That taste stays with a man, Miss Gertie. Like the feel of a woman's kiss.'

The hunger in Charlie's eyes wasn't just for food, but for kindness. Gertie recognised it well.

'Well now,' she announced with mock severity, hands planted on her generous hips, 'I might be making some tomorrow. If you gentlemen are passing by my boarding house around midday, I expect there'll be enough to spare.'

Frank pressed his hands together in exaggerated gratitude, while Billy's face lit up. Charlie attempted to come over as dignified but failed miserably.

'Can we help you with those bags?' Charlie offered, already reaching for her shopping with unsteady hands. 'Heavy load for a lady with such delicate arms.'

'My, what a gentleman you are, Charlie,' Gertie teased, her eyes gleaming with mischief. 'Sometimes I wonder what fine house you came from, with manners like that. Or what woman taught you to charm the birds from the trees.'

Something flickered across Charlie's face, a ghost of the man he might have been. He glanced away, suddenly finding the pavement fascinating. 'That's a story for another day, Miss Gertie. Preferably after several more bottles.'

'Everyone in the East End running from something, ain't that the truth,' she said softly. 'Though most don't run with a bottle in each hand like you three.'

An understanding passed between them. Charlie nodded, a moment of connection between two souls who recognised their own wounds in each other.

'Blessings upon you for the offer,' Gertie said, adjusting her grip on her bags, 'but these old arms still have plenty of strength. Got to keep my muscles.'

Charlie raised his bottle in a wobbly salute as she continued on her way. 'Tomorrow then, Miss Gertie! We'll bring our best manners and empty stomachs!'

Turning into a side street, Gertie hummed the upbeat hymn, 'I'll Fly Away', her sturdy shoes clicking against the pavement where tiny shoots of grass grew. The narrow road was unnaturally quiet for this time of day. No children playing hopscotch, no women gossiping on doorsteps with curlers in their hair. The sudden stillness raised the tiny hairs on the back of her neck in warning.

A man stepped from the shadows between two buildings, blocking her path with deliberate precision. Tall and broad, dressed in an expensive charcoal suit that couldn't disguise the predatory menace beneath. His eyes, cold and calculating, fixed on her with the focused intensity of a hawk watching prey.

'Miss Gertrude Watson.' The cultured greeting masked something far more dangerous in Miles Harker's tone. 'What an unexpected pleasure.'

The rhythm of Gertie's heart sped up, but she kept her expression neutral. 'Mr Harker. I thought our business was concluded.'

His smile was sharp-edged, refined cruelty wrapped in gentleman's manners. 'Concluded? Oh, my dear lady, I'm afraid you misunderstand the nature of our relationship entirely.'

Two more men materialised from doorways, cutting off her retreat. One was massive, with a face full of dead eyes. The other was wiry, nervous energy radiating from his twitching frame.

'You see,' Harker continued. 'What transpired at my establishment has been weighing heavily on my mind.'

Gertie gripped her shopping bags tighter. 'I don't know what you mean.'

'Don't you?' His cultured tone dropped to a hissed whisper. 'You walked into my club. My castle. You sat at my table and tried your best to turn me into a fool in front of my associates.'

The refined mask slipped slightly, revealing the savage fury beneath. 'Do you have any idea what that cost me? The whispers, the snickers, the hit my reputation took?'

'I simply played cards,' Gertie answered quietly. 'Nothing more.'

Harker's laugh was bitter. 'You humiliated me, you sanctimonious creature. Made me appear weak, gullible, a mark to be taken by some church-going immigrant woman.'

'I cleared my brother's debt fair and square.'

'Fair?' Harker bit out, tone rising before he caught himself, smoothing back his perfectly groomed hair. 'You played me for a fool, and now the entire underworld thinks Miles Harker can be conned by anyone with a clever scheme.'

The big man stepped forward, cracking his knuckles with deliberate menace. The sound echoed off the narrow walls.

'I'm afraid,' Harker informed her with mock regret, 'that your little performance requires a response. Something to restore the natural order of things.'

Gertie set down her shopping bags and reached into her handbag, pulling out her small Bible. Its worn leather cover was smooth beneath her fingers.

'The Lord protects His children,' she said firmly.

Harker's refined features twisted with disdain. 'Your God won't help you here, Miss Watson. This is about reputation, respect, and the price of making powerful men resemble dickheads.'

The big man knocked the Bible from her hands with casual violence. It hit the pavement, pages fluttering open.

The first blow caught Gertie across the cheekbone, snapping her head sideways. Pain exploded through her skull, bright and blinding. She staggered but remained standing, blood filling her mouth.

'The Lord is my shepherd.' Her prayer was strident despite the agony. 'I shall not want.'

Another hit, this one to her stomach, doubled her over. Her shopping scattered across the filthy pavement, tins rolling away, fish packaging coming undone, milk shattering into jagged fragments.

'He maketh me to lie down in green pastures.'

The smaller man pulled a polished wooden club from his coat, menacingly pounding it into his palm with violent intent.

'He leadeth me beside still waters.'

Gertie crashed to her knees, her hands scraping along rough, jagged stone. She saw her Bible on the ground, pages open to Psalms, and reached for it with desperate fingers.

'He restoreth my soul.'

The club came down.

***

Blood pooled in Gertie's mouth, thick and metallic. She spat it onto the pavement, watching it spread in a dark stain. Her battered body felt distant, disconnected, only the relentless pain anchoring her to reality. Sharp, throbbing waves that reminded her she was still alive.

She tried to lift her head. The simple movement sent lightning through her neck and shoulders. The world tilted, wobbled.

How long had she lain here? The merciless sun had shifted, casting longer shadows across the deserted street.

'Get up,' she told herself, her swollen lips forming soundless words. 'Get up now, right this minute, Gertrude Watson.'

She pushed up from the ground with trembling hands. Her left wrist collapsed, sending fresh agony shooting up her arm. Broken, maybe. The bones ground together, making bile rise in her throat.

Using her right arm, Gertie dragged herself forward, inch by excruciating inch. Her precious Bible lay just ahead, its leather cover smeared with dirt and blood. She reached for it, clutched it to her chest.

'The Lord is my strength,' she whispered through split lips. 'The Lord is my shield.'

She crawled forward, tearing her stockings on the pavement and the skin beneath. Biting back an agony of pain, her body silently screamed to surrender to the darkness pressing at her vision's edges.

A sound penetrated Gertie's fog of pain. Footsteps, followed by an alarmed sharp intake of breath.

'Miss Gertie! Oh God, Miss Gertie!'

Charlie.

His voice stripped of its earlier joviality. Then more footsteps, faster.

Gentle hands touched her, carefully turning her over. Charlie's weathered face swam into view, horror stamped into every line.

'Who did this to you?' He shook with rage. 'Who did this?'

Gertie couldn't answer. The words stuck behind the wall of pain and swelling.

'We need to get help,' Frank urged, his bloodshot eyes wide with panic. 'Billy, run to the police box on Whitechapel Road.'

'No.' The word tore from Gertie's throat. 'No police. Take me home.'

'You need a doctor,' Charlie insisted, his hands hovering over her broken form.

'My house,' Gertie repeated stubbornly. 'Ruddy will help.'

'No.' Charlie stood his ground, steady on his feet for the first time in a long time. 'You are badly hurt and we're taking you to the hospital.'

With infinite care, Charlie and Frank lifted her between them. Pain shot through Gertie's body, but she refused to cry out.

They carried her towards Whitechapel Road and the hospital. Gertie clutched her Bible tighter, drawing comfort from its familiar weight.

'Who did this, Miss Gertie?' Charlie asked again, his voice gentler now.

'Miles Harker.' Gertie tasted fresh blood. And righteous rage. 'He said I made a fool of him.'

When Bertram discovered what Harker had done to her, there would be hell to pay. And all her Christian charity couldn't make her entirely sorry about that fact.

# Chapter Twenty-Three

Brother Bertie tore through The Royal London Hospital's corridors, a man possessed. The stench of disinfectant burned his nostrils, made his stomach heave. Blood roared in his ears, drowning out everything but fear. His cherished Gertie lay somewhere in this cold, sterile place.

Broken.

Beaten.

'Slow down, bruv.' Jimmy struggled to keep pace. 'Your heart's going to peg out if you don't take a bloody breath.'

Brother Bertie couldn't slow down. Fear for Gertie propelled him forward. They burst onto the ward, his frantic gaze scanning desperately for his sister. A high-ranking nurse in a starched white uniform approached, her face grave.

'Bertram?'

'Sister Bailey.' He recognised her immediately. The Barbadian nurse who'd come to Sunday lunch at Gertie's boarding house more than once. 'Where's my sister? What's happened?'

Sister Bailey placed a gentle hand on his arm. 'She's been attacked. Badly.'

The words hit Brother Bertie with physical force. His legs buckled beneath him. Jimmy's strong hand on his elbow was all that kept him from crashing to the floor.

'Beaten?' The world spun, tiles and lights and faces blurring into a nauseating swirl. 'Who would mash up my sister? Everyone loves Gertie!'

'The men who found her said she was assaulted not far from her home. Three men.' Sister Bailey's eyes held a mix of compassion and suppressed fury. 'She's conscious but in considerable pain.'

Sister Bailey pointed to a bed at the far end of the ward, partially screened off for privacy. Brother Bertie moved towards it, each step heavier than the last. His heartbeat thundered in his ears, drowning out the hospital sounds around him.

Nothing had prepared him for the sight of Gertie.

His proud, strong sister lay broken against the white hospital sheets. Her face, normally so full of life and vigour, was bloated and discoloured. One eye was swollen completely shut, the skin around it a sickening shade of almost black. Her bottom lip was split, the wound held together with small strips of tape. Her left arm was encased in plaster, and vicious bruises marred every visible inch of her dark skin.

'Bumboclaat!' The Jamaican curse exploded from him, raw and primal. A violent tremor raced through his body. Bile surged up his throat, his stomach rebelling at the sight.

Behind him, Jimmy swore savagely. 'Jesus fucking Christ!'

Gertie's one good eye fluttered open. Despite everything, relief flooded her battered features. 'Bertram.'

His legs gave way entirely, and he collapsed to his knees beside the bed, taking her uninjured hand and pressing it against his face. His body shook with silent sobs, tears streaming down his cheeks, hot and unstoppable. Each breath became a stabbing pain in his chest.

'Gertie, who did this to you?' He choked on shocking pain and rage, the plea tearing out of him. 'Tell me who did this, sister!'

She tried to soothe him, her fingers weakly stroking his face. 'Hush now, baby brother.'

'Who. Did. This?' His teeth bared in primal fury.

Gertie's eye closed briefly, pain washing over her features. When she spoke, her voice was barely above a hush. 'The devil from Soho. Miles Harker.'

'I gwan murder that bloodclaat!' Brother Bertie stormed to his feet, Jamaican to the core. 'There's going to be a war inna England today! Raasclaat! I will cut him down where he stands!'

'Bertram, no.' Gertie's voice was stronger now, commanding despite her broken state. 'Vengeance belongs to the Lord.'

'The Lord wasn't there when they put their filthy hands on you!' He was shouting now, spittle flying from his lips, drawing stares from across the ward. His chest heaved with each ragged breath. 'The Lord didn't stop them from hurting my sister! But I will stop them from breathing, you hear me?'

'Please,' Gertie whispered, her strength flagging, eye drifting closed. 'No more violence.' The medication pulled her under, her hand going limp in his.

Brother Bertie stood over her, chest heaving, rage and grief tearing him apart. His vision tunnelled to red. Blind with fury, he headed for the door. One thought consumed him:

Find Harker, make him pay.

Jimmy intercepted him, both hands slamming into his chest, forcing him back. 'Bertie, wait.'

'Get out of my way, Jimmy.' His voice was a growl, unrecognisable even to his own ears. Every muscle in his body coiled, ready to explode into violence.

'Not until you tell me what the fuck is going on.' Jimmy's eyes were hard as flint, his jaw set in that stubborn Steele line that brooked no argument. 'What's this about a card game? Who's Miles Harker?'

Brother Bertie let the story spill out.

'Two hundred quid?' Jimmy growled when he'd finished, his face contorting with disbelief. 'Bloody hell! Why didn't you come to me?'

'I was embarrassed,' he muttered, not meeting Jimmy's eyes.

Jimmy studied him, sensing there was more. 'Time was, you wouldn't have thought twice about asking me for my help.' Something flashed across his face – hurt, suspicion. 'Something's changed between us, Bertie. I just can't figure out what.'

Staring back at Gertie's broken body, another terrible realisation crashed over him. This was his fault. His weakness for Sin had led to gambling, and gambling had led to this. He sagged against the wall, sliding down until he hit the floor. He clutched his head between his hands, digging his fingers painfully into his scalp.

'It's my fault,' he whispered, voice raw with anguish, body trembling. 'They hurt her because of me. Because I can't stop gambling. Because I can't...' He cut himself off, the confession about Sin dying on his lips.

His mind spun with self-loathing. His Gertie hurt, because he'd been weak enough to fall for his best friend's sister and too much of a coward to deal with it properly.

He jerked up, his face transformed by hatred. 'I keep a cutlas under my bed and it's marked for people like Harker,' Brother Bertie said, the words emerging with deadly calm. 'I'm going to chop his fucking raas into tiny little pieces.'

Jimmy crouched, gripping his shoulders, forcing Brother Bertie to meet him eye-to-eye. 'Not like this. Not half-cocked and off your head with rage. That's how you get yourself killed.' His fingers dug into Brother Bertie's flesh, a physical anchor to reality.

'I don't care!' Brother Bertie shouted, his features distorted with anguish.

'Well, I do!' Jimmy shoved him back against the wall. 'You're a brother to me, you daft git! You think I'm going to let you walk into Harker's den alone? We do this together. The Steele way.'

The determination in Jimmy's voice pulled Brother Bertie back from the edge of his fury. He drew a shuddering breath, forcing the red mist to recede. The trembling in his limbs gradually subsided.

'The Steele way,' he repeated, his voice steadier.

Jimmy nodded grimly. 'Harker has no idea who you're connected to. He thinks you're just some immigrant he can push around.' The disgust in his voice was palpable. 'Were going to make him pay.'

They left the hospital and, side by side with Jimmy, Brother Bertie stepped into the East End night, vengeance burning in his soul.

# Chapter Twenty-Four

Two days later, Miles Harker stood in the crowded bar of the Royal Oak Hotel with Rita clinging to his arm. He fancied himself as God's gift to the female population, a bloody magnificent specimen, he was. Built with a swagger that had charmed birds from all corners of London, well, that's what he told himself. At forty-three, he still had a reputation that preceded him, both for his violence and his bedroom prowess, and he made sure everyone knew it. According to Miles, he was the best fuck in London, and any woman lucky enough to sample his talents would be ruined for other men.

Tonight was just another conquest in his eyes. Rita had caught his eye because she was living in the flat above his club. He'd been sniffing around her for ages and finally she'd caved – no surprise there. Touching his thigh under the table, laughing at his crude jokes, hanging on his every word. Miles figured she was already mentally writing his name in her list of legendary shags. Women were ten a penny to a man with his magnetic appeal.

'Let's go upstairs,' Rita purred along the flesh of his thick neck, melting into his arm. 'I want you all to myself.'

Miles drained his glass, slamming it down with cocksure authority. 'Reckon it's about time I showed you what a real man feels like.'

Less than a minute later, the hotel room key jangled in his meaty hand as he fumbled with the lock, Rita's sharp nails digging into his broad back. Her intoxicating perfume filled his nostrils, and she snuggled even closer to him, all tits and hips wrapped in a tight red dress that left very little to the imagination.

'Hurry up, tiger.' The tip of her tongue flicked his earlobe. 'I can't wait much longer.'

The door finally gave way and they practically tumbled through it, Miles kicking it shut behind them. Crudely, he grabbed Rita, shoving her against the wall, mauling her mouth with his. Groping her arse, squeezing hard enough to bruise.

'You're a right fucking goer, you filthy slag.' He yanked down her dress strap, exposing a lace-covered breast. 'Knew you'd be gagging for it.'

'Let's get comfortable, shall we?' She pushed him backwards towards the king-sized bed, unbuttoning his shirt with practiced fingers. 'I know exactly what you want.'

His cock strained against his trousers. 'Bet you fucking do, darling.'

Rita guided him onto the mattress, crawling over him with feline grace. Her hands moved with expert precision, unbuckling his belt, sliding down his zip. Miles kicked off his shoes, helping her tug his trousers down his thick legs.

'Get 'em off, love. Daddy's got something special for you.'

She smiled, eying his erection straining beneath his Y-fronts. 'Oh, I can see that. But first, let me get more… comfortable.'

He licked his lips with small feral stabbing motions of his tongue, watching her stand and then reach behind to unzip her dress with agonising slowness. The red fabric whistled down her body, pooling at her feet. She stood there in just her stockings, suspenders, and a black lace bra that barely contained her impressive tits.

'Fucking hell, you're a proper sort,' Miles groaned, gripping himself through his pants.

'Not yet, darling.' Rita playfully batted his hand away. 'Let me do all the work.'

She reached for his underpants, pulling them down and off. Miles lay there, stark bollock naked, his hairy chest puffed out with pride while she admired his equipment.

'Now, I want to show you something special.' She turned around, bending over to slowly roll down one stocking, giving him a perfect view of her backside.

'Jesus fucking Christ,' Miles muttered, his hand moving to his cock.

Rita turned, wagging a finger. 'Uh-uh. Hands above your head, big boy. Rules are rules.'

Thinking it was all part of the game, Miles grinned and stretched his arms up. Quick as a flash, Rita had one silky stocking wrapped around his left wrist, securing it to the bedpost.

'Kinky little mare, aren't you?'

'You don't know the half of it.' Taking her other stocking, she secured his right wrist just as tightly. She tested the bonds, making sure they were secure.

Miles strained against them playfully, his cock standing at attention. 'Come on then, get those beauties out. I want to see what I'm paying for.'

Rita straightened, staring down at him with sudden coldness. Her face transformed, the seductive smile replaced by a hard, unforgiving line that could cut glass.

'What you're paying for?' She spat the words out with venomous intent. 'What about what Gertie Watson paid for when you and your two goons kicked seven shades of shit out of her?'

Miles blinked, confusion crossing his face before recognition dawned. His cock began to wilt as the blood drained from his face, leaving him pasty white.

'What the fuck are you on about?' But there was panic in his voice now. He yanked at his restraints, the silk stockings cutting into his wrists. 'Let me go, you fucking bitch!'

Rita slipped her dress back on with casual efficiency. 'I don't think so, dickbrains. You see, you made a terrible mistake beating an innocent woman. And that woman has a brother. A brother you know. What that thick noodle of yours probably hasn't worked out is that Bertie is an associate of the Steele family. Best mates with Jimmy Southpaw Steele.'

'Fuck off!' Miles roared, thrashing against his bonds. But Rita had done her job well; the more he struggled, the tighter the knots became.

A knock at the door.

Rita walked over and opened it without hesitation. Two men stepped inside. Miles recognised Brother Bertie immediately. But it was the man behind him that made Miles' bowels turn to water. Jimmy 'Southpaw' Steele, his silver-grey eyes cold as winter fog on the Thames.

Miles' eyes darted between them, realisation dawning with horrible clarity. 'Listen, this is all a misunderstanding. I didn't know she was your sister—'

'Bollocks,' Brother Bertie cut him off. 'She won that money fair and square at your own gaming table. But you couldn't handle being beaten by a woman, could you? So you came for her in Whitechapel with your gorillas.'

Rita gathered her handbag and gave Harker one last withering stare. 'You're a fucking monster.'

After she left, Miles tried a different tack. 'Look, lads, whatever this is about, we can sort it. I've got money—'

'Shut your fucking gob,' Brother Bertie snapped, followed by a menacing step forward. 'You think you can buy your way out of this?'

Miles swallowed hard, his throat working frantically. 'It was just business—'

'Business?' Brother Bertie's voice rose to a shout that bounced off the hotel walls. 'You call three men beating a woman half to death business?'

Jimmy stepped forward, his glare burning with cold fury. 'What kind of man goes after a woman in the street because she beat him fair at cards?'

Jimmy pulled a switchblade from his jacket, the steel glinting under the cheap hotel lighting. But instead of advancing on Miles, he began cutting the silk stockings that bound him.

'This isn't the place for what you deserve,' Jimmy said, his voice carrying deadly calm. 'Get dressed. We're taking a little trip down memory lane. Back to where scum like you belong.'

'Please, I can make this right. Name your price—'

Brother Bertie's fist connected with his jaw, snapping his head back with brutal force. Blood spurted from his split lip, spattering across the hotel pillows.

'Get your fucking clothes on,' Brother Bertie snarled. 'Unless you want to take this ride bare-arsed.'

***

The abandoned rum warehouse at Sugar Cane Wharf loomed before them in the desolate docklands, a decaying cathedral of misery perfect for tonight's sermon in pain. The heavy door groaned open to reveal a cavernous space illuminated by a single naked bulb swinging gently from the ceiling, casting monstrous shadows that danced across the walls.

Jimmy shoved Miles forward into the circle of sickly yellow light. The bastard's earlier swagger had evaporated completely, replaced by bone-deep terror that made his whole body shake.

'Sit,' Jimmy commanded, pointing to a sturdy wooden chair positioned in the centre of the space.

Miles hesitated, his gaze darting around the warehouse, searching for any possible escape. Brother Bertie grabbed him by the scruff of his neck and forced him down, rope appearing in his hands with practiced efficiency.

'You know what you did to my sister?' Brother Bertie's voice echoed through the vast space as he secured Miles' wrists and ankles to the chair. 'Three broken ribs. Fractured collarbone. Concussion that had her puking blood for two days.'

'I didn't mean for it to go that far—' Miles began.

Brother Bertie belted him a vicious one across his face, splitting his lip further. 'Lying bastard. You told them to make sure she remembered it.'

Jimmy emerged from the shadows carrying a large metal bucket, his movements deliberate and unhurried. The thick, cloying smell of molasses flooded the warehouse, sickeningly sweet.

'Know what happens to rats in the docks, Miles?' Jimmy circled the chair, his voice dropping to a whisper that carried more menace than any shout. 'They get what's coming.'

The bucket tipped, and dark, viscous molasses cascaded over Miles' legs, splashing onto the concrete floor and pooling around the chair. The sticky substance immediately soaked through his trousers, clinging to the skin beneath.

'What are you doing?' Miles' voice rose to a shrill scream, the chair creaking as he thrashed against the ropes binding his wrists and ankles. 'Jesus Christ! Please! I can fix this – I can make it right—'

'Too fucking late for that.' Brother Bertie's face was a mask of cold fury. 'Ever seen the wharf rats that live in these warehouses? Blood thirsty little bastards. They'd go mental for molasses. Loved the sweet stuff more than their own mothers.'

Miles' eyes widened to impossible proportions as understanding dawned with horrific clarity. A wet stain spread across his crotch, the acrid smell of urine mixing with the sickly-sweet molasses.

'Got me thinking,' Brother Bertie continued, crouching behind Miles' chair. 'Rat for a rat, eh? Only fitting.'

Jimmy disappeared into the shadows and returned with a wire cage. Inside, two massive wharf rats scurried about, sleek and fat, their dark eyes glittering with hunger in the dim light.

'PLEASE GOD NO!' Miles' scream tore through the warehouse, his body convulsing against the restraints. 'I'LL DO ANYTHING! CHRIST ALMIGHTY, PLEASE!'

'You already did everything, Miles.' Jimmy set the cage down just out of reach of the molasses. 'Thing about rats – once they get a taste of something sweet, they can't stop themselves. They lick and lick and then—' He made a vicious biting motion with his teeth. 'They want what's underneath all that sugar.'

Brother Bertie stood, his face carved from granite. 'This is for Gertie, you scum-sucking maggot. Every second of pain you're about to feel – that's for her.'

Jimmy flipped open the cage door. The rats hesitated for a moment, whiskers twitching, before the scent of molasses drew them forward with unstoppable hunger.

The first bite ripped a howl from Miles that barely sounded human. Blood welled up where tiny teeth had broken skin, mixing with the dark molasses in grotesque swirls.

'Right then,' Jimmy said, checking his watch with casual indifference. 'Let's give our friend some private time with his new mates.'

Brother Bertie spat on the floor near Miles' chair. 'Hope you enjoyed beating women, you worthless cunt. Because this is what it costs.'

They walked towards the warehouse door, Miles' increasingly desperate screams echoing behind them. The sound followed them even after the heavy door slammed shut, muffled but still audible through the thick walls.

Then the screaming stopped.

Miles Harker would never lay another finger on a woman again.

# Chapter Twenty-Five

*No going back now. It's Bertie or nobody.*

Sin had made up her mind. She had to do this.

Shivering in the evening chill, she stood outside Ade's gorgeous art deco apartment block in Bloomsbury. The grand building loomed above her, all clean lines and geometric patterns, mocking her while her life was a total mess.

Her low-heeled Mary Janes were soft against the marble-floored lobby. The brass lift gates closed with a satisfying clang, and she watched the needle tick to the second floor, each second bringing her closer to freedom. To Bertie.

But, oh God, what was she going to tell Ade? She felt sick with it. How do you tell a decent man that you're chucking him for someone else? That all those wedding plans, all those dreams he'd shared about their future together, meant nothing because you'd been living a lie the whole time?

For nights, she'd hardly slept, wrestling with how to break it off. He was such a good man, the best, and now it felt like she was going to rip his heart out and stamp on it. Her gut churned with guilt. Ade deserved better than this. He deserved a woman who loved him one hundred and ten percent, not some selfish cow who'd been using him as an escape route from all the rubbish in her life.

There was no easy way to do this. She'd have to hurt him to free them both.

The key, Ade's spare, slid into the lock. She hesitated before pushing the door open.

The flat stretched before her, bathed in soft lamplight, a bachelor pad with every mod con money could buy. Sleek record player, crystal decanters catching the light, leather chairs flanking a glass coffee table and burnt-orange wall-to-wall shag-pile carpet. Everything matched the glossy magazine spread Ade had shown her. 'Our future,' he'd called it.

'Adrian?' Her voice was stronger than the doubt swirling in her stomach.

Silence. Then a thud from the bedroom, followed by frantic rustling.

'Sin?' Ade hesitantly called out. 'That you, sweetheart? Wasn't expecting you tonight.'

Footsteps shuffled behind the bedroom door before it swung open. There stood Adrian, chest bare save for an unbuttoned shirt hastily thrown on, hair mussed, sweat beading his upper lip despite the cool evening.

'You all right?' Sin asked, alarm building in her chest. 'You look really peaky.'

'Fine, fine,' he bit out, which so wasn't his style. Even in the most stressful of situations, Ade kept it cool. Stepping into the hallway, he quickly pulled the bedroom door almost closed behind him.

His fingers tapped nervously against his thigh. 'Just wasn't expecting company tonight, love. Should've rung first.'

Her eyes narrowed, catching the shadow of movement behind him. The flutter of fabric, a soft gasp quickly silenced.

Rage flared white-hot all over her. 'What the hell is going on here?'

Before he could stop her, Sin barged past him, sending him stumbling into the doorframe. She yanked back the bedroom door.

Sin's jaw went south.

A woman stood there, back turned, frantically fastening a bra. Bubbly red hair flicking erratically against her shoulders.

The woman turned, clutching a blouse to her chest, eyes wide with horror.

Sin's throat closed tight, and her face become cold and ashen.

'Kath?'

*Christ almighty. My best mate. In Ade's bedroom. Half-naked. Flesh hanging out like a whore's washing.*

For one frozen moment, Sin couldn't breathe, couldn't think, couldn't move. Blood roared in her ears, deafening her. Her fingers curled into fists so tight her nails cut half-moons into her palms.

'Sin…' Kathleen pleaded, tears flooding her eyes. 'Oh God, Sin.'

***

Sin couldn't tear her eyes away from Kath. Her best mate stood there, fingers trembling buttoning up her blouse, missing a hole and making the whole thing crooked. Kath's usually perfect makeup was smudged, mascara trailing down one cheek. Her skirt was twisted around, zipper only halfway up.

Ade hovered between them, trousers on but belt unbuckled, dangling uselessly. His expensive shirt hung open, revealing the chest Sin had never actually seen naked, despite their engagement. His fancy cologne mixed with the unmistakable musk of sex, and fucking betrayal.

'Sin, please,' Ade broke the suffocating silence, voice pitched higher than normal, hands raised. 'This isn't—'

'Don't you DARE say this isn't what it looks like. Her shock hardened a cold, numbing sensation that spread through her chest, freezing her insides.

*My best mate and the man I was going to marry. You're having a laugh.*

Ade stepped towards her, hands outstretched. 'Sin, sweetheart, we need to talk about this.'

Sin backed away, bumping into the doorframe. 'Don't touch me.' Her voice dropped to a dangerous growl, skin crawling at the thought of his hands on her – the same hands that had just been all over Kath.

'We never meant for this to happen,' Kath whispered, tears streaming freely now. 'Sin, I swear to God—'

'Both of you shut up!' Sin bellowed, her voice bouncing off the walls of Ade's posh flat, fists clenched so tight her knuckles turned white.

She stormed back into the sitting room, needing space, air, anything to escape the suffocating betrayal. Ade followed, in a rush, hastily tucking in his shirt. 'Let me explain.'

'Explain what? That you've been shagging my best mate? Behind my back?' The accusations scalded her throat.

Kath appeared in the doorway, eyes red and swollen, arms wrapped around herself. 'Sin, I know you hate me right now. I hate myself.' She pulled in a shuddering breath. 'Adrian, could I speak to Sin alone?'

He looked between them, hesitating.

Sin planted her feet wide, fists still looking as if she was on the verge of swinging. 'If you've got any decency, you'll give us a minute.'

Ade nodded, grabbing his jacket. 'I'll be downstairs in the lobby.'

The door clicked shut behind him, leaving the two women facing each other.

'How long?' Sin finally asked, her voice stripped bare.

Kath sank onto the leather sofa, shoulders slumped in defeat. 'This was the first time between us, I swear on my mother's life.' She made the sign of the cross over her heart. 'But we've been… talking. Seeing each other.'

Sin grabbed the back of a chair to steady herself, knuckles white with pressure. 'While you've been helping me pick out wedding flowers and material for my wedding dress?'

'I'm so sorry,' Kath whispered, fresh tears welling. 'It wasn't planned. It just… happened.'

'Things don't just happen, Kath!' Sin's voice broke, betraying her.

'He was so good with Dilly,' Kath blurted, fingers twisting together anxiously. 'You remember that day at the park? The way he got down on her level, talked to her proper? Most blokes don't even acknowledge her, much less look at her, Sin.'

She paused, her gaze drifting, face softening. 'But it's more than that. Ade's gorgeous. I can't stop thinking about him. Can't stop dreaming about him. The way those eyes of his gaze at me…' Her voice trailed off, cheeks flushing. 'He feels the same way. We want to marry.'

Sin's anger flared hot and bright, a flash fire in her chest. 'Then why didn't you come to me? Tell me you had feelings for him?'

'How could I?' Kath's eyes were wild with desperation. 'You were tying the knot with him! What was I supposed to say? "By the way, I'm in love with your fiancé, mind if I have a go?"'

Sin paced the room. The shock was ebbing now because she realised that she should have figured this all out. Seen it because God knows it had been right in her face. The way Adrian had gone all twitchy when Kath barged in on them kissing. How he'd spent half the engagement party fussing over Kath and Dilly instead of his bride-to-be. The way Kath flew off the handle when she suspected that Sin had been with Bertie at her engagement party.

*I'm a proper* stupid cow. I should have twigged it ages ago.

A laugh bubbled up from deep in her chest, not bitter, but genuinely amused. 'Well, you can have him.'

'What?' Kath's mouth fell open, her breathing halting mid-sob.

Sin laughed again, this time with real mirth. 'The only reason I came here tonight was to break off the engagement.'

Kath's jaw dropped, eyes widening to perfect circles. 'You what?'

'I can't marry him,' Sin surprised herself with how steady her voice sounded. Relief flooded through her, tension melting from her shoulders. 'Not when I'm in love with another man.'

'Bertie,' Kath whispered, understanding dawning on her face.

Sin nodded, something loosening in her chest at finally saying it aloud. 'I couldn't keep living a lie,

Kath. I was going to tell him tonight that the wedding's off. I'm going to tell Bertie I love him, that I want to be with him, no matter what anyone thinks.'

Sin felt lighter than she had in months, the pressure of pretence finally lifted from her shoulders.

*Christ, this is mental. In actuality, Kath and Ade have done me favour.*

'You're not angry anymore?' Kath asked cautiously.

'I'm still narked you went behind my back,' Sin pursed her lips. 'You should have told me.'

'I know.' Kath's chin trembled. 'Ade wants to make a proper home for me and Dilly. No man's ever wanted that, Sin.'

'If you love him…' Sin began.

'I do. With my whole heart.' Her face melted into that of a woman in love. Then, 'But not at the risk of losing my best friend. You mean everything to me.'

Sin looked down at their hands, then back up at Kath's tear-streaked face. Despite everything, she felt the familiar tug of their lifelong bond.

'You daft mare.' Sin plonked herself down beside Kath and took her hand. Squeezed it. 'You know perfectly well I can't stay mad at you for long.'

Kath sent her a watery laugh, her grip tightening. 'I'll make it up to you, I swear.'

Sin took a deep breath, squaring her shoulders. 'You can start by telling me how the hell I'm going to find Bertie and convince him to take me back.'

Kath wiped her eyes, their old conspiratorial energy returning. 'You're really going to do it? Face down your father, Jimmy, the whole East End gossip mill? For Bertie?'

'Yes,' Sin responded without hesitation. 'I am.'

Just like that, they slipped back into their sisterhood, the betrayal not forgotten but set aside. Sin felt tears burning behind her eyes – not from anger anymore, but from the strange, bittersweet relief of knowing they would survive this.

When Kath opened her arms, Sin stepped into the embrace, hugging her fiercely.

'I love you, you daft sausage,' Sin whispered against Kath's hair.

'Love you, too,' Kath replied, squeezing her tighter.

When they pulled apart, Sin twisted off her engagement ring and placed it firmly in Kath's palm.

'There. Now it's official.'

Sin wore a smile that lit up her whole face. Finally, she and Bertie could be together.

# Chapter Twenty-Six

Sin practically floated up the steps to Gertie's boarding house, her heart hammering with wild hope. The gorgeous floral maxi dress she'd carefully chosen swished around her ankles. Victory was so close she could taste it.

She lifted back the knocker and let it fall, then smoothed her dress with trembling fingers. The lock clicked, and the door swung open.

Sin gasped when she saw Bertie. Gone was the sharp-dressed charmer with the cocky grin. His clothes hung off him and shadows ringed his bloodshot eyes. He was the picture of a man who had been destroyed.

Sin's greeting died in her throat. 'My God, what's happened?'

He blinked slowly, struggling to focus on her through a fog of misery. 'Sin.'

Just her name. No warmth, no light. The single word dropped between them and died.

Bertie felt his heart crack at the sight of her. Sin, gorgeous and glowing, standing on his doorstep. He wanted to sweep her into his arms, bury his face in her neck and never surface again. But the image of Gertie's broken face flashed in his mind, and he stepped back instead. His hands stayed rigid at his sides.

'Can I come in?' Sin's eyes searched his face, hunting desperately for the man she loved in this hollow shell.

He stepped back, letting her pass. His movements were wooden, mechanical. Inside, the normally bustling boarding house felt wrong – empty and cold.

'Where's Gertie?' Sin asked, dread crawling up her spine. 'It's not like her to miss greeting visitors.'

Bertie's face twisted, pain carving deep lines around his mouth. His hand shook as he rubbed it over his jaw. The mention of his sister's name didn't just hurt – it ripped through him.

'Hospital.' The word broke in his throat. 'Critical ward. Some men paid her a visit. A message for me about my gambling debt.'

Sin's hands flew to her mouth, horror flooding her system. 'Oh my God, Bertie. No.'

'They hurt her bad.' He gazed down. 'She might lose the sight in her right eye.'

Sin moved towards him. 'I'm so sorry. I had no idea—'

'No idea I'd been gambling?' A bitter laugh escaped him, the sound of something dying. 'Neither did I, until I couldn't stop.'

The coldness of that piercing laugh stopped Sin in her tracks. This wasn't her Bertie. The Bertie she knew – loved - had a laugh that warmed her from the inside out. This laugh was twisted, empty.

Sin's forehead creased. 'This isn't you. You never gambled big.'

'People change.' His gaze finally lifted to meet hers, and the emptiness there was complete.

Sin couldn't hold herself back any longer, so she rushed forward, throwing her arms around him. 'I've ended things with Adrian. The wedding's off. I want to be with you. Only you. Forever.'

She'd imagined this moment a thousand different ways. His face lighting up, his arms sweeping her into an embrace, his lips finding hers. Instead, his body went rigid against her. His arms remained at his sides, lifeless.

Every muscle in Bertie's body locked tight. How long had he waited to hear those words? And now she might as well have told him she'd come to kill him.

Pulling back, Sin searched his face. 'Did you hear me? I'm free. We can be together now.' Her voice rose, desperation naked in it.

Bertie stepped back. Sin felt the space between them expand into something unbridgeable. The rejection was a living thing, pressing down on her chest. Her ribs felt crushed, her heart squeezed until black spots danced at the edges of her vision.

*No. This can't be happening.*

'There can't be an "us", Sin.' Each word fell heavy and final.

'What?' Sin's throat closed around the question. 'Why not? I don't care what people think anymore. I don't care what my father thinks, what Jimmy thinks—'

'It's not about them!' The words exploded from him, his fist slamming against the wall. Blood smeared the wallpaper. 'It's about what happened to Gertie. It's about what I've done.'

The rage erupted from Bertie without warning. He'd spent days at Gertie's bedside, drowning in guilt, and now all that emotion detonated at once. Not at Sin – never at Sin – but at himself.

Sin flinched but held her ground. 'What are you talking about? What does Gertie have to do with us?'

Bertie's face twisted with fury and grief. 'Everything! When you ended things, when you threw our love away, I couldn't handle it. I started gambling. Big time. Desperate, stupid gambling. Trying to feel something again.'

He began pacing, movements frenzied and jerky. 'I lost more than I could ever pay back. And now Gertie's in hospital with her face beaten to a pulp because of me. Because of us.'

Each word tore from Bertie's throat. He didn't want to destroy Sin, but she needed to understand.

What they had was poisoned now, tainted by what had happened to Gertie.

Sin felt the ground open beneath her. The accusation didn't just slice through her, it gutted her completely. Her lungs struggled for air, each breath a battle.

'That's not fair. I didn't make you gamble—'

'When you're in love with someone who won't choose you, who keeps you as their dirty little secret, it breaks something inside.' Bertie's voice dropped to a whisper. 'I gambled because I was desperate to feel anything besides the agony of losing you.'

The words struck Sin with brutal force. The terrible truth of it, that she had kept him hidden away, that she had been too cowardly to choose him openly, shredded what remained of her composure.

Her eyes flooded with tears that spilled down her cheeks. She wanted to reach for him again, to smooth the lines of torment from his gorgeous face. But she held back, terrified of another rejection that might destroy her completely.

'But I have chosen you now,' she whispered, her voice breaking. 'I'm here.'

Bertie wanted her more than salvation itself. But when he closed his eyes, all he saw was Gertie's ruined face, swollen beyond recognition, her right eye bloated shut.

His fucking fault.

His catastrophic weakness.

Bertie's laugh was the sound of a soul being torn apart. 'Too late, isn't it? My sister's lying in hospital because of the choices I made. She might never see properly again because I couldn't bear losing you.'

Sin took a desperate step forward. 'We can fix this together.'

'I can't fix my sister's broken body!' His voice shattered completely. 'Don't you understand? Every time I look at you, I'll see Gertie's broken face. Every time I hold you, I'll feel her blood on my hands.'

Sin felt desperation clawing up her throat. Her vision blurred with tears until Bertie was little more than a wavering shape. She'd finally gathered the courage to defy her family, to face society's judgment – and now he was telling her it was all for nothing.

'But I love you.' The words emerged broken, hardly recognisable.

'And I love you.' The truth of those words burned in his chest. He did love her with a ferocity that frightened him. But love wasn't enough to wash away the blood.

'I'll love you until they put me in the ground. But love isn't enough. Not anymore. Not after what I've done.'

His fingers curled into fists so tight that his nails carved into his palms. The physical pain was nothing compared to the soul-destroying agony of denying himself Sin. He wanted to throw himself across the room, to gather her in his arms with such force they might merge into one being. The effort of restraint left him trembling, threatening to tear him apart.

Sin saw the war raging in him. She could read it in every line of his body, in the rigid set of his shoulders, the violent flex of his jaw, the way his eyes darted everywhere except to meet hers directly.

They stood separated by mere feet, but it might as well have been continents.

'Please,' Sin begged, her voice stripped raw. 'Don't do this. Don't throw away what we have.'

For one terrible moment, Bertie wavered. His resolve, built during endless nights at Gertie's bedside making desperate promises to be better, threatened to disintegrate. His hand rose, fingers stretching towards Sin's tear-ravaged face – then dropped back to his side.

The moment his fingers fell away, Sin knew with crushing finality that it was truly over. The realisation was a level of devastation she'd never felt before. The hope she'd carried up those steps, precious and so beautiful, didn't just die. It was murdered before her eyes.

'I need you to leave.' Brother Bertie's voice was hollow, empty.

'Bertie—' His name was a plea, a prayer, a final desperate reach.

'There is no "me and you", Sin.' The words were glass in his mouth, cutting him open from the inside. 'There can't be. Not anymore. Not ever again.'

Sin stood frozen, her heart being torn from her chest, still beating. The knowledge sank into her bones: his mind was set in stone. His guilt wasn't just powerful, it was all-consuming, a black hole that had swallowed the man she loved.

'So that's it?' Tears poured down her cheeks in rivers. 'You're giving up on us? On everything we could be?'

Bertie turned away, physically unable to bear the sight of her crumbling before his eyes. 'Gertie nearly died because of me. Because I made a mess of my fucking life.' Each word was a knife turned against himself. 'What kind of man would I be if I just forgot that? What kind of brother?'

Sin wanted to seize him, to shake him until his teeth rattled, to force him to see reason. But she knew it would only drive him further away. No way could she climb the wall of guilt he'd built around himself.

'You'll always be my Bertie,' she whispered, the words drowning in tears.

He didn't turn.

Wouldn't.

'Please go.' The words were barely audible, but their impact was deafening.

Sin stumbled towards the door, her vision so blurred she could barely see. She fumbled with the handle, her fingers numb and clumsy, desperate to escape before she shattered completely.

Outside, the bright sunshine was an obscene mockery of her grief. Sin made it three steps before her legs betrayed her. She collapsed against the wall of the boarding house, her body convulsing with sobs.

Inside, Brother Bertie listened to her footsteps fade away. He rushed up to his room and once inside, balled his hand and pounded it into the wall.

Again.

And again.

Then he collapsed on the bed, his head in his hands. Great, violent sobs tore through him, threatening to rip him apart. He'd done it. He'd done the right thing, the honourable thing. So why did it feel like he'd just lost his soul?

'I'm sorry, Gertie,' he whispered to the empty room, his voice already dead. 'I'm sorry, Sin.'

The silence swallowed his words whole, offering no comfort, no absolution, no hope.

# Chapter Twenty-Seven

Six weeks on, the battered Ford Cortina sat idling in a narrow side street three blocks from the Anglo-Merchant Bank, its dull brown paintwork blending with the other everyday motors. Jimmy drummed his fingers against the worn steering wheel, silver-grey eyes fixed on the corner where their target lay out of sight. Beside him, Brother Bertie adjusted his pork pie hat.

Jimmy shifted, muscles tense. 'You reckon we can trust her to get what we need? Rita's always been Danny's girl.'

Brother Bertie snorted, his usually warm eyes hardening. 'That's ancient history, mate. She's all West End now, ain't she? Too bloody posh for the likes of us.'

'If you two are finished assassinating my personality,' came a sharp voice from the back seat, 'I'd like to get on with it.'

Rita applied another coat of Revlon lipstick, rich brown with a hint of bronze. She wore a Russian sable fur jacket in deep chocolate, a heavy gold chain at her throat, and butter-soft kid leather gloves in caramel. She snapped her gold Stratton compact shut and slipped it into her Gucci bamboo-handled handbag. The real thing, not some Petticoat Lane knock-off.

'How's Gertie doing?' she asked Brother Bertie, straightening her gloves.

'Getting better,' he replied, his voice softening. 'Home now, thank Christ. Proper fighter, my sister is.'

Rita nodded. 'Good. She's a tough old bird.' Then her eyes narrowed with professional intent. 'I'll check out the layout, security positions, vault access. And look out for anything unusual.'

Rita leaned forward, expensive French perfume filling the car's interior. 'And let's not forget, unusual is what I specialise in.'

She stepped out and crossed the road, the fur jacket swinging elegantly around her.

***

Inside the Anglo-Merchant Bank, Rita approached reception, head held high. 'Good morning,' she purred, voice dropping to cultured tones. 'I'd like to speak with someone about establishing a private account. I've recently come into some family money and require more… discreet banking arrangements.'

'Of course, madam.' The receptionist nodded and smiled. 'Mr Turner will see you. He's one of our senior managers. For potential clients of your… calibre, he prefers to handle matters personally.'

Rita was led across the marble expanse, trained eyes scanning everything. Security guard positions, cameras, staff protocols. She noted the heavy oak door that likely led to the vault area.

Edward Turner rose from behind his mahogany desk on the second floor. He looked like a right jobsworth, Rita decided, in his round glasses and his forgettable face. But his suit screamed Savile Row money. Oh, Rita knew how to spot money.

'Ms…?' he enquired, extending his hand.

'Huntington-Smythe,' Rita supplied smoothly. 'Eliza Huntington-Smythe.'

'Edward Turner. Though everyone calls me Teddy.'

Once she took her seat, Rita didn't waste time spinning her concocted story. 'As I mentioned, I've recently come into some family money. My late uncle's estate in Berkshire has finally cleared probate.' She sighed dramatically. 'The solicitors have been absolute beasts about it all. Nevertheless, I find myself in need of proper financial management.'

Teddy nodded, bland features arranged in professional sympathy. 'Discretion and security are our hallmarks at Anglo-Merchant.' He leaned forward, lowering his voice. 'Perhaps you'd care to see our facilities? Many clients find it reassuring to witness our security protocols first-hand.'

'That would be lovely,' Rita purred. 'I'm particularly interested in your safety deposit services. I have certain family heirlooms that require secure storage.'

Well, that was music to his ears, and he led her back downstairs where Rita made sure she took in every security detail she could.

'Our vault,' Teddy announced proudly as they approached the heavy oak door. He nodded to the guard, who stepped aside respectfully.

He entered a code, then used a large brass key. 'Dual authentication,' he explained reverently. 'No single person can access the vault alone.'

The vault door was massive, fifteen inches of solid steel with polished brass face bearing the Chubb logo.

'1966 model,' Turner said, pride evident. 'The most advanced currently available. Time-locked as well – cannot be opened outside banking hours, even with correct codes and keys.'

Inside, the vault was brightly lit and spacious. One wall contained teller drawers for cash reserves. The other three walls were lined with safety deposit boxes.

'Our standard boxes are available for an annual fee,' Turner explained. 'The larger ones are for premium clients only.' His eyes assessed Rita's worth with cold calculation. 'I suspect you would qualify.'

Rita smiled, letting him believe his flattery worked. 'I would require one of the larger boxes, yes. What's your security protocol for access?'

After the vault tour, Turner escorted her back upstairs, continuing his sales pitch. Rita was half listening, her mind already fitting pieces together.

When she emerged into the main banking hall, a movement near the private client corridor caught Rita's eye. She turned slightly, then froze.

*Bloody hell. Bloody, bloody hell.*

Iris Steele. Danny's supposedly submissive, gin-soaked wife was being escorted by an elderly, distinguished banker. Iris was dressed conservatively but expensively in tailored wool, her normally dull blonde hair freshly styled, posture straight and confident. Nothing like the downtrodden woman Rita knew.

'Is everything all right, Ms Huntington-Smythe?' Turner asked, noticing her stillness.

Rita recovered instantly, sending him a smile of reassurance. While they walked back, Rita angled to keep Iris in view. The elderly banker was speaking with unmistakable deference, holding a leather portfolio stamped with the bank's crest.

'…your father's trust continues to perform exceptionally well, Mrs Steele,' Rita caught. 'The quarterly dividends have been transferred as usual.'

You what? Rita couldn't believe her ears.

A trust fund? Iris Steele had a bloody trust fund?

And she would bet her last shilling that Danny knew sod all about it. The implications were staggering.

Back in Turner's office, Rita completed the charade, discussing rates and investments with just enough knowledge to be convincing. She promised to return with documentation, accepted a leather folder, and allowed Turner to escort her out.

'I look forward to welcoming you to the Anglo-Merchant family, Ms Huntington-Smythe,' he said, his hand lingering on hers.

Rita leaned closer, voice dropping to an intimate murmur. 'I believe this may be the beginning of a very productive relationship, Mr Turner.'

***

'Well?' Thrown at Rita once she was back in the car.

Rita gave them the lowdown on what she'd seen and found out, but she couldn't get Danny's wife out of her head. From the looks of things, Iris Steel was a very wealthy woman.

When she'd finished, Jimmy asked, 'You see anything else interesting?' His penetrating gaze meet hers in the rearview mirror with unsettling directness.

Rita hesitated. The image of Jimmy's mother burned through her brain.

Jimmy caught her hesitation, eyes narrowing. 'What is it? You saw something.'

'Spill it, Rita,' Brother Bertie added. 'If you're holding out on us…'

Rita made her decision, smoothing her features into practiced innocence. 'Yeah, I saw something. Not about the bank itself, but…' She paused, manufacturing uncertainty. 'One of my former clients from the Sing-Song Lady was there. High-roller type, used to come in regular. Don't think he spotted me.'

That got them off her back.

On the drive back to the East End, Rita gazed out of the window, thinking about secrets and the power they held. In her world, information was currency. But some things were worth more than money.

*Sorry, Danny,* she thought, a small smile playing at her lips. *Some secrets belong to us girls.*

# Chapter Twenty-Eight

*Jesus Christ. This bumbling fool shares my blood,* Lord Xander thought, eying the pathetic figure in front of him with undisguised contempt. Thank God the Blacklock ancestors, who gazed down at them from their lofty positions in the portraits in his study, weren't alive to witness this disgrace.

He found it strange to believe that he and his nephew shared the same blood. When he'd strode into the drawing room, his sister's son had jumped up from the wingback chair, nearly upending a small, antique table in his haste. Total disaster. Annoyed beyond belief Xander hadn't acknowledged his presence, and instead had moved to the drinks cabinet and poured himself a generous measure of aged single malt Macallan Whisky, deliberately not offering one to his visitor.

Xander took his time, swirling the alcohol, inhaling its peaty aroma before taking a lingering, savoury sip. Only then did he lower himself into a leather armchair with exaggerated slowness. He didn't invite his nephew to sit.

Let the spineless worm stand. Just like his mother—weak to the core.

'Did you find anything?' Xander finally asked, his voice silky smooth but edged with steel.

His nephew's glasses slid down his nose, and he shoved them back up with trembling fingers. 'N-no, Uncle. I've searched through Mother's things thoroughly. She hasn't got anything concerning this matter.'

The mention of his sister made Xander's lip curl. Eleanor. Another disappointment in a long line of them. Xander restrained from hurling the glass at the wall. If word got out about this…

All these years he'd assumed that his brother, Rufus, who lived the high life in Jamaica, had the papers. But when his brother had died last year it materialised that he didn't have the documents after all, they were tucked up in a safety deposit box in the Anglo-Merchant Bank. A box that he couldn't legally access.

But Daniel would soon have that covered. The robbery was this week, and soon those documents would be in his hand. And when he got them he was going to burn them in the fire.

Still, he had to ensure that there was no other evidence about this that his sister was keeping. Hence, why he needed the help of his tomfool nephew.

'Are you absolutely certain there was nothing?' Xander's laser-like stare pierced through the younger man. 'Because you wouldn't want me coming over there to check for myself, would you?'

His nephew flinched, then swallowed hard. 'Actually, Mother's been asking for you,.' He appeared steadier, his anxiety calming down. 'She wants to see you.'

Xander waved a dismissive hand, ignoring the unexpected pang in his chest. 'I may come. I may not.'

He knew it would be a not. He hadn't seen Eleanor in years and wanted it kept that way.

He took another sip of booze, letting the silence stretch uncomfortably. His nephew shifted his weight from foot to foot, clearly desperate to escape.

'Keep looking,' Xander said finally, his face darkening as he leaned forward. 'What are you waiting for?' He slammed his glass down. 'Get out.'

His nephew scurried away with the speed of a frightened rabbit, stumbling over his own feet in his rush to escape, the door banging shut behind him.

Xander knocked back the last of his single malt, savouring the tang of it passing down his throat. Not a tremor in his hand, not a flicker across his aristocratic features. To any observer, he appeared the epitome of composed nobility – a man without a care in the world, certainly not one facing the potential ruin that tomorrow's bank robbery could bring if it failed and his name was linked to it.

He'd perfected this mask over decades, this ability to bury every emotion beneath layers of breeding and cold calculation.

Never let them see weakness, Alexander.

His father's voice echoed from the grave, as sharp and cutting as it had been forty years ago. Lord Fitzwilliam Blacklock had been a towering giant of a man, built like a prize fighter but dressed in Henry Poole & Co perfection. Icy blue eyes that could strip flesh from bone with a glance, a mouth that rarely curved except in cruel amusement.

Xander had been twelve when he'd made the mistake of crying in front of the privileged old cunt. Some entanglement with the housekeeper's boy – he couldn't even remember what now – but he'd arrived home with tearstained cheeks and a bloody nose, seeking comfort from a father who viewed emotion as a contagious disease.

'Tears?' Fitzwilliam's voice had been arctic. 'In my house? From my heir?'

The beating that followed had been methodical, precise. Not the wild fury of a common brute, but the calculated violence of a man who understood exactly how much pain he could inflict without leaving permanent damage. Each blow accompanied by lessons delivered in that same conversational tone.

'A Blacklock does not weep. A Blacklock does not show fear. A Blacklock certainly does not display weakness to lesser mortals who would exploit it.'

When it was over, when Xander lay gasping on the Turkish rug, his father had straightened his cufflinks and delivered the final lesson: 'Compose yourself. We have guests arriving in an hour, and you will join us for dinner. If anyone asks about your appearance, you fell from your horse. And Alexander – if you ever again disgrace this family name with such a pathetic display, the consequences will be far more severe.'

Xander had learned well. By the time dessert was served that night, he'd been the perfect young gentleman, charming the ladies, discussing politics with the men, his bruised ribs hidden beneath impeccable tailoring and iron self-control.

Now, setting the glass down with steady hands, Xander allowed himself a thin smile. Only a few days now and the contents of the deposit box would be in his possession.

His bastard son, Danny, might be crude East End scum, but he'd never failed him yet.

# Chapter Twenty-Nine

Sin almost turned tail and ran when she arrived outside the red door. But she didn't. She made herself take a deep, fortifying breath to slow down her heart and calm her nerves. Then she pressed the bell for the flat upstairs.

And waited.

Sin's tummy tightened, making her nerves worse, and the throbbing in her head started up again. The door opened.

Rita appeared in the doorway, her willowy figure wrapped in midnight-blue silk. An Embassy cigarette dangled from her red-lacquered fingers, tendrils of smoke curling upwards past her face.

'Well, well.' Rita's pink lips parted in surprise, and she surveyed Sin with a sharpness that left her uncomfortable. 'Jimmy Steele's little sister, Danny's Steele's little girl. I had no idea you knew where to find me.'

Truth was, Sin hadn't crossed paths much with Rita. They lived very different lifestyles.

Sin tried to speak, but the words she'd rehearsed dissolved on her tongue.

Rita exhaled a plume of smoke, her gaze never leaving Sin's face. 'You look like death warmed up, girl.' She stepped back, the silk dressing gown whispering against her thighs. 'Come in before you fall down.'

Rita's new home wasn't the tacky place Sin associated with a working girl. It was tasteful and simple. Neat and clean. The only bit of flash was a tray with a decanter and a set of pretty glasses. Cleo Laine's mellow voice floated form a record player in the corner.

'Park yourself,' Rita ordered, gesturing towards a plush velvet sofa. 'You're white as a ghost.'

Sin sank into the cushions, her knees suddenly boneless. The enormity of why she'd come crashed over her, driving the air from her lungs. Her hands trembled in her lap, and she clasped them tightly together.

*I can't do this. I can't bloody do this.*

Rita returned with two delicate teacups. 'Get this down you.' She placed one in Sin's unsteady hands. 'Proper English breakfast with enough sugar to stand a spoon in. Good for shock.'

Sin gripped the warm cup, inhaling the sweet, comforting steam. 'Thanks.'

Rita settled into an armchair opposite, crossing her long legs. She studied Sin with piercing intensity. 'Right then. Out with it.' Her voice softened a fraction. 'Whatever mess you're in, it won't fix itself while you sit there all glum like the world's about to cave in.'

Sin fixed her gaze on a spot on the carpet, unable to meet Rita's eyes. 'I'm in trouble.'

'An unexpected arrival in the oven?' Rita's blunt words slammed into Sin like a physical blow.

Sin's head jerked up, her eyes wide. 'How did you—'

'Seen that look a thousand times.' Rita set her cup down with a decisive clink and leaned forward, elbows on knees. 'How far gone?'

Sin stared down at her white knuckles. 'Nearly eight weeks.'

*Our baby. Bertie's and mine.*

'I need to…' God, she couldn't say the words.

So Rita supplied her own version. '…get rid of it.'

Sin nodded numbly and carried on, with a bite to her tone. 'I know the laws changed, but fat lot of good that does me. Need two doctors willing to sign off. Need the right reasons – mental health risks, foetal abnormalities, social hardship. Need appointments and records and questions. Might as well put an announcement in the *Sunday Times*.'

Rita finished the last of her smoke and mashed it out in a decorative ashtray. 'And you thought because of the business I'm in, I'd be able to help sort you out.'

Sin placed the cup down. Her fingers locked together in her lap. 'Can you help me or not? I need someone… discreet.'

Rita rose and crossed to a walnut writing desk, extracting a slim silver key from her dressing gown pocket. She unlocked a drawer and removed a small black address book.

'Two options.' Rita flipped through the pages. 'Dr Marsden in Kensington. Clean office, proper equipment, trained medical staff. He charges a hundred quid cash.'

Sin's heart plummeted. 'I haven't got that kind of money.' The entire sum she'd saved from her hairdressing job, tucked away in a box beneath her bed, amounted to less than forty pounds.

'Thought not.' Rita nodded, turning another page. 'Second option. Mrs Eliza Bellamy in Stepney. Former midwife. Thirty quid. She's done hundreds, knows her onions better than most doctors.' A shadow crossed Rita's face. 'Used her myself, years back.'

'Is she safe?' Sin pressed, her mouth bone-dry.

Rita's dark eyes met hers unflinchingly. 'Safer than most. She's clean, careful. But she's not a hospital, Sin. There's always risk.'

Sin's heart thundered. She'd heard the whispered stories – girls carried away in the night, bleeding and feverish, found dead in abandoned buildings or floating in the Thames.

'This new law,' Sin said, her voice catching. 'It was supposed to fix things. Stop women dying.'

Rita's laugh held no humour. 'Oh, sweetheart.' She settled back down. 'Laws aren't made for women like us. Middle-class birds with nice GPs who'll sign the forms, sure, they're sorted. Working girls, East End girls, coloured girls?' She shook her head. 'We're still on our own, just like always.'

'It's not fair,' Sin choked out, her voice catching with the bitter truth of it.

'Life rarely is for our sort.' Rita's voice wasn't unkind, just matter-of-fact. 'Not many options for women, are there? Marry well if you're lucky, work your fingers to the bone if you're not. And God help you if you step out of line.' She gestured to the opulent room around them. 'Find me one woman in a hundred who gets to choose her own path.'

Sin dragged hard on her cigarette, the smoke burning her lungs. 'I thought I was choosing. With Adrian. A way out of the East End. Away from my father.' A harsh laugh escaped her. 'And here I am, more trapped than ever.'

Rita studied her face. 'Why not keep it? Tell your salon man it's his?'

'He's found love with someone else.' Sin replied, her voice rough. 'Besides which, Adrian's a decent bloke. He doesn't deserve a lie that big.'

'Noble of you,' Rita remarked, not unkindly. 'Most wouldn't think twice.'

Sin closed her eyes briefly, misery clenching her heart. 'I don't have a choice.'

Rita was quiet for a long moment, before she rose and returned to the desk, scribbling something on a piece of paper.

She handed it to Sin. 'So it's Mrs Bellamy, then,'

# Chapter Thirty

Unfolding the scrap of paper with the address, Sin's hand trembled. She'd deliberately worn her plainest dress, a drab brown thing that wouldn't draw attention, and pulled a headscarf low over her forehead, tucking her distinctive blonde hair out of sight.

Number forty-seven was eerily quiet, leaving a strange, unsettled feeling twisting in Sin's gut. Unlike some of the run-down buildings surrounding it, this house gleamed with fresh paint, windows polished to a sparkle. Pretty lace curtains hung inside, drawn shut against prying eyes.

Her legs felt like lead. She climbed the short flight of steps to the front door. Before she could knock, a wave of nausea hit her. She doubled over, hand pressed against her mouth, fighting the urge to vomit all over Mrs Bellamy's immaculate front step.

*Baby don't want to be here either.*

Straightening, Sin forced air into her lungs. Her fingers brushed against her still-flat stomach. No outward signs yet, nothing but the constant nausea and bone-deep exhaustion to indicate the life growing inside her.

*Bertie's baby. Our baby.*

Sin raised her fist and rapped sharply. For a wild, desperate moment, she considered running, disappearing into the night.

Too late.

The door swung open silently, revealing a young woman, barely out of her teens in the well-lit hallway. She wore a pristine white apron over a plain dress, blonde hair scraped back in a severe bun. Her face remained blank, expression wiped clean of any emotion.

'Come in.' The girl stepped aside. 'The missus will be with you shortly.'

The hallway stretched before Sin, wallpapered in delicate floral patterns. A small table held a vase of fresh-cut flowers, their sickly sweet scent filling the air. The girl quickly ushered Sin into a small waiting room, opening the door just enough for Sin to slip through before promptly closing it behind her.

'Please wait here.'

Sin perched on the edge of a plush sofa with antimacassars adorning its arms. Everything gleamed with polish, not a speck of dust in sight. Porcelain figurines lined the mantelpiece above a spotless fireplace.

A sound from upstairs made her jump. A muffled cry, quickly silenced. Sin froze, ears straining. Nothing followed. The house settled back into unnatural stillness.

Her gaze drifted to a side table beside an armchair. A basin sat there, partially hidden by a folded newspaper. Sin leaned forward, squinting in the dim light. A cloth soaked in dark liquid lay inside.

Blood.

Sin recoiled, bile rising in her throat. The room suddenly felt colder. She wrapped her arms around her middle. Footsteps approached, and Sin straightened, hands clasped tightly in her lap to hide their trembling. The door opened to reveal a small, plump woman with silver hair pulled into a neat bun. Her face was lined with age, cheeks flushed pink, eyes welcoming. She was a dead ringer for someone's gran.

'I'm Mrs Bellamy.' Her voice was warm, motherly.

Sin nodded wordlessly.

Mrs Bellamy settled into the armchair across from Sin, hands folded neatly in her lap. A gold wedding band gleamed on her left hand, though Rita had mentioned she was a widow.

'And you are?' she asked gently.

'Mary,' Sin lied, the name of her childhood doll springing to her lips. 'Mary Smith.'

Mrs Bellamy's eyes crinkled, suggesting she'd heard countless 'Mary Smiths' before. 'Don't you worry, dear. Women have been helping other women since time began. God gives us burdens, but he also gives us ways to lighten them.'

She rose, smoothing her skirt. 'I'll need the payment now, if you don't mind.'

Sin reached into her handbag with numb fingers, extracting the envelope of carefully counted notes. Almost her entire savings. Mrs Bellamy took it, not bothering to count, tucking it into her cardigan pocket.

'Come with me, dear.' She moved to the door, gesturing for Sin to follow.

Eventually, Mrs Bellamy pushed open the door to reveal a kitchen. Unlike the pristine sitting room, this space had been transformed. The cheerful domesticity stripped away, replaced by clinical efficiency.

The large wooden table dominating the centre had been covered with a white cloth. Metal instruments gleamed under harsh electric lighting, arranged in neat rows on a side table. The smell hit Sin immediately. Bleach, stronger here, attempting to mask something darker beneath.

A drain in the tiled floor. Rubber sheeting. A leather strap folded neatly at the head of the table.

Sin's breath caught in her throat. Sweat beaded on her forehead as reality crashed over her.

*This is happening. Really happening.*

'Remove your undergarments and lie on the table.' Mrs Bellamy's voice had changed, professional now, all warmth drained away. She turned to a sink in the corner, scrubbing her hands with harsh soap. 'It won't take long.'

'Come now, don't dawdle.' Mrs Bellamy had donned a white apron over her grandmotherly outfit, the incongruous image sending chills down Sin's spine. 'The sooner we start, the sooner it's over.'

Sin's feet carried her forward as if controlled by someone else. She reached the table, hands braced against its edge. The wood felt cold beneath her palms.

*One decision. One moment. After this, there's no going back.*

'Lie down, dear.' Mrs Bellamy crossed the room to the kitchen door and quietly closed it. The lock clicked with terrible finality. 'Let's begin.'

Sin stared at the ceiling, its once-white paint yellowed with age, a hairline crack running from corner to corner. Her body trembled with fear.

A tear escaped, tracking silently down her temple and into her hair.

Mrs Bellamy reached for the first gleaming instrument.

# Chapter Thirty-One

The sawn-off shotgun stared back at Brother Bertie from the open holdall bag, its twin barrels gleaming dully in the morning light. Beautiful, deadly, illegal. His finger traced the cold metal, feeling every nick and scratch on its surface.

Today was the day. They were going to turn over the Anglo-Merchant Bank. He was going to meet Jimmy in about an hour.

Brother Bertie wrapped the shotgun carefully in a soft cloth and nestled it back between boxes of cartridges. His stomach twisted into tight knots. He hadn't slept well last night, too tense.

The thunderous banging on the front door downstairs nearly stopped his heart.

Brother Bertie froze, heart hammering against his ribs. The Old Bill? Had they rumbled the job before it had even started? No, coppers would've kicked the door clean off its hinges.

The pounding continued, wild and desperate.

Brother Bertie hurried down the stairs. He paused at the door, composing himself before yanking it open.

'Who the bloody hell—'

Kath Doherty stood on the doorstep, her chest heaving with exertion. And panic, she was in a proper flap.

'Brother Bertie!' She could barely get his name out. 'Thank God you're here.'

'Kath? What's happened? Is it Dilly?' His mind immediately went to her sister.

Kathleen pushed past him into the hallway, her body vibrating with tension. 'We need to talk. Somewhere private, like.'

Once in his room upstairs he said, 'You're scaring me, Kath. What's going on?'

Her chest rose and fell rapidly, lips parting and closing several times before words came.

'Sin's pregnant.'

The floor seemed to drop away beneath Brother Bertie's feet. His legs weakened, forcing him to grab the edge of the dresser to steady himself.

'What did you just say?' His voice emerged as barely more than a whisper.

'Sin's pregnant,' Kathleen repeated, tears welling in her reddened eyes. 'With your baby.'

Brother Bertie sank onto the edge of his bed, the springs creaking under his weight. The room tilted and spun around him, Kathleen's pale face blurring in and out of focus.

'That's not possible,' he managed, his throat bone-dry.

'Eight weeks,' Kathleen insisted. 'Her engagement party. When you two…well, you know what, in that hotel room. I clocked you going down in the lift.'

His breath came in short, shallow gasps. Blood rushed in his ears, drowning out everything but the thundering of his heart. Sin carrying his child. Their child. A tiny life created from their forbidden love, growing inside her at this very moment.

'Brother Bertie, listen to me.' Kathleen seized his hands, her grip ice-cold and desperate. 'She's going to get rid of it. Today. This morning.'

His head snapped up, eyes locking with hers. The words landed, driving the air from his body.

'What?' Blood drained from his face. 'No, she can't—'

'She thinks she's got no choice,' Kathleen's voice fractured, tears spilling over onto her cheeks. 'Said you turned your back on her.' The last she uttered with outrage on her friend's behalf.

But Kath wasn't done. 'And before you ask, it isn't Ade's. They never…' She pursed her lips significantly. 'And I should know because he's my fella now.'

His heartbeat stuttered. The reality of it crashed over him in suffocating waves. Sin. Pregnant. With his child.

'Where is she?' he demanded, surging to his feet.

Kathleen dug in her coat pocket with trembling fingers, producing a crumpled piece of paper with the particulars.

Brother Bertie had to stop Sin.

But Jimmy was waiting for him.

Sin. Jimmy. The baby. The job.

But if he didn't get to Sin…

A child. His child. Growing inside the woman he loved.

Sin. Our baby.

Jimmy.

The job.

Time to choose.

# Chapter Thirty-Two

Brother Bertie shot up the short flight of steps of the house in Stepney in two furious strides and pounded on the door with enough force to make the brass knocker rattle. His body shook with fear.

*Please don't let me be too late!*

The young woman who opened the door, her eyebrows shot up with shock at the sight of him. 'Sir, we do not receive gentlemen callers here—'

He barged past her, ignoring her startled protests. 'Where is she?' His gaze searched wildly around. 'Where's Sin?'

'Sir!' The girl grabbed at his arm. 'You can't just—'

'Sin!' His voice echoed through the quiet house. 'Cynthia!'

A door at the end of the hallway opened, and an older woman emerged, silver-haired and grandmotherly in appearance. Her eyes narrowed behind wire-rimmed spectacles.

'Young man, this is a private residence,' she said, voice hard beneath its honeyed surface. 'I must insist you leave immediately.'

Brother Bertie moved towards her, desperation making him reckless. 'Not without Sin.'

The woman's face hardened. 'I don't know any—'

'Bertie?'

The voice stopped him cold. Sin stepped into view from behind the older woman, coat draped over her arm, handbag clutched in white-knuckled fingers. Her face, usually glowing with vitality, looked hollow-cheeked and ashen. Dark circles shadowed her eyes, which widened with shock, then narrowed with fury.

'What… What are you doing here?' Her lips wobbled like she was on the point of crying. Her hand instinctively rested against her tummy.

A wave of relief crashed through him that she was standing there alive, not the victim of a botched back-alley abortion.

'You can't do this.' His plea broke with raw emotion. 'Sin, please. Our baby. It's part of us both.' His hand reached towards her instinctively, every fibre of his being strained towards her, as if by sheer will he could jerk her away from the brink of this terrible choice.

'I know I've no right to ask anything of you, not after I walked away. But this—' His voice faltered, eyes sparkling with tears he fought hard to hold back. 'This innocent life deserves a chance. We deserve a chance.'

Mrs Bellamy looked between them, understanding dawning in her shrewd eyes. 'I think you two need to sort this out elsewhere.'

Neither of them moved. 'I couldn't go through with it,' Sin confessed, her hand gripping the strap of her bag.

Brother Bertie crossed the space between them and took her elbow to guide her out of the house.

Outside, the morning sunlight felt too bright, too cheerful for the storm raging inside them both.

'How did you find me?' Sin asked, voice barely above a whisper when they were inside his car. Before he could respond, she raised her hand. 'No, let me guess. Kath.'

A heavy silence fell. Then her face crumpled, tears suddenly streaming down her pale cheeks. Her body folded forward, breathless sobs tearing through her, violent and raw, her shoulders shaking with the force of them. The heartbreak she'd kept bottled up burst from her like blood from a wound.

'Shit, Sin.' He reached for her, gathering her trembling figure against his chest. 'I've got you. I've got you now.'

Her fingers dug, claw-like, into his jacket, holding on for dear life as she buried her face against his neck.

The warm dampness of her tears seeped through his collar.

'I didn't know what to do,' she choked out between ragged breaths. 'I was so scared, Bertie. So fucking scared.'

His throat tightened painfully. 'Why didn't you come to me? Jesus, Sin, why didn't you tell me?'

Easing back, Sin stared up at him, her face blotchy, eyes swollen. She'd never looked more beautiful to him.

'You didn't want me anymore,' she whispered, the words cutting and so painful for her to remember. 'You told me to get lost like I was nothing. Like *we* were nothing.'

Brother Bertie's face twisted with pain. He brought his hands up to cup her face, thumbs brushing at the tears that wouldn't stop flowing.

'I never stopped wanting you,' he confessed, voice thick. 'Not for a single bloody second.'

Fresh tears spilled over his thumbs. Sin's hand came up to grip his wrist, her touch electric on his skin. Then her touch transferred to trace the line of his jaw, the curve of his lips. His skin burned under her touch.

'I still love you,' he whispered hoarsely, his declaration ripping from somewhere deep in his gut. 'Never stopped. Not for a day, not for an hour.'

Sin's breath hitched. 'I tried to stop loving you. God knows I tried.'

'And?'

A sad smile curved her lips. 'Failed miserably, didn't I?'

He crushed his mouth to hers with hunger and desperation. Sin responded hungrily, her lips parting, feverish fingers knocking his hat off to tangle through his curls, clutching him closer as if she could crawl inside him.

The kiss was greedy and desperate, both of them pouring every ounce of loss and longing into it. When they finally broke apart, both gasping for air, Brother Bertie touched his forehead to hers, unwilling to let even an inch separate them.

'Our baby,' he breathed, his hand moving down to rest on her flat stomach. 'Our baby, Sin.'

She covered his hand with hers, a fresh tear rolling down her cheek. 'I was so afraid. I still am.'

'I'm here now,' he promised fiercely. 'And I'm not going anywhere. We'll figure this out together.'

'How?' Reality crashed back in, fear shadowing her eyes. 'My dad will go mental. Jimmy will never forgive either of us. We can't just—'

'We can,' Brother Bertie insisted, gripping her hand tightly. 'We can go somewhere else. Start fresh. Birmingham, Manchester, fuck it – Scotland if we have to. Anywhere but here.'

Hope flickered in Sin's eyes, fragile and tentative. 'Just up and leave? Everything? Everyone?'

'What's keeping us here except fear?' His hand tightened on hers. 'We deserve a shot at happiness, Sin. Our baby deserves better than growing up in the shadow of your father's world.'

Sin stared at him, conflict written across her face. 'You'd leave it all behind? Jimmy? Gertie?'

Pain flashed in his eyes. 'It would kill me to leave Gertie. But she'd understand. She's always wanted what's best for me.' He swallowed hard. 'And Jimmy… he's been my brother in everything but blood, but I can't choose him over you. Not anymore.'

Sin's eyes welled with fresh tears. 'I never wanted to come between you.'

'You didn't. This world did. The rules we never made but have to live by.' His jaw set with determination. 'But we don't have to play by those rules anymore.'

Brother Bertie glanced at his watch, and his expression shifted. 'Shit.'

'What is it?'

He hesitated, conflict etched in the lines of his face. 'I'm supposed to meet Jimmy. There's this job—'

Sin's fingers tightened around his. 'What kind of job?'

His answer was to thoroughly kiss her. 'I love you, Sin Steele. You and our baby. Don't you ever doubt that again.'

'Just come back to us,' she whispered against his lips. 'Promise me.'

'Wild horses couldn't keep me away.' Brother Bertie reluctantly pulled back, starting the engine. 'Go straight to Kath's. Don't stop anywhere else.'

Sin nodded, reaching for the door handle.

'Sin,' he called as she stepped out. When she turned back, he took one last look at her – tearstained and beautiful, carrying his child – and burned the image into his memory. 'Everything changes today. For the better.'

He checked the time.

If he didn't reach Jimmy the whole bloody bank job was fucked.

# Chapter Thirty-Three

'Everyone on the fucking floor! Faces down! NOW!'

Jimmy crashed through the double doors. His command exploded through the bank. Adrenaline surged through his veins, electric and raw.

Brother Bertie burst in beside him. Coal-black stockings stretched taut across their features transformed them into nightmare visions of bulging eyes, distorted nostrils, mouths twisted into permanent snarls. Through the mesh, only the glint of their determined eyes showed. Jimmy's fitted navy peacoat couldn't disguise his boxer's build, but that hardly mattered now.

*This is it.*

Women screamed. A man in a pinstripe suit dropped his briefcase in shock, his face draining white. Jimmy spotted the security guard's hand creeping beneath his desk…

Fuck! The alarm!

Before Jimmy could move, Brother Bertie was there in three fluid strides. He pressed the cold metal barrel of his sawn-off hard against the guard's spine.

'Easy now, sunshine,' Brother Bertie warned, his accent thick and menacing, his Jamaican roots disguised. 'Want your missus measuring you for a pine box? Thought not.'

A heavy-set bank manager stumbled backwards, sending a brass-potted fern crashing to the marble floor. The sound triggered another scream, heavy breathing from an elderly customer.

Jimmy's massive frame cast a shadow over the cowering customers.

'Shut your bleeding noise!'

No one dared move.

Sweat darkened the nylon where it clung to his lips. The taste of fabric filled his mouth, cheap and chemical. 'Anyone makes another sound gets a face full of buckshot!'

He gripped the shotgun, knuckles bone-white against the metal. The terrified pregnant woman cowering in the corner made his gut twist, her hands protectively cradling her belly. Jimmy swallowed hard behind his mask. The thrill had already soured.

He vowed there and then that this would be the last armed robbery he ever did. There were other ways of making money and building an empire in the gangland underworld.

But first he had to get this one finished.

Chrissie dropped to her knees with practiced perfection, her heartbeat kicking harder and harder. The thrill surged through her veins hotter than any drug. The danger was real now, not just planning. Her red-tipped fingers splayed against the cold marble. She stole a glance at Teddy, trembling by the manager's office. His wire-rimmed glasses slid down his nose. Thinning hair plastered to his forehead.

Jimmy stalked towards Chrissie. She steeled herself for what was coming. The stocking transformed Jimmy's face into something barely human.

'You.' He jabbed the shotgun in Chrissie's direction. 'Up.'

She played her part to perfection. Eyes wide, hands visibly shaking, rising on unsteady legs. Terror bled through every trembling syllable. 'Please, I've got children waiting at home—'

The crack of his hand against her cheek echoed through the bank. Not a gentle stage slap. She'd told him it had to be real. Her head snapped sideways, the force sending her staggering. Chrissie clutched her face, tasting blood where her teeth had caught the inside of her cheek. The sting was real, the performance flawless.

Everyone in that bank witnessed it. Every copper who interview them later would hear about the brutal bastard who'd walloped a defenceless woman.

'Did I ask for your fucking life story?' The threat slithered between his teeth. 'Now for the money.'

Brother Bertie herded three security guards into a supply cupboard, his movements economical and practiced. A telephone lay ripped from the wall, wires dangling uselessly.

He set the shotgun down within easy reach, worked fast to bind the guards' wrists with rough hemp rope, then snatched the shooter up again. The whole process took less than a minute.

'Nobody tries to be a hero, nobody gets carried out in a wooden box,' he announced to the prone customers. 'This is a simple business transaction.'

He vaulted over the teller counters, canvas bags in hand. 'Fill it to the top, darling,' he instructed the first teller. 'Notes only.'

Her hands moved fast, stuffing bundles of crisp notes into the bag. Every teller surrendered their money.

Jimmy's fingers dug into Chrissie's arm with bruising force, the cold steel of the shotgun pressed against her temple.

'Where's the vault?' he demanded, spittle flying through the stocking mask.

Teddy's eyes darted between Jimmy and Chrissie, genuine terror mingling with their rehearsed plan. She gave him the slightest nod, maintaining her terrified facade even as power surged through her. Even now, with a gun to her head, she was pulling the strings.

'D-downstairs,' Teddy stammered 'I can… I can take you there.'

'Too right you will,' Jimmy growled, shoving him hard enough to send him stumbling into a desk. 'And she's coming with us. Insurance policy.' He looked over his shoulder at Brother Bertie. 'Keep this lot quiet.'

Brother Bertie nodded, prowling the perimeter of the room, his shotgun sweeping across the prone bodies.

Jimmy forced them towards the stairs. Chrissie caught the gleam of sweat on Teddy's neck, a droplet running down to darken his starched collar. She kept her head down, shoulders hunched, the picture of a terrified hostage. Her cheek throbbed where Jimmy had struck her, but the pain was nothing compared to the savage excitement building within her.

Teddy led them down narrow spiral stairs of worn marble, each footfall echoing. Iron railings, painted institutional green decades ago, guided their descent into the bank's bowels. Naked lightbulbs in wire cages cast harsh shadows.

'Move faster.' Jimmy gave Chrissie a theatrical shove that sent her careening into Teddy's back.

The banker steadied himself against the cold stone wall. Rapid, shallow breaths misted in the cool air. 'Almost there.'

At the bottom stood a heavy metal door with a combination dial. Teddy's fingers trembled. He approached the combination dial, fumbling with the sequence. Once, twice, three times he failed to align the numbers properly.

'Bloody hell,' Jimmy hissed, prodding the shotgun harder into Chrissie's spine. 'Sort it out or I'll blow her fucking head off.'

He wiped his palms on his trousers and tried again. This time, the tumblers clicked into place. He grasped the large steel wheel and turned it with visible effort. Muscles strained beneath his tailored suit.

The door swung open with a deep, pressurised hiss, revealing the Anglo-Merchant Bank's inner sanctum.

The vault room was a monument to Victorian engineering with walls lined with thick steel plates, rivets the size of fifty-pence pieces studding the seams. The ceiling arched overhead, supported by decorative iron columns. Hundreds of deposit boxes lined the walls, each with its own brass plate and keyhole. A massive free-standing safe commanded the centre of the room.

'Lock the door,' Jimmy ordered. The command bounced off steel walls, amplified by the vault's acoustics.

Teddy pushed the heavy door closed, the mechanism engaging with metallic clanks.

'Box 718,' Jimmy demanded. 'Now.'

Chrissie and Teddy sent each other an urgent glance of confusion. In fact, Teddy's face had lost its colour. This wasn't part of their plan. Suddenly, Chrissie didn't feel in control anymore.

'718?' Teddy swallowed hard. 'It's… it's on the upper tier.'

He pointed to the far wall, where the highest boxes gleamed dully. The numbers etched in their brass plates barely visible from the floor.

Jimmy dragged Chrissie along, keeping her pinned against his side.

'Get it open,' Jimmy demanded. He shoved Teddy towards a rolling ladder attached to tracks along the wall.

Teddy positioned the ladder and climbed unsteadily. Keys jangled in his sweaty palm. The ancient ladder creaked ominously under his weight.

'Hurry the fuck up,' Jimmy barked, his trigger finger twitching.

'The master key doesn't work on these,' Teddy called down, his words quavering. 'We need the customer's key, too, or—'

'Pick it,' Jimmy cut him off. 'There's a set of picks in my inside pocket.'

His free hand dipped inside his pocket and he tossed a slim case up to Teddy who surprisingly caught it with one hand. A great catch for a man who was so nervous. Chrissie frowned.

'You know how to use those?' Disbelief dripped from every syllable.

'I-I've seen it done,' Teddy stammered. He unrolled the case to reveal slender metal tools. His hands shook violently.

'Two minutes,' Jimmy warned. 'Then I start shooting fingers off her hand.'

Teddy's hands shook so badly he dropped the first pick. It clattered to the marble floor, the sound amplified by the vault's acoustics. He selected another. His movements were clumsy, unpractised. Metal scraped against metal.

Chrissie counted the seconds silently, weighing her options. Whatever game Jimmy was playing hadn't been part of their arrangement.

Was this Danny's doing? Her fucking double-crossing brother? Then she allowed herself a small smile. He wasn't the only one with a surprise up his sleeve for the heist…

After an agonising minute of scraping metal and muttered curses, the lock finally surrendered with a soft click. Teddy slid the long drawer from the wall and peered inside.

His expression shifted from fear to confusion. 'It's… it's empty.'

Jimmy's grip on Chrissie's arm tightened painfully. 'What?' The word came out strangled, disbelieving.

'There's nothing here,' Teddy hesitantly insisted, tilting the metal drawer to show them. Not even dust lined its bottom.

Jimmy's breathing accelerated, rage rolling off him in waves. He shoved Chrissie aside and took two menacing steps towards the ladder. 'Check again.'

Teddy ran trembling fingers along the interior of the box. 'I swear, there's nothing—'

'GET DOWN HERE!' Jimmy roared, aiming the shotgun upwards.

Teddy scrambled down, nearly falling in his haste. Blood rushed to his face. 'Someone must have emptied it already.'

And that's when everything started going wrong.

A dull thump from above shook dust from the ceiling. Then another. Then the unmistakable sound of shouting, muffled but urgent.

Jimmy's head snapped upwards. 'What the fuck?'

Another booming sound – a shotgun blast – followed by screams.

'Shit!' Jimmy spun towards the vault door, momentarily forgetting his rage. 'Something's happening upstairs.'

He stormed to the door, spinning the wheel to unlock it. Turning back to them, shotgun levelled, he said, 'Don't fucking move. Either of you.'

Then he was gone, taking the stairs two at a time, racing towards the chaos that had erupted on the main floor.

# Chapter Thirty-Four

No fucking way. Jimmy's disbelieving mind railed.

Three hulking shadows in stocking masks stood with sawn-offs levelled across the marble counter. Another fucking crew had muscled in on his bank. Behind splintered desks, Brother Bertie crouched with his shotgun raised, bulging canvas bags scattered at his feet.

The scene held deadly still. Five trigger fingers twitching. Five hearts thundering. Death hanging by a thread.

Jimmy stepped forward, molten rage almost suffocating him. Some other crew muscling in on his territory? His job? The fucking audacity burned through him.

'Who the fuck do you think you are?' Jimmy's outraged growl echoed against the marble like a gunshot.

The leader of the rival gang swivelled, twelve-gauge aimed at Jimmy's gut. 'That's my fucking question,' he snarled back, voice muffled but carrying a guttural rasp that scraped across Jimmy's memory.

Recognition slammed into him, a heavyweight's punch.

That voice. That stance. His despised father-in-law himself.

His dad's archenemy.

Batters Rogers.

The bastard seemed to register it, too, his body stiffening beneath the dark overalls. 'You?' The word dripped venom. 'What in Christ's name are you doing in my bank?'

'Your bank?' Jimmy's laugh came out harsh and brutal. 'You've lost your fucking mind, old man. This job's been set for weeks.' His voice lowered for their ears alone. 'A Steele score.'

Batters yanked his stocking mask higher, revealing a mouth twisted with hate. His face flushed violent crimson, veins bulging like they might burst. 'Fucking bollocks! We've been working this over for months. Your daddy send you to sabotage me, did he?'

The mention of his father sent Jimmy's blood pressure rocketing. 'Keep him out of this. This ain't his play.'

Brother Bertie edged sideways, weapon never wavering, and whispered, 'Something rotten as week-old fish happening here.'

Jimmy's gaze flicked to the giant beside Batters – Lucas, unmistakable even beneath the mask. Mini's brother. The gentle giant who'd whispered sweet words about his sister years ago. Now pointing a shooter at Jimmy's chest.

'Fuck. Off.' Jimmy snarled. 'Find another bank to knock over.'

Batters scoffed. 'Three of us, two of you. My boys eat little shits like yours for brekkie. So why don't you crawl back to Daddy and tell him his scheme fucked up proper?'

Brother Bertie hissed, 'We been played, bruv. Set up like bowling pins.'

The brutal truth hit Jimmy that someone had orchestrated this collision. But who had the reach – and the brass bollocks – to play them both?

Batters jabbed his shotgun forward. 'Tell your mate to drop his hardware first.'

'Not in this fucking lifetime.' Jimmy's finger found the trigger.

Sweet Christ, how easy it would be. One squeeze and Batters' brains would paint the marble red. After everything that bastard had done to Mini. Disowning her, turning his back when she needed family most, treating her like she was dead. The old cunt deserved it.

*Do it,* his mind screamed. *End this piece of shit right here.*

Jimmy's finger tightened. The trigger began its deadly travel.

*One pull. That's all it takes.*

Slicing through the deadly silence, police sirens wailed in the distance.

Naked panic flashed across Batters' face. 'You brought the fucking filth?'

'Don't be thick,' Jimmy spat, reluctantly easing pressure on the trigger. 'Why would I call coppers on my own job?'

The sirens multiplied, growing louder, closer. Blue death racing towards them.

Brother Bertie's eyes flickered towards their bags of cash. 'Jimmy! We need to move! Now!'

Lucas snarled behind his mask, 'We gotta scarper, Dad. This is fucked six ways from Sunday.'

For five excruciating heartbeats, nobody moved. The banking hall became a pressure cooker, hatred and greed and fear building to explosion point.

The sirens screamed closer, mere streets away.

'Time to go!' Jimmy roared at Brother Bertie.

Batters' crew bolted towards the main entrance, heavy boots pounding marble. Brother Bertie hurled a bulging canvas bag towards Jimmy, who caught it one-handed without breaking eye contact with his father-in-law.

'This ain't finished,' Batters promised, backing towards the door. 'Not by fucking miles.'

'Take that to the bank,' Jimmy whispered, voice dropping to a killer's promise.

As Jimmy hefted the bag's weight – Christ, it was heavy with stolen cash – and grabbed another from the floor, his mind raced. Two bags loaded with money, Brother Bertie armed and ready, but how the fuck were they getting out of here?

The sirens grew deafening. Seconds away.

# Chapter Thirty-Five

'This way!' Brother Bertie grabbed Jimmy's arm, urgent beneath his stocking mask. 'Gents' toilet! Maintenance access!'

The money bags thumped heavy against their legs as they bolted across the marble floor, shoes skidding on blood and broken glass. Behind them, chaos erupted; someone had triggered the alarm, its banshee wail cutting through the air with scalding intensity.

They burst through the door marked 'Gentlemen'. The pristine porcelain and polished brass fixtures stood in surreal contrast to their sweat-streaked, stocking-masked faces. Jimmy slammed the bolt home, buying precious seconds.

Both men yanked off their stocking masks… and breathed.

'Here!' Brother Bertie shoved aside a wooden panel behind the last stall, revealing a maintenance shaft plunging straight down into blackness. 'This is it, the access I told you and Danny about.'

Jimmy remembered Bertie mentioning that Central Line trains ran beneath the building. 'You sure this leads to the Tube?'

'Fuck no.' Brother Bertie swung his legs over the edge. 'Pray to the good Lord it's the Underground and not some forgotten sewer.'

Brother Bertie lowered himself first, feet finding rungs hammered into the shaft wall. His bag scraped against the narrow walls, shotgun clattering. The shaft dropped straight down, blacker than hell.

Jimmy followed. Cold air rushed up from the depths, carrying the stench of decay and electricity. Were those train sounds or just water through ancient pipes?

Twenty feet down, Brother Bertie's boot slipped on a wet rung. He swung out, suspended by one hand, legs kicking at empty air. The money bag nearly dragged him into the abyss.

'Blood fire!' His desperate grunt echoed in the shaft.

Jimmy lunged down, grabbing Brother Bertie's wrist just as his grip failed. 'Got you, bruv!'

For terrifying seconds, Jimmy supported both their weights plus the cash. His shoulder joint screamed in protest. Brother Bertie's boots scrambled for purchase against the slick walls.

'There!' Brother Bertie found the rungs again. 'Thought I was brown bread.'

They descended deeper. Thirty feet. Forty. The shaft walls wept with condensation. Jimmy's bag caught on a protruding bolt, nearly yanking him backwards into the void.

A distant rumble shook the walls. Train or police? Jimmy's throat went dry.

Then – blessed relief. The shaft opened onto a narrow ledge. Beyond it, the familiar curved tiles of an Underground tunnel. Train tracks gleamed dully in the distance.

'Central Line!' Brother Bertie's grin split his face. 'We fucking made it!'

They emerged onto the service walkway. The tunnel stretched in both directions, disappearing into darkness. The third rail hummed with lethal electricity.

'Which way?' Jimmy hefted his bag, muscles bunching and protesting.

'Bank junction's east.' Brother Bertie pointed right. 'Rita's waiting two streets up.'

They walked the narrow ledge, trying not to look at the live rail. One slip meant instant death. The tunnel amplified every sound, their breathing, their footsteps, the distant rumble of approaching trains.

A maintenance ladder led up to street level. They climbed in silence, bags weighing heavier with each rung. Emergency exit markings pointed the way to salvation.

The heavy iron grate at the top resisted Brother Bertie's shoulder. Rust flakes rained down. Jimmy braced beneath him, taking the weight.

'Now!' Jimmy grunted.

Brother Bertie heaved. The grate shrieked open. Hauling themselves into a narrow alley behind a row of shops, daylight blinded them.

'Where the hell are we?' Jimmy stripped off his mask, stuffing it deep in his bag.

Brother Bertie checked the street signs. 'Rita should be two streets over.'

They walked fast but didn't run. Running drew eyes.

The gleaming burgundy Jaguar idled exactly where promised, engine ticking impatiently. Jimmy rapped twice on the passenger window, relief flooding through him.

The glass slid down, revealing Rita behind the wheel.

'You're late,' she snapped, every syllable cutting. 'Get in. Now.'

Jimmy yanked open the rear door, shoving Brother Bertie inside before diving in himself. No time for pleasantries. Sirens wailed in the distance, growing closer.

'Drive! Bloody drive!' Jimmy barked, already reaching for the suit bags Rita had prepared.

Rita shifted into traffic, her movements precise and controlled. She glanced in the rearview, those hawk-sharp eyes missing nothing. 'Change of clothes in the bags beside you. Move fast.'

In the confined space, they stripped with desperate efficiency. Rita had thought of everything – pinstripe suits, crisp shirts, gold cufflinks, expensive ties. Jimmy threw on the jacket, amazed at the perfect fit.

Brother Bertie struggled into his suit, cursing at his elbow hitting the window. The transformation was remarkable. Two bank robbers becoming City gentlemen in minutes.

'Shooters and overalls in the canvas bags.' Rita navigated through the warren of streets. Police sirens faded and swelled around them. 'We get stopped, you're international businessmen. I'm your… escort. Use the handkerchiefs in your breast pockets to wipe all that nasty sweat off your faces.'

Jimmy dabbed at his forehead, mind racing through what had gone spectacularly wrong. The empty safety deposit box. The other crew. This stank of setup from top to bottom.

Rita's knuckles tightened on the steering wheel. 'Filth ahead.'

A police roadblock materialised at the end of the street, two uniformed officers flagging down vehicles. Rita's face remained carved from marble, but Jimmy caught the almost imperceptible tightening around her eyes. She was good, ice where others had blood, but this was bad.

Banged up for two score prison-sentence bad.

'Act natural.' Jimmy smoothed his hair back with trembling hands.

Brother Bertie looked about ready to jump from the moving car, sweat pouring down his broad face in rivers.

Rita's head whipped around, eyes flashing lethal. 'Don't you tell me what to do, Southpaw. I was handling sticky situations when you were still pissing your nappies.'

The Jag rolled to a gentle stop. A fresh-faced copper leaned down to the driver's window, notebook in hand, eyes scanning the vehicle's occupants.

Then recognition flashed across his boyish features. 'Miss… Lawless?'

Rita's entire being shifted in an instant. A seductive smile spread across her face, eyes suddenly warm as brandy. 'Why, Officer Jenkins. Fancy seeing you here.' Her tone dripped honey and forbidden promises.

The copper's face flushed crimson from collar to hairline. His partner, older, paunchy, with suspicious eyes, moved closer and peered inside.

'You know this woman, Jenkins?'

Jenkins shifted uncomfortably. 'She's, ah, an acquaintance. From The Sing-Song Lady. Down at Sugar Cane Wharf.'

Understanding spread across the older police man's face, followed swiftly by a knowing smirk. 'I see.'

Rita leaned further out of the window, her blouse putting her assets on display. 'I'm just taking these international gentlemen for a… lovely London welcome.' She gestured to the back seat where Jimmy and Brother Bertie sat rigidly, attempting to appear every inch the wealthy businessmen despite their thundering pulse rates. 'They've paid very handsomely for my time.'

Jenkins looked ready for the street to swallow him whole. 'The thing is, Miss Lawless, we've had a bank robbery nearby. Two gangs, if you can believe it. We're stopping all vehicles.'

Rita's laugh tinkled, expensive crystal. 'Bank robbers. Officer? Really?' She nodded towards the back seat, then pushed her chest further forward. 'With assets like these?'

Jimmy nearly choked. Brother Bertie coughed violently into his handkerchief.

Jenkins went from red to purple. The older copper snorted, clearly enjoying his partner's discomfort.

Jimmy forced his face into a bored, aristocratic mask, willing Brother Bertie to follow suit. Years of watching his father deal with posh twats finally paid dividends.

The older copper leaned down, eyes narrowing, studying the both of them. 'You gentlemen enjoy your visit to London, then.' He straightened up.

The Jag pulled away from the roadblock. In the rearview mirror, Jimmy watched the officers grow smaller, until they disappeared around a bend.

The tension snapped. Brother Bertie slumped against the leather seat, a half-laugh, half-sob escaping his lips. 'Thought we were nicked.'

'Saint Rita.' Jimmy's admiration coloured his tone genuine. 'Proper miracle worker.'

'Someone played us,' Brother Bertie aired what was on all their minds. 'The question is, who?'

# Chapter Thirty-Six

'It was h-h-horrible,' Chrissie wailed at the police, shaking with manufactured sobs. 'They just burst in with those g-g-guns.'

She was sitting in Teddy's office chair, pressing a trembling hand to her heart, her face blotched and peaky. Her scarlet trouser suit, the one that had turned heads this morning, now sported a tear at the shoulder and a smudge of something that might've been blood but was actually her own cleverly applied lipstick.

Detective Abbot was squat with a tummy that obviously loved a pint or two, while his partner, Detective Long, was exactly that – long and thin with eyes that a would look right at home on a fox.

While Abbot scribbled in his notebook, Long circled the plush office with a vulture's eye. Teddy sat behind his desk, the thick lenses in his glasses making his eyes appear overly large. He backed her up one hundred percent by nodding gravely.

These two coppers were lapping up her account of events, big time. Chrissie had always been a bloody brilliant actress. Every tear, every quiver of her bottom lip calculated for maximum effect. These dim-witted sods couldn't spot real distress if it bit them on their arses and did a bloody tap dance. Well, that was her smug opinion.

'Did you recognise any of the perpetrators, Miss Wilson?' Abbot asked.

'*Armed* perpetrators,' Long corrected, emphasising the word with a theatrical flourish of his bony hand.

Chrissie unleashed a fresh torrent of crocodile tears, her shoulders heaving dramatically. 'They could've killed us all!' Her voice wobbled perfectly on the last word. 'I thought they were going to...' lowering her tone theatrical perfection, she added with horror, 'violate my person.'

Abbot sighed, his patience clearly wearing thin. 'Which brings me back to my question – did you recognise anyone?'

Chrissie stared back at him like he'd landed from Mars. 'They were wearing masks! Horrible, terrifying stocking things!' She touched the angry red mark on her cheek where Jimmy had slapped her. She'd made sure to enhance it with a bit of makeup before the coppers arrived.

'See what one of them did to me! I could've been murdered, right here in my place of work.'

'Did either of you notice anything suspicious before the robbery?' Long queried, his beady eyes darting between them. 'Any unusual customers? Strangers hanging about?'

'Nothing out of the ordinary, Detective,' her lover answered. 'Tuesday mornings are typically quiet.'

Chrissie had to give Teddy his due, his hands clasped together, he appeared as cool as they come. She'd thought he would be a nervous ninny by now and more likely to give the game away. Not so much as a bead of sweat on his forehead or a tremble in those soft hands. If she didn't know what an absolute car crash he really was she'd put money on him having more bottle than most of the hard-faced nutters she'd grown up with on the docks.

Long abruptly speared Chrissie with an intent stare, his brow furrowing into deep trenches, while his eyes narrowed to calculating slits. 'Hold on a minute. Don't I know you from somewhere, Miss Wilson?'

The room went deathly quiet. Chrissie felt Teddy stiffen beside her.

Fan-fucking-tastic.

Einstein is on the case!

She did not need this.

He could recognise her from anywhere. Being a member of the Steele family, the stint she did in Holloway two years back, being a general bloody nuisance known to the police. This was where others would fall apart.

Not Chrissie Steele.

She tilted her chin up, eyes wide with mock innocence. 'Well, Detective, if you frequent Madame Miranda's establishment on Greek Street, you might've seen me there.' She leaned forward conspiratorially, breasts straining against her blouse. 'I do charity work with the working girls. Teaching them to read. Serving soup. Saving souls.'

Batting her eyelashes, she suddenly gasped and whispered, 'Now you talk about recognising someone, you weren't that paying customer who came back last week? In which case, how's that nasty rash? Cleared up, has it?'

Long's face went beetroot-red. Abbot coughed violently to cover a snort of laughter. Teddy's jaw dropped in horror before he caught himself.

That'll teach the nosy git to ask questions. Nothing shuts a man up faster than suggesting his knob's been in places it shouldn't.

'I – that's not – I've never—' Long spluttered, his mouth opening and closing like a fish on a slab.

'Must be mistaken then.' Chrissie sniffed primly, straightening her shoulders. 'I do have one of those forgettable faces.'

Abbot cleared his throat, eager to move the conversation along. 'Well, at least there's some good news for the bank. According to their initial inventory, it appears nothing was taken from the safety deposit boxes. One box was empty, but there was paperwork verifying the contents had been signed out before the robbery. All aboveboard, apparently.'

'Nothing taken?' Chrissie blurted, her performance momentarily forgotten.

*That can't be right.*

Teddy said he'd fleeced some of those boxes as bare as Mother Hubbard's cupboard. Said there were thousands missing that would be discovered during the next audit. The whole bloody point of this circus was to cover his tracks.

After Jimmy had left them in the vault, she and Teddy had opened all the other boxes, tipping some over to give the impression that they'd been rifled through.

'Thank God.' Teddy exhaled heavily, relief washing over his plain features. 'The boxes belong to our high-end clientele. They will be so relieved.'

Chrissie stared at him, fighting to keep the confusion off her face. He seemed genuinely relieved. Not like a man whose plan had gone tits up. Not like a thief who'd been caught with his hand in the till.

After the detectives finally departed, Chrissie rounded on him, with daggers in her eyes.

'Nothing stolen?' she ground out. 'You confessed to me, point-bank, that you'd been pilfering those boxes blind for months!'

Teddy removed his glasses, polishing them on his tie. 'I-I don't understand it either, Chrissie. I swear.' He placed his glasses neatly back onto his face. 'I suspect that the bank has gone into saving reputation mode. If word gets out to their wealthy clients that they've been robbed, those clients will take their business elsewhere. They will replace the money themselves. It's all about maintaining the facade of security.'

Chrissie eyeballed him. 'You better not be playing me for a tit and a git,' she warned.

'I would never lie to you, petal,' he protested, reaching for her hand. 'You know how I feel about you, Chrissie.'

She let him take her hand, but every alarm bell in her head was going mental. Like trying to count cards when someone's nicked half the deck and replaced it with jokers.

# Chapter Thirty-Seven

The three hard bangs on the front door of her house in Molasses Quay went right through Mini. She had been expecting this. Knew exactly who was at her front door.

She took a deep breath, released it, and opened the door with a beaming smile.

Two men in cheap suits stood on her doorstep, radiating the unmistakable stench of Old Bill. Mini had expected the plod to turn up. But just not these two.

Abbot and Long. The two numbnuts coppers who'd tried to shake down Jimmy and Brother Bertie over that stolen Aston Martin two years back. They'd been nursing a grudge ever since, vowing to get payback the first chance they could.

Behind them, two unmarked Fords sat at the kerb, each bulging with plainclothes detectives trying, and failing, to appear inconspicuous.

'Gentlemen, can I help you?' Mini innocently asked, voice sweet as spun sugar, head tilting slightly in rehearsed confusion.

'Did you hear that, Long?' the shorter one said, words dripping with sarcasm. 'She wants to know if she can *help* us.'

The tall one snorted, a malicious expression twisting his face. 'Fancy that. Right helpful all of a sudden, ain't she, Abbot?'

Before she could respond, they barged past her, shoulders deliberately clipping hers. The force nearly sent Mini sprawling against the hallway wall.

'Oi!' she snarled, East End roots flaring through her carefully constructed housewife veneer. 'Who the fuck d'you think you are, barging into my house like that? My kids are here, you rude bastards!'

Abbott smirked. 'Language, Mrs Steele. Not very ladylike.'

Long added, already poking his ferret-like face into her front room, 'Question is, where's that tea-leafing husband of yours?'

Mini stood staunch and strong. 'You've got some nerve. Who the bloody hell do you think you're talking to?'

Abbott flashed a warrant card in her face. 'Detective Inspector Abbott and Detective Sergeant Long, Serious Crimes Unit. And we're here because your old man has been busy today.'

'That right?' Mini folded her arms across her chest, chin jutting defiantly. 'And what's my Jimmy supposed to have done, then?'

Long leaned in, his breath reeking of stale cigarettes and cheap coffee. 'He knocked over the Anglo-Merchant Bank this afternoon. Him and that darkie mate of his.'

Mini's hand flew to her mouth, eyes wide with shock. She'd practiced this expression a thousand times in the mirror. 'Jimmy? Rob a bank? You've got it wrong, Detective. Dead wrong. My husband's been here all day.' She gestured down the hallway. 'Don't believe me? Come and see for yourself.'

She turned on her heel, not waiting for a response, and marched towards the dining room, moving with righteous rage. Behind her, the detectives exchanged glances laden with suspicion, but they followed.

With a fuck-you flourish, Mini pushed open the dining room door, revealing a scene straight from a *Woman's Weekly* magazine. The long table groaned under a proper spread of the Fray Bentos steak and kidney pie everyone was raving about, accompanied by Yorkshire puddings, chips, veg, and gravy.

And around the table sat the Steele family in all their glory.

Jimmy at the head, with his father and mother to the side of him. On the other side was Sin and Brother Bertie. Danny Steele himself, knife and fork in hand, halfway through cutting a slice of beef. The children, Violet, Robbie, and little Harry completed the picture of harmonious domesticity.

'We've got visitors,' Mini announced, as if she were introducing the vicar for Sunday tea.

Every head turned, performances clicking into place with practiced ease. Only Harry continued smashing peas with his spoon, oblivious to the drama unfolding.

Jimmy stood, brows fiercely pleating together. 'What's the meaning of this interruption? We're having a family dinner.'

'When did you get here?' Abbott stalked closer to Jimmy.

Iris answered before her son could speak. 'They've been here since this morning, Detective. Helped me prepare the vegetables.' She took a delicate sip of gin. 'Jimmy was particularly helpful with the potatoes. Always had a knack for peeling them since he was a boy.'

'That right?' Long prowled around the table like a starving alley cat. 'Funny, because we've got witnesses placing two men of your descriptions at the Anglo-Merchant Bank this afternoon. During a rather nasty armed robbery.'

'Must be my handsome mug,' Jimmy replied, sitting himself back down and vigorously cutting into his Yorkshire pudding. 'Gets mistaken for all sorts of villains.'

'And I do have a rather distinctive hat,' Brother Bertie added, grinning. 'I'm assuming one of your witnesses described a black man wearing a hat?' Catching the flash of consternation that passed between the cops, he raised a brow. 'Because, you can ask far and wide, I am never seen outside my home without my hat.'

Violet stared up from her plate, eyes wide with curiosity.

'Mummy, what's a robbery?'

Danny's booming laugh cut through the tension. 'Nothing you need worry about, princess. These gentlemen are just confused, that's all.' He locked eyes with Abbott, the genial grandfather mask slipping just enough to reveal the hardened gangster beneath. 'Aren't you, Detective?'

Long started towards the sideboard. 'So you won't mind if we search the premises?'

'Actually, I do mind.' Mini stepped forward, playing the outraged housewife to the hilt. 'You got a warrant?'

'Don't need one when we're in hot pursuit.' Abbott grinned nastily.

'Hot pursuit?' Jimmy raised an eyebrow. 'Of what? The last brussels sprout?' He speared one and popped it in his mouth for emphasis.

After sending Jimmy a dirty look, Long told his partner, 'Get the men in here. Turn this place upside down.'

For going on half an hour, the police tore through the house with the intent of terriers after rats.

'Get on and eat,' Danny instructed the family. 'There's nothing to see here.'

Jimmy and Brother Berrie had been careful. The stolen money was stashed at Rita's place, the shooters were long gone. The stolen clothes burned to ash.

But one slip was all it would take…

The detectives returned, faces twisted with furious frustration. The fucked off expression that passed between them spoke volumes. They knew they'd been outplayed but couldn't prove it.

Gloating, Danny slowly raised his glass. 'If you've finished trampling mud through my son's house, perhaps you'd like to leave us to our precious family time?'

Abbott snarled, 'The next time—'

'The next time what?' Danny cut in with deceptive ease. 'The next time your ticker gives out during a raid? How many of those little white pills you got stashed in your inside pocket right now, Abbott?'

Abbott froze, his hand unconsciously moving towards his chest before he caught himself.

'That's right,' Danny smirked for all he was worth. 'Heard you collapsed at that warehouse bust in Hackney last month. Sergeant Willis had to radio for an ambulance while you was gasping on the floor like a landed fish.' He took a leisurely sip of whisky. 'Heart condition, ain't it? The kind that gets a copper stuck behind a desk pushing papers till retirement.'

Long urgently glanced at his partner, confusion etched across his face. 'Abbott?'

'Pure fiction,' Abbott muttered, but the sheen of sweat on his forehead told a different story.

'Your governor, Commander Hawthorne's real strict about physical fitness these days, I hear,' Danny mused, examining his glass. 'Be a right shame if someone grassed you up to the governor about your dodger ticker. Thirty-eight's awful young for a medical discharge, but better than dropping dead chasing villains, eh?'

Abbott's jaw clenched so tight it looked like it might shatter. 'We're leaving.'

'Smart lad.' Danny nodded approvingly. 'Do take care of yourself. All that stress… can't be good for a dicky heart. Mind your step on the way out.'

Long's radio crackled to life. While he listened intently to the voice on the other end, his body suddenly sprang back into life, a dog catching a scent.

'That right?' Long spoke into the radio. 'You're sure? Good.'

Conversation over, he turned back to the table, a slow, cruel smile spreading across his thin lips. He marched over to Brother Bertie. 'You're nicked, son.'

All hell broke loose.

# Chapter Thirty-Eight

The hefty London telephone directory slammed full force into Brother Bertie's kidneys with a dull thud, Detective Abbott's meaty fist driving the impact through five hundred pages of business listings. Fire erupted through his core, a white-hot explosion that stole the oxygen from his lungs and sent black spots dancing across his vision. His teeth clamped down so hard he tasted blood from his bitten cheek. Every muscle in his body contracted at once, his spine arching involuntarily against the metal chair. Not a mark would show. Not a bruise would form. Just pure, clean agony.

'Let's try this again, shall we?' Abbott growled, his bulbous face inches from Brother Bertie's. Spittle flew from his lips, landing on Brother Bertie's cheek. 'What were you doing at Anglo-Merchant Bank yesterday afternoon? Your fingerprints were found at the scene.'

The cramped interview room at Rosewater Police Station reeked of stale sweat and decades of fear. The walls had heard all manner of confessions – real and invented. Local whispers called it 'The Butcher Shop', though the only meat tenderised here was human. This particular station had earned a notorious reputation for suspects who mysteriously 'fell down the stairs' or 'walked into doors'. The pretty name – Rosewater – couldn't disguise the corruption that festered within its walls.

Brother Bertie straightened in the hard metal chair, lungs struggling to remember their purpose. His stomach muscles spasmed, his kidneys throbbed like they'd been set alight. Sweat drenched his shirt despite the room's chill.

'Like I told you,' he managed through gritted teeth, 'paying in money to my sister's account… two months back. Used the gents while I was there.'

Detective Sergeant Long circled behind, the Yellow Pages held between his skeletal fingers, ready for his turn. 'Funny thing about that,' he hissed, breath hot on Brother Bertie's ear. 'Your fingerprints turned up on the maintenance hatch in the gents' toilet. Right where someone cut the alarm wires.'

'I told you, I used the facilities when—'

The second blow caught him mid-sentence, Long's knuckles driving through the directory into his shoulder blade. Brother Bertie's world exploded into fragments of agony. His throat closed around a scream that never emerged. Every nerve ending between his shoulder and fingertips ignited, as if someone had replaced his blood with petrol and struck a match. His handcuffed hands jerked involuntarily, metal cutting into his wrists.

Abbott planted his palms on the table, leaning his considerable weight forward. 'Nobody's coming to save you. Not your friends, not those Steele criminals. Nobody.'

'Search the security cameras,' Brother Bertie insisted, each word battling the waves of pain washing through him. 'You'll see I was there on behalf of my sister, who has an account there. Turns out I wasn't feeling well, so I paid a visit to the gents and then left.'

In his head, Brother Bertie reflected on how the shameful act of trying to steal from his sister might now save his skin. Life had strange ways of evening the score.

'Lying piece of shit,' Abbott snarled, nodding to Long.

This time they positioned the phone book against his ribcage. The impact drove his body back with force into the chair. The pain radiated through his chest, transforming his lungs into burning sacks that refused to fill. His diaphragm seized, caught in a vice of agony. Every shallow breath sent fresh lightning bolts of pain through his torso. Sweat poured from his forehead, dripping into his eyes and down his neck. He fought to remain conscious; grey shadows crept in from the edges of his vision.

'No bruises,' Long taunted, tapping the directory on Brother Bertie's chest. Each light tap reawakened the screaming tissue beneath. 'No marks. Just your word against two decorated officers of the law. Who do you think they'll believe?'

Trying to straighten up, a spasm of pain rippled through Brother Bertie's torso. Muscle and bone protested the movement. 'I've told you the truth,' he wheezed, tasting copper with each laboured breath.

Abbott's piggy eyes narrowed. 'You know what happens to little girls when their daddies go to prison?' His pudgy lips twisted cruelly. 'Precious, isn't it? Sweet name for a sweet little girl.'

Cold fury flooded Brother Bertie's system, drowning out the pain. His daughter's name in this filthy pig's mouth snapped something inside him. With a thunderous roar that tore from deep in his gut, he lunged forward, his handcuffed wrists limiting his movement but not his rage.

'You fucking leave my daughter out of this!'

Long anticipated the move, slamming Brother Bertie back into the chair with practiced efficiency. Abbott's fist connected with Brother Bertie's stomach – no phone book this time – doubling him over. The impact reignited every injury, creating a symphony of agony that threatened to black him out completely. Brother Bertie's world narrowed to a pinpoint of light surrounded by darkness, his consciousness hanging by a thread.

'Assaulting a police officer,' Abbott crowed with gleeful satisfaction. 'That's another charge to add to your growing list.'

Brother Bertie gasped for air, every breath setting off fresh explosions through his damaged ribcage. 'I won't… sign… anything.'

'Oh, you will,' Long promised, fingers digging into Brother Bertie's shoulder. 'They all do eventually.'

The interrogation room door didn't just open – it blasted off its hinges with the force of a bomb detonation.

The sudden crack of wood against concrete sent both detectives leaping backwards as if electrocuted. The door ricocheted off the wall, revealing a silhouette that seemed to fill the entire frame.

Commander Hawthorne stood frozen in the doorway, statuesque and imperial, radiating a cold fury that dropped the temperature in the room by ten degrees. His iron-grey hair and knife-edge uniform creases seemed carved from marble. The very air around him crackled with authority.

Abbott's ruddy face drained of colour so rapidly he resembled a deflating balloon. Long's skeletal frame went rigid, his throat bobbing with a desperate swallow. Their transformation from predators to prey happened in an instant – cornered animals suddenly facing an apex predator.

The silence stretched to breaking point, tension filling the room like cement hardening around them. No one moved. No one breathed.

When Hawthorne finally spoke, his words sliced through the silence with surgical precision.

'Release him.'

Two words, delivered with such absolute command that they seemed to physically compel obedience.

Long's fingers fumbled with the keys, suddenly clumsy with dread. 'But, sir, this suspect—'

'Was at the bank two months ago, exactly as he claims,' Hawthorne cut in, each syllable another nail in their coffins. 'Security footage verifies his presence and the date. I've just viewed it myself.'

Abbott's mouth worked soundlessly, a fish snatched from water. 'But the fingerprints—' he finally managed, his voice unnaturally high.

'On a maintenance hatch he leaned against while waiting to use the facilities,' Hawthorne finished. His gaze cut to Brother Bertie's restraints. 'Cuffs. Off. Now.'

The detectives knew better than to defy a member of the top brass.

'Out,' Hawthorne commanded once the cuffs were off, his gaze never leaving Brother Bertie.

The detectives slunk from the room, whipped dogs, Abbott's shoulders hunched in defeat, Long's frame vibrating with thwarted rage.

When the door closed, Hawthorne's penetrating gaze bore into Brother Bertie. Recognition flashed between them – the Aston Martin, the dismembered body in the boot, the commander's son-in-law who had beaten his daughter once too often. The mess that

Brother Bertie and Jimmy had helped clean up without questions, without judgment.

'Mr Watson,' Hawthorne said, using Brother Bertie's legal surname. 'You did me a good turn once. I'm merely repaying the favour.' He straightened, his imperial bearing returning. 'We're even now.'

But the top cop wasn't done with him. The older man leaned in close, his breath hot in Brother Bertie's face. 'I need you to deliver a message for me. If you ever cross paths with the animals who did this, you must tell them that the people who work in the bank were terrified, especially the women. And you, of all people, are aware that I detest men who prey on innocent women.'

He drew in his breath, lengthening his neck. 'Tell them that if they do this again, I'll burn through every favour, call in every debt, break any rule. I won't stop until they're buried so deep in Wormwood Scrubs that their own mothers wouldn't know where to lay flowers.' His furious eyes never left Brother Bertie's face. 'You understand me, don't you, Mr Watson?'

Brother Bertie nodded limply.

Lips pursed, Hawthorne stood, straightening his jacket. 'Good. Please collect your hat at reception. This arrest never happened. I was never here.'

# Chapter Thirty-Nine

The front door of Gertie's boarding house creaked despite Brother Bertie's careful efforts. He winced, both from the noise and the stabbing pain in his ribs. The hallway stretched before him, dark and welcoming. Just a few more steps to the staircase, then up to his room where he could collapse and let the agony take him properly.

'Bertram? That you?'

His sister's voice floated from the kitchen at the back of the house, stopping him in his tracks. Brother Bertie closed his eyes briefly. Of course she'd hear him. Even with her injuries, Gertie possessed a sixth sense where he was concerned.

'Just going up, Gertie. Talk tomorrow, yeah?' He tried to keep the pain from his words, failing miserably.

'You come in here right now, Bertram Cornelius Watson.'

Her tone brooked no argument. The same voice that had ordered him to wash his hands for dinner as a boy and scolded him for mud on his school uniform. Some things never changed.

Sighing, Brother Bertie adjusted his pork pie hat and limped towards the kitchen. The warm light spilled into the hallway, carrying with it the comforting smell of roti and chicken curry – a recipe one of her Trinidadian sisters from the church had taught her, that Gertie made when deeply troubled.

She sat at the kitchen table, her solid frame wrapped in a practical floral house dress, a steaming pot of curry cooling beside her. The kitchen was warm and clean as always, pots gleaming on their hooks, wooden table scrubbed to pale perfection.

'Sit down before you fall down,' Gertie instructed, gesturing to the chair across from her.

Brother Bertie eased himself onto a kitchen chair, biting back a groan of protest from his battered body. His sister was recovering well, but it still made him bleed inside to see the effect the attack had on her, like being forced to cook sitting down instead of standing.

Her left arm hung slightly stiff at her side, the cast recently removed but the limb still favouring caution. His throat closed as though a fist squeezed it. Brother

Bertie dropped his gaze to the table, unable to look at what he'd caused.

'Police?' Gertie asked, carefully reaching across the table to place a steaming mug of sweet tea before him.

He noticed how she kept her left arm close to her body, the way someone does when bones are still remembering how to be whole again.

He nodded, wrapping his hands around the mug for warmth. His knuckles were scraped raw from where he'd fought against the handcuffs.

'They use the phone book?' Gertie asked matter-of-factly.

Brother Bertie's head snapped up, momentarily forgetting his guilt. 'How'd you—'

'Sister Mava's boy got the same treatment last year. Not a mark showed, but his insides were mashed like overripe plantain for weeks.' She adjusted herself in her chair, wincing slightly as her left arm protested the movement. 'The robbery at my bank, then?'

The directness of the question cut through him. He couldn't meet her eye, shame burning him from head to toe.

Gertie's face hardened. 'Lord have mercy, Bertram. Armed robbery? With guns? Have you lost your soul entirely?' She studied him, disgust and heartbreak warring in her expression. 'This wouldn't have happened if you'd stayed away from those Steeles and their criminal enterprises.'

His beloved sister, who'd never asked for anything in return except that he live a decent life. Now she was wounded and in pain because of his choices. Sick guilt twisted his gut.

'I'm sorry, Gertie,' he whispered, the words pathetically inadequate. 'What they did to you—'

Gertie cut him dead, her good eye blazing. 'You think I don't know what drove you to that card game? What drove you to gambling away money you didn't have? What nearly made you steal from your own blood?'

The shame burned hotter than his physical pain. Brother Bertie stared into his tea, unable to meet her gaze.

'You still carrying a torch for *that* gal?' Gertie continued, her words edged with steel. 'After everything. After what it cost you. After what it cost me.'

Brother Bertie's throat tightened. Perhaps it was time to tell her the truth about him and Sin, to lay bare the secret that had been eating at him these past days.

'Gertie, I—'

An urgent knocking at the front door cut him off. Three sharp, insistent raps that echoed through the quiet house.

Gertie's good eye narrowed. 'Who comes calling at this hour?'

Before Brother Bertie could rise, his sister pushed back from the table with effort, her chair scraping against the floor. Her footsteps moved towards the hallway, slower than her usual brisk pace but still determined. He heard the front door open, followed by muffled voices – one his sister's, measured but tight with tension, the other higher, urgent, familiar in a way that made his heart stutter.

The voices grew louder, sharper. Not quite an argument, but heading that way.

Brother Bertie stood up, the movement sending fresh waves of pain through his battered body. He'd made it halfway to the hallway when Sin burst through the kitchen doorway.

Her face was pale, her usually perfect hair dishevelled. She saw him and froze for half a heartbeat, relief washing over her features before she launched herself into his arms.

'Thank God,' she gasped, her body trembling in his arms. 'When I heard the police had taken you, I thought…' She clutched at his jacket. 'Jimmy said you'd been released, that you were here.'

Brother Bertie held her close, ignoring the screaming protest from his ribs. Behind Sin, he could see Gertie had returned to the kitchen doorway, one hand resting on the frame for support, her expression a mixture of disappointment and resignation.

His heart clenched, seeing his sister and the woman he loved in the same room, the physical evidence of his divided loyalties laid bare. Sin must have felt the tension radiating from him. She pulled back slightly, becoming conscious of Gertie's presence. Her fingers tightened on Brother Bertie's arms, but she didn't step away.

Brother Bertie felt the weight of the moment. The crossroads he'd been approaching for two years finally reached.

No more hiding.

No more pretending.

He drew Sin closer to his side, one arm around her waist, and stared his sister straight in the eye.

'We're having a baby,' he announced, his voice steadier than he felt. 'And getting married.'

Sin's body stiffened in his hold, her head snapping up sharply, eyes widening in genuine shock to meet his gaze.

'Married?' she whispered, the word carrying equal parts wonder and confusion.

The silence that followed was absolute. Even the old house seemed to hold its breath, the usual creaks and sighs of the timbers falling silent.

Gertie's gaze moved from Brother Bertie to Sin, then back again. Something shifted in her expression, not softening, exactly, but a subtle change, like stone weathering under years of rain.

'I will pray for you,' she said simply, and turned away, leaving them alone in the warm kitchen with nothing but the scent of curry and the weight of things that could never be undone.

***

Marvin Gaye's smooth vocals flowed from Brother Bertie's record player, the needle catching occasionally on a worn groove of 'I Heard It Through the Grapevine.' The soft lamplight cast golden shadows across the small bedroom, hiding the peeling wallpaper and water stains in the corner.

Sin nestled into Brother Bertie's embrace, her head resting in the crook of his arm. His palm spread gently across her still-flat belly, fingertips making small circles on the silk of her blouse. The brutal interrogation at the cop shop felt distant now, the pain in his ribs dulled by her warmth melting into him.

'You feel anything yet?' Brother Bertie murmured, his breath stirring her hair.

'Too early, you daft banana.' Her carefree laughter vibrated through him. 'Ask me again in a few months.' She paused, then lifted her head to level him with an intense stare. 'Did you mean what you said downstairs? About getting married?'

Brother Bertie shifted, wincing at the movement. With careful, deliberate motions, he disentangled himself from Sin and slid off the bed, dropping to one knee beside it despite the protest from his battered body. His eyes, warm and serious, held hers.

'Every word,' he said, taking her hand in his. 'I should've done this proper before now.'

Sin's eyes glistened in the dim light, her free hand moving to cover her mouth.

Brother Bertie glanced around his room, then reached for his bedside drawer. From it, he extracted a small brass curtain ring that had fallen behind the drawer months ago. The tarnished metal caught the lamplight, humble but honest in his palm.

'I know it's not exactly Hatton Garden,' he said, his voice thick with emotion. He held up the simple circle. 'But it's round, it's mine, and right now it's all I've got to give you.'

Sin's laugh bubbled up, bright and tearful at once. 'You absolute madman.'

Holding the makeshift ring between his thumb and forefinger, Brother Bertie gazed up at her, his expression solemn yet radiant. 'Cynthia Steele, will you marry me? Proper and legal, in front of God and whoever else dares to show up?'

Sin's laugh was half-sob, half-wonder. 'Yes, you magnificent fool. Yes.'

He slipped the curtain ring onto her finger. It was slightly too large, but Sin closed her fist tightly around it, as if afraid it might vanish. The tarnished brass seemed to glow in the amber light.

'One day I'll get you proper gold,' Brother Bertie promised and pulled himself back onto the bed, drawing her close again.

'This is perfect,' Sin whispered against his chest. 'It's us.'

For several minutes, they simply held each other, the reality of their commitment settling around them like a blanket.

Finally, Sin's fingers traced the bruises on his face, her expression darkening. 'What are we going to do about Jimmy? And my father?'

The question hung between them, weighted with all the complications of their tangled lives.

'You know we have to tell them,' Brother Bertie said gently. 'And soon. But we'll need to wait until the heat of the bank business cools down,' he promised, pulling her closer. 'Then we tell Jimmy first, together. He deserves that much from me. From both of us.'

Sin nodded, her hand joining his over their unborn child. The record clicked to its end, filling the room with soft static. Neither moved to change it, content in the cocoon of warmth they'd created against the world waiting outside.

His fingers traced lazy patterns along her spine, counting the delicate knobs of vertebrae through the thin fabric of her blouse. Sin's breathing slowed and deepened, her lashes flickering on his neck.

Brother Bertie stared at the ceiling, mapping out invisible futures where they could exist without shadows. Where their child wouldn't carry the weight of crossed lines and old hatreds. Where love might be enough.

For now, with Sin's heartbeat steady pressed to his own, he allowed himself to believe it might be possible.

# Chapter Forty

'He's going to kill you one of these days,' Ruddy told Lady Pru, her features pinched with concern.

Ruddy shifted to face her employer, making the leather seats of the Rolls-Royce creak. Outside the window, Belgravia's grand white stucco townhouses stood tall and pristine, their elegant façades gleaming in the pale winter sun. The exclusive neighbourhood, with its private garden squares and wide, tree-lined streets, remained a bastion of aristocratic wealth even as other parts of London embraced the swinging sixties.

Lady Prudence smoothed an invisible wrinkle from her tweed skirt. 'You're being alarmist, Ruddy. Xander has a temper, I grant you, but—'

'Alarmist?' Ruddy interrupted, her beehive hairdo bouncing as she shook her head vigorously. 'I've seen his kind before. Doesn't matter if they're from the Old Kent Road or bloody Buckingham Palace. Men like him are only interested in getting what they want, and they'll squash anything – or anyone – who gets in their way.'

Prudence opened her mouth to respond, but her words died in her throat. She gasped, pressing her hand against the window. 'Stop the car! Stop immediately!'

Before the chauffeur had fully braked, Prudence had flung open the door. 'There!' she yelled, pointing frantically down the street. 'Look there!'

Ruddy scrambled out after her. A thin elderly woman in a silk dressing gown and bedroom slippers wandered aimlessly in the middle of the road, oblivious to the honking cars swerving around her.

'Not again,' Prudence muttered with dismay.

They rushed forward together. As they drew closer, Ruddy's heart twisted. Lady Eleanor's silver-white hair hung loose around her shoulders instead of in its usual elegant chignon. Her delicate frame trembled violently in the bitter winter air.

'Lady Eleanor!' Prudence called gently. 'It's Pru, your sister by marriage. Xander's wife.'

The elderly woman turned, confusion clouding her once-striking green eyes. 'Is the car here already? I mustn't be late for the ball. The Savoy will be absolutely buzzing tonight.'

'Yes, love, we're here to take you,' Ruddy said, draping her own coat around Eleanor's shoulders. 'Your fingers are frozen solid! How long have you been out here?'

Despite her dishevelled state and confused mind, there remained an undeniable grace about Eleanor. Beneath the hollow cheeks and paper-thin skin, Ruddy glimpsed shadows of the beauty who had once captivated London society.

'My party dress,' Eleanor murmured, plucking at her dressing gown. 'This won't do at all.'

'We'll find you something much nicer at home,' Prudence assured her, gently guiding her towards the waiting Rolls-Royce.

Twenty minutes later, they arrived at Eleanor's Georgian townhouse. Though smaller than many Belgravia residences, the home emanated quiet elegance, with its symmetrical windows and wrought-iron railings. Inside, polished antiques and tasteful artwork reflected a refined sensibility rather than ostentatious wealth.

The part-time housekeeper rushed towards them, relief breaking across her worried face. 'Oh thank heavens! I've been beside myself with worry. I went to check on her after bringing up tea, and she was gone! I called the police—'

'It's all right now,' Prudence reassured her. 'We've found her. Please prepare a warm bath and make some hot tea.'

When the housekeeper hurried off, Prudence turned to Ruddy. 'She's been wandering off more frequently lately. We'll need to keep the doors locked.'

Settled in a wingback chair by the fire, wrapped in blankets with a cup of tea warming her hands, Eleanor appeared marginally better. Ruddy knelt beside her, helping her hold the cup steady.

'Her son is absolutely devoted to her,' Prudence said quietly. 'He visited Xander at the house just the other day. I hate how Xander treats him, like he's nobody. Just because he's not part of the aristocracy.'

'Why does Lord Xander dislike his sister so much?' Ruddy asked, careful to keep her voice down.

Prudence frowned, her brows drawing together. 'I don't know the full story. The only time he answered that question, he said his sister was a disgrace.' Her voice hardened with anger. 'If Eleanor hadn't had a trust that left her this house, I'm certain Xander would have let her and her son live on the street.'

Eleanor's teacup clattered against its saucer. For a moment, startling clarity returned to her eyes as she glanced directly at them both. 'I've got a secret Xander wants no one to know.' Her voice, though frail, carried absolute conviction.

Then, as quickly as it had come, the moment of lucidity vanished. Eleanor's gaze drifted towards the window, her thoughts once again lost in the labyrinth of her failing mind.

Ruddy and Prudence exchanged a worried glance, the weight of Eleanor's words hanging in the silence between them.

***

'You've got it for me then, Danny?' Triumph filled Xander's face, his teeth gleaming in a wolfish grin. 'I knew you wouldn't let me down.'

He was cloaked in the shadows in the exclusive section of the Voodoo Lounge, the low lighting catching the aristocrat's gold cufflinks.

Danny's gut tightened. He'd rehearsed this moment a dozen times on the drive over, but now his throat dried up. The expectant expression on his father's face made everything worse.

Drumming his calloused fingers on the table, Danny cleared his throat. 'There's been a complication.'

Xander's smile vanished. 'What kind of complication?'

'The deposit box was empty.' Danny watched his father's face change, a storm gathering in his eyes. 'Someone got there before us.'

'Empty?'

Danny watched carefully because he'd never seen the old bastard this flustered.

'That's not possible,' Xander incredulously continued.

'Empty as a docker's wallet on payday.'

'You took it.' Xander leaned forward, the action turning his accusation into a verbal spit.

That put Danny's temper on the rise. 'What did you just say?'

'I said,' Xander repeated, 'you took it. Where is it, Danny?'

The rage bubbled up from Danny's chest, hot and volcanic. 'Are you accusing me of stealing from you? The fucking nerve! After everything I've done? Every sodding thing?'

Inside, Danny reeled. Sure, he was a villain, but steal from this man? Never! He wouldn't take a single hair from his head. Why was it his own father expected him to prove himself all the time? He was sick to the back teeth with it.

That crushing sensation of inadequacy came back, the one he had no control over when it came to this man.

Xander laughed, the sound knifing Danny even more. 'You're not exactly a choirboy, are you? If you've taken it—'

'You'll what?' Danny erupted, surging forward, until his face was inches from his father's. Glasses toppled on the table, spilling liquor across the polished wood. 'Tell me what you'll fucking do. I'm all ears, Your Cunty Lordship.'

Snarling, he jabbed a dangerous finger in Xander's astonished face. 'I've torn men apart for less than what you're suggesting. You think because you've got blue blood running through your veins you can talk to me like I'm something you scraped off your fancy shoe?'

Pushing his neck back, Xander ran his palms down his immaculate jacket, brushing away invisible dirt. The cool aristocratic mask slipped back into place.

'Now, Danny, I wasn't accusing you of anything.' Xander's voice shifted back to its smooth, cultured tone. 'Merely exploring all possibilities. Information gathering, that's all.'

His breathing heavy and ragged, hesitating for a moment, Danny retreated.

*Some day one of us is going to have to die because there won't be space for us both anymore.* Danny knew this with a certainty in his bones.

Suddenly, Xander turned a sickly grey. 'That pathetic weasel…'

He stood abruptly, knocking his chair backwards, and turned to leave. Danny's hand shot out, fingers digging into the expensive fabric of his father's sleeve.

'What little weasel? Who you talking about?' Danny's features contorted with fresh anger. 'You been keeping things from me?' His grip tightened. 'Like hedging your bets by sending in another criminal gang to do your bidding?'

Xander's jaw dropped, genuine shock spreading across his features. 'What? Are you completely mad? Another gang?'

The surprise in his father's eyes told Danny everything. Xander wasn't behind Batters showing up at the bank. This was something else entirely.

'What was in that safety deposit box?' Danny demanded, keeping his voice low but deadly serious. 'What's got you rattled enough to make threats against your own son?'

Xander's face remained pale, gaze darting around the club as if searching for invisible enemies. Without answering, he wrenched his arm free and stormed towards the exit, leaving Danny alone with his tumultuous thoughts.

Danny drained his rum, the burn in his throat nothing compared to the fury in his chest. Whatever his father was hiding, it was big enough to make a man who appeared to fear nothing turn white with terror. Gut instinct told him it had everything to do with what was stashed in that safety deposit box.

And he wouldn't rest until he'd uncovered what it was.

# Chapter Forty-One

'So you two want to tell me how fucking Batters Rogers turns up at exactly the same bleedin' bank, same fucking time as us?' Danny's voice was deceptively soft, but he was consumed with fury.

And to top it off, his mood was made fouler by being in the one place he never wanted to be.

The hidden tunnel that led from Jimmy's house in Molasses Quay to the river. Not his son, nor anyone else knew what had happened to him here when he was a kid. The tunnel's musty stench of river water and decay dragged him back to childhood nightmares. A baby screaming. His mother pleading for mercy for her child.

Blocking out the past, Danny peered through the shadowy light from the single battery-operated lamp at his son and Brother Bertie. Jimmy stood big and large in the light, back at the wall, while his friend sat rigid on a crate.

The canvas bags stuffed full of stolen banknotes sat in neat piles not far from where Jimmy stood, a fortune in dirty money that should have been theirs alone. Instead, they'd nearly lost their necks because some crafty sod had played them for mugs.

'Could be coincidence,' Jimmy insisted, sending his dad a penetrating glance.

'Coincidence?' Danny butted in, mouth twisted with naked contempt. He leaned forward, thrusting his scarred face into the light. 'In our game? Don't talk fucking bollocks.'

*Something stinks worse than low tide at Wapping,* Danny decided, his criminal instincts screaming. Thirty years running the docks had given him a nose for treachery, and right now the stench was overwhelming.

Brother Bertie spoke. 'Two rival firms hitting the same target at the exact same time?' He shook his head slowly, his usually animated features grim. 'Danny's right. Someone's playing us off against each other.'

'Question is, who's the crafty cunt pulling the strings?' Danny peered at them hard, his patience, never his strong suit, beginning to fray. 'Either of you tossers running your mouths before the job?' he demanded, his eyes narrowing to dangerous slits. 'Anyone get wind of our plans?'

'What?' Jimmy's head snapped up, the flush of anger darkening his cheeks. 'You calling us grasses?'

Brother Bertie's outrage quickly backed him up. 'In all the years you've known me, Danny, have I ever snitched?

Danny wouldn't leave it alone. 'Bertie, maybe your tongue got loose with one of them fancy birds you knock around with.'

'You what?'

Despite his vehement protests, Bertie made the mistake of tensing his jawline, his gaze shifting away for a split second. If this man only knew he was thinking about how he'd not long made sweet love to his daughter, how she was carrying his baby.

Danny pounced on the change in Brother Bertie's demeanour. 'Pillow talk, was it? Couldn't keep your gob shut when some tart was stroking your ego?' He turned vicious. 'Maybe you thought you'd make yourself look the big man in her eyes, eh? Flash bastard showing off about pulling a proper job. Had to let her know what a tasty piece of work you are, did you?'

Brother Bertie saw red and was on his feet in a second flat. He yanked up his shirt, displaying his washboard stomach covered in bruises. 'I've just taken a pasting from the Bill for us, and this is how I'm treated?' He could barely control himself. 'Not once did I open my trap. I stayed schtum while they battered me every which way to Sunday.'

The tunnel fell silent except for the steady drip of water and Brother Bertie's ragged breathing. The air crackled with barely contained violence.

It was Jimmy who dissolved the situation with, 'Bertie, calm down. Dad never meant anything by it.' He sent his old man a pointed stare. 'Did you?'

He got a grunt back for his troubles, but the tension eased.

Jimmy said, 'We can either stay here tearing each other apart, or do something about it.'

He hauled over one of the money bags and took out three items. Sawn-off shotguns, their shortened barrels promising brutal, up-close carnage.

Danny's face filled with a cold grin. 'And I know exactly where we can get those answers from.'

***

The three men slipped through the maze of narrow cobblestone streets, their footsteps echoing off brick walls slick with river damp. A thick fog had rolled in from the river. Danny moved with the confidence of a man who'd learned these streets when he still had milk teeth, leading them through the labyrinthine passages.

'Watch yourselves now,' Danny growled, the sawn-off shotgun hidden beneath his coat. 'We're crossing the line.'

The acrid smell of coal smoke mingled with the briny stench of the river as they turned down a particularly narrow alley. Rubbish crunched underfoot, rats scurrying into the shadows at their approach. Since the docks closed, Sugar Cane Wharf had become a corpse of its former self. Empty warehouses standing like tombstones, broken windows staring blindly at streets where proud working men once walked with purpose. The heart had been ripped clean out of the community.

They pushed on in silence. The building they were after rose before them, its brickwork blackened by decades of industrial grime.

'Round the back,' Danny quietly ordered, leading them towards a rusted metal door that faced the river. The wind picked up, whistling through the stacked crates and abandoned machinery, carrying the creaking sound of boats straining against their moorings.

Jimmy tested the door handle. Locked tight. No surprise there. He took out the assortment of lock picks he'd forced Teddy Turner to use in the bank's vault and made quick work of the door. The door swung inwards with an ominous creak.

They were in.

Cautiously, they slipped inside, finding themselves in a narrow corridor, the smell of alcohol and cleaning fluids high.

Danny pulled the shotgun from beneath his coat, his hands steady as stone. 'This is it, boys. No turning back.'

They crept forward, the floorboards protested beneath their weight. A single light beckoned from beneath a door at the far end of the room. Next to it was a slim wooden staircase that spiralled down into darkness. The smell of damp earth and mould wafted up from below, along with the faint glow of light.

They went down, slowly, quietly. At the bottom, they found themselves in a cavernous underground room, its vaulted brick ceiling marked with decades of water damage and neglect.

A solitary lamp cast long shadows across the space, illuminating the room's grotesque centrepiece:

A wooden gallows.

A hangman's noose swinging gently from it in an unfelt breeze. The thick rope's shadow danced across the wall, stretching and contracting with the flickering light.

Jimmy froze, cold sweat breaking out across his forehead as memories slammed into him. The last time he'd been here, he'd been forced to his knees beneath that same gallows. The humiliation burned through him afresh, along with the desperate terror he'd felt with that rope hanging above his head.

Brother Bertie scanned the room, muscles tense. 'Where is he? Something don't feel right.'

The desk beneath the gallows was empty, papers scattered across its surface. A half-drunk glass of whisky sat beside an ashtray with a still-smouldering cigar.

'He's been here,' Danny said, his finger brushing the glass. 'Still warm.'

A subtle, sinister click from behind froze them in place.

'Well, well, well,' a gravelly voice announced from the stairway. 'If it isn't the has-been hisself, paying a social call.'

They turned slowly to find the stairs packed with bodies.

Batters stood at the front, a vicious grin splitting his face, flanked by his towering son, Lucas. Behind them, a half-dozen hard-faced bastards aimed guns at Danny and his crew.

'Three rats in my trap.' Batters chuckled, his back gold tooth glinting in the lamplight. 'Must be my lucky day.

# Chapter Forty-Two

The click of half a dozen pistols being cocked echoed off the damp walls. Jimmy held his breath. Batters' men had them surrounded, faces twisted with anticipation, trigger fingers all ready to get happy.

Danny stood deathly still beside him, emotionless and calculating, surveying the situation with merciless eyes. It wasn't the first time he'd had a gun aimed at his heart and, you could bet your life, it wouldn't be the last. Brother Bertie's breath came in controlled, measured pulls beside him.

'Lower your shooters.' Batters' instruction surprised them all. 'Now!'

His men hesitated, confused glances passing between them, the animal hunger for blood still bright in their eyes. A moment stretched into eternity before they reluctantly obeyed, weapons dropping to their sides but fingers still caressing triggers. The underground room beneath the Dockside Devil pub fell into an uneasy silence broken only by the distant gurgle of the Thames against ancient pilings.

Batters stepped forward into the room where he cut his dodgy deals and those who crossed him disappeared. 'Been a long time since you darkened my door, Danny boy.' His words carried old wounds, festering grudges.

Jimmy and Brother Bertie moved warily to the cold-brick, far wall, keeping an alert watch on the armed men. Brother Bertie's fingers twitched along his thigh while Jimmy betrayed nothing, a skill learned from years of observing his father.

They might be dead men before dawn.

Lucas towered beside his father, massive arms folded across his chest, his gaze never leaving the intruders. The rest of Batters' crew formed a loose circle around the room.

But between the two gang leaders, the bitter taste of bad blood contaminated the air. Decades of cutthroat battles, spilled blood, and murderous vengeance crackled between them. Batters and Danny weren't just gangland rivals, they were former friends, brothers-in-arms turned deadliest enemies.

'Whisky?' Batters pulled a bottle from his desk drawer, the amber liquid catching the lamplight. The label was worn but still legible – Macallan, the good stuff, not the watered-down piss served in Soho clubs.

He set out two glasses with deliberate calm, thick-knuckled hands steady despite the tension.

Danny nodded once, his features remaining neutral. 'Why not?'

If word got out about this sit-down, half of London would swear you were talking bollocks. Danny Steele and Eric 'Batters' Rogers in the same room without bullets flying? Not in this life or the next. These two titans had carved their territories into the flesh of East London with blood and brutality, their feud legendary.

Batters poured two generous measures of amber liquid, the bottle neck clinking against glass, breaking the silence. His yellowed eyes never leaving his rival's face, he slid one glass across the desk, the whisky sloshing up the sides.

'Drink up. You never know, it might be your last.'

Danny eased himself into the chair opposite, leather creaking beneath his weight. Every muscle knotted and ready. Jimmy noticed his father's right hand stayed below the table edge – likely resting on the pistol Jimmy knew he carried at all times. Trust had never been their currency.

Danny took the glass without hesitation, knocking it back in one fluid motion. The empty glass hit the desk with a decisive thunk. 'Thought you'd have upgraded to something better by now. Still drinking the same piss you did thirty years ago.'

A muscle twitched in Batters' jaw which twisted into a hard grin. 'Some things don't change.' He knocked back his own drink before refilling both glasses, the bottle hovering longer over Danny's. Old habits, always making sure his enemy's glass was fuller, always watching for the slightest flinch, the smallest sign of weakness.

Reaching into his breast pocket, Batters produced a mahogany cigar case, its corners worn smooth from decades of handling. He selected a dark Havana Montecristo, thick as a man's thumb and smuggled in through the docks like everything else valuable in this part of London. He ran it beneath his nose and inhaled deeply, nostrils flaring with pleasure. The flame from his gold lighter danced across his scarred knuckles as he drew the smoke in, thick and heady. The rich tobacco scent filled the room, the burning ember illuminating the deep lines etched into his face, mapping decades of violence and power.

'Remember that bombed-out watchmaker's on Commercial Road? Winter of '40?' Batters asked, blue smoke curling from his lips, voice momentarily softening with the memory of youth. His eyes took on a distant look, seeing ghosts from another time.

Danny settled deeper into his chair, every movement calculated, his fingers tracing the rim of his glass. The whisky had left a golden sheen on his lips that he didn't bother to wipe away. Two predators circling, neither willing to expose their throats. 'The Blitz. Blackout was a gift to men like us.'

Batters nodded, tapping ash into a heavy crystal ashtray. 'Three watches and a music box.' He chuckled, the sound rusty with disuse. 'Thought we'd struck gold until…'

'Until you triggered the bloody unexploded bomb in the rubble,' Danny finished, his mouth curving into something almost resembling a smile, crow's feet deepening at the corners of his eyes. 'Never seen a man move so fast.'

'Didn't stop you running your mouth the whole way down Cannon Street,' Batters countered, gesturing with his cigar, trailing smoke like memories through the air.

'What was I supposed to do? There we were, two up-and-coming twats from the East End, scrambling across rubble in the dark like frightened schoolboys while the fucking Luftwaffe dropped their load overhead.'

'And you with your trousers torn right up the arse,' Batters added, bracing forward. 'Your lily-white cheeks shining in the moonlight brighter than a bloody air-raid signal.'

A bark of genuine laughter erupted from Danny's throat, deep and thunderous, shaking his broad shoulders. Batters joined in, his guttural howls filling the room, cigar temporarily forgotten between thick fingers.

Jimmy and Brother Bertie exchanged what-the-fuck glances. They'd never heard Danny laugh like this, unguarded, genuine, not his usual manipulative chuckle. Lucas shifted uncomfortably, too, his scowl deepening at the sight of his father sharing anything with their sworn enemy.

'Coldest winter of my life, bollock naked from the waist down.' Danny shook his head, memory momentarily softening his granite features, a ghost of the younger man visible beneath the hard-earned lines. 'The look on that ARP warden's face when we tumbled into his shelter…'

Tears formed at the corners of Batters' eyes, his body shaking with so much laughter, the cigar smoke billowed around his head, a demonic halo.

Abruptly, the guffawing died in Batters' throat, his gaze hardening. ''I never figured out until it was too late that you always wanted what was mine. Always.'

Danny set his glass down with a sharp click, all traces of warmth vanishing from his face. 'Wanted? I call it opportunity. That's business.'

'Business?' Batters' features turned sour. 'Is that what you did to me?'

'Speaking of business.' Danny tilted his head, his stare running icy-cold. 'Funny thing you and your gorillas turning up at the same bank job.'

'Thought that was your doing,' Batters replied, suspicion darkening his expression. He leaned forward. His chair squeaked. 'Setting me up for a fall.'

'Wasn't me.' Danny's voice dropped to a near whisper. Everyone strained to hear. 'Someone knew both our plans. Down to the minute.'

Batters tapped ash from his cigar, eyes narrowing to dangerous slits. The air in the room grew heavier, charged with new tension. 'Who knew about your end?'

'Just Jimmy and Bertie here. My most trusted.' Danny waved towards the pair without looking at them. 'Your side?'

'Lucas. Two others.' Batters drummed thick fingers on the desk, the rhythmic tapping a time bomb counting down. 'No one talks out of school in my firm. I'd have their tongues nailed to my wall.'

'Then we've got a problem.' Danny reached for the bottle, refilled both glasses without asking. The whisky splashed loudly in the tense silence. 'We've been had. Someone played us.'

Both men fell silent, mental gears turning, trying to figure this one out.

'Has to be someone who knows both our operations,' Batters finally said, his voice thick with realisation. 'Someone with connections on both sides.'

The men stared at each other, pieces falling into place. Jimmy watched his father's expression change subtly, until it abruptly darkened, realisation dawning across his features.

The same name formed in both their minds, understanding hitting them simultaneously.

Batters and Danny growled the name together.

'Chrissie.'

# Chapter Forty-Three

Run.

That single word consumed Chrissie's thoughts, her hands shaking while she crammed silk lingerie into the baby-pink Samsonite vanity case. Her fingers fumbled with the delicate fabric, adrenaline making her clumsy. Two gangs would be hunting her soon. Danny's crew and Batters' firm. The most vicious bastards in East London.

The zipper stuck halfway, and she cursed under her breath, yanking at it with desperate fingers. Every sound from the street below made her freeze. Was that footsteps on the stairs? A car door slamming? Her heart pounded so hard she could feel it in her throat.

Time was running out.

Quick as a flash, she snatched up perfume bottles and her slap from the dressing table. Something was properly bent about that empty deposit box. And Teddy's explanation about the other deposit boxes – she didn't believe a word of it.

Chrissie zipped the case shut with one smooth movement, then caught her reflection in the mirror and barely recognised the fear-stricken woman staring back at her.

*Pull yourself together, girl. You've been in tighter corners than this.*

She enveloped herself in a fur jacket while her hair disappeared beneath a Hermès silk scarf, knotted tightly under her chin. The final touch: a pair of oversized Courrèges sunglasses with their distinctive white frames and enormous oval lenses that obscured half her face.

Chrissie yanked open the door, case swinging… and almost tripped over her heels, staggering back at what was waiting for her.

'Going somewhere?'

Danny.

Her brother's voice was cold and unnerving. But it wasn't her brother's presence that made her blood freeze. It was the man standing beside him.

Batters.

The two men who'd spent decades trying to kill each other were now united in the doorway of her flat, wearing identical expressions of deadly calm.

Chrissie's throat went drier than the bottom of an empty gin bottle.

***

Ten minutes later, Chrissie sat with the stiffness of a board on the edge of the plush settee, but the confidence that usually radiated from her was nowhere to be seen. Danny sat opposite, elbows on knees, and for the first time in years, she couldn't read his expression. That scared her more than Batters looming behind her like the angel of death.

'Chrissie love, Chrissie love.' Danny sighed, shaking his head. 'What am I gonna do with you?'

She pursed her lips and flicked her hair. 'I don't know what you're on about. Can't a girl take a little holiday?'

Batters snorted. 'You've been stirring in both our camps. Whispering in my ear, then your brother's. There's only one person who could've put us both in the bank at the same time. You.'

'You've got the wrong end of the stick,' Chrissie protested, a hardness creeping into her tone. 'I admit working with both of you to turn over the bank, but how was I to know you'd both pick the same day to knock it over?'

Danny's fist smashed down on the coffee table, making her jump out of her skin. 'Don't piss on my back and tell me it's raining.'

Chrissie lifted her chin defiantly. 'It was bad luck, is all.'

Danny glared at his half-sister. If it had been anyone else they'd already be six feet under in Epping Forest with their knackers stuffed in their gob.

But this was Chrissie. *His* Chrissie. The wild one. The unpredictable one.

She smugly stared him out, like she had him under her thumb. 'Let's save ourselves a lot of time because you'd never hurt me.'

Danny stood slowly, his eyes dangerously hooded. 'You know what? You're right. I wouldn't hurt you. You're my baby sister.'

Relief flashed across Chrissie's face. 'Exactly. Now can we—'

'But he will.' Danny nodded towards Batters.

Chrissie went white, stricken with outrage. 'You what?'

'You crossed a line this time, girl.' Danny's voice turned ice cold. 'You set me up, your own flesh and blood. So I'm gonna stand there and watch while Batters asks you a few questions.'

'Danny!' Panic shredded her voice. 'Danny, you can't!'

Batters' meaty hand closed around Chrissie's upper arm, yanking her to her feet. The mink coat slipped from her shoulders. He dragged her towards the bathroom, her heels skittering uselessly against the floorboards.

'You think I won't do it, love?' Batters growled, his voice thick with menace. 'I've been waiting to teach you a proper lesson since you did the dirty on me two years ago.'

The bathroom light flickered on. Batters shoved her towards the porcelain sink, one hand holding her in place while he slammed the plug into the drain and cranked the cold tap to full.

Danny casually leaned against the doorframe, arms folded across his chest.

'Get off me, you animal!' Chrissie thrashed to break free from Batters' grip, fingernails clawing at his wrist, leaving bloody marks that he didn't even notice.

'Last chance, darlin'.' Batters' breath was hot in her ear.

'Go fuck yourself sideways,' she spat.

His hand tangled in her platinum hair, forcing her head down towards the rising water. Chrissie fought hard, heels slipping on the tiled floor as she struggled.

'Danny!' she screamed. 'DANNY! Don't let this knob-gobbler touch me!'

Danny did nothing.

Batters pushed her face into the freezing water. The cold punched through her skull, straight to her brain. Water flooded her nose, her mouth, rushing down her throat. Her chest squeezed tight, lungs burning for air that wasn't there. Her heartbeat pounded in her ears, drowning out everything else. She kicked wildly, rising dread overtaking every rational thought.

Just when the darkness started to crowd in, he yanked her head back up. Chrissie gasped desperately, water streaming from her hair, her nose, her mouth. She didn't need a mirror to tell her she was a mess.

'Ready to stop playing the gobby mare and tell us what we want to know?' Batters asked.

Chrissie coughed violently, water spewing from her mouth. 'F-fuck you.'

Down she went again, deeper this time. This time the sensation of drowning was unbearable. The second time he pulled her up, she couldn't even curse him. She just hung in his grip, retching and sobbing.

'Dying ain't pretty, Chrissie,' Danny observed flatly from the doorway. 'Third time under usually does for most. Brain damage starts after about four minutes.' He checked his watch with theatrical care.

'Teddy!' The name tore from her throat like it was ripped out with pliers. 'For crying out loud, it was Teddy! Edward Turner.'

'The banker?' Danny stiffened with tension.

'He's… he's my lover.' Chrissie gasped, hair plastered to her skull, lips blue with cold. 'Got me this flat, bought me things. I just wanted to help him.'

'Load of cobblers,' Batters growled, pushing her head back towards the water. 'Give us the straight goods or I'll hold you under till Christmas.'

'I'm being straight!' Her palm came up. 'Teddy told me he'd been nicking from deposit boxes for months. Said thousands would be found missing at the next audit.'

'So you set us up to take the fall,' Batters snarled. 'Hung us out to dry like yesterday's knickers.'

'It wasn't bloody personal!' She gestured frantically towards the opulent flat. 'Teddy set me up here, didn't he? If I helped him, I could keep the lifestyle. Can't go back to being skint in the East End, can I?'

Eyes narrowing to dangerous slits, Danny stepped closer. 'Since when do you help anyone without getting something proper tasty in return? You'd skin a turd for a farthing if you thought there was profit in it.'

'You expect me to swallow that horseshit?' Batters quickly added.

'I swear on Mum's grave!' Chrissie pleaded, her eyes wild with terror.

He dunked her again without warning. This time the water pressed against her eardrums, filled her mouth, stole what little breath she had. Her body thrashed with primal panic, lungs screaming for air that wasn't coming. The cold penetrated her skull, an ice pick driving straight through her brain. She felt herself slipping away, the edges of everything going soft and black.

When he pulled her up, she vomited water before he'd even asked a question.

'Nothing was stolen from the deposit boxes! Turns out there was no upcoming audit either.' She sobbed, her whole body trembling violently. 'The only thing that was missing was the contents of one box. The lying toerag's been feeding me a load of old cobblers from day one!'

Danny pushed off from the doorframe, suddenly alert. 'Box number 718.'

Chrissie briskly nodded. Batters let her go, and she staggered into the wall, her teeth chattering.

Batters grabbed a towel and tossed it at her. 'Clean yourself up.'

Danny moved to loom over her. 'Where's lover boy live?'

# Chapter Forty-Four

Batters' Merc screeched to a halt outside the elegant Georgian townhouse in Belgravia. Chrissie stumbled from the back seat, her platinum hair still damp, black mascara tracks staining her pale cheeks. Danny and Batters flanked her, prison guards escorting a condemned prisoner.

'This is it,' she rasped, her voice raw from coughing up water. 'Teddy lives here with his mother.' She pointed towards the pristine white facade with its glossy black door. 'Poor woman's dying. Something growing in her brain.'

Danny's eyes narrowed. This was a proper toff's residence, this. The kind of place where East End boys only ever entered through the service entrance.

Through the rain-streaked windows, shadows moved within. A man's voice, sharp with anger, pierced the evening quiet. Then came a woman's sob, a sound so laden with anguish it made Danny's skin prickle.

'Sounds like someone's beaten us to the party,' he muttered, exchanging dark glances with Batters.

Batters didn't waste time with niceties. His boot connected with the front door, wood splintering around the lock with a satisfying crack. The door flew open, revealing an elegant entrance hall with a sweeping staircase.

Following the sounds of confrontation, they thundered up the carpeted stairs to a set of double doors at the corridor's end. Danny shoved them open without hesitation.

Not much shocked Danny, but the scene before him did.

Lord Xander.

What the eternal hell was his father doing here?

The old man stood in the centre of the richly appointed room, his aristocratic face twisted with rage, teeth bared. His manicured hands gripped the collar of a bespectacled man, lifting him half off the floor. In the corner, an elderly woman cowered in a wingback chair, tears streaming down her refined face.

'That's Teddy,' Chrissie confirmed beneath her breath.

Danny thought quick: now why would his father be here roughing up one of the senior members of the bank?

'I've had enough of your interference, boy!' Xander snarled, spittle flying from his lips. 'You think I don't know what you did?'

The intrusion went unnoticed until Chrissie's face contorted with protective fury. Without hesitation, she yanked off her stiletto heel, its four-inch spike glinting under the chandelier light. She launched herself across the room, surprising agility in her battered body.

'Get your filthy hands off him!' The heel connected with Xander's temple with a sickening crack.

He staggered sideways, releasing Teddy. He clutched his bleeding head. When he straightened, his eyes widened with shock, blood trickling down his patrician face.

'Danny?' Recognition dawned in his eyes, quickly followed by calculation. 'What the hell are you doing here?'

Teddy straightened his glasses, his shoulders squaring. The mild-mannered banker vanished, replaced by someone harder, colder, who positioned himself protectively before the weeping elderly woman. His transformation was so complete, it gave even Danny pause.

'Everyone shut their goddamn mouths!' Batters bellow rattled the antique chandelier. 'Someone better start explaining what's going on before I begin breaking things, starting with necks.'

Lord Xander dabbed at his bleeding temple with a monogrammed handkerchief, cold eyes calculating every angle. 'This is family business. Nothing that concerns you lot.'

'Family business?' Danny's voice dropped dangerously, the muscles in his jaw working overtime. 'Since when is Edward Turner family to you?'

A cruel smile twisted Xander's lips, his gaze sweeping contemptuously over the assembled East Enders. 'He's my nephew. My sister's son.' He gestured dismissively towards the woman in the corner. 'Eleanor always did have appalling taste in men.'

The revelation sent a shock wave through the room. Chrissie's mouth fell open, her gaze darting between Teddy and Lord Xander. Teddy stepped forward, his previous meekness stripped away completely.

'Why don't we all sit down?' His polished accent cut through the tension. 'This situation requires clarification.' He clenched his fists, visibly restraining himself from launching at his uncle. 'I need to settle my mother first. She's distressed enough without this circus.'

He approached Lady Eleanor, crouching beside her chair with gentle care. 'It's all right, Mother. These people won't harm you. I promise.' He helped her to her feet with reverence, supporting her frail body. 'Let me take you to your room. You need to rest.'

Guiding her towards a side door, Teddy paused, turning back to face the room. 'Make yourselves comfortable.' His eyes threw daggers at his uncle.

'Perhaps he would be so kind as to explain why he's been hiding my mother's first-born child from her for over thirty years?'

***

'What is it with you and hiding kids?' Danny scoffed at his father. And before the other man could answer he added, 'And let me guess, Teddy, your nephew, was the weasel you referred to during our last meeting.'

Lowering himself into a Chippendale chair, Lord Xander compressed his lips, stubbornly refusing to answer Danny. Batters remained standing, his massive frame blocking the exit, while Chrissie collapsed into a velvet armchair.

Minutes crawled by before Teddy reappeared, his shoulders slumped with exhaustion. The vulnerability vanished the moment his attention fell on Lord Xander, replaced by cold hatred.

'You've terrorised her enough for one day,' he said, voice tight with controlled fury. 'She should be resting, not reliving her nightmares because of you.'

'She brought it on herself,' Xander snapped, wincing at the pain caused by his forceful movement. 'The family name—'

'Shut your mouth before I shut it permanently.' Teddy's sudden vehemence silenced even Lord

Xander. The banker's hands trembled with rage, and he took a seat opposite his uncle. Chrissie looked on in shock at Teddy's toughness. That's when she knew she'd been well and truly had.

'You've been screwing me over from the start, haven't you, Teddy? You poxy wanker.' Her accusation was loud. She whispered to the empty doorway, 'You never stole anything from those boxes, did you? There never was an audit. Of course, you did need me to get two gangs in the bank to create chaos and blame them for what was stolen from box 718.'

Teddy's gaze softened when it landed on her. 'I'm sorry, Chrissie. I needed a cover story that would motivate you.'

Danny's hard stare bore into his father's. 'You better start loosening your tongue about what was inside that box.'

Before Xander could respond, a frail voice came from the doorway. 'The truth. That's what was in that box. The truth.'

Lady Eleanor stood in the entrance, her silver-white hair loose around her shoulders, her nightgown elegant despite its simplicity. In contrast to her frail body, her eyes blazed with sudden clarity.

She moved with painful slowness towards her son, each step deliberate. Teddy rushed to support her, taking her arm to steady her. He guided her towards her chair, his tenderness was palpable. When she reached up to caress his cheek, his eyes closed briefly, and he leaned into her palm with the trust of a child. He kissed the inside of her hand before helping her sit.

'No mother could ask for a better son than my Edward,' Lady Eleanor declared softly, a glow of love transforming her features.

Danny shifted uncomfortably, unused to such naked devotion. A complex knot of emotions twisted in his gut. He'd never known such tenderness from Xander, never would. Batters stared at the carpet, suddenly interested in its pattern. Only Chrissie watched openly, hunger for such unconditional love evident in her eyes.

'Mother, you should be resting,' Teddy protested gently.

Lady Eleanor patted his hand. 'There's precious little time left for rest, my darling.' She turned to face the room, settling a scathing stare on her brother. 'They deserve to know what kind of man you are, Alexander.'

The room waited, held captive by the quiet dignity of this dying woman. Her rheumy eyes seemed to look beyond them, into the past.

'I was twenty-two when the Americans came to England,' she began, her voice gaining strength with each word. 'Everything was changing. The old rules, the rigid hierarchies, they suddenly seemed so pointless with bombs falling on London.' A ghost of a smile touched her lips. 'Thomas was a pilot. So handsome in his uniform. So kind. So different from the stuffed shirts I'd been paraded before.'

Lord Xander made a disgusted noise. Lady Eleanor ignored him.

'When I discovered I was pregnant, I wrote to Thomas. But he was shot down over France.' Old grief surfaced, a sob escaping her. 'My father was already dead. Alexander had become the new Lord Blacklock. Head of the family.'

She turned wounded eyes towards him. 'You said you would help me. Instead, you sent me away to that horrible place for "fallen women". You took my baby the moment she was born. I barely saw her face.' Her composure fractured, tears spilling down her lined cheeks. 'I never knew who adopted her.'

Teddy's arm went protectively around his mother's shoulders, his face a mask of fury aimed at his uncle.

'You brought shame to the family,' Xander hissed, unmoved by her tears. 'A Blacklock breeding with some colonial nobody—'

'You had no right!' Teddy exploded. 'But that wasn't enough for you, was it? You had her committed. Had her locked away in an asylum for "unstable women" when she wouldn't stop asking about her child.'

Danny's face darkened with disgust. The man he'd spent his life trying to please, whose approval he'd craved since childhood, had committed his own sister – his own flesh and blood – for the crime of loving the wrong man. The realisation sank into Danny's bones, cold and horrifying. All those years of desperate loyalty, of doing Xander's dirty work, suddenly felt like chains around his neck. What kind of man could lock away his own sister?

Even Batters, hardened by decades in the criminal underworld, looked sickened. Chrissie shook with righteous indignation, her fingers digging into the armrests.

'You spineless, gutless bastard,' she spat at Lord Xander, half rising from her seat. 'To do that to your baby sister!'

Lady Eleanor raised a trembling hand, quieting the room. 'For years, I thought our middle brother, Rufus, might have the adoption papers. He'd been kind to me, visited me in that dreadful place until Alexander forbade it. But Rufus moved to Jamaica, and we lost touch.' Her gaze drifted to her son. 'When Rufus recently died, Alexander discovered he'd kept the papers in a safe deposit box at the bank. What he didn't realise was that Teddy knew this, too.'

Teddy knelt beside his mother's chair, taking her fragile hands in his. Tears shone in his eyes, no longer hidden behind his glasses. 'All Mother wanted was to know what happened to her child. She's dying…' His voice broke. 'She has a right to know.'

Chrissie launched to her feet, pointing an accusing finger at Teddy. 'So you used me to get two gangs to raid the bank! There's me thinking I'm helping you create chaos so we blame the robbers for taking things from the deposit box. When in fact, you just needed to blame them for taking the stuff in only one box.'

'And Xander,' Danny added grimly, 'wanted me to get the same papers.' He glared at Lord Xander, a lifetime of complicated emotions churning in his gut. 'To keep your dirty secret buried.'

Lady Eleanor's eyes suddenly took on a dreamy, distant quality. 'My baby lives in New York with her husband and two children. She seems happy.' The clarity in her face dimmed, her words becoming slurred. 'My little girl… all grown up…'

Teddy squeezed his mother's hand as she drifted away from them, retreating back into the fog of her illness. He continued where she'd left off, his voice thick with emotion.

'My father was a doctor at the asylum. He realised a terrible injustice had been done to her. He helped her escape, married her, gave her a good life.' He looked up, tears streaming unashamedly down his face. 'But she never forgot her first child. Not for one day in thirty years.'

He stood, advancing on his uncle with such menace that Lord Xander shrank back in his chair. 'You are the most despicable excuse for a human being I've ever encountered. You ruined lives to protect your precious family name.'

'I couldn't agree more,' Chrissie declared, turning to Danny and Batters. 'I say we kick his bleedin' balls off.'

The threat hung heavy in the air. Lord Xander's face paled, his eyes darting nervously to Danny. The unspoken secret crackled between them like electricity.

Chrissie suddenly began to clap, slow and deliberate. Her gaze shifted to her one-time lover, a reluctant admiration sparking in her eyes. 'Bravo, Teddy. You played a blinder. All along you were the one pulling the strings, getting us all to dance to your tune.'

Teddy stared at her with defiance. 'I would have done anything for my mother. '

To everyone's surprise, she laughed, a genuine, throaty sound. 'Forget it. I would've done the same in your shoes.' She cast a tender glance at Lady Eleanor, who had drifted into a light doze in her chair. 'For someone I loved? In a heartbeat.'

Chrissie suddenly stood, her body rigid with righteous fury. 'This,' she announced with relish to the room, 'is for Lady Eleanor and all the other women who get fucked over by their families.'

She strutted over to Xander with deadly purpose. Before anyone could react, she delivered a lethal right hook to his jaw, her knuckles connecting with bone in a sickening crack.

Lord Xander crumpled in his chair, sliding sideways onto the expensive carpet, out cold.

Chrissie shook out her hand. 'Sweet dreams, Your Lordship.'

# Chapter Forty-Five

'You absolutely certain about this?' Brother Bertie leaned forward, his voice dropping to that low, velvety tone that always made Sin's heart skip. 'Once we go down this road, there's no turning back. No pretending. No going back to stolen kisses in dark corners.'

The faded yellow light of Gertie's boarding house kitchen cast long shadows across the worn wooden table between them. Sin sat opposite, tension carved into every line of her beautiful face. Her fingers twisted nervously around each other, betraying the fear she was trying so hard to hide.

'I'm carrying your baby, Bertie,' Sin reaffirmed with intense emotion.

Instinctively, her hand moved to her still-flat stomach, a protective gesture that stirred something primal inside him. 'I'm not ashamed of loving you. But Christ, I'm terrified.'

Reaching across the table, Brother Bertie captured her restless hands in his with reassurance. The warmth of her touch still stunned him, even after all this time. His thumb traced gentle circles across her knuckles, trying to calm the tremors he could feel beneath her skin.

'We're in this together and need to go into this with our eyes wide open.' The words came out rougher than he'd intended. 'Danny Steele doesn't take kindly to anyone taking what he considers his. And you, sugar, you're his precious princess.'

Imagining her father's reaction Sin's throat constricted, bile rising. 'I'm not his property.'

'To him you are,' Brother Bertie ground out. 'His daughter. His to control. His to decide who touches you. And me?' His voice turned bitter. 'I'm good enough to be a friend, but never good enough to be family.'

Sin shoved back her chair abruptly, the legs scraping across the linoleum with a sound that grated on both their nerves. Rising, she paced the small kitchen with jerky, agitated movements, her arms wrapped protectively around herself. Her breathing grew shallow and quick with memories of the belt crashing down on her skin from Jimmy's hand, while her father stood by goading him.

'And Jimmy—' Brother Bertie began, the words sticking in his throat. His best friend. His mucker and mate. The betrayal would cut Jimmy to the bone.

'My brother loves you,' Sin cut in, her words tumbling out in a desperate rush. She wheeled to face him, her chin lifting with defiance even while terror darkened her eyes. 'You're his best friend. His blood brother.'

'It's not me I'm worried about, sugar.' His expression crumbled into tenderness, brows slanting upwards, vulnerability replacing his usual swagger. 'If your father lays a hand on you because of this—' his voice turned deadly quiet, 'if he so much as makes you shed a single tear, I don't care if he's your blood. I'll end him.'

His fierce protectiveness made Sin's heart clench painfully, her breath catching in her throat.

'They need to know that I chose you.' Her voice strengthened with each word, steel entering her spine. 'That I'll always choose you.'

Brother Bertie bent his head, touching his forehead to hers with infinite tenderness. 'No matter what happens,' his breath warmed her skin, 'we face it together.'

Sin's fingers tightened around his until her knuckles went white. 'Together.'

His lips found hers, the kiss desperate and hungry. When they finally broke apart, both were breathing heavily, their hearts one.

'Jimmy first,' Brother Bertie decided, though the tension coiled in his shoulders betrayed the casual tone he attempted. 'He deserves to hear it from us before anyone else.'

He took her hand, their fingers intertwining like a promise, and together they moved towards the door.

Whatever storm was coming, they were in this together.

***

The closer they got to Jimmy's home, the more Sin's tummy tightened and knotted. Her hand clamped onto Brother Bertie's with vice-like force. She could feel the sweat between their palms. The truth they were about to drop was going to shatter everything, no two ways about it.

Brother Bertie's mouth was dry, his heartbeat going so crazy, so hard he was surprised Sin couldn't hear it. This was it then, the moment that would either make or break everything.

'Whatever kicks off in there,' he muttered, 'we face it together, yeah? No running, no backing down.'

Sin nodded, though her stomach kept churning. She'd rather face down a gang of tooled-up thugs than see the look on Jimmy's face when they told him the truth. But there was no going back now. They'd made their bed, and now they had to bloody well lie in it.

One final reassuring glance between them, they paused at the bottom of the steps leading to the imposing riverside property. Both steeled themselves for the conversation that would change everything.

Then they heard it. Children crying. Not just crying – wailing. The kind of raw, primal screaming that came from deep terror.

'Jimmy! Mini!' Brother Bertie bolted the remaining distance. He took the front steps two at a time, his fist pounded against the solid oak door with desperate fury. 'Open the bloody door!'

Something was badly wrong here. Every instinct screamed danger.

Sin pushed past him, pressing her face to the frosted glass panel. 'I can see movement. The children, but no adults. Christ, Bertie – where are Jimmy and Mini?'

Brother Bertie stepped back, sizing up the door with grim determination. 'Stand back.'

He slammed his shoulder against it with brutal force. The impact jarred every bone in his body, sending shock waves of pain down his arm, but the thick, weathered door didn't budge. He tried again, throwing his full weight behind it, muscles straining. Still nothing.

'Fuck's sake!' Pain shot through his shoulder, but desperation trumped discomfort. Rage at his own helplessness burned through him. 'This fucking door!'

Sin tugged at his arm, her face drained of all colour. 'The side entrance, through the kitchen. Now!'

They sprinted around the side of the house, their footsteps echoing off the cobblestones. Through a gap in the curtains, they caught flashes of small bodies moving frantically inside, shadows dancing with panic.

Brother Bertie stripped off his jacket, wrapping it around his fist with quick, efficient movements. Without hesitation, he smashed it through the kitchen window. The sound of shattering glass exploded in the quiet street, sharp and violent. Shards rained down, glittering wickedly in the afternoon light.

'Watch your hands,' he warned, methodically clearing the jagged edges from the frame. Blood welled from small cuts on his knuckles, but he ignored it. Forcing the wooden sash upwards, he groaned in protest. He hoisted himself up and through, glass crunching beneath his shoes. Heavy landing, but he was through.

Sin followed with surprising agility, her face set in grim determination.

'In here!' That was Violet's voice, shrill with terror, calling from the front room.

The sound cut through them both.

They found her and Robbie standing helplessly around a body sprawled on the carpet. Robbie was rocking back and forth, his small hands pressed over his ears. He needed to block out reality. His face was streaked with tears and snot. The body was their mum.

Mini.

She wasn't moving. Her skin had a waxy, grey pallor that made Brother Bertie's blood turn to ice.

'No! No!' Brother Bertie dropped to his knees beside her, his breathing high and ragged with disbelief. Cold sweat beaded across his brow. He pressed trembling fingers to her neck, feeling desperately for a pulse. His hands shook so badly he could barely feel anything.

Thank Christ! It fluttered beneath her clammy skin – weak and thready, but she was still with them. Still breathing, just about.

Sin stood frozen in the doorway, her hand flying to her mouth to stifle a cry of horror. The scene before her was every parent's nightmare.

'Mini? Mini, love, can you hear me?' Brother Bertie tapped her face gently, then more firmly. No response. Her eyelids didn't even flutter. Panic clawed at his throat.

Violet, her small face ravaged by tears, choked out between ragged sobs, 'Mummy fell down. She was making tea and she just… fell. I tried to wake her up. I shook her and shook her, but she wouldn't wake up.'

Robbie's eyes were wide and unseeing, lost in the kind of terror no child should ever know. His voice came out in a broken whisper. 'Is Mummy dead? Is she going to die?'

Sin dropped to her knees, opening her arms wide despite the tremor in her own hands. 'Come here, my loves,' she called, her voice breaking with barely controlled emotion. 'Come to Auntie Sin.'

Sobbing, the children stumbled into the safety of her embrace. The tremors of their small bodies went straight through her. 'Your mummy is sick,' she soothed, pressing fierce kisses to their damp heads. 'But we're going to help her, I promise. Your mummy is so strong. Where's Harry?'

It was Robbie who answered through his tears, 'Asleep upstairs. He doesn't know.'

Brother Bertie gathered Mini's limp body into his arms, her head slumping against his shoulder. She felt too light, too fragile. 'I need to get her to hospital. Now.'

Sin nodded, holding the children tighter. They shuddered into her chest. Tears welled in her eyes, but she blinked them back fiercely. These children needed strength, not more fear.

'I'll look after the children. Go! Don't waste another second!'

Robbie wailed louder, his small fists clutching at Sin's blouse with desperate intensity. 'Don't let Mummy go! Don't let her go!'

'Your mummy needs a doctor, sweetheart,' Brother Bertie explained, his voice catching despite his efforts to stay calm. Each sobbing child was a knife twisting in his gut. 'Your Auntie Sin will stay with you, but I need to take your mummy now.'

Violet, trying to be brave beyond her years, pulled her brother closer with shaking arms. 'It's okay, Robbie. Uncle Bertie will make Mummy better.' But her trembling lower lip betrayed her own terror.

'Tell Jimmy—' he started, then stopped. There wasn't time.

'Just go!' Sin cut him off, already gathering the children closer, whispering soothing nonsense into their hair. 'Keep her alive, Bertie. Don't let anything happen to her. Don't you dare let her die.'

Brother Bertie's jaw clenched with determination. He would not let Mini die. Not on his watch.

# Chapter Forty-Six

Jimmy frantically took The Royal London Hospital stairs three at a time. His lungs burned, his heart pounded with enough force to break free. *Sweet Jesus, let her be all right.* He reached the top and powered through the swing doors into the ward.

Brother Bertie and Sin sat huddled together on a hard wooden bench, their faces marked with worry. After leaving the children with their grandmother, Sin had quickly followed Bertie and Mini to The London.

Relief flooded through Jimmy at the sight of them, followed immediately by fresh terror. If they were out here…

'What the bloody hell happened?' Jimmy's face drained of all colour, panic causing sweat to bead on his forehead. 'Where is she? Where's my Mini?'

Brother Bertie rose, his usual swagger nowhere to be seen. 'Jimmy, mate, we found her collapsed in the house. She was—'

'I don't want the bleedin' details!' Jimmy's hands shook as he raked them through his hair. 'Where is she now? Is she all right?'

Sin stood, pale, features stark. 'Jimmy, Bertie got her here in a flash—'

'Mr Steele?'

The voice that cut through held professional authority. Jimmy spun round to see a tall, grey-haired doctor approaching, his face wearing that careful neutral expression that made Jimmy's stomach plummet. Behind him walked Sister Bailey, the no-nonsense Bajan nurse he recognised from when Gertie was attacked.

'I'm Dr Morrison,' the doctor introduced himself. 'I wonder if we could have a word? Privately?'

The word 'privately' hit Jimmy like a physical blow. In his world, private conversations meant bad news. Terrible news. The kind that changed everything.

'Whatever you've got to say, you can say it here.' His confused desperation came out as pent-up aggression.

It was his sister who calmed things down with, 'Best go with them, Jimmy, eh?'

After exchanging a glance with Sister Bailey, the doctor quickly jumped in. 'Perhaps it would be better if we stepped into the family room.'

Family room. The phrase sent ice through Jimmy's veins. He'd heard about those rooms, places where doctors delivered news that shattered worlds. But his legs moved anyway.

The small room was white, four chairs, and a crucifix on the wall. Jimmy remained standing, his fists clenched, every muscle in his body twisted tight.

The doctor cleared his throat, sensing there was no point asking Jimmy to sit. He chose his words very carefully. 'Your wife is very unwell. The tests we've be running—'

'Whatcha mean, running?' Jimmy looked from one to the other.

It was Sister Bailey who quietly, and with such compassion, answered. 'Jimmy, Mini has been coming to the hospital for tests for the last three months. It took a while to know what was happening. But we now know why Mini has been so ill.'

Three months. Tests. Very unwell.

Jimmy could barely take it in. His Mini would've told him. Then his mind shot back to the day she could hardly get out of bed and he had to see to getting their kids ready for school.

With a huge breath, Jimmy gathered his courage. 'What are you telling me?'

'Your wife has a brain tumour.'

Oh my God! Jimmy couldn't breathe.

'A rather aggressive one, I'm afraid.'

The words bounced off Jimmy's mind without sticking.

Brain tumour. Aggressive.

The room tilted sideways, and he gripped the back of a chair to steady himself.

'Nah.' The word escaped his lips in a whisper. 'No, you've got it wrong. She's tired, that's all. Three kids, running the house… she's just knackered.'

Dr Morrison's face softened with practiced compassion. 'I understand this is difficult to process, but the results are quite clear.'

'I said no!' Jimmy's voice exploded through the small space. 'She's twenty-six years old! She's got babies to raise! You've mixed up the bloody files or something!'

Sister Bailey stepped forward. 'Jimmy, she doesn't have long.'

His world stopped.

There was a buzzing in his ears. The walls seemed to press inwards, the crucifix on the wall blurring.

Mini. His Mini. The tiny force of nature who'd turned his life from black and white to full colour. The woman who'd given him three perfect children and a reason to be become a better man. The girl who had given up her own flesh and blood for him.

'Sadly, she inherited the same condition that her mother had,' the doctor explained.

The cruelty of it staggered him. Jimmy lurched back. 'Where is she? Where's my wife?'

Sister Bailey moved towards the door, her voice steady. 'I'll take you to her.'

Jimmy followed blindly, his wobbly legs moving without conscious thought. The corridor stretched endlessly ahead, each step taking him closer to a reality he couldn't accept. He didn't register Brother Bertie or Sin as he passed them or the naked distress contorting their faces. Nothing existed except the need to see Mini, to prove the doctor wrong, to make this nightmare disappear through sheer force of will.

***

Jimmy paused at the doorway, his hand gripping the frame. The sight that greeted him punched the air from his lungs.

Christ almighty.

His Mini, his fierce, unstoppable spitfire was disappearing before his eyes. The hospital bed swallowed her tiny frame whole. Her once-plump cheeks had hollowed out, the skin stretched paper-thin over cheekbones that jutted sharp and pronounced. Dark-purple shadows pooled beneath her closed eyes. Her hair lay limp and colourless against the stark white pillow. She looked ancient. Decades older than her years.

Panic clawed at his throat. His hands trembled, and he forced them into fists, nails cutting crescents into his palms. The physical pain was nothing compared to the agony crushing his chest. A vice squeezing his ribs inwards, making each breath a struggle.

But he couldn't let her see. Not his devastation. Or his terror. She needed his strength now.

Jimmy slapped on his game face and stepped into the room, summoning his trademark East End swagger.

'Afternoon, beautiful,' he called softly, injecting warmth into his voice.

Mini's eyelids fluttered, then opened. The fierce spark was still there in her eyes, blazing through the illness.

A fighter to the last, his gorgeous girl.

'Gonna stand there gawking all day, or what?' Her voice was reed thin, but the sassy tone was pure Mini.

Jimmy's face lit up in a one hundred watt cheeky smile. 'Just admiring the view, ain't I?'

Mini's lips spread into a grin. 'Got a face that would stop traffic, and you know it.'

He laughed, louder than necessary, desperate to fill the space with something other than the beeping machines and her laboured breathing. Moving to her bedside, he reached for her pillows, plumping them with gentle hands.

'There you go, love. Better?'

She nodded, watching him fuss around her bed with knowing eyes. When he finally settled into the visitor's chair, he took her hand, folding it between his massive palms. Her fingers felt brittle, so cold despite the ward's stuffy heat. He pressed his lips to her knuckles, and lingered there, never wanting his mouth to let go.

Mini's free hand reached up, trembling with effort, to touch his face. Her fingers traced the stubble on his jaw. 'Jimmy, love…' Her chest rose with a ragged series of breaths.

He kissed her palm, his eyes burning. 'Not much longer now, eh? The quack says you'll be right as rain in no time. Ready to come home to me and the kids.'

The lie hung between them, heavy and suffocating.

'Jimmy Steele.' Her voice strengthened, that no-nonsense tone that had kept him in check for years. 'Look at me proper.'

He forced himself to meet her gaze. Her eyes were clear, determined, and suddenly he knew what was coming.

Jimmy shook his head violently, so hard his neck cracked. He wanted to clap his hands over his ears, block out whatever truth was coming next. His mind screamed against it. He couldn't bear to hear the words that would make this real. If she said it aloud, there'd be no going back, no pretending anymore.

'You'll be back at your sewing machine before you can blink. Making them fancy frocks for them dolly trolleys from Up West.'

Despair, bewilderment, grief, it all bundled into a choking mass in his throat. His jaw worked, but no words came out. He ground his teeth so hard his back molars groaned.

A tear escaped, tracking down his cheek. Mini caught it with her finger.

'Don't you go soft on me now, Southpaw.'

Jimmy's chest heaved, fighting for control, but Mini's expression suddenly grew strained. The playful mask slipped away, revealing raw fear beneath.

'Jimmy, love… it won't be long now.'

'No.' The word exploded from him. 'Don't you bloody dare—'

But Mini summoned every ounce of strength left in her wasted body, her trembling hands gripping his face, forcing him to look at her. Her fingers pressed into his cheeks with desperate urgency.

'Listen to me,' she whispered, her tone forceful despite its weakness. 'It's in my breathing, Jimmy. There's a rattle… it's coming for me now.'

'Stop it!' Jimmy tried to pull away, but her grip was surprisingly strong. 'You're going to be fine. The doctors said—'

He couldn't go on. His face crumpled with utter devastation.

'I want you to take me.' Her voice was barely a breath now, but each word carried absolute conviction. 'I want you to take me home, Jimmy. Now.'

He couldn't deny her.

With infinite tenderness, he peeled back the blanket and slid one arm beneath her knees, the other supporting her back. She weighed nothing, a collection of bones beneath hospital cotton.

Mini snuggled into the love of her life, her head finding its familiar place in the crook of his neck.

'Mr Steele! What do you think you're doing?' Sister Bailey's outrage rang through the quiet.

Jimmy turned, Mini cradled in his arms, his face set in granite. 'I'm taking my wife.'

'This is absolutely unacceptable!' Hands on her hips, she threatened, 'I'll call security!'

Mini's fingers curled into Jimmy's shirt. He could feel her heart fluttering, frantic and weak.

'Call whoever you bloody want,' Jimmy growled. 'But I'm walking out that door with my wife.' He caught the anxious stricken stares of his best mate and sister. 'Anyone tries to stop me, they'll regret it.'

Jimmy strode towards the exit, his precious cargo secure in his arms.

Mini's eyelids were growing heavy again, but a smile played at the corners of her mouth.

'My big, strong man,' she murmured. 'Always saving me.'

Jimmy's throat closed up. If only that were true. If only he could save her from this.

'Anything for you, Mini,' he promised, his voice cracking. 'Anything in this world.'

# Chapter Forty-Seven

It was their last dance. Down by the river, just where she wanted it.

Nestled and safe in her husband's arms. Jimmy took care stepping through the French windows and onto the terrace. Mini adored it out here. Some days he'd come home to find her doing a spot of hand sewing. The Thames stretched before them, a ribbon of murky green-brown catching the afternoon light. Jimmy set her down gently, keeping his strong arms around her waist to hold her upright.

'Remember this one, love?' he asked, his voice thick with emotion. He began to hum 'She Loves You' by The Beatles, their song from that magical summer of '63 when they'd first locked eyes across a crowded dance hall.

Mini's heart swelled at the memory. *My handsome Jimmy. Just as easy on the eyes now as he was back then.* Despite everything that had happened between their families, they'd chosen each other. Batters Rogers and Danny Steele – sworn enemies – but their children had found love. Funny how life worked out.

Despite everything, she felt safe wrapped in his embrace, his body radiating warmth into her cold bones. The solid wall of his chest, the familiar scent of his aftershave mixed with cigarettes – it anchored her to this moment, to him.

'You couldn't dance for toffee back then,' she whispered, her words barely carrying over the breeze.

'Still can't,' Jimmy admitted, swaying them slowly.

Mini had explained it to him years ago. If her time ever came, she wanted to be right here by the river. The Thames had flowed through generations of her family, same as the blood in her veins. The Rogers had worked on these docks for over a hundred years. It was part of her East End heritage, part of who she was.

Jimmy twirled her in a careful circle, supporting her weight as her feet barely touched the ground. His movements were gentle; he was afraid she might break. Mini closed her eyes, feeling the breeze brush her face. For a precious moment, the pain retreated. She wasn't a skeleton wrapped in paper-thin skin. She wasn't dying. She was just a woman dancing with her husband.

She wanted to memorise every second of this. The feel of his beautiful heartbeat beneath her cheek. The gentle strength in his arms. The sound of his breathing. Soon she'd have to leave him. The thought of it tore at her. Who would look after him? Who would make sure he didn't become like his father? And the children – her precious babies. She wouldn't see them grow up. Wouldn't hold Violet's hand on her wedding day. Wouldn't see little Robbie become a man. And Harry – barely three years old – might not even remember her.

'Not too shabby for a Rogers girl and a Steele boy,' she murmured with pure East End pride.

His arms crushed her closer. 'They never stood a chance against us, did they?'

The sunlight warmed her face, but darkness hovered at the edges of her vision. A bone-deep exhaustion swept through her, worse than before. Her time was running out.

'Jimmy, I need to sit down.'

Without question, he guided her to the wooden chair he'd brought up earlier. He sat first, then gathered her onto his lap, cradling her to his chest like a child. Her head found its place in the hollow of his neck.

Mini felt the subtle tremors running through him. He wasn't crying, but every muscle in his body warred with his grief. His chest rose and fell unevenly, breath catching, then releasing in controlled measures. His face buried into the top of her head, lips moving in what might have been a prayer.

This magnificent, unbreakable man. Her protector. Her love. How would he manage without her? She had to say it now, while she still could.

'Jimmy,' she whispered, 'promise me something.'

'Anything,' he answered immediately, his voice breaking.

'The kids. Look after our babies. Don't let your dad get his claws in them. Raise them right. Make sure they know how much their mum loved them.'

He feverishly caressed her arm, her cheek, her hair – as if through touch alone he could keep her tethered to this world. His palm was rough from years of dock work and fighting, but so gentle on her skin.

'I promise,' he said, the words a vow carved in stone. 'I swear on my life.'

That was all she needed to hear. Mini gazed out at the river one last time. The water glittered with afternoon sunlight, boats drifting past. The tide was coming in, the water rising steadily against the quay wall. Always moving, always changing, yet somehow always the same.

*Oh, my Jimmy. My love. I'm sorry to leave you.*

The darkness crept closer, soft and insistent. Mini didn't fight it.

***

A chill ran through Jimmy, blood draining from his face as he looked down at Mini. Her eyes were closed, her face peaceful.

'Mini?' *No! No!* 'Mini, love?'

No response.

*God, no. Please God, no. Not yet. We need more time.*

'Mini!' He shook her gently, then with more urgency. 'Wake up, darlin'. Please.'

Nothing.

'No, no, no.' His voice rose with each word. 'Don't you dare. Don't you bloody dare.'

*She can't be gone. She can't.* Mini never gave up on anything in her life. The stubborn, beautiful force of nature who'd dragged him kicking and screaming into being a better man. The only person who'd ever seen past his Steele reputation and loved the man beneath.

He pressed his fingers to her neck, searching for a pulse. Were his hands trembling too much to feel it? Was it there, but too faint? *We still have so much living to do. The kids need their mum. I need you, Mini. I don't know how to do this without you.*

'Let me see what's what, son.'

Jimmy's head snapped around. His mother, Iris, stood at the edge of the terrace, with his father, Danny, and Brother Bertie behind her. He hadn't heard them arrive, too lost in his world of two.

Iris crossed the terrace with quick, practical steps. She knelt beside the chair, her experienced fingers finding Mini's wrist. After a moment, she moved them to Mini's neck, her touch gentle but certain.

The seconds stretched into eternity.

*Please find something. Please tell me she's still here. I'll do anything. I'll give anything. Just don't take her from me.*

Iris looked up at her son and slowly shook her head, her silver-grey eyes – so like Jimmy's own – swimming with tears.

*This isn't happening. This can't be real. We were supposed to grow old together. We were supposed to watch our children grow up. We were supposed to have more time.*

Jimmy gathered his soul mate closer to his chest, burying his face in her hair. The pain exploded inside him, tearing through every defence, shattering every wall he'd ever built. He opened his mouth and let out a terrible roar that echoed across the river – raw and primal, the sound of a heart breaking beyond repair.

# Chapter Forty-Eight

The Dockside Devil's doors crashed forward, banging against the wall with a splintering crack. Conversation died instantly. Glasses froze midway to thirsty mouths.

Lucas filled the doorframe, and the sight and state of him made many gasp. Six-foot plus of solid muscle. Angry muscle. His massive chest heaved with each ragged breath, making the straining buttons of his shirt threaten to burst. Cold sweat plastered his dark hair to his furrowed forehead despite the bitter December chill. His bloodshot eyes swept across the hushed room, wild and unfocused.

'She's dead.'

The devastating words fell heavy into the unnatural silence. Hardened regulars shrank back because they'd seen Lucas in terrifying rages before. When the giant lost control, smart men cleared a hasty path.

In the shadowed corner, Batters stubbed out his cigar and slowly rose from his usual table. His hand still clutched a half-gone glass of whisky. Three of his most trusted men sat frozen around him.

Confusion creased his leathery face. *Dead? She? What's the bloody boy going on about?*

'What's got your knickers in a twist, son?' His puzzled question came out sharper than intended.

Lucas thundered forward. Fist pumping violently by his side. Wary and frightened punters scattered before him, pressing themselves against walls.

'Mini.' He rocked with rage in front of his father. A thick vein pulsed in his corded neck. 'Your daughter. My sister. Gone.'

Batters' glass slipped from nerveless fingers, smashing with a crack onto the scarred table. The deafening rushing in his ears drowned all other sound. His dry mouth opened but produced nothing.

Mini. His little girl.

Blood drained rapidly from his face, leaving it grey as dockyard slurry. He gripped the edge of the rough table with desperate strength.

'She went the same way as mum.' The son's jaw clenched so tight that twitching muscles jumped beneath his flushed skin. 'I should've known. She weren't herself the last time I clapped eyes on her.' His lips curled. 'My sister's been suffering for agonising months while you sat drinking in this bloody boozer.'

The older man stared at his boy's contorted face, unable to process the devastating words. Her mother? Mini? The room seemed to tilt and spin around him.

'At Mum's grave she saw you.' Lucas slammed his massive fist onto the fragile table. Wood splintered loudly. Heavy glasses toppled and shattered. 'And you turned her away. Again. Not just her, but her little ones, too. Your own precious flesh and blood.'

The brutal accusation pierced right through Batters' heaving chest. His frantic heart pounded against brittle ribs, threatening to crack ancient bone. But he stood his ground. He'd done what he needed to do. And he didn't owe an accounting for his actions to no one.

But Mini… gone?

'Nah, you're lying—'

The vicious punch caught him square in the unprotected jaw before he could finish. Blinding pain exploded through his skull as he staggered backwards, crashing heavily into the sticky bar. His loyal men jumped up but froze at his quick, commanding hand gesture. Nobody interfered in sacred family business.

His dad barely raised his arms before his raging son smashed into him. Despite his advanced age, decades of brutal dock fights had kept Batters dangerously hard. He caught Lucas with a savage uppercut. His son's head snapped back violently, but his massive body barely registered the powerful blow.

They collided with the crowded bar, fragile glasses smashing around them. Batters landed a crushing hook to his son's exposed ribs, feeling young bone give beneath his scarred knuckles. Lucas answered with a devastating blow that drove all precious air from the father's straining lungs.

Hot blood sprayed from the old man's split lip. He spat crimson onto the filthy floor and drove his hard forehead into Lucas' unprotected nose. Fresh blood streamed down his boy's twisted face, turning his thick beard slick and bright red.

'I watched her waste away.' Lucas landed another crushing blow, filled with white-hot fury that sent his father reeling backwards. 'While you nursed your stupid, pointless grudge.'

Each condemning word hit harder than any physical blow. Batters fought mechanically, his battered body remembering what to do while his shocked mind reeled.

Lucas caught him by the vulnerable throat, powerful fingers lifting the older man until his feet barely touched the sticky floor. His massive hands tightened mercilessly.

'Your own innocent daughter.' Furious spit and bright blood flew from Lucas' twisted mouth. 'She still loved you after all that you did to her.'

Batters clawed frantically at his son's iron grip. His burning lungs screamed for precious air. Then, something profound broke inside Lucas. His crushing grip loosened suddenly. His massive body began to tremble violently, not with blinding rage but something deeper entirely.

Without conscious thought, he wrapped his shaking trembling arms fiercely around his boy, jerking him close with desperate paternal strength. His calloused hands cradled his sobbing boy's massive frame with fierce tenderness that surprised many who were watching because they didn't know that Batters had that level of love left in him. He hadn't held his boy like this since he was a young un in school.

Batters wouldn't let his son go.

He held on tight to the only flesh and blood he had left.

# Chapter Forty-Nine

The Steele home was a house in mourning.

Iris sat rigid in her armchair, the familiar comfort of the worn upholstery now a prison. Across the sitting room, Danny occupied his usual chair, but there was nothing usual about the hollow-eyed statue that had replaced her husband.

Violet and Robbie huddled against her skirts like frightened puppies. Mini's poor mites! Violet looked so lost, while little Robbie, kept asking when his mummy was coming home. Harry squirmed in her arms, mercifully unaware that he'd never remember his mother's face.

They hadn't spoken for hours. What was there to say when the world had collapsed?

Iris twisted her hands in her lap. Strange how her fingers didn't reach for the gin bottle on the sideboard. For the first time in years, she needed clarity, needed every sharp edge of this agony. Some burdens you had to carry with a clear head.

*That's what mothers do, ain't it?* The thought came unbidden. *We hold the bleeding pieces together while everything falls apart.*

In the East End, when tragedy struck, the women became the backbone. The men might run the streets and the business, but in times of grief, the women ran everything else. They cleaned, they cooked, they arranged, they comforted.

And now it was her turn.

Three beautiful children. Mini's beautiful children. Without a mother.

'Where's my daddy?' Violet's trembling question broke the silence. Her eyes were red-rimmed from crying.

'He'll be back soon, love,' Iris soothed comforting fingers through her hair.

The truth was, nobody knew where Jimmy was. Gone, vanished into the evening light. Not a word to anyone, just the slam of the door. Brother Bertie was out looking. If anyone could find Jimmy, it was the man he was connected to deeper than blood.

A thunderous knock shattered her thoughts. Three hard blows that seemed to rattle the foundations of the small terraced house.

Iris' eyes snapped to Danny's. A silent conversation passed between them in that single haunted glance. They both knew who probably stood on their doorstep.

Danny gave a single, grim nod.

Rising with Harry still clutched to her chest, Iris made her way to the front door. Her hand trembled slightly when she turned the lock.

As expected, Mini's father and brother filled the doorway. From the state of them, both of them had been in a right old ding-dong.

Iris felt the weight of a hundred hidden eyes watching from behind twitching curtains. Batters standing hat in hand at Danny Steele's door… this was a moment the gossips would feast on for years.

'In you come.' She beckoned quietly, stepping back to allow them entry.

The men hesitated, each seeming to gather strength before crossing the threshold. The narrow hallway of the terraced house suddenly felt airless with the addition of their massive frames.

Danny appeared in the sitting room doorway, shoulders squared. For a heartbeat, the old enemies stared at each other.

Then Batters broke the spell.

'Where is she?' he forced out. 'Where's my girl?'

Iris shifted Harry in her arms and nodded towards the stairs. 'This way.'

She led them up the narrow staircase, the wood groaning beneath their heavy tread. The landing seemed to shrink with three adults crowded upon it. Carefully, she turned the handle to the bedroom where Mini was laid out.

'I've been waiting for you before calling the undertakers,' she said softly. 'You have the right to see before she goes.'

The curtains were drawn, casting the room in muted shadow. A single lamp cast a gentle glow over the bed where Mini rested. Even in death, she was beautiful. The cancer that had ravaged her body hadn't touched the peaceful expression on her face. Sin had brushed her dark hair until it shone, had dressed her in one of Mini's legendary creations, a soft, flowing mint-green chiffon empire dress.

Iris stepped back, allowing the men to enter.

Batters approached the bed with the dazed tread of a man walking to the gallows he kept in his den at the Dockside Devil.

'Fleur's family,' he said, his voice thick, 'they had this way about them. She told me they always purify the departed with water. To wash away earthly suffering.'

With trembling hands, he reached for the small basin of water on the nightstand.

'Her mother should be here to do this,' he continued, his words choked. 'But I have to do it. It's what my Fleur would have wanted. The water cleanses,' he whispered. 'Prepares the spirit for its journey home.'

With infinite tenderness that belied his hulking frame, the battle-scarred gangster touched the damp cloth to his daughter's forehead. His massive hand was strangely gentle and steady. A gentle stroke over

Mini's closed eyes, her peaceful cheeks, her still lips seeming to physically pain him.

'May the blessed water take away your pain,' he whispered, repeating words Iris suspected he'd heard from his wife decades ago. 'May it wash you clean for your journey across the great water.'

The simple ritual complete, father and son sank to their knees on either side of the bed. Lucas reached across his sister's still form to grasp his father's hand. Their fingers interlocked over Mini's heart.

The wrenching sobs that tore from both men were ripped from the depths of their souls. Quietly, Iris backed out of the room, pulling the door closed to give them privacy in their devastating grief. She leaned against the wall, baby Harry having fallen asleep in her arms.

Little lives go on, even when big ones end.

She closed her eyes, the grief too massive to contain.

# Chapter Fifty

'He'll do himself a mischief,' Micky Hall, the owner of the boxing gym muttered from across the room. 'He's been at it for over two hours.'

Blood from Jimmy's shredded knuckles spattered the floor with each brutal impact. Crimson flecks marked a violent half-circle around the punching bag. His breathing came in harsh, ragged gasps. Sweat poured down his face, stinging his eyes, but he didn't pause. Stopping meant thinking. Thinking meant feeling. Feeling meant acknowledging she was gone.

*Mini. My Mini.*

The Bethnal Green Boxing Club beneath the railway arches hummed with tension. Each time a train rumbled overhead, the building shook, but Jimmy didn't even blink. The musty stench of sweat and liniment hung in the air. Faded posters of champions lined the damp-stained walls, including one of him, young and full of promise.

Jimmy pounded the bag with another punishing combination. Left hook. Right cross. Left again. Each blow harder than the last, his technique nothing but raw animal fury now.

The other boxers had stopped their training to watch. These hard bastards, with their battered faces and calloused hands, stood in quiet solidarity. Until two years ago he had been their champion. Now they watched their hero battle something no fist could touch. Word about Mini had spread through the East End faster than winter flu. Everyone knew. Everyone knew the great love this man had had for his woman.

'Southpaw,' Micky called out, approaching cautiously. 'That's enough now.'

Jimmy didn't hear him. Just kept walloping and walloping. His white vest was soaked through, streaked with crimson where he'd wiped his hands.

The gym door banged open with a thunderous crack. Jimmy didn't turn. Didn't break rhythm.

'Blood fire!' Brother Bertie's concern rang out across the silent gym. 'How long's he been going?'

'Too bloody long,' Micky answered. 'Can't get through to him.'

Brother Bertie's footsteps approached, deliberate and measured. Jimmy sensed his friend moving into his peripheral vision but kept up his punishing routine, his arms heavy now, each punch weaker than the last.

'All right, bruv,' Brother Bertie's voice cut through the haze, firm but gentle. 'Your form's gone to shit. My granny could dodge those punches, and she's been pushing up daisies for twenty years.'

Another punch. Another spatter of blood.

'Your kids need a father.'

Jimmy faltered for half a second, then resumed his assault.

Brother Bertie stepped closer, right into Jimmy's space. 'Mini would give you hell for trying to bash yourself half to death.'

Jimmy's next punch missed the bag entirely.

'Don't.' Jimmy's growl was raw, it's tone a terrible thing. 'Don't you fucking dare.'

'What? Speak the truth?' Brother Bertie squared up to him, unflinching. 'You think this is what she'd want? While your kids sit at home wondering if they've lost their dad, too?'

'SHUT UP!' Jimmy roared, rounding on him, chest heaving, face contorted with grief-fuelled rage.

'Come on then. If you're determined to hurt something,' Brother Bertie challenged. 'Might as well be me. At least I can hit back.'

The two men stood toe-to-toe, breathing hard, the air between them electric. The other boxers tensed, ready to intervene. But after a long, dangerous moment, something in Jimmy's posture crumpled. The rage drained out of him, leaving nothing but hollow exhaustion.

'Everyone back to work,' Micky barked. 'Show's over, ladies.'

Jimmy raised his head and, for as long as he lived, Brother Bertie would never forget that look in his eyes. It was like his friend's heart had been ripped out.

'That house on Molasses Quay,' Jimmy said jerkily. 'It was her dream. A palace by the river. Mini colour-coded everything. Even the bloody tea towels. Who the fuck colour-codes tea towels?'

'Only Mini,' Brother Bertie agreed with a sad smile. 'Remember how she organised the cupboards? Labels facing front, everything in perfect rows?'

'With miliary precision.' Jimmy nodded, the ghost of a smile touching his lips, which soon faded away. 'How am I supposed to walk through that door every day knowing she'll never be there again?'

'One day at a time,' Brother Bertie answered simply. 'And you won't be doing it alone. I'll be there. Sin. Your mum. Even that headcase dad of yours.'

Jimmy clenched his jaw, fighting the crushing pressure in his chest. 'I don't know how to be here without her, Bertie. I don't know who I am if I'm not Mini's husband.'

They leaned forward until their foreheads touched, like they use to in the old days. Then the weight of everything crashed down on Jimmy all at once. His shoulders shook, then his whole body, and suddenly he was falling into his best friend's arms.

'I can't,' he sobbed into Brother Bertie's shoulder, the words torn from somewhere deep inside him. 'I fucking can't do this without her.'

Brother Bertie held him tight, his own eyes burning with unshed tears and buried guilt. 'You can, brother,' he whispered fiercely. 'You can. And I'll be right there with you, every step of the way.

Brother Bertie inhaled a deep punch of air. 'I swear it on my life, I will never leave you.'

# Chapter Fifty-One

Mini Steele was only twenty-six years old. No one could believe they were burying her today.

The rhythmic thunder of hooves on cobblestones echoed through Sugar Cane Wharf, each strike hammering grief deeper into Jimmy's broken heart.

Four magnificent black Friesian stallions stepped in perfect unison, their glossy coats gleaming under the grey sky, elaborate white plumes dancing from their proud heads. The ornate Victorian hearse they pulled was made of a shiny carved mahogany and gleaming brass, its glass sides revealing Mini's small white coffin buried beneath a sea of white roses and lilies.

Jimmy walked directly behind the hearse, his face a stoic mask of control, his youngest child cradled against his chest. Violet clutched his free hand with her cold and trembling fingers, while Robbie held tight onto her hand. The children's confusion tore at Jimmy's soul worse than any physical beating he'd ever endured.

*Hold it together. For them.*

*For Mini.*

Brother Bertie walked beside him, steady and silent, occasionally reaching out when Jimmy's step faltered. Behind them came the Steele family. Danny in his finest black suit; Iris, pale and trembling, dabbing at red-rimmed eyes; Sin, beautiful and haunted, her face a canvas of grief and guilt; and Chrissie, who hid her face behind a black veiled hat.

The entire Sugar Cane Wharf community had turned out, giving Mini a proper East End send off. Three deep they lined the narrow streets. Former dockers, shopkeepers in their best Sunday clothes, women clutching soaked handkerchiefs to their streaming faces, children standing solemnly beside their parents. Curtains hung closed in every window. Not a soul dared speak above a whisper.

Some paid quiet tribute as the hearse went past:

'She was such a tiny thing, but Christ, what a fighter she was.'

'Beautiful little sparrow, that one. Too good for this world.'

The slow cortège wound through the familiar streets where Mini had run as a child, where she'd met Jimmy, where she'd found forbidden love. Jimmy's throat constricted. Every memory was a knife twist. Every step took her further away from him.

A sudden ripple moved through the crowd ahead. The whispers started low, then spread like wildfire through the gathered mourners.

'Bloody hell… Rogers… it's Lucas Rogers… Didn't know if he would show his face… Bad blood between the families…'

The electric tension crackled through the air. People craned their necks, murmuring anxiously. Some stepped back, others pressed forward, all waiting to see what would happen. Jimmy looked up to see the massive frame of Lucas pushing through the crowd, his face ravaged with grief, tears streaming down his craggy cheeks. Mini's brother moved with hesitant steps, clearly uncertain of his welcome, his huge hands shaking.

The crowd held its collective breath.

Would Jimmy Steele turn away his dead wife's brother? Would the bad blood win out even here, even at Mini's funeral?

The procession slowed. Jimmy felt every eye upon him, waiting, watching. Lucas stopped at the edge of the crowd, towering over the other mourners, his bloodshot eyes fixed on the white coffin that held his baby sister.

She'd died estranged from her father, cut off from half her family because she'd chosen love over loyalty. He wouldn't let that poison follow her to the grave.

Jimmy gave a slight nod.

Permission granted.

Lucas stepped forward, his massive frame shuddering with sobs. 'I promised our mum I'd look after her,' he choked out, his voice breaking. 'Swore on her deathbed I'd keep Mini safe. I failed her.'

'You didn't fail anyone, Lucas.' Jimmy's voice came out raw, barely audible. 'You were always there for her. Always.'

Lucas fell into step beside the Steele family, united in grief for the woman they had all adored and loved.

Jimmy clutched his children tighter and followed his wife towards her final rest, the weight of loss threatening to crush him with every breath. But he walked on, because that's what she would have wanted. Because he had to be strong for their babies. Because in the East End, you honoured your dead by carrying on, no matter how much it destroyed you inside.

***

St Nicholas of the Sea was the church where Mini had been christened, where she had married Jimmy, and now it would be the place where she would be laid to rest.

The ancient stone walls had witnessed more grief than any building should bear. Those same Gothic arches had echoed with Mini's laughter on her wedding day in 1963, when the Rogers and Steele families had nearly torn each other apart before God's altar.

Now she was coming home for the final time.

The church was packed beyond capacity, mourners crammed into every pew, standing shoulder to shoulder along the walls, spilling out into the courtyard. The air hung thick with the scent of lilies and burning candles, hundreds of flickering flames casting dancing shadows across the stone pillars. Mini's white coffin sat before the altar, draped in white roses, looking impossibly small in the vast space.

Jimmy sat in the front pew, Harry, snug and sleeping on his chest, Violet pressed protectively to his left side, Robbie clinging to his right arm. Gertie, Ruddy, and Rita sat together, in the pew behind.

Father Casey, the same priest who had united Jimmy and Mini in union here, stood at the pulpit.

'Beloved congregation,' Father Casey began, his voice cracking, 'we gather today to celebrate the life of our dear Annabelle Steele. She will always be Mini to us all. A wife, a mother, a daughter—'

The massive oak doors at the back of the church slammed open with a thunderous crash that echoed through the sacred space.

Batters Rogers staggered in, clothes dishevelled, face flushed with booze and grief-madness. The entire congregation turned, gasps rippling through the church. Horrified at his dad's appearance, Lucas half rose from his seat in alarm.

'YOU KILLED HER!' Batters roared, stabbing an accusing finger at Jimmy. His voice shattered the reverent silence. 'MY LITTLE GIRL! If she'd never married you, she'd be safe at home!'

The children started crying. Harry wailed. Women in the congregation pressed handkerchiefs to their mouths in shock. This was a house of God, a funeral, and everyone knew the explosive hatred between the Steeles and Rogers.

Batters stumbled down the aisle, grief and rage contorting his features into something terrifying. 'She'd be ALIVE if it wasn't for you and your fucking criminal family!'

Jimmy's control finally snapped. He handed Harry to Brother Bertie and rose slowly, his silver-grey eyes murderous. The congregation held its collective breath, sensing violence about to erupt in God's house.

'You want to do this here?' Jimmy's voice was deadly quiet, more terrifying than any shout. 'At her funeral? In front of her children?'

'I'll kill you for what you've done to her!' Batters lunged forward, his massive frame bearing down on Jimmy.

Just as the two men were about to clash, a voice cut through the chaos with unexpected authority.

'ENOUGH! Both of you!'

Iris Steele stood, her voice carrying a power that froze everyone in place. The gentle, gin-drinking housewife had vanished, replaced by something formidable and fierce.

'This is Mini's day,' she reminded one and all. 'Her little ones are watching. Have you no shame?'

Batters stopped, swaying, suddenly seeing scared faces of the grandchildren he had never acknowledged.

Head held high, Iris approached him calmly, fearlessly. 'Eric, she loved Jimmy. You know she did. She chose her life, and she was happy. Don't dishonour her memory like this.'

Lucas moved quickly to support his father, his face stricken. 'Dad, please. Not here. Not like this.'

The fight drained out of Batters. His massive shoulders sagged, fists unclenching as the rage that had sustained him for so long finally abandoned him. For the first time since he'd burst through into the church, he truly saw what surrounded him - the horrified faces of mourners, his weeping grandchildren, the priest clutching his Bible. The sacred space he'd violated with his grief and fury.

'She was my baby girl.' His broken admission hung in the air, heavy with years of regret. 'My little Mini… and I threw her away.'

Lucas and Iris gently guided him towards the back of the church, the big man suddenly shrunken and older, crushed by grief. Jimmy remained standing, his whole body vibrating with rage and sorrow.

Brother Bertie rose and carefully guided him back to his seat, placing Harry back in his arms. The living warmth of his son was the only thing keeping Jimmy from completely falling apart.

Jimmy clutched his precious children closer, fighting the horrifying sobs that wanted to break free.

# Chapter Fifty-Two

The church was silent.

Everyone had gone, giving Jimmy the privacy he needed for his final goodbye.

Jimmy stood alone in front of his wife's coffin. He placed his open palm on the front of it for and then closed his eyes. He stood there for a time, just him and Mini. When he opened his eyes again, his trembling hand reached into his jacket pocket, fingers closing around the precious photograph he'd been carrying all day.

The photo was from A.P. Griffiths Studio off Roman Road. It was their first proper family portrait, and Mini's pride and joy. She'd insisted they all dress in their finest clothes, had fussed over the kid's hair. It was their first colour photograph together: Jimmy in his best suit, Mini radiant in her homemade yellow dress, baby Harry on her lap, Violet and Robbie beside them.

'You loved this so much,' Jimmy whispered, his voice cracking in the empty church. 'Said it proved we were a proper family, didn't you?'

He placed the photograph gently on her coffin, right over her heart. The glossy surface caught the candlelight, making their smiling faces glow warmly in the sacred space.

'Look at you in this picture, Mini. Look how beautiful you are. How happy.' Jimmy fought hard to get the words out. 'You were always the beautiful one. From the first moment I saw you at that boxing match, you took my breath away. Still do.'

Jimmy's hands gripped the edge of the coffin, his knuckles white with the strain of holding himself together.

'You were the bravest woman I ever knew. Married me against your father's wishes. Stood up to my dad when he tried to intimidate you. Never backed down from anyone.' His voice grew thick with emotion. 'My little spitfire. Because you had more fight in your tiny body than most men twice your size.'

The tears he'd been holding back all day finally began to fall, cutting hot tracks down his cheeks.

'You made me a better man, Mini. Made me want to be worthy of you. And now…' His voice broke completely. 'Now I don't know who I am without you.'

The dam burst. All the strength he'd been forcing himself to maintain crumbled.

'Mini, how am I going to bring our kids up right without you?'

Jimmy's big body convulsed, then crumpled forward onto the coffin. His arms wrapped around the cold wood with a brutal desperation as if sheer force could bring Mini back to him. The sounds that tore from him weren't human, animal howls of agony that ripped through the silence, echoing off the stone walls. His massive frame shook with brutal sobs with such crushing grief even the stone angels seemed to weep.

# Chapter Fifty-Three

The house on Molasses Quay groaned under the weight of mourners, their voices creating a low hum that drifted through the rooms. Jimmy had thrown open his doors to anyone who wanted to pay their respects to Mini.

In the kitchen, a physically and emotionally exhausted Sin stood beside her mother, mechanically arranging plates of sandwiches and pouring drinks. Her face was pale, dark circles shadowing her eyes, but she moved with purpose. Anything to keep busy. Anything to stop thinking about the gaping hole Mini's death had torn through all their lives.

'Look at them tucking in,' Sin murmured to Iris, nodding towards the sitting room where the mourners had descended on the spread with East End zeal. 'You'd think they hadn't eaten in weeks.'

Iris managed a watery smile. 'That's what we do in the East End, sweetheart. When death comes calling, we rally round. A cup of tea, a sandwich, a kind word – it's how we show we care. Nobody grieves on an empty stomach. Besides, Mini would have wanted a cracking old knees-up.'

Through the doorway, they could see old Mrs Craxton, three sheets to the wind on gin, attempting to demonstrate the Charleston to a group of scandalised church ladies. Her ancient legs wobbled precariously while she kicked and swayed, her hat tilting at a dangerous angle.

'Blimey, someone better catch her before she goes arse over tit,' Sin said.

The old woman executed a particularly ambitious spin, lost her balance entirely, and toppled backwards into the arms of the shocked woman from the corner shop. Both women went down in a tangle of black skirts and flying handbags. Mrs Craxton let loose with Mad Hatter laughter of drunken delight.

'I've still got it, girls!' she cackled. 'Seventy-three and still dancing rings around you young 'uns!'

'Sin.' Brother Bertie's voice was soft behind her. 'Can I have a word?'

She turned, seeing the same grief etched in his features that she felt cutting through her own chest. Without a word, she followed him through the crowded rooms and up the stairs to the sitting room, where the large French doors stood open to the balcony, letting in what little light the grey day offered.

The terrace beyond gazed out onto the Thames, and she could hear the water slapping angrily against the stone steps that led down to the shoreline. Everything about the day felt ominous, heavy with more than just grief.

Brother Bertie closed the door behind them, shutting out the noise from below. They stood facing each other, two people drowning in sorrow, and then she was in his arms, clinging to him while the tears finally came.

'I can't believe she's gone,' Sin sobbed against his chest. 'She was so young, Bertie. Too bloody young.'

'I know, sweetness. I know.' His hand moved instinctively to her belly, where their secret grew beneath the black fabric of her funeral dress. 'She would have been over the moon about the baby.'

Mini would've been the first one knitting booties and planning the christening. Now she'd never even meet her nephew or niece.

Sin covered his hand with hers, feeling the slight swell that would soon be impossible to hide. 'We need to tell them soon. I'm starting to show, and people will suss it out.'

'After this week,' Brother Bertie agreed, his thumb stroking gently across her stomach. 'We'll sit down with Jimmy and your parents. Do it properly.'

'Are you ready for the explosion that's coming?' Sin's voice was barely a whisper. 'Dad's going to go mental. And Jimmy...'

'Jimmy will understand. He has to. He loves you, and he loves me. Once he gets over the shock—'

Brother Bertie's words were cut off by Sin pulling his face down to hers, kissing him with desperate need. His hands tangled in her hair, kissing her back for all he was worth. His palm stayed pressed against her belly, protective and possessive, when the door suddenly flew open.

'Bertie, Mum said she saw you come upstairs. I need you to help me move—'

Jimmy's voice cut off abruptly. He stood frozen in the doorway, his face cycling through confusion, disbelief, and dawning horror. He took in the scene before him – his best friend with his arms around his sister. Bertie's hand resting intimately on Sin's stomach. The unmistakable posture of two people who'd been kissing.

'What the fuck's going on?'

The words exploded from Jimmy's throat with such fury that both Sin and Brother Bertie jerked apart. Jimmy's silver-grey eyes were wild with shock, but his confused brain was still in denial.

Jimmy's hands curled into fists at his sides. His breathing came in short, sharp bursts. 'Answer me! I want to know what the bollocks is going on here!'

Sin's skin had drained of all colour. She looked like she was about to throw up.

Brother Bertie stepped defensively in front of her, and that small gesture nearly sent Jimmy over the edge completely. The protective stance. The way his body shielded her. It was intimate. Screamed, 'She's mine.'

Brother Bertie raised his palms in a calming gesture. 'Jimmy, we were going to tell you—'

'Tell me what?' Jimmy's voice climbed higher, more dangerous. 'Tell me WHAT, exactly?'

The penny dropped with a crash that nearly floored him. Jimmy's gaze flicked between them, seeing the protective way his best friend guarded Sin, the guilt written across both their faces, the obvious intimacy that couldn't be explained away.

'You and Sin.' The words came out strangled. 'You and my sister.'

*They've been at it. Behind my back. Made a laughingstock of me.*

'We were getting ready to tell you,' Brother Bertie said steadily, though his heart was hammering against his ribs. 'After the funeral, when things settled down—'

'We love each other, Jimmy,' Sin spoke up, her voice shaking but determined. 'We have for years.'

*Years? YEARS?*

Jimmy's gaze dropped to where Brother Bertie's hand had been resting, and his face went white. 'Why were you… Christ, why was your hand on my sister's belly?'

The silence stretched between them, heavy with the weight of the secret that could no longer be hidden.

'You've knocked her up.' It wasn't a question. Jimmy's voice was deadly quiet now, which was infinitely more terrifying than his shouting. 'You've fucking knocked up my sister.'

*My sister's up the duff. With my best mate's kid.*

Brother Bertie's jaw tightened. The accusation and disgust set him off, the anger he'd been carrying for two years ready to pour out. He straightened to his full height and took Sin's hand in his, a gesture of defiance and protection.

'Yeah, we're having a baby,' he stated proudly, his feet widening in challenge. 'And I'm going to marry her.'

Jimmy felt like someone had just ripped the ground from under his feet. Everything he'd believed was bollocks. Everything he thought he knew about the two most important people in his life had been a lie. And then another realisation hit him, even more devastating than the first.

'It was you!' His voice was barely a whisper. 'Two years ago, when Sin was seen with a black man. It was you.'

All this time. All this fucking time.

Brother Bertie lifted his chin, meeting Jimmy's horrified gaze without flinching. 'Yeah. It was me.'

'You were the man she was seeing when—' Jimmy couldn't finish the sentence, couldn't voice what he'd done.

But Brother Bertie had no such problem. Two years of repressed rage and guilt exploded from him with volcanic force.

'When you beat her with a belt? When you whipped her bloody because your racist fucking father told you to? Yeah, Jimmy, I was the man she was in love with. I was the man she was protecting when she took that beating from her own brother.'

'She was my sister! I was protecting her!'

'Protecting her?' Brother Bertie's voice rose to a roar. 'You twisted bastard. You nearly broke her! You left bruises on her back that took weeks to heal! You tortured the woman I love because she had the audacity to fall for someone with darker skin!'

'It's got fuck all to do with colour. You've crossed a line!' Jimmy shouted back, his control finally snapping completely. 'You're my best friend! You don't sleep with my sister! You don't sneak around behind my back! You don't betray me!'

'Betray you?' Brother Bertie stepped closer, his eyes blazing. 'I fell in love, Jimmy. But you? You're the betrayer here. You betrayed every principle you claim to have when you picked up that belt.'

They were nose to nose now, decades of friendship crumbling into violence and recrimination. Sin tried to step between them, but Jimmy was beyond reason. The truth was eating him alive, but he couldn't face it. Couldn't admit what he'd become.

'Fuck off out of my house,' he snarled. 'Both of you. Fuck. Off. Out.'

'Jimmy, please—' Sin begged.

'No! You betrayed my trust—'

Brother Bertie's fist connected with Jimmy's jaw before he could finish the sentence. Jimmy staggered backwards, tasted blood, then launched himself forward with a roar of pure rage.

They crashed through the open French doors onto the terrace, with the stone steps that led downstairs to the shore of the river below. Their bodies slammed into the stone balustrade. Below, shocked gasps rose from the mourners who had spilled outside, drinks forgotten while they watched the two men who'd been soul mates try to destroy each other.

Jimmy landed a vicious uppercut that snapped Brother Bertie's head back, but Bertie recovered quickly, driving his knee into Jimmy's ribs. Grappling, they tumbled down the stone steps in a brutal mess of limbs and blind fury. They punched and rolled until they crashed onto the small golden beach at the river's edge.

'Someone get Danny!' a voice shouted from above.

'Get Gertie!' another called.

On the beach, Jimmy straddled Brother Bertie, his hands closing around his former best friend's throat. 'You fucking bastard! You betrayed me! You betrayed our friendship!'

Brother Bertie bucked and twisted, trying to break free, his face turning red while Jimmy's grip tightened. 'I… loved… her… first…' he gasped.

Jimmy's hands squeezed tighter, two years of pain and now fresh betrayal fuelling his rage.

'I'm going to kill you!' he screamed, pressing harder, eyes bulging with rage. 'KILL YOU!'

Brother Bertie's struggles were growing weaker when a sharp voice cut through the violence.

'Oi!'

Chrissie stood at the top of the stone steps, formidable in her fury, with Rita beside her. Both women looked ready for war.

'You fucking dare!' Chrissie blasted with enough outraged authority to stop anyone dead. 'At Mini's funeral? With the whole community getting a front-row seat?'

Her words broke through Jimmy's madness, and he released Brother Bertie's throat. The shame crashed over him. He'd nearly murdered his best friend at his wife's funeral.

His best friend? Fuck him!

Both men struggled to their feet, still glaring at each other with murderous intent, but Chrissie was already striding down the steps with Rita close behind.

'Try it!' She stabbed a warning finger at them. 'Just fucking try it, and I'll brain both of you with my handbag.'

Danny appeared at the top of the steps, Iris beside him, both looking shocked and furious. Sin stood sobbing in the doorway, her hands pressed to her mouth.

Seeing her, Jimmy spat at his sister, 'You need to go.'

People gasped in disbelief.

Brother Bertie pulled himself upright, blood streaming from his nose, and held out his hand to Sin. 'Come on, baby. We don't need them.'

Sin looked between her family and the man she loved, tears streaming down her face. Then she walked down the steps, took Brother Bertie's outstretched hand, and let him lead her away along the riverbank.

The mourners watched in stunned silence while the couple disappeared around the bend, leaving behind a family torn apart by secrets, betrayal, and the kind of love that destroyed everything it touched.

Jimmy stood there, blood on his knuckles, watching his sister walk away. The woman was carrying his future nephew or niece, and he'd just thrown her out like rubbish.

*I'm my father's son after all.*

# Chapter Fifty-Four

'I'm done crying.'

Sin's voice was hoarse from tears but steady now. She sat on Brother Bertie's bed at Gertie's boarding house, her head resting on his shoulder, arms wrapped around his waist. The small room felt cramped with grief and uncertainty, but it was theirs. Safe.

Brother Bertie's hand moved gently through her brown hair. 'We'll figure this out, darling. We'll stay here with Gertie until something better comes up.'

'What if nothing does?'

'I've applied to the council for a flat.' His voice carried quiet determination. 'I'll make sure you and the baby want for nothing.'

Sin lifted her head to look at him, studying the bruises blooming across his jaw from Jimmy's fists. 'Do you regret it? Any of it?'

'Loving you?' Brother Bertie cupped her face in his hands. 'Never. Not for a second. I'd fight him and the Devil himself again tomorrow if it meant keeping you.'

'Even if it costs you everything?'

'You are everything.'

***

Jimmy sat in the middle of his children's bedroom, arms wrapped around all three of them. The house felt hollow without Mini's laughter echoing through the rooms.

Mini's death had gutted him. Now Sin and Brother Bertie's betrayal had finished the job, carving out whatever remained of his heart.

'Why was Auntie Sin crying?' Violet's tiny voice cut through the silence.

Jimmy's throat burned. 'Sometimes grown-ups make choices that hurt the people they love.'

'Is she coming back?'

Jimmy couldn't find the words.

Robbie looked up at him, innocent and trusting. 'Are you going to leave, too, Daddy?'

The question nearly destroyed him. Jimmy crushed them closer, feeling their absolute dependence on him. They'd lost their mother. Now their aunt. Brother

Bertie, who'd been another father figure, was gone, too.

'It's just us now,' Jimmy whispered into their hair. 'Just us four. But I promise you, I'm never leaving. Never.''

# Chapter Fifty-Five

Iris swayed slightly on her feet while the darkness crept across the docks like a thief, stealing the last scraps of daylight. Danny had thrown open the doors of the River Rat to stragglers of the mourners left from Mini's funeral. She'd needed some fresh air, to get her head around the shocking turn of events with Jimmy, Sin, and Brother Bertie. If Jimmy and Danny thought they were going to lord it over her, putting their foot down that she cut off her daughter, they had another think coming.

And a new, gorgeous grandbaby was on the way… Iris grinned happy and wide.

She fumbled with the silver flask hidden in her black-and-gold box handbag, the gin burning a comforting trail down her throat. Her heart hurt that

Mini was no longer there to enjoy her dream house. The house on Molasses Quay was never meant to be for her son on his own. Jimmy had no idea she was the anonymous person who had gifted her son and wife their home by the river. No one knew.

It was her secret.

A shadow peeled away from the narrow passage beside the pub. Iris' heart jack-knifed against her ribs. A figure stepped directly into her path.

'Danny!' His name erupted from her lips before she could stop it, her hand flying to her throat. 'You nearly frightened the bloody life out of me!'

Danny's face split into a grin that didn't touch his eyes. 'Sorry, love. Didn't mean to make you jump.'

*Something's wrong.* The thought dropped into her stomach heavier than a brick in the Thames. Danny was never sorry for anything.

'What are you doing skulking around outside?' Iris demanded, the gin making her bolder than usual. 'Thought you'd be inside making sure the drink was flowing.'

Danny moved closer, his cologne mingling with the sour stink of whisky. He reached for her hand, his fingers closing around hers with peculiar gentleness. 'Come on.'

But instead of leading her towards the pub's entrance, he tugged her deeper into the shadows, guiding her around the back of the building where the lights couldn't reach.

'Danny, where are we going?' Iris dug her heels in, suddenly wishing she hadn't had that last nip of gin.

The world tilted slightly, making her stomach lurch. 'The pub's that way.'

'Just want a private word, is all.' His grip tightened painfully around her wrist, jerking her forward.

The glow from the River Rat fell away behind them, plunging them into near darkness. Ahead, Iris could make out the glint of moonlight on water, and her blood turned to ice in her veins.

The Executioner's Steps.

*Oh God, no.*

The ancient stone steps, worn smooth by centuries of use, led down to the hungry Thames waters. Pirates had swung from gibbets here centuries past, their bodies left to dangle as warnings until the tide claimed them. Now, it was where East End 'accidents' happened. Like young Pete two years back, found at the bottom with his neck broken and his first baby on the way.

'What's going on?' Iris wrenched her arm free, backing away. A savage chill raced up and down her spine, refusing to stop. 'I'm not going down there.'

Danny's face emerged from the shadows. The moonlight carved his features, his lips twisted back over bared teeth, nostrils flared wide, eyes narrowed to glittering slits. A muscle jumped and twitched in his jaw, his forehead creased with deep furrows.

'Didn't you think I would find out?' he hissed, his voice barely recognisable.

Iris edged backwards, her heel scraping against the top step. Nowhere to go but down. 'Find out what? You're not making any bleedin' sense.'

'That blag on the bank unearthed some interesting things.' Snarling, Danny crept closer. 'Interesting information. Papers with your name on them.'

Oh Christ. The world contracted to a pinprick of terror. He knew. After all these years, he'd discovered her secret.

'A trust fund.' Danny confirmed with venom. 'Set up by your bloody father behind my back. All this time, you've been sitting on a fucking fortune while I've been grafting my fingers to the bone.'

*Danny Steele hasn't grafted a day in his fecking life,* Iris thought with sudden clarity. *The only grafting he's done is to take what doesn't belong to him.*

Iris swallowed hard. Fear coated her mouth, metallic and bitter, burning the back of her throat. Decades of submitting, of hiding gin in teacups, of turning a blind eye to his tarts littered across London.

Finally something snapped in Iris.

'So what if I have?' Her chin jutted out defiantly. Her backbone went ramrod straight, an unfamiliar posture after decades of hunching to make herself smaller around him. It had been a long time since her spine had grown that tall. 'A woman's got a right to money of her own.'

Fury distorted Danny's face into something ugly. 'Rights? You think you've got rights that don't come from me?'

'My father knew what you were. Wanted to make sure I had something if I ever found the guts to leave you.' Iris felt reckless now, decades of suppressed rage bubbling up and spitting out.

'You want to know something else?' She was feeling very brave indeed. 'It was me who bought the house for Jimmy and Mini. With *my* money. So you couldn't get your filthy hands on it.'

Danny's eyes widened, genuine shock flashing across his face before something darker, more primitive took its place. 'You sneaky, scheming bitch.' His voice dropped to a deadly whisper. 'All these years, making a mug of me.'

His hand shot out, a striking snake, fingers digging into her arm with bruising force. Yanking her towards him, Iris cried out, her husband's malicious face inches from hers.

'No one makes a fool of Danny Steele. No one.'

With a vicious shove, he pushed her down the first few steps. Iris windmilled her arms, struggling for balance, but Danny was on her in an instant, dragging her further down the slippery stairs.

'Danny, please!' Terror clawed at her throat, the black water of the Thames coming closer. 'It's me – Iris! Think of the children!'

His only answer was a snarl. He wrapped his hand in her hair, yanking her head back. 'I'll show you who's the bloody man of this house.'

Iris fought like a cornered animal, nails raking across his face, drawing blood. But Danny was stronger, always stronger. He slammed her, bang, into the wall, knocking the breath from her lungs.

'Your dad always looked down his snobby nose at me.' Danny's breath was raging hot, burning her face, spittle flying from his lips. 'Thought his precious daughter was too good for the likes of me. Where's your high-and-mighty father now, eh?'

Through the haze of pain and fear, a strange calm settled over Iris. She stared directly into the eyes of the man she'd spent her life fearing and found her voice one last time.

'You're nothing, Danny Steele. A scared little boy playing at being a man.'

Something primitive flashed in Danny's eyes. A hatred so pure it transcended simple rage. With a roar, he grabbed her by the hair and smashed her head into the jagged rock at the water's edge.

Pain exploded behind Iris' eyes. Once, twice, again and again, each impact sending white-hot shards through her skull. Blood, warm and thick, coursed down her face, into her eyes, her mouth. The taste of it mingled with the brackish river water splashing the stairs.

Her last thought, before consciousness slipped away, was of Jimmy. Of Sin. Her beautiful children. The only good things Danny had ever given her.

He stood, panting, staring down at what remained of his wife. Iris Steele lay broken and still, her face unrecognisable, her silver-grey eyes – the ones Jimmy had inherited – staring sightlessly at nothing. The tide came in, greedy fingers of black water pulling at her body, washing away her blood as it had washed away the blood of so many others before her.

Iris Steele was gone.

***

Fuck. Fuck. *Fuuuck.*

*What have I done?*

Danny Steele stood over the broken mess that used to be his wife. His body vibrated with rage, great bloody waves of it washing through him while the water lapped at Iris' crumpled form. Blood swirled in the greedy Thames, a dark cloud spreading then disappearing into the murky depths.

The enormity of what he'd done crashed down on him. Not some docker who'd skimmed off the top. Not some rival muscle trying to cut in on his territory. His wife.

His hands wouldn't stop shaking. He sucked in a sharp breath, his racing heart gradually slowing, his mind clearing. His expression hardened, mouth twisting into a cruel line.

The duplicitous bitch had it coming.

All these years, sitting on a fortune while he'd sweated his nuts for every penny. Using her daddy's money to buy that devil house on Molasses Quay, the same house that haunted his nightmares. Worse, she'd used it to steal Jimmy away from him, to weaken his control over his own son.

Fresh anger surged through him, hot and thick. He drew back his foot to kick her lifeless body, then stopped himself.

No point wasting good energy on the dead.

Danny's manipulative mind clicked into gear. No need for the usual cleanup. No need to pour booze down her throat like he'd done to Pete. Iris already stank like the Truman's Brewery in Brick Lane. The coppers would take one sniff and write her off. Another boozy tumble down the Executioner's Steps. Back in the day she been called One O'clock Iris behind her back for a reason, knocking the hard stuff back some days so much she didn't get out of bed until one in the afternoon.

All he had to do when she didn't come home was raise the alarm, lead the search party himself. Play the worried husband. Nobody would question Danny Steele.

'Worked out for the bloody best,' he muttered, straightening his jacket.

The Steele empire was growing, changing. Moving beyond the stink of the dead docks. A man in his position needed a different sort of wife. Someone with class, not some gin-soaked skeleton in the closet who might spill her guts after one too many.

He pictured himself with a younger model. Someone who'd know her place, unlike Iris with her secret stash and sneaky purchases.

Danny ran his fingers through his hair, brushing away invisible evidence. Below, the tide tugged at Iris' body, her silver-grey eyes thankfully shut.

For the briefest moment, something that might have been regret flickered across Danny's face.

Then it was gone, quick as a flash.

'Should've known your place, love,' he whispered. His voice carried no tenderness, only cold finality.

Danny Steele turned and walked away, leaving his wife's body to the Thames. By the time he reached the top of the stairs, his mind had already moved on to the big announcement he was about to make.

Less than a minute later, Danny swaggered through the back door of the River Rat, his kingdom. He plastered on his most convincing smile, the one that had charmed dockers and coppers alike for decades.

'Charlie! How's it going, mate?' He clapped a firm hand on a regular's shoulder. 'Jonsey, pour us a Clarke's Court rum,' Danny instructed the barman.

The pub was packed to the gills, black-clad mourners huddled in grief-stricken clusters. Mini's wake – perfect bloody timing. Couldn't have arranged it better if he'd planned it. If anyone started asking awkward questions about Iris, fifty witnesses would swear Danny Steele had been right here, drowning his son's sorrows.

His shrewd eyes narrowed, scanning the crowd until he spotted Jimmy. His son sat hunched at the bar, shoulders slumped, knuckles white around a glass of scotch. The poor bastard looked broken, hollowed out. Losing a wife could do that to a man – not that Danny would know.

Danny felt a strange mixture of pride and pity seeing his boy devastated. Jimmy had buried Mini today, the mother of his children, taken too young by a cancer that ate her alive from the inside out. Then came the bombshell about Sin and Brother Bertie's secret love affair. His own sister and his best mate, carrying on behind his back. The ultimate betrayal.

*Family's supposed to be everything,* Danny thought bitterly. *The ones who've got your back, who you can trust above all else. But they're the ones with the sharpest knives, ain't they? Always ready to stick it in when you're not looking.*

*Good riddance to the lot of them,* Danny thought, weaving through the crowd towards his son. And now he'd gone and got rid of another traitor.

'All right, boy?' Danny slid onto the stool next to Jimmy, signalling Jonsey for another round. 'Holding up?'

Jimmy nodded mutely, staring into his glass like it held the answers to life's mysteries.

'Listen, Jimmy.' Danny draped a comforting arm around his son's shoulders, lowering his voice to a conspiratorial rumble. 'You're better off without that slag sister of yours and that so-called best friend.' His fingers tightened, feeling the raw grief radiating off his body. 'We're Steeles, you and me. We stick together. All you need is family. *Blood and guts* family.'

A flash of red caught Danny's eye. He glanced down at his hand on Jimmy's black suit and froze. A single spot of blood – bright, damning – stood out on his signet ring.

*Iris' blood.*

His heart skipped a terrified beat. Danny snatched his hand away, rubbing the ring frantically against his trouser leg.

'You all right, Dad?' Jimmy frowned, his bloodshot eyes focusing for the first time.

'Course I am,' Danny snapped. He forced out a laugh that sounded fake even to his own ears. 'Just remembered I need to check on your mum later. She wasn't feeling too clever earlier.'

Suddenly, the pub door burst open with a thunderous bang. A gust of cold air swept through the crowded room, silencing conversations mid-flow. Heads turned towards the commotion.

A piercing scream of horror tore from one of the female mourners.

Danny shoved his way forward, Jimmy close behind. The crowd parted like the Red Sea, revealing the impossible.

Danny's legs turned to jelly. The colour bled out from his face like he'd seen a ghost – which he had.

Iris.

She stood swaying in the doorway, barely recognisable. Her face was a pulpy crimson mess, one eye swollen completely shut. Blood matted her hair and soaked her once-elegant black dress. Somehow, she'd dragged herself up those stairs, through the streets, to find him.

Her hand rose, and a trembling, bloody finger pointed directly at him, an executioner identifying her mark.

Iris was still alive.

# Chapter Fifty-Six

*What if the bitch fingers me?*

Danny Steele paced the sterile corridor of the London Hospital, his polished brogues squeaking against the linoleum with each agitated step. Twenty-four hours it had been since they'd wheeled Iris through those double doors. Twenty-four hours of him playing the devastated husband to perfection.

The waiting was torture, worse than any kicking he'd taken. His mind kept circling back to the same terrifying thought: what if the duplicitous cow woke up and grassed him up?

He'd be trading his handmade suits for prison stripes faster than you could say 'Old Bailey.'

'Dad, you're wearing a hole in the floor.' Jimmy's soft complaint cut through his spiralling panic.

Danny glanced at his son, slumped in one of those uncomfortable plastic chairs that made your arse go dead. His looked absolutely knackered, the weight of losing Mini still crushing his broad shoulders. Poor bastard had barely slept since they'd put his missus in the ground yesterday.

'Can't help it, son. Worried sick about your dear ole mum, aren't I?' Danny forced the right amount of concern into his voice, the same tone he'd perfected, back in the day, sweet-talking the dock management. 'She's all I've got.'

Jimmy threw his head back and shut his eyes for a moment. 'Hate this bleedin' place. The smell, the sounds…' He trailed off, thinking of the last time he was here seeing Mini, a few hours before she'd left him.

'Your mum's a fighter. Tough old bird, she is. Takes more than a tumble down some steps to finish off a Steele woman.'

A young doctor with glasses emerged and came striding towards them. Dr Patterson, that was his name. Danny had barely registered it when they'd first arrived, too busy calculating how to spin Iris' 'accident' if she didn't pull through.

'Mr Steele?' The doctor's eyes found Danny's. 'Your wife is awake.'

Danny's heart dropped. Fuck!

He was going down, no word about it. He counted himself a lucky man, but this time his luck had surely run out.

'Can we see her?' Jimmy was already on his feet, desperation written across his exhausted face.

'Of course. But please, she's extremely weak. Try not to overwhelm her.'

Danny hung back, wiping his sweaty palm across his face. His legs felt unsteady, treacherous. Every instinct screamed at him to scarper, to leg it before Iris could destroy him with a few choice words. But that wasn't his way, he faced his problems head-on. Always had.

Iris lay propped up against starched white pillows, her face a mess of bruises and bandages. One eye remained swollen completely shut, the other barely a slit. Tubes snaked from her arms to various machines that beeped and hummed with mechanical persistence. She looked fragile, breakable, nothing resembling the defiant gin-soaked bitch who'd faced him down last night.

Christ, he'd really done a number on her.

Jimmy rushed to her bedside. 'Mum? Mum, it's me. It's Jimmy.'

Iris' good eye fluttered, focusing with obvious effort on her son's face. Her split lips moved, barely producing sound. 'Jimmy?'

'Yeah, Mum. I'm here.' Jimmy took her hand gently, pressing it to his stubbled cheek. 'You're safe now. You're in hospital, but you're safe.'

Danny stepped forward, arranging his features into the covered deceit of a devoted husband. Time for the performance of his bleedin' life.

'You gave us a proper scare.' He mustered with fake concern. 'The coppers said you fell down the Executioner's Steps. Must have had a few too many at Mini's wake, eh? You know how you get when you're upset.'

Perfect. Plant the seed that she'd been pissed as a newt. Everyone knew Iris liked a tipple.

Iris' eye tracked slowly towards him, blinking with obvious confusion.

Danny held his breath.

*Here it comes.*

*She's getting ready to point the finger of guilt at me. Grass me up.*

Instead, Iris stared at him with vacant bewilderment.

'Who are you?'

The words hit Danny harder than a brick to the skull. He blinked, certain he'd misheard. 'What?'

'Are you a doctor?' Iris' voice was barely a whisper, but the confusion in it was unmistakable.

Danny's mouth opened and closed without sound. The room seemed to tilt, the beeping machines growing louder, more urgent.

'Mrs Steele.' Dr Patterson stepped forward, his expression grave. 'This is your husband, Danny. Do you remember him?'

Iris shook her head slowly, wincing at the movement. 'I… no. I don't…'

'Mr Steele, could I have a word?' The doctor's tone was carefully neutral. 'Outside?'

Danny nodded mutely, his legs moving without conscious thought.

'I'm afraid your wife appears to be suffering from a certain type of amnesia,' the doctor explained. 'It's not uncommon with head injuries of this severity. The trauma has affected her ability to recall some memories from before the accident. She knows your son but not you.'

Danny's pulse quickened. Could his luck really be this good? 'How… how long will it last?'

The doctor adjusted his glasses, choosing his words carefully. 'Sometimes these things resolve themselves in days or weeks. The brain can be remarkably resilient.' He paused, studying Danny's face. 'Sometimes the memories never come back, Mr Steele. I'm sorry.'

Danny bit down hard on the inside of his cheek to keep from grinning. The pain helped him maintain his devastated husband act. Inside, he was doing bloody cartwheels.

'Never?'

'We'll monitor her progress closely. For now, she needs rest and familiar faces. You and your son will be crucial to her recovery, assuming she can form new memories with you.'

A commotion erupted near the ward entrance. Raised voices, someone having a right barney with the nurses. Danny turned to see a flash of chestnut hair, a familiar defiant stance that made his blood pressure spike.

Sin.

She pushed past a protesting nurse, her face streaked with tears and smudged mascara. 'I want to see my mother! Let me through!'

He couldn't have that girl of his here. But Jimmy was already moving. He stepped out of Iris' room and positioned himself in the doorway, his muscular frame blocking Sin's path completely. His face was cold and unforgiving.

'Please, Jimmy,' Sin pleaded, her face twisted with pain. 'I need to see her. I need to know she's all right.'

Jimmy stared at his sister for a long moment. The silence stretched, thick and poisonous. When he finally spoke, his voice carried no emotion at all, flat and final.

'My mother doesn't have a daughter.'

He stepped back and closed the door in her face.

# Epilogue

1970

The amber-gold whisky caught the afternoon light streaming through the grimy windows of Odds On, and Jimmy savoured the burn as it slid down his throat. His office above the betting shop on Commercial Road wasn't much to look at but it was his kingdom now.

A Cuban cigar smouldered in the ashtray, sending lazy spirals of smoke towards the yellowed ceiling. The ledger spread across his huge desk told the real story, the big and little wrinkles he has his fingers in.

Heavy footsteps echoed up the narrow staircase, followed by a respectful knock.

'Come,' Jimmy called without looking up.

One of his runners appeared in the doorway, cap in hand. 'Beggin' your pardon, but there's a delivery from the brewery. Where d'you want the barrels?'

'Round the back,' Jimmy said. 'And make sure the Old Bill don't see nothing.'

'Right you are.'

The runner disappeared downstairs, and Jimmy returned to his books. Through the window, he could see the bustling Commercial Road, the different types of people going about their business. His business now. They all knew who controlled this stretch of pavement, who decided which bookies operated and which protection rackets ran smooth.

A car backfired in the street below, and Jimmy's hand instinctively moved towards the desk drawer where he kept his shooter. Old habits. In this game, paranoia kept you breathing.

The phone rang, jarring him from his thoughts.

'Odds On,' he answered, voice steady and controlled.

'Is that Jimmy Southpaw?' The voice was nervous, deferential.

Jimmy smiled, stubbing out his cigar. Nobody called him Jimmy Steele anymore. He was Jimmy Southpaw now, and that name meant respect.

***

The key turned in the lock with a satisfying click, and Brother Bertie pushed open the door to their new council flat on the Isle of Dogs. A maisonette was what the council called it with its upstairs-downstairs, and good-sized three bedrooms, kitchen, and sitting room. The standout feature was a private balcony that faced the Thames, where container ships drifted past like floating cities in the distance.

'Welcome home, little man,' Sin whispered to the bundle of joy in her arms, her voice thick with emotion.

Baby Isaac – Izzy, they'd already taken to calling him – slept peacefully against her chest, tiny fists curled beneath his chin. At eight days old, he was perfect in every way that mattered. Dark curls like his father's, Sin's delicate features. Their beautiful boy.

Brother Bertie dropped their cases by the door and crossed to the window, pulling back the thin curtains to let in the morning light. He was done with the bad-boy life. Only legit work for him. That's what he'd promised Sin.

This was their chance to build something real for his family.

Sin joined him at the window, Izzy still sleeping in her arms. The sunlight caught the simple gold band on her finger. They'd married quietly at Whitechapel Registry Office with only Gertie and Kath, and Dilly, of course, as witnesses. No fuss, no family drama, just two people promising to love each other through whatever came next.

Sin leaned into his warmth, feeling unwanted tension spoil her good mood. 'Sometimes I can't help thinking about Jimmy, about—'

'Jimmy made his choices, just like we made ours.' Brother Bertie's voice was gentle but firm. 'We can't live in the past, sweetness. This little one deserves better than that.'

Izzy stirred in Sin's arms, making soft baby sounds that melted their hearts.

Brother Bertie pressed a kiss to the top of Sin's head, breathing in the scent of her hair. 'The future's going to be good, Sin. I promise you that. We've got each other, we've got our son, and we've got this place to call home. That's more than most people get.'

Outside, a tugboat's horn echoed across the water, welcoming them to their new beginning.

# Next in the Love and Hate Series

Are you ready for Book 3 in the love and Hate Series?
SECRETS AND LIES

Available on Amazon and FREE on Kindle Unlimited

Book 1: Love and Hate is also available
LOVE AND HATE

# Free Novella

Join Our Exclusive Book Club

Plunge into the gangland world where the Steele and Watson Crime Family Drama started

# Dangerous

A LOVE & HATE SERIES PREQUEL

**Fate throws them together. The streets try to tear them apart.**

Brother Bertie, newly arrived from Jamaica, finds himself on the run in London's gritty East End. Jimmy Steele, son of a feared gangster, is bleeding out in a warehouse after a botched heist. Their paths cross in a twist of fate that will change their lives forever.

As Bertie's Jamaican street smarts clash with Jimmy's East End savvy, they form an unlikely alliance. But with rival gangs closing in and dangerous secrets coming to light, their newfound friendship is put to the ultimate test.

In this thrilling novella, loyalties are tested, blood is spilled, and love is pushed to its limits in the unforgiving world of London's underworld.

Visit www.dredamitchell.com

**In gangland men reign but it's the women who rule**

**Big Mo Series**

Enter a world of ruthless ambition and deadly family feuds!
The Steele and the Watson families are back in the epic Big Mo Gangland Series
Available on Amazon and FREE in Kindle Unlimited.

Dirty Tricks
Fight Dirty
Wicked Women
Play Dirty
The Big Mo Series

# Check out Amazon for all our books

Dreda Amazon Books UK
Dreda Amazon Books US

Reviews: We write for you!
We adore hearing what you think about our books. Reviews help other readers find books. So do please leave a review.

For news and staying in touch head over to: www.dredamitchell.com including signing up to our newsletter for goodies and free stories.
https://www.facebook.com/dredasaymitchell/
https://www.tiktok.com/@dredaryanauthors?lang=en

# All About Dreda & Ryan

Her Majesty Queen Elizabeth awarded Dreda an MBE in her New Year's Honours' List, 2020! She has appeared on Queen Camilla's Reading Room.

Ryan and Dreda are a wife and husband team who write across the crime and mystery genre - psychological thrillers, gritty gangland crime and fast-paced action books.

She scooped the CWA's John Creasey Dagger Award in 2004, the first time a Black British author has received this honour.

Spare Room, their first psychological thriller was a #1 UK and US Amazon Bestseller. Lee Child, named her 2022 novel, Say Her Name his best book of the year so far. She is one of the twelve acclaimed female authors of International Bestselling, Marple, a new reimagined Miss Marple anthology. Dreda is a passionate campaigner and speaker on social issues and the arts. She has appeared on television, including Celebrity Pointless, Celebrity Eggheads, BBC 1 Breakfast, Sunday Morning Live, Newsnight, The Review Show and Front Row Late on BBC 2. She had Fun! Fun! Fun! With Alan Carr on documentary series, Alan's Adventures with Agatha Christie, Channel 4.

Dreda's Black History Month short story about the remarkable Althea McNish was narrated on Amazon's Alexa by Sir Trevor MacDonald. Ryan and Dreda both performed a specially commissioned monologue on the ground-breaking SkyArts50 on Sky TV. She is a judge on the Women's Prize, Discoveries initiative for new writers, 2025.

Dreda has been a guest on many radio shows and presented BBC Radio 4's flagship books programme, Open Book. She has written in a number of leading newspapers including The Guardian and was thrilled to be named one of Britain's 50 Remarkable Women by Lady Geek in association with Nokia. She is a Trustee of The Royal Literary Fund and an ambassador for The Reading Agency.

Some of their books are currently in development as TV and film adaptations.

Dreda's parents are from the beautiful Caribbean island of Grenada. Her name, Dreda, is Irish and pronounced with a long vowel ee sound in the middle!

Printed in Dunstable, United Kingdom

67656654R10275